Beyond the Mists of Katura

ELVES

BOOK 3

Beyond the Mists of Katura

ELVES
BOOK 3

James Barclay

GOLLANCZ

LONDON

The right of James Barclay to be identified as the author
of this work has been asserted by him in accordance with
the Copyright, Designs and Patents Act 1988.

First published in Great Britain in 2013 by
Gollancz
An imprint of the Orion Publishing Group
Orion House, 5 Upper St Martin's Lane, London WC2H 9EA
An Hachette UK Company

A CIP catalogue record for this book is available
from the British Library

ISBN 978 0 575 08523 7 (Cased)
ISBN 978 0 575 08525 1 (Trade Paperback)

1 3 5 7 9 10 8 6 4 2

Typeset at The Spartan Press Ltd,
Lymington, Hants

Printed and bound at CPI Group (UK) Ltd
Croydon CR0 4YY

The Orion Publishing Group's policy is to use papers that
are natural, renewable and recyclable products and made
from wood grown in sustainable forests. The logging and
manufacturing processes are expected to conform to the
environmental regulations of the country of origin.

www.jamesbarclay.com
www.orionbooks.co.uk
www.gollancz.co.uk

For my father, Keith,
who is the greatest man I have ever known.

Chapter 1

Only in the direst need does the TaiGethen body first seek its full potential through the subconscious mind.

Auum, Arch of the TaiGethen

Ollem prayed that his feet would find safe purchase on the sodden, sucking ground and pushed yet harder through the slapping leaves and whip-like vines of the dense rainforest growth. The sudden downpour was both blessing and curse, obscuring his scent and sound from the quartet of rogues hunting him while misting the way ahead and turning the ground to a dangerous sludge.

He was tantalisingly close to safety. To reach the cliff tops of the Verendii Tual and begin his descent there would allow him to escape the rogues' jaws. But they were fast and merciless, too fast for a TaiGethen to outrun, and they would tear him apart if they brought him down. The temptation was to climb to evade them, but the boughs of the banyans were broad and low to the ground and the rogues would be able to follow him into the trees.

Ollem ducked a branch and jumped down a steep bank into a stream which was already swollen with rainwater, the current running swiftly over the slick stones. His right foot slipped momentarily before finding new purchase and he hurried on. In the stream he was free from the snagging foliage, but much easier to see.

Easier to kill.

The stream he had chosen cascaded over the cliffs into the River Shorth hundreds of feet below, but in the fog of the rain he couldn't tell how far he was from sanctuary. Ollem pumped his arms harder, trying to find that fraction more speed. He leaned forward, taking the risk that his feet might slip again but knowing, deep inside, that to risk anything less would be to fail.

He cursed his fortune. Had he achieved the state of shetharyn already he would have escaped the rogues comfortably. But here he was, seven days into his emergence cycle and not yet feeling the joy of it, the sheer speed and clarity of it. When Ollem had begun the cycle he'd had no idea what would happen to him . . . but it shouldn't have involved rogues. No one controlled them. And there was no one nearby to save him.

Ollem quashed any thoughts of injustice. He was TaiGethen. He would save himself if it was possible to do so. Chanting prayers to Yniss that were lost in the thunder and rain, he ran on. His ears twitched at a whisper to his left and he glanced over his shoulder.

A low dark shape was streaking through the forest above the stream gully, slipping easily through the packed undergrowth, gaining on him pace by pace. Ollem didn't need to look behind or to his right. He knew the pattern: one on each flank to get ahead of him and the other two behind. Once they surrounded him, the kill was inevitable.

He had no option but to carry on running and pray he would reach sanctuary. Ahead, the rain and low cloud disguised his path. Ollem found himself laughing deep down in his throat, imagining himself escaping the jaws of the rogues only to fall to his death on the rocks that bordered the Shorth.

He heard a roar behind him, close and loud. A shiver ran the length of his spine but he kept running. Through the din of rain on rock Ollem could hear the splash of paws, fleet through the stream. To his right, the rogue was now level with him and moving ahead fast, its sleek dark body hard to follow as it wove through the trunks and bushes that bordered the gully.

Not long now.

Ollem ran on, experiencing a growing anger at his fate coupled with a refusal to believe he could not avoid it. It burned at him, sending needles through his body, re-energising his aching limbs and sharpening his vision. And there, through the mist and rain, he caught a glimpse of the edge of the cliff. There was still a chance.

The first pair of rogues leaped down into the gully ten paces ahead of him and turned to face him. Ollem screamed in frustration and slithered to a halt, his chest heaving. Behind him, the other pair slowed. They knew he was dangerous; they recognised his garb, the paint on his face and the twin scabbards on his back. But he was cornered. They knew they would kill him; they just wanted to do so without being injured themselves.

Ollem weighed them up just as they did him. They were panthers,

black and slate-grey, which had shunned the touch of the Claw-
Bound and chosen to run free. There were few rogues but they were
exceptionally dangerous. They followed his every move, every twitch
of his hands. Ollem glanced back to see the pair behind him had
stopped and were hunkered down, tails twitching, waiting their
moment to strike.

Ollem took a deep breath and looked beyond the pair ahead of
him. The safety of the cliff face was close enough that if he could
evade them just once, he would save himself. Even so, he reached for
his blades. The rogues growled in response and settled themselves for
the charge. Ollem let his hands fall back to his sides.

'Yniss guide my steps.'

Ollem ran at the rogues, veering to the left to reduce the chances
of both hitting him simultaneously. The panthers crouched to spring;
he saw their muscles bunch and their eyes fix on his head. Ollem's
body chilled with the certainty of his death. Yet, in his mind, a voice
insisted that this was not his time and that there was a way to
survive. He felt energy surge within him from his toes to the top of
his shaven head.

Ollem relaxed and his body felt fluid and clean, his movements
suddenly easy, free of tension and the fear of death. In front of him,
the scene cleared; the rogues were moving slowly, their paws making
lazy splashes in the stream, their mouths opening as if in a long,
luxurious yawn.

He smiled, seeing the beauty of their movement and the shimmer
of muscle beneath their shining coats. He could see the individual
drops in the teeming rain and could pick out the sound of each drop
as it struck rock or water. He could feel his body moving faster than
he'd ever experienced, reacting instantly and balancing perfectly.

Ollem swayed left and saw the panthers track his movements. One
of them, its claws outstretched and its teeth bared, travelled steadily
through the air. The other was leaping too, aiming to pin his legs
while the first took his head.

He ducked and turned a forward roll through the stream, feeling
the rush of water across his already soaked body. The first panther's
jaws snapped shut on fresh air. Ollem came to his feet and jumped
high, seeing the second rogue pass beneath him, his momentum
carrying him well beyond it. He spread his arms wide and dropped
gracefully back into the stream.

Ollem spun round. The rogues were already twenty paces from

him, almost as if they'd stopped to watch him. They were regarding him cautiously, no longer approaching, no longer a direct threat. Ollem frowned and began to walk back towards them, not reaching for his blades.

'You cannot harm me,' he said. 'And I am not your enemy.'

The rain was falling in a blurring torrent once more. The panthers ran easily out of the gully, and Ollem watched them go, feeling the energy settle in his body but not leave it entirely. It remained at rest, ready to be called on at will. The panthers disappeared into the forest and the calls they sent up were carried by the voices of elves too. They were calls of celebration.

Ollem frowned and turned back towards the Verendii Tual cliffs. Two elves stood there, their arms wide in a gesture of welcome. One was a ClawBound, tall, thin and with half his face painted white and the other covered in piercings and tattoos. The other was TaiGethen.

'Auum?'

Auum smiled and walked towards him.

'Welcome to the ranks of the emerged,' he said. 'Welcome to a joy so pure you will wonder how you existed without it. Welcome to a new phase of your life with the TaiGethen.'

'The rogues—' Ollem began, his heart racing and his excitement barely in check.

'Claws can imitate their lost brothers and sisters much as we can ours,' said Auum.

'I thought they were going to kill me.'

'As you were meant to,' said Auum. 'Because only in the direst need does the TaiGethen body seek its full potential through the subconscious mind. Only then can a TaiGethen emerge and join the shetharyn.'

Ollem shook with relief and tears began to flow down his cheeks. Auum took his head in his hands and kissed his eyes and forehead.

'I'd begun to question everything,' said Ollem. 'I had no idea seven days spent alone could seem so long.'

'And now you need never fear isolation. You are joined with the energies of the earth and can never truly be alone.' Auum smiled and stepped back. 'Now, come and speak with Serrin. I always let him tell the emerged why they must never reveal the secret to any yet to enter the cycle.'

'Why Serrin?'

'He is the most persuasive,' said Auum. Ollem shuddered.

'Remember that fear and respect it. You might be faster than a rogue but you are not faster than him. Never him.'

Ollem followed Auum along the path to his new life.

Nerille was ancient. She was surely the most long-lived Gyalan in the bloody history of the elves. Had she been Tuali, she'd be old . . . and even as one of the Beethan she'd be getting on in years. She'd outlived all of her children, and the only mercy in that was her six grand-children, all of whom were still alive though well into middle age themselves.

She was sitting on a bench in front of the flagpole as she had so often during the long centuries of her life in Katura. Today she was here for the last time. Around her she could still picture the bustle of the market, the scents of spice and herb and meat, the chatter and bustle of offer and deal, laughter echoing from the walls of the buildings surrounding the central circle.

All gone now, of course, consigned to memory just like the rowing tournaments, the excited babble of children during the lake race, the climbing tournaments and the feasts; all the things that spoke of a city blossoming in the wake of war. Nerille smiled to herself and pressed her shaking hands to her mouth.

She should have known it wouldn't last for ever. With the rout of the humans and the freeing of the enslaved cities seven hundred years ago, their reasons to come here, to live in the Palm of Yniss, were gone. And one by one the Katurans had felt the call to return home. She couldn't blame any of them for desiring a return to their old lives.

Thousands had left after the war, choosing to help rebuild Tolt Anoor, Deneth Barine and the capital, Ysundeneth. And over the years the trickle had continued until it became clear that Katura was unsustainable. So the city had been dismantled, timber and stone, and the materials taken to help rebuild elsewhere, cities whose repair was yet to be completed. It never would be. The scars of man would always remain.

All that remained of Katura now was the Wall of the Fallen, which held the names of every elf from every thread who had given his or her life to the cause: for the salvation of the elven race. The wall had been built from the temple stones and was a spiral structure that led to a central shrine to Yniss and all of the elven gods. The flagpole stood proud above the shrine.

There was not a day that Nerille had failed to walk the spiral, her trembling hands trailing over the thousands of names, the memories of struggle still fresh despite the passing of the centuries. They mingled with more recent acts, equally brave though not undertaken in warfare. The images that played in her mind gave her a reason to draw her next breath.

Nerille never ceased to be amazed at how quickly Beeth's root and branch had returned to the deserted city, grabbing greedily at the land vacated by the elves and erasing the wounds of civilisation. The wall and flagpole would soon be covered, hidden beneath vine and leaf, and that was as it should be.

The mists that dominated the Palm of Yniss had already returned, sweeping from the cliffs and sitting on the lake, swirling around her ankles and giving the ground in all directions a ghostly, ethereal aspect. As the vegetation gained ground, so the mist would deepen.

'Nerille?' She started and looked up. The silhouette of a tall elf was before her. 'I'm sorry, I didn't mean to startle you.'

The figure approached and knelt before her, revealing the face of an old Tuali warrior, Arch of the Al-Arynaar until his advancing years had forced him into a very active retirement. His eyes were hooded and his hair all gone but still he pulsed with a zest she envied.

'Hello, Tulan. I hadn't thought to see you here again.'

'How are you feeling?' he asked, taking her hands in his and raising them to dry lips.

Nerille thought for a moment and shook her head.

'I don't really feel anything,' she said. 'Is that bad?'

Of all the things she had expected – sorrow, relief, even a weary acceptance – it certainly wasn't this.

'Nothing you have ever done or felt could be described as bad,' said Tulan. He levered himself back to his feet and sat beside her. 'All that Katura and its people have become since the war is because of your work and your sacrifice.'

Nerille could feel herself blushing, and her smile was warm with the recognition of her efforts.

'You came all the way from Aryndeneth to embarrass me?'

Tulan laughed. 'In front of who, the macaques?'

'So why are you here? Bit old for a bodyguard, aren't you?'

'That depends how slow the attacking animal is. I'm still more than a match for any sloth.'

'Well, that's a relief.'

Nerille looked at Tulan, saw the smile cracking his face and laughed hard, her shoulders shaking and tears filling her eyes at the idea of a ferocious battle against a sloth.

'And I'm still highly skilled at crushing ants.'

'Stop!' said Nerille, smacking his arm with a bony hand. 'I've missed you, Tulan. You were always too long away from here.'

Tulan's smile faded. 'I know. I could hide behind my duties, but the fact is that when you started dismantling the city it became too hard to come back here and see what was happening. I still think it's a mistake.'

'You and me both, but we are very much in the minority.'

'I still feel the pain of Pelyn's death and that was seven hundred years ago. She died protecting Katura, and we've abandoned it.'

'No, Tulan,' said Nerille. 'I wanted Katura to survive because it was my home. But the fight was never for the city, it was for the elven race. That's what Pelyn died defending, not the buildings.'

'But this place should have become the focus of our renewal. The energy and harmony should have been the beacon for all to follow.'

'Yes, but it was the same in all the cities. After all, in the end humans managed to do more for elven harmony than Takaar ever managed. And, romantic though our notions were, Katura is just too distant and difficult to reach.'

Tulan shrugged. 'I know you're right but it still doesn't feel . . . fitting. Not elven.'

'The memories will always be here for those who wish to find them,' said Nerille. 'So tell me, what *are* you doing here?'

Tulan smiled again. 'Sloth attacks notwithstanding, I'm not here as your bodyguard. Honour guard would be a more accurate description.'

Nerille felt heat in her cheeks. 'There you go again, making me blush. It's lovely of you, Tulan, though you didn't have to. There are seventy or so of us making this final trip after all.'

'Respectfully I must disagree,' said Tulan. 'This is one journey I would not miss for all the years of an Ynissul. And I'm not the only one.'

Tulan pointed behind them at the wall, where two elves stood studying the names and whispering prayers when they touched that of a loved one. Nerille gasped to see them and her hand went to her mouth. She felt giddy as a youngster excited at the sight of a hero, and she was most certainly in the presence of heroes.

Nerille pushed herself to her feet, feeling a moment's unsteadiness. She reached out a hand, which Tulan took, and the pair walked to the wall together.

'This is where we met for the first time,' said Auum, not turning.

'Not precisely,' said Nerille. 'You were balanced atop that flagpole after all.'

'Will you ever let me get away with the slightest inaccuracy?'

Auum turned, Ulysan with him, and Nerille shook her head.

'Not while I draw breath,' she said. 'Gyal knows it's good to see you.'

Auum embraced her, and Nerille clung to him hard, feeling the lack of strength in her arms and remembering the energy she used to have.

'There was nowhere else I could be.'

'Don't you start,' said Nerille.

Auum broke the embrace and kissed her eyes and forehead.

'What do you mean?'

'Ask Tulan. What are you doing here, then? Come to watch me walk extremely slowly into the forest?'

Nerille studied Auum's face. How old he must be. He'd witnessed thousands of years and yet he retained such vitality. And it would be thousands more before he showed the signs of a tiring body. But his would never deteriorate like hers, to the point where death seemed a sensible option. She knew why and she envied him the sheer joy that serving his faith gave him. Every day in the rainforest was a renewal. How magnificent to be inspired that way.

'I heard a rumour that the Mother of Katura felt she was unlikely to survive the trip to Aryndeneth. I am here to ensure that she reaches her destination very much alive.'

'Blabbermouth grandchildren,' muttered Nerille, but she could not stop a smile crossing her face. 'Well, whatever the reason, I'm . . .'

It hit her then – the enormity of today and what it meant to have the Arch of the TaiGethen escort her away. She stepped away from Auum and looked quickly around at the huge open space where Katura had once stood and where the lines of foundations still ran like veins across the ground. A cascade of memories ran through her and with it came the tears, the weakness in the legs and Tulan and Auum's arms about her, supporting her body and soul.

'I don't want this to end,' she managed eventually. 'I should have died here.'

'Yniss blessed you with long life. So this is not an ending; it's another step on the journey for you, and for Katura.'

Nerille composed herself, taking her time to wipe the tears from her face and stand unsupported again with her skirt smoothed and her shirt arranged properly about her shoulders.

'You talk such rubbish sometimes, Auum,' she said. 'Still, at least you stopped my whimpering. Let's go.'

'It's a long way,' agreed Ulysan. 'Best not waste time.'

'That has nothing to do with it,' said Nerille, recovered and beginning to feel mischievous like she was a child once more. 'I fear staying here might lead to more pomposity from the Arch, and no one deserves having to put up with that.'

Chapter 2

All that I see is my gift to the elves, yet still I am reviled. Such is my eternal punishment.

Takaar, Father of the Il-Aryn

Takaar looked down from the top of Crier's Mound and found his sense of satisfaction and achievement undiminished by the passage of time. Indeed it had probably grown, intensified by the progress of all those he surveyed today and those further away, working with all he had taught them.

Laughter rose on a light breeze, dissipating into a clear blue sky.

'And to think this was all my gift.'

That is an interesting interpretation of history.

'I brought them to this place and look what they have achieved.'

No, Auum exiled you here with all your dribbling sycophants.

Takaar began to walk down the slope of the mound. The sun blessed the ground of the Ornouth Archipelago this morning. The sands sparkled, the channels between the islands shone and here on Herendeneth, the largest of the islands, the sounds of joyous life filled the air.

'We needed a secluded place in which to do our work for the benefit of all elves. I was already considering this place.'

I might be mistaken, but I thought the last time you spoke to Auum he said you and the Il-Aryn would never have a place in the lives of elves and that the best thing you could do was draw a hurricane down on yourselves to rid the world of your dangerous meddling. I paraphrase, obviously. Expletives are so distasteful, aren't they?

'And I can't believe that after seven hundred years you still think you can get a rise out of me with all this.'

You're right, it's a waste. All I have to do is quote the names Auum and Drech, don't I?

Takaar said nothing but could not stop his jaw tensing. Instead of replying he focused on the extraordinary school he had created. What had begun as a simple wood and thatch house was now a sprawling mansion of stone and slate, robust enough to withstand all that the Sea of Gyaam could throw at them when the storm season came.

Over the centuries a large settlement had grown up around the mansion and at its height more than a thousand adepts and teachers had lived here. That number was currently a little over seven hundred because of the deal Takaar had brokered with the college city of Julatsa on Balaia. He expected the benefits of it would be felt over the coming decades as elven magical power and understanding grew exponentially.

Only you could believe that. Everyone else knows they are just cheap fodder when the humans go to war again.

'That is a laughable accusation. Even for you it sounds desperate.'

Takaar walked past groups of students gathered in the open spaces laid out for range and area castings. Lectures were ongoing in the amphitheatre built into the southern face of the Crier's Mound, and Takaar knew that under the domed roof at the centre of the mansion new adepts were taking their very first steps into the world of the Il-Aryn. It was their most dangerous time, and the sanatorium was ever busy with those unfortunates whose minds could not cope.

Takaar took comfort every day from the sheer energy he felt from each of those lucky enough to study here. It was an intellectual paradise, and those Gyalans and Ixii who tested themselves, then learned how to harness and to use their power, were unendingly grateful to him. Meanwhile he walked the paths of Herendeneth seeking new inspiration and moved among his people to better disseminate that wisdom.

Your people?

'It is how I am viewed. I am the father of the Il-Aryn.'

Oh yes, the mystical leader . . . Why not go the whole way and deify yourself? Then you can wander among your flock, blessing the chosen with knowledge, power and the pure joy your presence brings them.

Takaar felt a shiver of anger but forced a smile onto his face. His passage down the slope and into the midst of his students was drawing the usual attention, and he was always serene when in the company of the Il-Aryn.

*Of course you do find it difficult to remain in their company for all
that long, don't you?*

'We all need our solitude,' muttered Takaar. 'Places where we can
think and be inspired to learn.'

*Those outbursts of yours against Drech have nothing to do with it,
then?*

'Those will always be a matter of regret.'

Much as is your jealousy.

'Be silent,' hissed Takaar. 'I have places to be and I do not need
your insidious comments.'

He was nearing the grand main doors of the mansion, which were
intricately carved hardwood set in a stone frame decorated with the
symbols of elven magic. They were pulled open from within as he
approached and a trio of his most promising adepts raced out,
shrieking his name. They were *iads*, bright with excitement, and
they crowded around him all speaking at once.

Takaar's first thought was to step back, but the first faint laughter
was already on his tormentor's lips so he stood his ground and held
up his hands.

'Please, my children, songs of my mind . . . Cleress, Aviana,
Myriell . . . one at a time.' Whatever the excitement was, it was
infectious, and Takaar felt his heart beginning to race. 'To where
must I come, and why?'

'We've got one!' said Cleress, grabbing his hand and pulling him
towards the doors. 'Just now. Ephy is keeping him in the air!'

'Slow down, slow down,' said Takaar. 'One what, my child?
Aviana, take a breath and start from the beginning.'

Cleress and Myriell looked to Aviana, the eldest of them by all of
three years and ever the most eloquent. She was the most beautiful
too, though none of them lacked attention. Their innocence had to
be protected until they had reached the maturity of their powers, and
the more persistent *ulas* had been warned as much. A heightened
emotional state in combination with the volatile nature of their
abilities would be a terribly dangerous mix.

Aviana bowed her head and placed the tips of her fingers to her
forehead.

Why does she do that?

'That is not necessary, Aviana,' said Takaar, lifting her chin with
his left hand. 'We are friends, are we not? Now.'

'We, well Ephemere mainly, were working on your Ixil transfer theory with Drech, trying to sustain one of his castings as he withdrew from it. She heard a call through the energy lines and, as she already had her focus, she switched to him. He's a long way away and he's almost spent, but she's keeping him in the air and bringing him here. She needs help, though. Will you help us?'

Takaar felt the thrill of righteousness. Just one more thing Drech didn't believe was possible and had only researched under protest.

'Who is he?'

'We don't know,' said Aviana. 'But he's a human, he's injured and probably unconscious by now, and he's still days out to sea. He's coming from Balaia.'

Takaar smiled. 'Perfect. Show me the way. We must not fail.'

Congratulations.

Takaar almost tripped over his own feet in surprise.

The quartet of black orbs, each the size of a catapult stone, wove through the air and smashed into the stern mast in quick succession. The magical fire consumed the sail canvas in the space of a breath, the blaze shedding wisps of ash to fall like feathers across the ship. A fifth orb struck. Flame roared down the mast and a wall of heat slammed into Stein, picking him up and hurling him back.

Stein raised his hands to protect his face and felt the skin blister on his palms and forearms. His hair was scorched from his head and his heavy leather coat smouldered and blackened as he flew through the air. He landed on his backside and slid hard into the port rail. He ignored the pain across his body and gathered his legs under him, staring back at the aft deck.

The captain and helmsman were gone, both taken by fire. A black stump was all that remained of the wheel, and the deck was awash with dark flames grabbing voraciously for new fuel and growing in intensity.

'Where was the shield?' Stein asked of any who might listen.

But precious few were left. A handful of sailors were heading aft with buckets in a futile attempt to extinguish the fire. Survivors of the mage teams hurled flame and ice at the trio of enemy ships closing on them and a small knot of defensive casters raised a new shield over the main deck.

The ship yawed, rudderless now and prey to the fifteen-foot swell. She swung broadside on and wallowed, shattering the concentration of the casting mages. Stein grabbed the rail with his burned hands.

The vessel steadied momentarily and he pushed himself off, wincing at the pain.

Across the shortening distance to the nearest enemy, he could see shamen readying again and the ranks of Wesmen crowding the rails, eager for their chance to taste blood. He knelt by the knot of defensive mages and joined their casting, seeing the mana shape flicker before it steadied and deepened, widening to encompass the mid-mast and the deck on which their entire surviving mage strength was now gathered.

'Brace yourselves,' said Stein. 'Here they come.'

Orbs of dark fire raced across the sky. Stein could sense their force through the mana spectrum as they flew for the shield.

'Steady,' he whispered.

The orbs struck the shield with the force of a cavalry charge. The shield shivered and every mage was driven back across the deck. Black tendrils of shaman magic searched the invisible barrier, seeking weakness. The shield held.

'Well done,' breathed Stein. 'Let's keep it strong.'

Stein took a breath and looked aft. The fire was raging over a third of the ship now. Sailors still tried to beat out the flames but it was a hopeless task. Clouds of smoke billowed across the deck and out over the ocean. The ship would sink. The only question was whether or not they could cover an escape.

'Incoming!'

The ship wallowed again, affording Stein a view of another enemy ship horribly close to their stern. Spells spiralled from her bow, slamming into the unprotected aft deck and burning mast. Stein felt every blow through his feet. He heard the cracking of timber and the sharp whip of lines torn from their stays . . .

. . . as the aft mast fell along the length of the ship, colliding with the mainmast, bringing down rigging, pulleys, spars and sail on the defensive mage group.

'Break!' roared Stein, scrambling away. Others weren't so quick and were able only to cover their heads as the avalanche of heavy rigging fell on them. 'Dammit!'

Stein and a handful of crew ran back to try and pull the mages clear, but all three enemy vessels were on them now, their shamen preparing to cast the killing spells and the Wesmen ready to mop up any survivors. Stein felt a hand on his shoulder and spun to face the first mate.

'You have to go.'

'No,' said Stein. 'We can't leave anyone. They'll offer no mercy.'

'Casting inbound!' yelled a voice.

Spears of black fire tore into the ship, ripping up timber, throwing deadly splinters into the air to bury themselves in the bodies of the mages still at the rails, trying to fight back. More dark orbs crashed into the mainmast and landed nearer the bow. The ship shuddered and Stein fell. The mate dragged him back to his feet.

'It's too late for the rest of us. Go. Now. Someone has to take the message south.'

'I—'

'Stein! We knew what we were facing. I am proud to die for my college and my country.'

Stein stared into the first mate's eyes and saw belief shining through fear. Stein nodded, bit down on his guilt and began to cast. 'The council will hear of your courage.'

Another volley of spells crashed into the ship, and water burst through already shattered deck timbers. The first mate turned from Stein, took a single pace forward and was struck by a tongue of flame. His burning body was flung clear over the port rail, his screams lost in the tumult of the dying ship.

Stein cast his Wings of Shade and shot straight up into the air. Fingers of black fire chased him, ripping into his boot and up his left leg. He screamed and barely clung on to the casting, feeling the wings gutter on his back and his stomach lurch as he lost altitude, plunging back towards the deck.

Black smoke billowed across the ship. He could just make out some of his mages trying to cast, but the shamen were too close and the dark fire was all-consuming. Stein focused, strengthened the spell and climbed once more, orbs still chasing him into the heavens but unable to reach him before they fell back to the ocean.

Below him the wreckage of his ship was sinking fast while the three enemy vessels circled like sharks contemplating their kill. Stein banked and flew south. They had been six days' sail from Calaius – an enormous distance for a fit mage, and Stein was far from fit. His head and arms were burned and raw and his left leg was a throbbing agony. The spells he had cast had depleted his stamina and he felt a gnawing shock at the ease with which the enemy had caught and destroyed them.

Stein focused on managing his stamina, trying hard not to think about the futility of his escape attempt. He tried even harder to stop making bets with himself about how long it would be before his wings flickered out and he plunged into the southern ocean. Instead he concentrated on the feeling of the air across his face and the chill in his hands, using it to remind himself he was still alive.

Stein lost track of time fairly quickly once he'd been through one night. The endless ocean below him had started to look like the most comfortable of blankets beneath which to sleep.

Stein welcomed the pain of his injuries because it kept him awake. His left leg was a particular torment, constantly prey to the buffeting of the wind. The cloth of his trousers was burned into his flesh, and his boot had contracted around his foot to create a hideous throbbing that sent pain all the way up to his hip.

His face and arms were raw and blistered. The rain that whipped into him periodically made him cry out, begging for it to stop. But at least it meant he was still alive, still flying, even though he knew it could not last. It was a shock when he noticed how close he was to the waves. His speed was barely above a trotting run and the shape of his spell had become so ragged that his wings were holed and torn in sympathy with his concentration.

Stein had absolutely no idea how far Calaius was and he found no satisfaction in the knowledge that he had tried to deliver his message. He had failed and he would drown; the elves would never know of their peril in time. The thought made Stein angry, and he shouted with both voice and mind even though none would hear him barring the gulls following him.

'*Congratulations, Ephemere. Note that following my teaching produces wonder, excitement and progress simultaneously.*'

Stein gasped and almost dropped into the ocean. He was sure it was his mind playing tricks but it sounded so real . . . so close.

'*We've got him. I don't believe it, we've got him.*'

'*There was never any doubt in my mind that this would work.*'

(*Laughter*)

'*It's amazing. Is he still conscious?*'

'*Barely, but it doesn't matter. We can sustain the casting for two reasons: it is a very basic construct, and we can feed the necessary strength through the energy lines I always told you were there.*'

'*I wonder why he's coming here?*'

'*I don't care. This is purely an experiment in energy transfer. And it is one that will succeed. It really doesn't matter whether he lives or dies.'*

'You have no heart.'

'There is no room for heart. You've felt the sickness in the north. We have to be ready, and that means we have to understand our craft more keenly than they do theirs.'

'Then we need him to live, don't we? He might have critical information about why our voices in the north can no longer be heard.'

'I already know why.'

'You know the answer to absolutely everything, don't you?'

'Almost.'

The voices stopped after that, and Stein's consciousness slipped away.

Stein had an itch. Actually his whole body itched but his face was the worst. He put his hands to his cheeks then pulled them away with a start. Strange. Stein opened his eyes, blinking against the light and waiting while they dragged themselves into focus. He was bandaged from fingertips to elbows. This was not death as he had imagined it.

Stein closed his eyes. He was lying down. He'd got the impression of a small room filled with a drumming noise and possibly with two or three people staring down at him. It felt hot and humid too. He opened his eyes again and found he was right on all counts.

He was in a small room with wooden walls. Curtains billowed before an open window beyond which he could see rain falling in sheets. The odd drip was coming through the thatched roof above him. He was lying in a bed and there were three people gathered about him. One of them had a wild and unkempt aspect and his eyes would not stay still. Nor would his mouth, as if he was in constant conversation though there were no words.

There was another man there – no not a man, an elf, a male elf. Male elves were called *ulas*, weren't they? Whatever, he was a stern-looking individual, and whenever he looked at the unkempt one, which he seemed to do a lot, he scowled. The third was a female, an *iad*. She was young and bright and excited, and when she spoke to the stern one and he answered, he realised he'd heard their voices before.

'Where am I?' asked Stein, using the elvish that he and thirty-five generations of his family had been tasked to learn.

'You are on Herendeneth, largest island of the Ornouth Archipelago, north of Calaius,' said the stern one.

Stein relaxed back into his pillow.

'I made it,' he breathed. 'It's a miracle.'

'I'm so glad you're alive,' said the *iad*. 'I'm Ephemere; pleased to meet you.'

'The credit should be given to those of us who found you and brought you here, not to some ethereal notion.'

Stein turned to the unkempt one, and knowledge clicked in his head, knowledge that had been passed down over seven hundred years of family secrets.

'You are Takaar,' he said. 'Your name and face are noted in the historical records of my family.'

Takaar, for it was Takaar, paused and his eyebrows rose in surprise.

'And your name is . . . ?'

'Stein.'

There was a silence and Takaar hissed a breath in and out.

'Then your arrival is welcome but the message you bring is not,' he snapped.

'Didn't you mention that Stein's survival was irrelevant to the experiment that brought him here?' asked the stern one, a smirk on his face.

'Your tongue will bring you to harm one day, Drech,' said Takaar.

'What is it you came all this way to say?' asked Ephemere, her smile bright and fragile amid the sudden tension.

Stein looked at Drech and Takaar, waiting until they were both paying him their full attention and the atmosphere had softened a little.

'War has engulfed my country and it is a war we're losing. You must help us, or when they are done with Balaia, they will visit their fury and revenge on Calaius next.'

'Who are "they"?' asked Takaar.

'The Wytch Lords,' said Stein.

'You speak that name as if it should chill our souls,' said Takaar.

'Ystormun is a Wytch Lord,' said Stein, and he saw Takaar's expression change from confidence to anxiety in a kind of weary slow motion.

Drech and Takaar exchanged a glance.

'We must speak to Auum,' said Drech.

Takaar spun on his heel and left the room.

Chapter 3

We must never turn away from faith in however small a measure because to lose faith is to lose both belief and hope.

Auum, Arch of the TaiGethen

Despite the slow pace, the ox dragging a comfortable litter behind it, and the focused ministrations of the finest elven healers, Nerille's condition had deteriorated throughout the journey to Aryndeneth. Auum did not think it had anything much to do with the journey itself, more that the increasing distance from Katura was breaking her heart.

The sadness was infectious. Auum had thought to engender a light spirit on the long days of walking and sailing, but even the normally effervescent Ulysan was muted and introspective. Auum found himself walking next to Nerille's litter, as he had for large parts of each day, trying to treasure each moment as if that might banish the sombre mood.

'I'm sorry to bring you all down,' said Nerille suddenly.

Auum looked down at her and smiled. 'I hadn't realised you were awake.'

'I rarely sleep. I just watch very quietly or listen with my eyes closed. And I feel a great deal, Auum, and I am sorry that I agreed to this journey. It has caused such sadness.'

'Of all of us you have the least need to apologise. Katura has been your life. And your leaving is the passing of something into history that touches us all. Every elf living and every elf yet to be born owes you a debt of gratitude they cannot hope to repay.'

'I won't be around long enough for a start. That's a lot of gratitude.'

Auum chuckled and a smile broke briefly on Nerille's face.

'Well, hang on until we get to Aryndeneth, at least, could you? I'd hate to think all this was a waste.'

'I'll remind myself to keep breathing.'

'You know what I believe?' said Ulysan.

'Enlighten us,' said Auum, glad the big TaiGethen had joined the conversation.

'We built Katura in the Palm of Yniss. And Yniss favours those who fight to save his children. That's what you did, Nerille, and so he blessed you with long life. Life enough to see all your efforts bear fruit, enough to see your achievements gloried. Now you've left the palm, those energies will be withheld until you reach Aryndeneth. There you will live for ever.'

'Dear me, I do hope not,' said Nerille and she reached out a hand to Ulysan. 'But you say the most wonderful, uplifting things. Thank you.'

'I'm right, you know,' said Ulysan.

Deep in the forest an ululating cry grew in volume. It was taken up by others from all points of the compass. The roars of panthers rose and fell in concert with the cries of the elves. The sound shattered the ambience of the rainforest as every one of Tual's creatures paused to listen. Auum felt a shiver pass through his body and a great weight settle on his shoulders.

It had been seven centuries since this call had echoed beneath the canopy, and it brought back memories of invasion, war and extermination. Only in the bleakest times was the ClawBound call to muster the TaiGethen sung in this way. It chilled Auum's blood to hear it again.

'We're still six days from Ysundeneth,' said Ulysan.

'No,' said Auum. 'Eight. I will not fail in this, the happiest of tasks, in order to seek out the grimmest.'

'Don't be ridiculous, Auum,' said Nerille. 'Unless my ears have failed me, that was the call of mortal threat. You can't delay answering it, not by a day, not even by an hour. The Al-Arynaar will see me safe to Aryndeneth.'

Auum shook his head. 'After seven hundred years of unfailing service to the whole of elven kind, if their salvation cannot wait another two days it is already beyond us. But, if you'll forgive me, Nerille, we will increase our pace.'

The disappointment Auum felt at their arrival in Aryndeneth would live with him for ever. All that he had planned had been ripped to shreds by the ClawBound call. There was no honour guard of

TaiGethen to see them to the doors of the temple. There was no feast of welcome. There would be no ceremonial prayers to dedicate the Palm of Yniss back to Tual's denizens.

Nerille's arrival, marking the end of one of the more glorious chapters of elven history, passed almost unnoticed.

The grand old Gyalan elf was helped from her litter, determined to walk across the apron and into the temple to pray. Auum and Ulysan flanked her. Tulan and the Al-Arynaar walked behind them. Early evening sunlight was warming the forest after a brief deluge. Steam rose into the canopy, shafts of sunlight sparkled against the multi-coloured glass tiles in the temple roof. Aryndeneth should have been at peace.

Auum looked around him. The usual TaiGethen guards were already gone to join the muster. Inside the temple the atmosphere was subdued and anxious. Prayers were being led by senior priests, and the sounds of light and laughter that Auum associated with the temple were muted. Auum laid his hand on the shoulder of a young priest kneeling by the harmonic pool. The *iad* looked up, her smile brittle.

'Auum.' She rose to her feet and her smile broadened. 'Nerille? We are honoured you have chosen to come and live with us. I am Tanyse. Welcome to Aryndeneth.'

'Thank you, Tanyse,' said Nerille. 'Now I wonder if you could find me a place to lie down. I crave a proper bed and mattress after the hammocks Auum has made me sleep in all the way here.'

Tanyse laughed, and it was a sound that danced across the dome, lightening the atmosphere.

'He really should have brought a bed with him,' said Tanyse.

'I wanted to but Ulysan refused to carry it,' said Auum.

'Only because the frame got caught in the lianas the whole time,' said Ulysan.

Tanyse held out her hand. 'If you'll do me the honour, I'll show you to your rooms in the village. The bed there holds the prayers of every priest in Aryndeneth.'

'Bless you, Tanyse,' said Nerille taking her hand. 'I think we are going to get along.'

'Tanyse,' said Auum. 'Where is Onelle?'

Tanyse nodded towards the back of the temple. 'She's in the chamber of light. What's going on, Auum?'

'I hope she might be able to tell me. Has she heard from Drech?'

'I think so,' said Tanyse. 'She hasn't spoken much since.'

'Bless you,' said Auum. 'Nerille, you are in the best of hands. I'm sorry your arrival was not greeted with the ceremony you deserve.'

'Gyal's tears, I'm not,' said Nerille. 'Look in on me before you head off to save us all, will you?'

'I would deem it a crime not to do so,' said Auum. 'Ulysan, check on the Al-Arynaar numbers and come back to me at evening prayer.'

Auum trotted into the lantern-lit corridor beyond the statue of Yniss and up to the door of the chamber of light. It was a large chamber, set with windows in both outside walls and in the ceiling. Mirrors further reflected the natural light that came in, bathing the small shrine and its mats and benches with a warm gentle glow.

Onelle was sitting on a bench looking out into the rainforest. When the training of mages had been moved to Herendeneth she had elected to remain here, ostensibly to welcome and orient potential adepts before their travel to the island. But the truth was she didn't feel safe anywhere else. Some memories would never fade.

'I'm not sure even the prayers of light can help, can they?'

Onelle turned from the window. 'We must never turn away from faith in however small a measure. That's your teaching, isn't it, Auum?'

Auum inclined his head in acknowledgment.

'You know why I'm here, don't you?' he asked.

Onelle nodded and stood up. She looked well, if you saw past the worry on her face. Her hair was lustrous and she carried her frame proudly. Peace at Aryndeneth had been very kind to her.

'I had contact yesterday at dawn,' she said. 'Takaar has brought a human to Ysundeneth. He is warning of another invasion. It's stirred up quite a panic in the city.'

'I bet it has,' said Auum. 'Takaar's understanding of the word discretion is sadly lacking. Who requested the ClawBound to call the muster?'

Onelle swallowed. 'Takaar did.'

Of all the names Auum had expected to hear, his was not among them.

'What?'

'Drech says that Takaar is foretelling an end to the elves.'

Auum sighed and rubbed his hands over his face. 'I don't believe this. Why did the ClawBound listen to him?'

'I've no idea,' said Onelle.

'Who is this human anyway? Garan come back from the grave to haunt us? Did Drech say?'

'Drech didn't know much except his name.' Onelle searched her mind briefly for the detail. 'It was . . . curse my leaky brain . . . *Stein*, that was it. Stein.'

Auum felt cold and his fury towards Takaar evaporated while a pain grew in the centre of his chest. 'Are you sure?'

'Certain,' said Onelle. 'Why?'

'I have to get to Ysundeneth.'

'What is it?' asked Onelle. 'What's wrong?'

Memories long buried clawed their way back to the surface. Fears long forgotten started his hands trembling and made his heart quicken.

'Don't leave here. Not unless you hear a general call to evacuate everyone south. Takaar may not have been overreacting.' Auum kissed Onelle's forehead. 'Pray, Onelle. Pray this Stein is a fraud and Takaar has been fooled. I'll send word when I can. Look after Nerille. She's old and frail and I want to see her again before she dies.'

Onelle had tears on her cheeks.

'You can save us, can't you, Auum?'

'I don't know.'

The palace and temple of Parve was grand beyond the comprehension of all of those who had been forced to build it, all of those summoned to worship there and all of those who could not avoid seeing it every single day. Those who dwelt within it cared nothing for it, only for the power that smouldered within its walls and seeped through the stone flags on the floor.

Parve, the only great city of the Wesmen, was largely deserted and had fallen into disrepair as the unity of the tribes had crumbled in the wake of the Sundering at Triverne and the destruction of the Wytch Lords' greatest power base. But now it was complete, an aura of strength was building within the temple. Already the first strikes had been made into the east.

The ill-advised unveiling of the apocalyptic spell Dawnthief by Septern had forced the Wytch Lords' hands but their agents had failed to capture the mage or his creation. The subsequent assault on Septern's mansion and workshop had yielded nothing but had cost a large number of Wesman lives. Those were acceptable losses, but the disappearance of two agents was disappointing.

Ystormun had a great deal more to ponder than that and much to answer for on a personal basis. He had never regained his true status since his return, in a decidedly withered form, from Calaius more than seven hundred years ago. His reincarnation had been greeted with disdain by the cadre, and his efforts to retake his power had been thwarted at every turn.

He was the first to arrive at the meeting in the Hexerion chamber, and he could still find the energy to raise a smile at its stunningly naive design. In the mistaken belief that all Wytch Lords considered themselves equal, the room was a perfect hexagon with identical panels each containing a door and a fireplace. The table which dominated the centre of the room was a marble hexagon mounted on a granite plinth.

A six-spoke iron chandelier hung low over the table, its candles spilling yellow light not quite far enough. The six chairs were ident-ical: high-backed, winged and leather-upholstered. The tapestries hung on each wall depicted the imagined glories of the Wytch Lords.

It was a ridiculous room, but strangely conducive to the matters of dominion so beloved by the Wytch Lords. And so they endured the chill of the table, the poor light and the erratic heat of the fires because it was within these walls that they could hate each other with particular acuity.

Ystormun brushed down his thick woollen robes. He pulled his cloak about him and sat in his chair. He closed his eyes and found the trails of the other five as they meandered or strode through the ether to the Hexerion. All of them felt angry, all of them were prepared to blame one another, and all of them would have particular vitriol for Ystormun.

Before long, all of the soulless immortals were present, and the table had been set with spirits, wines and meats. Ystormun rested his head against the back of his chair, finding that the wings obscured him from the glares of the vain black-skinned Belphamun on his left and the venous mottled sack of bones that was Giriamun on his right.

Opposite him, Pamun gazed at him with undisguised loathing. His skin seemed tighter than ever over the angled bones of his skull, and the ever-present skullcap had not been pulled down far enough to hide the pulse in his temple. He was flanked by Weyamun, who boasted downy white hair on his ridged skull, and Arumun, whose eyes were the bleakest of them all and set deep and close above his narrow nose.

'I presume your early arrival was to give yourself time to properly reflect upon your latest failure,' said Pamun, his voice quiet malice.

'It is a setback, nothing more.'

'Stein escaped,' rasped Belphamun.

Ystormun did not turn towards his voice. 'He was badly injured and flying south. Only the most deluded among you could believe he is still alive. Even a fit and fresh mage could not stay on the wing for five days straight.'

'We felt fingers of energy reaching out from the south, from the heart of elven magical power,' said Pamun.

'Which proves nothing,' said Ystormun.

'Yet we must now assume the elven race is aware of our plans for them,' said Giriamun.

'Perhaps we should also pause to dissect Giriamun's progress and achievements in capturing Dawnthief?' said Ystormun. 'It will not divert us for long, after all.'

Ill feeling flashed around the table, dragging a harsh silence in its wake. Ystormun spoke into the void.

'It is the single most important task, is it not? Perhaps Giriamun is not up to it. Perhaps another should take the reins.'

'And who would you suggest? You?' Giriamun spat the word out as he would rotten meat. 'You who cannot kill one mage on a defenceless ship?'

'No, my brother, not I,' said Ystormun and he smiled and leaned forward. 'I am sworn to defeat the elves and so I shall. But I am surprised there is no dissent from around the table. No doubt expressed, no blame to be attached for your abject failure? If we believe the elves are alerted to our intentions, should we also assume Xetesk has captured Dawnthief?'

'ENOUGH!' Belphamun's voice shivered the air. Fires guttered and spat. 'Are we children squabbling over scraps? How long have we lived, how long have we survived, how much power do we wield only to bicker like women over grain?'

Ystormun hunched back into his chair while the echoes of Belphamun's voice faded against the stone walls of the Hexerion. Across the table from him, Pamun's fingertips were pressed hard together and sparks of mana played across his nails.

'Errors have been made,' continued Belphamun. 'Our gambit for

Dawnthief has failed. The elves might be aware of our plans. Are these mortal blows? Focus, brothers, on our next actions. Actions we must execute without error.'

'The march towards dominion of this dimension is in hand,' said Arumun, waving a hand dismissively.

'Plainly not,' said Belphamun. 'Or, if it is, it is a fragile and shaking hand. Here is what must be done—'

'Have I missed something?' Weyamun rested his ancient arms on the table. 'I had not understood you to be the speaker of the cadre.'

Ystormun felt Belphamun's weary anger deepening.

'Each of us knows that we are all equal within the walls of this chamber,' said Belphamun. Ystormun had to bite back a bitter retort. 'I will, with your permission –' and frost from his fingers rimed the table '– put forth my opinion for you to challenge should you feel so inclined.'

Weyamun actually growled, and the smell of mana fire came from within his pale grey robes, but he said nothing. Ystormun steepled his fingers and settled back more comfortably into his chair, considering where he might seek allies when the time came.

'Forget Dawnthief. Accelerate the unification of the tribes, drive the shamen harder and invade before our enemies can ready themselves. Remember that for all our weaknesses they have been weakened too, and they do not have the resources we enjoy. Nor do they understand the magnitude of our powers.

'And because they must not gain allies, we must snuff out the elven threat as a matter of urgency. Ystormun, I remain confident you can meet this challenge. Or does another wish to come to his aid?'

Ystormun laughed into the silence. 'For all your vitriol, you have not a single spine between you.'

'I will oversee your efforts,' said Pamun. 'But I will not stand by your side.'

'*Oversee?* Look to your own problems, Pamun. Why aren't the lords of every tribe awaiting us in the rotunda? Where are the legions of shamen to lead our tide of destruction?' Ystormun turned to Belphamun and met his gaze. 'We all have our tasks, brother. Leave me to complete mine.'

'Do not fail us again,' said Belphamun.

'Nor you us.'

Belphamun bridled. 'I have not—'

'You have no idea if Dawnthief is ours, is lost or rests in the hands of Xetesk.'

'My agents are in the field as we speak.'

'But they have not found an answer, and so we are vulnerable. Hence you have failed. I accept the shortcomings of certain of my actions, brother. Why don't you?'

Ystormun pushed back his chair and stood.

'There is much to be done,' he said, feeling the weight of their combined hatred like a collar around his neck. 'Sadly, the elves will not exterminate themselves.'

'A shame since that appears to be your brightest hope,' said Arumun.

'You possess so much bitterness, Arumun,' said Ystormun. 'It blights what would otherwise be the delightfully pathetic collection of bile, bigotry and ignorance making up your character.'

'Ystormun,' said Pamun. 'The business of the Hexerion is not yet done. And we all must have the opportunity to comment on Belphamun's ideas. And you *shall* listen, Brother. And hear how success sounds. Sit.'

Ystormun bit his lip. With the eyes of the cadre on him he had no choice but to lose face. He sat. Giriamun chuckled.

'Error upon error,' he hissed.

Pamun's eyes closed briefly. His door opened and the stench of Wesman flooded the chamber. Weyamun gestured his displeasure with a flap of a hand in front of his nose. Giriamun coughed.

'Could you not have had it bathed?'

'Come, Sentaya. Stand among us. Show us your faith,' said Pamun.

The man walked forward to stand between Pamun and Weyamun. He was shaven-headed, dressed in warm woollen clothes and his shoulders were draped in a lined cloak. He was of average height and appeared past his physical peak though his neck was still thick with muscle.

Ystormun could not see his face until the Wesman leaped on to the table and turned a slow circle, taking them all in. It was weathered, tanned dark, scarred and flat. His eyes were brown, defiant and hard. He displayed no fear.

'My name is Sentaya. I am lord of the Paleon tribes and rightful lord of all the tribes of the Wes.' He continued to turn his slow circle. 'My faith is in my gods and in the strength of my arms. It is in the blood coursing through my veins and the veins of every man of Wes.

We seek to destroy a common enemy. Without me, you cannot unite the tribes and bring them to the gates of the colleges in numbers that will break them. Without you, we cannot be certain of defeating their magic.

'But we are not your servants. I am not your slave. It shall always be this way.'

Sentaya stopped turning and stared at Pamun. Ystormun could see the fury in the Wytch Lord's face. He smiled as dark sparks flashed in Pamun's palms.

'We are your masters,' said Pamun. 'Your lives are in our hands to be snuffed out as and when we choose.'

Sentaya shrugged. 'I do not fear death. But you surely fear being exiled here for eternity.'

Ystormun stood once more.

'So this is success? We have discovered a whole new definition. Well met, Sentaya, lord of the Paleon. And now, with or without your permission, brothers, I am leaving. There is work to be done.'

Chapter 4

When the muster is called, the TaiGethen answer.

Unattributed

Ysundeneth was in ferment.

Auum and Ulysan had run hard from Aryndeneth, hearing the call to muster repeated over and over. It haunted Auum's waking hours and woke him from his brief moments of sleep. Auum ran up to the top of the cliffs surrounding the Ultan to look down on the city before going in, and what he saw took his breath away.

Like an invasion was already under way, ordinary elves were flooding out of Ysundeneth and into the dubious security of the rainforest. He could see hundreds of sails, big and small, heading along the coast to the east and west. Elves thronged the streets doing whatever it was that panic prompted.

But there were no human ships outside the harbour; none on the horizon either. All the same, elves with no experience of living beyond the city were still throwing themselves on the mercy of the forest in fear of what might be coming. And Takaar had fuelled it all, whether by accident or design hardly mattered.

'Why do they listen to him?' whispered Auum. 'You'd think no one else knew he's insane and given to outbursts and fabrications. What a mess.'

'Where do you want to go?'

'The temple of Yniss in the piazza. That's the only place we'll get a level-headed appraisal of the situation.'

The Ultan bridge was thronged with people in the process of making themselves refugees. A few Al-Arynaar were with them, trying to direct them to the surer forest paths.

Auum ran along the handrail and swung about the flagpoles set along its length looking at the upturned faces as he passed. Two out of ten of them would fall prey to bite, claw or sting. No one with them had any knowledge of herbs or roots, barks or flowers.

Auum called for them to go home, to listen for the TaiGethen order to evacuate, if it ever came. But a greater power, a greater charisma at any rate, had voiced fear enough to drive them into the rainforest's dangerous embrace. Takaar: they loved and hated him in equal measure, but they always believed him.

The temple piazza was full to bursting with elves desperate to pray in their temple, seeking guidance from their priests or simply looking to share their fear with each other. Auum and Ulysan headed to the temple of Yniss, skirting the piazza to avoid getting stuck in the desperate heaving crowd.

Auum was uncomfortable this close to a crowd; too many memories, too many harsh sounds at odds with the purity of the rainforest. He led Ulysan down the left-hand side of the temple. It was quieter here. The walls were painted the colours of the forest and Auum instantly felt calmer. He indicated upwards, Ulysan following his gesture.

Perhaps seventy feet up, lantern light was spilling from a circular opening.

'Think she's up there?' asked Ulysan.

'Race you to find out,' said Auum.

Ulysan was strong, fast and had a long reach. Auum had often likened him to a monkey, and the big TaiGethen delighted in the gentle jibe. He leaped, found a tiny fingerhold in the timber work and cruised up the outside of the temple as if he was scaling a ladder. Auum smiled and followed as quickly as he could. He was still a good ten feet behind when Ulysan disappeared through the opening. By the time he'd turned a roll over the sill to land in Lysael's dedication chamber, Ulysan was sitting in a chair reading a book.

'Very funny,' said Auum.

'I thought we should attempt to alleviate the tension for a moment,' said Lysael, moving into view from behind a screen, cinching her pale grey robes with a braided red cord. 'You are most welcome, Auum.'

Auum knelt and Lysael kissed the top of his head. He stood and the two of them embraced, Auum kissing her eyes and forehead and she returning the gesture.

'Please tell me you know what's going on,' said Auum. 'All I know is a human mage called Stein has contacted Takaar and he has reacted with the proper urgency but without the proper tact.'

Lysael turned to a tray and filled three carved wooden goblets with sweet red wine. Ulysan rose and bowed his head as she offered one to him. Auum raised his goblet and muttered a prayer of thanks before taking a sip.

'We're in trouble. Whether an invasion fleet is headed this way or not, you've seen the effect the rumours have had. Takaar has brought Stein here. Pretty much every Il-Aryn too. But he needs swords, and that's why he persuaded the ClawBound to muster the TaiGethen. He says he wants the Al-Arynaar too, and many of them are already with him.'

'To do what, exactly?' asked Auum. 'We already have plans for defending the cities.'

Lysael swallowed the remainder of her wine and headed back to the jug for more.

'That isn't what he wants. He's equipping ships.'

Ulysan coughed, spitting out a mouthful of wine and mumbling an apology. Auum could do nothing but stare at Lysael, trying to unpick the confusion of thoughts crowding his mind. Finally, he managed to get one of them out.

'He's planning an invasion?'

The question sounded ludicrous even as he was voicing it, and he was momentarily happy to see Lysael shake her head.

'Not even he is quite that delusional,' she said. 'Though Yniss knows he's dangerous when his other voice gets the upper hand. No, it seems he is planning a rescue.'

Auum put his goblet down, fearing he might drop it if the revelations got any more astonishing.

'But who is there to rescue?'

Lysael paused as if weighing up what to say, or perhaps how to say it. She pressed her hands together and took a deep breath. Auum frowned, glad he'd put down his goblet.

'He's been sending Il-Aryn adepts to train in Balaia.'

'*What?*'

'Why?' asked Ulysan.

'You'll have to ask him, but, whatever the reason, now they're trapped and Takaar wants to rescue them.'

'Well, he'll be doing it without the TaiGethen,' said Auum.

He was finding the whole scene surreal: the wailing out in the piazza a backdrop to Lysael's words, which echoed in his head like statements of creeping madness. Even the wine tasted bitter.

'Where is he?' asked Ulysan.

'He'll be on the docks. He's stationed himself at the harbour master's house and he's using the Herendeneth warehouse for staging people and supplies. The TaiGethen are there.'

Auum closed his eyes, hoping it was all a ridiculous nightmare. But when he opened them again, the fact that a Stein was here meant that, whatever perverse actions Takaar was taking, the elves were almost certainly facing a mortal threat.

'We'd better go,' said Auum.

'Front door?' asked Ulysan.

'I don't think so,' said Auum. 'I prefer our private route.'

'Not before we share a prayer you don't,' said Lysael. She held out her hands to the TaiGethen and the trio knelt facing each other. 'And we'd better hope Yniss is listening.'

Auum felt his heart skip as he reached the docks at Tual's Wharf by the harbour master's house. Amid the chaos engulfing the greater part of the docks, as people sought escape, this was an oasis of industry and organisation.

Laden carts stood by the doors to the Herendeneth warehouse. A chain of workers passed crates, barrels and nets inside. Four ships were tied up along the length of the wharf, their crews busy organising cargo into holds and checking sails, rigging and timber. Gang masters sang orders, their gangs responded in kind.

Ulysan grabbed Auum and pointed towards the warehouse. Faleen stood in the doorway. At the sight of him, she shouted over her shoulder and ran across the cobbles. Her face was bright with excitement.

'So many have come ready to fight,' she said. 'It is the greatest muster for seven hundred years. A meeting of friends and a renewal of vows, joy amid the danger. How did you know to call the muster? I thought you were in Katura . . . What's wrong?'

Auum took Faleen's shoulders and kissed her eyes.

'It is good to see you, old friend. It's been too long. But I did not call the muster. Where's Takaar?'

Faleen frowned.

'He's inside . . . but . . . He didn't, did he?'

'Forgot to mention that, did he?' said Ulysan.

'What possessed you to think I'd agree to the TaiGethen sailing for Balaia?' asked Auum.

'We didn't understand it,' said Faleen. She shrugged. 'But when the muster is called, the TaiGethen come.'

Auum nodded. 'Yniss bless you, Faleen. How many of us are here?'

'Two hundred and twenty-seven.'

Auum blew out his cheeks not knowing whether to be furious or impressed. He settled on the latter. The TaiGethen never failed to respond. But Takaar had much to answer for.

'I'll talk to you all in due course. But I need to see Takaar and this Stein first.'

The TaiGethen were gathered to welcome Auum when he walked into the warehouse. He acknowledged their cheers and the songs with a wave but his eyes were fixed on the elf who stood behind a long table covered in parchments. He straightened and spread his arms in a gesture of welcome with that damned beatific smile on his face.

'Auum. More trials await the greatest among elves. And we must greet such challenges with energy, humour and an unswerving faith in our power and our gods.'

'I feel sure the entire elven nation is calmed by the knowledge that you have stepped up to marshal the defence of Calaius.'

Takaar's smile flickered briefly before firming once more. 'I have merely done what needed to be done while awaiting your arrival.'

'Really?' said Auum.

He walked up to the table and cast his gaze over the parchments, seeing cargo manifests, lists of names, racking plans and what appeared to be a list of ingredients for some of Takaar's most potent poisons. Some ingredients were ticked, many were not.

'On learning of a threat to Calaius, would you not have mustered the TaiGethen and made this place your centre of operations?'

'What I would have done is not panic the entire city! There is an evacuation going on without any order and without a plan. Thousands are putting themselves at needless risk by fleeing to the rainforest totally unprepared. Do you have a parchment dealing with that?'

Takaar looked at him blankly. 'We have enemies to face. Our people must be trusted to look after themselves.'

'We must keep them safe from harm. That is our duty. You have pushed them into harm's way. All the Al-Arynaar you have gathered will be redeployed to advise and aid the population of Ysundeneth.'

Anger flashed across Takaar's face. 'They have more important tasks.'

'There is no more important task than the safety and security of our people.' Auum sighed. 'Look, let's not do this wrong. Right now I can see panic across the city, ships in the harbour and my people gathered here for no particular purpose. Talk to me, Takaar. What do we face? Where is Stein?'

'See, I told you he would believe me,' said Takaar, looking to his right, apparently addressing his other self. He frowned. 'Tell him, Auum. You do believe me, don't you?'

Auum noted Takaar's lieutenants – Drech was one, he didn't recognise the other – switch their attentions to the table. Drech gave the merest shrug and Auum wished, not for the first time, that he was more than the tacit leader of the Il-Aryn.

'I believe that not even you would call a muster without cause.'

Takaar looked to his right again.

'Well I *would* call it a ringing endorsement. And we must be ready or we will be swept aside.'

Auum waited while Takaar descended into spitting and muttering, the mad elf's hands clenching a piece of parchment and finally ripping it into pieces.

'Takaar, where is Stein?' asked Auum gently, cursing himself for a fool for not seeing Takaar's delicate state sooner. 'Why did you send your adepts to Balaia to train with humans? With our enemies?'

Takaar focused on him briefly before laughing at something his other self had said.

'Well we can agree there,' he said. 'No combat magic on Herendeneth. Only place to go is Julatsa.'

Auum frowned. 'And Julatsa is . . . ?'

'The human magical college and city most closely aligned to the Il-Aryn in terms of ethics and magical constructions.'

Takaar was so far within himself, Auum doubted he had heard Drech's answer. With a tip of his head he indicated Drech should come around the table and speak with him. But before he moved, Auum pointed at Takaar's other lieutenant.

'You, make sure he has water to hand and a place to sit when he comes back to himself.'

The *iad* bobbed her head nervously. Takaar stared at Auum through faraway eyes.

'Where are you going? We have so much to discuss. So much work to do.'

'It's all under control,' said Auum. 'Just one question: how many of your adepts are in Julatsa right now?'

Takaar smiled broadly. 'The programme is working so well. Our adepts have been welcomed by the Julatsans. They have shared their knowledge in return for the best of training in key castings where our lore and energies connect.'

Auum felt his heart rate increasing and a crawling sensation across his shoulders.

'How many, Takaar?'

'Our current success currently numbers four hundred and seventeen.'

Auum gaped, he couldn't help himself. He licked his lips, trying to frame a response, but his mind was struggling to comprehend the ramifications of that number. It was beyond his darkest fears, potentially catastrophic beyond measure. And all the while Takaar smiled at him as if he'd made a decision that would bring them peace for eternity.

'It is truly amazing, isn't it?' said Takaar. 'What do you say, Auum?'

Auum felt his control slip and he had no desire to regain it. He reached out and grabbed Takaar by his collar, hauling him across the table. Papers and weights scattered across the stone warehouse floor. Takaar's feet caught on the table edge, tipping it over to hit the ground with a resounding crack.

Auum turned and pushed Takaar ahead of him, pushing him up against a wall with enough force to shake off dust and rattle the contents of nearby shelving. Takaar's smile was gone now, replaced by an expression of pained confusion. Auum spoke quietly though he knew every eye in the warehouse was on them.

'I'll tell you what I say. I say that you have trapped more than half of your magical strength on an enemy continent an ocean away from here. Four hundred and more who you have promised to the defence of Calaius should the day come. I say that you have left our people vulnerable, and yet your answer is to send more of our defenders after those surely already lost.

'I say that once again you have demonstrated your utter

unsuitability to be in any position of influence or power. I am done with you.'

Takaar laughed in his face. 'You should be pleased, shouldn't you? Four hundred of the adepts you so hate and wish had never been created, able to cast the magic you despise and deny can help us, are overseas. Now's your chance to show us how the mighty TaiGethen alone can defend Calaius from what is coming.'

'And what is coming?' asked Auum. 'No, strike that. I don't want to hear any more from you. I'll ask the question of someone capable of answering it.'

He let Takaar go and the mad elf sank to his haunches, back to the wall. Auum turned on his heel and strode towards Drech, who was standing with Ulysan and a human: Stein. Auum ignored Takaar's taunting and abuse and the angry stares of his acolytes.

'Get him out of here,' said Auum to Ulysan.

'Got a point, though, hasn't he?' said the big TaiGethen.

Auum shrugged. 'Yes. Magic is damaging, as he proves daily. Those four hundred should be wearing the cloak of the Al-Arynaar, shouldn't they? I wish they were not Il-Aryn but they are. And at the base of it all, we need bodies here when our enemies attack.'

Another tirade of abuse struck Auum's broad back.

'I'll find him a place to lie down,' said Ulysan.

Auum turned to Stein, appraising the human carefully. He was a confident man, confident enough not to be cowed by the presence of the TaiGethen. His bearing was proud and his features, bold and prominent, reminded Auum of his ancestor of seven hundred years past. But it was his eyes that truly marked him of the line of the first Stein. And it was the birthmark across his palm that granted him the right to speak.

'Sorry about the altercation,' said Auum. 'Takaar and I have our . . . differences. What is it?'

Stein was smiling and he was shaking his head gently, musing on something.

'I'm sorry. This may be hard for you to comprehend, but you and Takaar are elves whose tales have been told, whose names and deeds have been passed down through the generations of our family for hundreds and hundreds of years. And here you stand, free of the ravages of time, at least physically. For me it is simply amazing that you can have lived for so long. For you, of course, it is normal.'

Auum thought for a moment before holding out his hand in the way he remembered humans did. Stein took it and shook it, a broad smile breaking out on his face.

'If my history is correct, you would not shake the first Stein's hand.'

'Perhaps I've grown soft over the centuries,' said Auum. 'You risked your life to come here to warn us of invasion or worse. For that I thank you.'

'Yes, but it isn't altruism that brought me here. We need your help. We must have your help. And whatever else you believe about Takaar, he is right about the need to take ship.'

'Why?'

'Because you cannot beat what is coming on the shores of Calaius.'

'And you're honest too. Your elvish is excellent, by the way,' said Auum. He glanced about him. Ulysan was leaning over Takaar, speaking quietly and firmly. 'This is not the place for this discussion. We'll go to the harbour master's house. Drech, I need you too. Faleen, take the rest of the TaiGethen, find as many cloaks as you can. We need to quell the panic. Tais, my friends, we move.'

Chapter 5

Potential is as dangerous as it is exciting; a very difficult child.
Septern, Master Mage

Auum sat at an ancient pitted and scarred wooden table in the harbour master's kitchen. The master had a cauldron of guarana and lemon-grass infusion on the embers and all three present had steaming mugs of the invigorating drink in front of them. Stein had eyed his with some suspicion but on trying it declared himself an instant convert.

The harbour master having withdrawn and with Ulysan standing just outside to deflect Takaar after his avowed intent to join the meeting, Auum, Drech and Stein could talk openly.

'If there was one thing you humans taught us during the decades of slavery it was that we cannot afford to kill each other,' said Auum. 'Yniss knows we struggle with this every day, but at last the threads work together and they have done ever since the filth of your past left us. In all the time your people were occupying my country, only two of you showed you had a soul. Garan, who I will admit was misunderstood in his dealings with Takaar, and the first Stein. You might be the third.'

Stein nodded but could not keep the hurt look from his face.

'I understand that the memories of our past atrocities are still fresh for you but you have to understand—'

'I have to understand nothing. I have some respect for you, but I will not commit any forces to your aid unless I believe there is a direct threat to the elves. Takaar believes there is, and that worries me. Now you have to lay out the facts and convince me.'

Stein held up his hands. 'That is nothing more than I had expected to do.'

'Good. Your war should have ended with your Sundering battles hundreds of years ago. Perhaps you should have learned our lesson, eh?'

'Some of us did, believe me. And now we are forced into alliances much as you were.' Stein paused to take a lengthy swallow of his infusion and looked over at Drech. 'Before I start, how much have you discussed our magic colleges with Auum?'

'I have never spoken about human magic with either Drech or Takaar. It is of no interest,' said Auum flatly.

Stein opened his mouth and then closed it again, getting a little edgy. Auum knew he was being confrontational but it did no harm for the human, however welcome, to understand where he was and in whose presence he sat.

'Right,' said Stein and a brief smile played over his face, masking his anxiety. 'With respect, Auum, I think you need to know a little background before I can properly explain the magnitude of the threat that we, and as a direct result you, now face.'

Auum shrugged. 'If you must.'

'I'll be brief. The Sundering was the inevitable consequence of our differing approaches to magic, its learning and its casting. Four schools of thought, ethics and morals emerged over the course of time; then there are your old friends Ystormun and the Wytch Lords.

'I doubt there would have been a battle, let alone a full-blown mage war, if the Wytch Lords had not been determined to cling on to Triverne. Obviously, that could not be allowed.'

'Obviously,' said Auum.

Drech chuckled. 'It was the location of the heartstone – the artefact that focuses all human magical power.'

'Was?' Auum felt cheered by the implication.

'During the conflict Triverne and the stone were destroyed. It set back magical research and use by – I don't know – three hundred years.'

Auum bit back a childish comment and suppressed a smile too. Instead, he spread his hands.

'Let's skip to the outcome, or by the time you get around to our problems your enemies will be docked at wharf one.'

'As was already agreed, each faction set up its own college, but there was no stone to split so we all had to make our own. They were the work of generations. But at least the Wytch Lords had been defeated, diminished and banished way into the west to dig dirt with the Wesmen.'

Auum let the reference to Wesmen go. 'So what happened? I had no idea Takaar was sending elves to Julatsa – your college, I presume? – but not even he would send them into the teeth of a breaking war.'

Stein blew out his cheeks. 'The first adepts arrived a hundred years ago, well before any conflict could be foreseen. But the latest arrived less than a hundred days ago. You'll have to make your own judgement.'

'I wish I could believe he wouldn't ignore the warnings. If there were any?'

Stein flinched under Auum's bleak gaze.

'There were warnings. But the tide rolled in so quickly. The Wytch Lords had been building their strength of magic and arms beyond the curtain of the Blackthorne Mountains, but their chosen moment to strike should have been foreseen.'

'We are all guilty of not seeing the obvious at times,' said Auum. Stein inclined his head. 'What was the trigger?'

'Our greatest mage, a man called Septern, created a spell to prove a theory. Once he'd announced his success to a four-college meeting it quickly became clear they would all fight to get it.'

'Must be some spell,' said Auum.

'It is. It's Dawnthief.'

'That's supposed to mean something, is it?'

'Dawnthief,' repeated Stein. 'An extraordinary construct. Septern made the impossible possible. He demonstrated that, in theory, magic can do absolutely anything.'

'I think that's too great an assumption,' said Drech, his enthusiasm for this debate only marginally less than Stein's. 'Dawnthief can, in theory, remove all light and air from an entire dimension. That does not prove that magic can, say, grow crops from seeds in a fraction of the usual time.'

'What?' said Auum.

'It's a matter of perspective,' said Stein, turning to Drech, his hands making a globe, his fingertips together. 'If you take our dimension as a single entity, then a spell that can remove all light, air and life from that dimension must, at its core, understand that life. Hence it could potentially give rise to any spell for any purpose you care to mention.'

'What!?' said Auum, hoping he was mishearing but knowing he was not.

'That doesn't follow,' said Drech. 'If my understanding of Dawnthief is correct, it merely, if I can use that word in this context, removes light and air and hence life. You do not have to understand the basis of the genesis of life to know how to remove it from something that is living.'

The slap of Auum's palms on the table overturned all three mugs and jolted Drech and Stein from their ridiculous discussion. Both looked at him like guilty schoolchildren, Stein's expression instantly became anxious. There was silence but for the *drip-drip* of spilled infusion from the table to the floor. Auum's face was hot with anger.

'And there you both sit. Smug examples of exactly why magic is so dangerous and its practitioners must be treated with maximum suspicion. One of your own has developed a spell that, unless I misheard you, can kill everything in a heartbeat, and yet you sit there and discuss the finer points of the theory?

'How can you have been so . . . *careless*? Yniss preserve us, but I thought I'd heard it all. But in all the thousands of years I have enjoyed blessed life, I have never been so astonished, so *furious*, that another sentient being could do something so . . . so *stupid*!'

Auum pushed back and got up, unable to sit any longer. He walked around the kitchen, trying to get his thoughts in order and failing completely.

'To be fair, we weren't the ones who were careless,' said Drech.

'It's the whole sorry lot of you!' Auum shouted. 'Don't you understand? This is the curse of magic. It endangers innocent people all over Balaia and Calaius. I don't care if you call yourself a mage or Il-Aryn, you are all complicit in this. Of course Ystormun and the Wytch Lords want Dawnthief. Why by all the gods of elves and men did you let this Septern create this thing and, worse, allow it to be announced to the entire dimension?'

Auum rubbed his hands over his face as if that would cleanse him of this reality. But when he looked back at Drech and Stein his anger intensified.

'Have you really nothing to say?'

Stein had a sheen of sweat on his brow and was rubbing his hands together.

'The spell is hidden. The Wytch Lords can't get their hands on it.'

'They are fighting a war to do just that,' said Auum. 'Clearly they think otherwise.'

'They have no choice,' said Drech. 'They need to get to the spell before any of the other colleges.'

'And are you lot going to fight for it too? Can any of you resist such power?'

Stein didn't reply at once, considering his next words carefully.

'It is only natural that the colleges should seek the spell. Not to use for destruction but to analyse, research and to keep safe against those who desire its capacity for destruction.'

Not carefully enough.

'Do I have IDIOT tattooed on my forehead?' demanded Auum, tapping it. 'I must do if you expect me to swallow that cup of frog poison. "Not to use for destruction"? Yniss bless me, but Takaar is sending adepts to Julatsa to learn battle magic. It is *what you do*. And if you captured the spell that could devastate your enemies you expect me to believe you wouldn't use it to gain more power?'

'It's a moot point,' said Stein, shifting nervously. 'None of us know where it is.'

Auum had emitted a derisory laugh before he could swallow it.

'Then praise be to all we hold dear, we're all saved. Stand down the armies, go back to your homes and tell your children they are safe for eternity!' Auum leaned over the table and shouted straight into Stein's face. 'How can you know that the Wytch Lords can't find it if you don't know where it is! In case you didn't learn this in your history lessons, we had a hundred and seventy years to understand the tenacity of that utter, utter bastard Ystormun. And now all six of them are chasing the damned thing. It doesn't matter if your precious colleges can't find it, *they will*. They will never give up and they will never, ever stop. Not unless you stop them.'

Auum half sat, half fell back into his chair, his energy and his ire well and truly spent.

'Unless we stop them,' he muttered. 'Yniss save us all, but this is a nightmare.'

'I'm sorry,' said Stein. 'I wish it could have been any other message I carried.'

Drech was frowning. 'If Auum is right –' Auum growled, Drech smiled briefly '– and we must assume he is, why are the Wytch Lords fired up about invading Calaius? They should be focusing all their efforts on finding Dawnthief.'

'It's not that simple,' said Stein. 'The Wytch Lords, even backed by Wesmen muscle, are by no means certain to gain the victories that would leave them free to search for the spell. And now they see an alliance between Julatsa and Calaius, they see you as a threat. They want to snuff out that threat.'

'You're saying that us sending Il-Aryn to Julatsa has led directly to the Wytch Lords planning another invasion?' asked Drech.

Auum shook his head.

'Actually, I think it's far simpler,' he said. 'We remain the resource-rich land the Wytch Lords need to fund their war effort. And Ystormun hates us with a passion I'm sure has remained undimmed across the centuries. It's the simplest of equations. He's been waiting for his chance and now you idiots and your precious Dawnthief have presented it to him.'

Auum grabbed his mug, tossed out the few dregs remaining after the spill and refilled it at the cauldron.

'Well, thanks for placing everything I've striven to achieve over the last seven hundred years at mortal risk. And on behalf of every innocent elf and human, thanks for creating the means to kill us all on a whim. Now I need time to think. Alone. One last thing: how long have we got?'

'Until what?' asked Stein.

Auum blinked. 'You really need me to clarify that?'

Stein blushed. 'No, sorry. They could be at sea now. We were attacked on our way to warn you they were preparing ships, ready for their strike. I've been here for three days, plus four on the wing. I think it's safe to assume they're either on their way or leaving imminently.'

Auum nodded. 'Go,' he said.

Stein was out of his chair with the speed of a panther. Drech stood too, but a little more slowly.

'While you're thinking, there's something else you should add to the mix,' he said.

'Oh yes?' said Auum. 'Please heap on more reasons to hate you.'

'It's obvious we'll have to travel to Balaia with Il-Aryn and the TaiGethen.'

'Very obvious.'

'We have to take Takaar with us.'

Auum's heart was stone. 'Absolutely not. If I have to kill him myself to stop him boarding a ship, I will.'

'I know how you feel about him, Auum, but without him, you will not bring half the adepts with you. You'll be ignoring the extraordinary talent he possesses.'

'He will undermine everything we try to do. He'll undermine you, Drech, you know he will. And sometimes he won't even mean to. He isn't strong enough to fight in Balaia. Yniss knows I'm not sure I am. I don't care that he's the most talented, or that he's your spiritual leader, we're going to be sailing into the teeth of a massive conflict, and if he freezes or disappears inside his head at the wrong moment it could be catastrophic.'

'And if he doesn't come, every adept who still agrees to travel will sail with little or no confidence.'

Auum sucked his top lip. All those centuries of bizarre behaviour, and there must have been many more episodes than Auum was aware of, and still they held him in mythical, almost godlike awe. The only one of them who had really seen the light was Drech, and Auum pitied the path he trod, notionally leading the Il-Aryn but playing a poor second to Takaar at the mad elf's whim.

'What does he know about Dawnthief?' asked Auum.

'As much as any of us,' said Drech. He nodded at Stein. 'Julatsa shared the text of the theory with us, and he's certainly read it.'

'And that doesn't worry you? It doesn't make you wonder why he's so intent on getting to Balaia?'

'He wants to rescue the adepts trapped in Julatsa,' said Drech.

'And you don't think he'll be after the spell too?' Auum searched Drech's face for support but even he seemed blind to the obvious. 'What an opportunity this gives him. Balaia presumably in total chaos, all eyes on the Wytch Lords and none focused on the search? For anyone with the ability, this is a good time to make progress unnoticed.' Auum sighed. 'Look, Drech, I don't think for one moment that Takaar would want to cast the spell, even if he were able to. But I think he'd tinker with it, try and understand it, and he is not of sound mind. Worse, he's clever enough to uncover it and deranged enough to leave it for someone else to pick up. On every level I can think of, we cannot afford his sort of liability.'

Drech shrugged. 'I'm sorry, Auum, he has to come.'

Auum jabbed a finger at Drech. 'Then he's your patient. Keep him out of my way and off whatever ship I find myself on. And when he detonates, as he is sure to do, pray that you can confine the blast.'

Chapter 6

An elf born to life beneath the canopy is uncomfortable beyond it.
You wear clothes. Would you feel at ease if they were denied you?
Lysael, High Priest of Yniss

Ystormun's consciousness travelled inside the body of a shaman and with the strike force sailing across a heavy sea to Calaius. The Wesman spiritualists had proved so amenable to mind control and so accepting of Wytch Lord magics. They were given little choice of course, and the effects of long-term use of their minds and bodies were unfortunate, but there were plenty of other subjects available when they were beyond use.

It amused Ystormun to watch the Wesmen work. They were unskilled as sailors, particularly of ocean-going vessels, but they were enthusiastic and strong, and their sheer energy made up in good part for their lack of experience. Enough skilled sailors had been put on board each of the ten ships to ensure they could survive the crossing, and the rest was left to the fates. Not even Wytch Lords could tamper with the elements. Not yet, anyway.

Ystormun walked his host body all the way to the prow. Wesman sailors and soldiers alike made a path for him, seeing all the signs of possession in his face. He stared through the shaman's keen eyes and could just about make out the dark on the horizon that was Calaius.

He found himself experiencing a thrill that pushed aside the thoughts of revenge and the memory of his humiliation. Ystormun found he could recall the scents of the rainforest and the sounds echoing night and day in the deeps of the canopy. He could taste the sweetness of Calaian fruit and herbs, the potency of their root alcohols. And he could hear the screams of elves dying at his behest.

Ystormun allowed himself the briefest of hidden smiles. Incredibly, he had actually *missed* the place, and there was some form of faint excitement at the thought of his return, however vicarious.

How long he had waited for this moment to come; his pleas to the cadre, his plotting and planning, his aborted attempts to defy them and mount an invasion of his own to make himself independent from them. And now, thanks to Septern, his spell and the wars engulfing Balaia, the full force of his fury could be unleashed. This time slavery would be replaced with the glory of genocide. Wesmen would sail the barges, wield the axes and skin the animals for their rich fur. This time Calaius would be the wealth mine it would already have been but for the cadre's endless meddling.

But first the elves would suffer, and he would force two of them to watch it all before he freed them. Free to endure their failure for the rest of eternity, to know that their gods had deserted them. Ystormun had pondered so many excruciating tortures but none other would provide the end he desired for them: endless mental pain, now that was a delicious thought.

Ystormun let their faces play in his memory one more time and their names touched the shaman's lips.

Takaar and Auum: the twin architects of his diminution. If they still lived, and he had no doubt that they did, he would visit upon them such misery as to eclipse the sun and leave them only darkness on which to feed. It would be the crowning moment of his life. It would satisfy his every craving.

Ystormun withdrew from the shaman to rest.

He did not hear the shout of warning from the crow's nest.

Auum spent most of his time in the mainmast crow's nest because only there could he imagine he was above the canopy, taking in the elements unfettered by his beloved rainforest. It also gave him peace from the bedlam on board ship. The creaking of the timbers wasn't as permeating of his consciousness; the rattle of rigging up and down the length of the vessel was muted by the roar of the wind and the snap of sails in his ears. And he was away from the claustrophobic presence of so many elves in such a confined space.

It didn't matter that many of them were his people. Enough were Il-Aryn or sailors to ensure he constantly felt uncomfortable. He had trouble sleeping, his appetite was gone and he craved the room just to *run*.

Auum looked down past the sail canvas to the deck over a hundred feet below. The ship was in a light swell, the yawing exaggerated way up here. Faleen was engaged in combat training with her Tai, inviting them to attack her two on one. He watched them for a while, smiling at their instant innate balance despite the shifting of the deck at the sea's whim. Sailors with a lifetime on the ocean had nothing like the same skill. Such was the talent of the TaiGethen.

Having seen Faleen's Tai dumped on their backsides twice by their veteran leader, Auum sat down facing aft, his legs stretched out before him. He studied the sky, watching gulls circling overhead waiting for scraps while the high cloud whipped across the heavens. Three days was the longest Auum had ever gone without feeling Gyal's tears, and it did nothing to improve his mood.

Ulysan's head appeared through the hole in the centre of the crow's nest, a broad smile on his face.

'Still alive, then,' he said.

'Did you miss the part where I said I wanted total solitude up here?'

'Nope,' said Ulysan, heaving his body though the gap. 'Budge up, budge up.'

'Beeth drop a branch on your head, Ulysan, what are you doing? I'm trying to think up here.'

'Carry on, I won't interfere.'

Ulysan sat down opposite Auum and stared intently at the knots in the wooden frame of the nest. Auum tried to muster some genuine anger but succeeded only in feeling a sense of relief he was not alone. He scowled at the big TaiGethen nonetheless.

'All right, what are you really doing up here?'

'Making my morning report, my Arch.'

Auum snorted to hide a laugh and played his part.

'Ships still afloat?'

'All four, skipper.'

'TaiGethen still on board?'

'No reports of any individuals attempting the swim home, skipper.'

'Il-Aryn still puking their guts up?'

'Unfortunately there has been some improvement in that area. The seagulls have lodged a complaint. We suspect some form of casting might be settling stomachs.'

'Sorry to hear that but you can't have everything.'

'Indeed you can't.'

The friends fell silent for a time.

'Thank you, Ulysan,' said Auum.

'What for?'

'For not letting me retreat too far inside myself.'

'It's not good for you, you know, spending all this time up here. Not good for our people, either.' Ulysan raised his eyebrows. 'It's about time you shared whatever's got you so worried.'

'Is it that obvious?'

'It is to me.'

Auum sighed. 'We don't have a plan. We've rushed out to sea because Stein says there's probably a fleet headed our way and if we meet them we know what to do, but what about when we get to Balaia? We've scarcely discussed it, and I'm as much to blame as anyone. It's like we're hoping it'll all be laid out for us like a recipe for bread.'

'I think you're being a little harsh.'

'Really? We don't know the size of the forces against us. We don't know where they are. We don't know the true state of alliance between the four colleges of idiots. We only know the geography of this accursed place through a very poor map and Stein's guesses of distances, heights and terrain. We can speculate endlessly about all these things but we have to make a plan.'

Ulysan frowned. 'But we do know what we're doing, don't we? We're going to Julatsa, we're rescuing our adepts and we're leaving. Right?'

'That's just naive, Ulysan, and you know it.'

'I'm just making the point that it's not quite so bleak as you paint it.'

'Not quite. I'm starting to regret not being on the same ship as Drech and even Takaar. At least then we could make a few decisions. I'm feeling in limbo and I shouldn't. I'm Arch of the TaiGethen.'

'This isn't really about the lack of a plan though, is it?' said Ulysan.

'Isn't it?'

'We all feel the same to a greater or lesser degree. Most of the TaiGethen spend most of their time below decks trying to remember the canopy over their heads. You're up here trying to escape the crowds. We're born to the rainforest and we're heading for a barren wasteland.

'It's natural to be fearful, to try to cling to tight organisation. But if we place faith in our gods, keep Yniss in our souls every step of the way and believe in our skills, we'll prevail.'

'Bless you, Ulysan,' said Auum, feeling his spirit flicker more strongly than it had in days.

Ulysan stood and stretched, looking forward. He stilled, staring into the distance.

'What is it?' asked Auum.

'Dust off your jaqruis,' said Ulysan. 'Stein was right. I see sails.'

Auum and Ulysan trotted aft to the wheel deck. Halfway there, Auum stopped and stared about him at his surroundings, the vastness of the Sea of Gyaam and the ships flanking them.

'What is it?' asked Ulysan.

'I've spent too much time up top,' said Auum, his eyes tracking a wave, the pitch of a ship and the crew busy with such focused purpose.

'We've just been through this,' said Ulysan.

'I've been blind to how majestic it is, how quiet and how very, I don't know . . . *efficient.*'

Four ships had sailed from Ysundeneth, each with a crew of sixty, a TaiGethen contingent of thirty and forty Il-Aryn. Plenty more had been left on the dockside, and despite Takaar's outbursts, there they remained to defend the capital should this expedition fail.

There was a bleak beauty to the scene of white canvas, dark-stained wood and grey sea. It was so different from the rainforest and its multitude of greens and browns studded with colours as vibrant and wonderful as new birth. Auum's nose was full of the scents of sea spray, fresh paint and oil; his ears found joy in the sounds of the ocean passing beneath them, the creak of timbers and the snap of sailcloth.

Elven cargo ships were lower, longer and faster than their human counterparts but not as reliable in heavy seas and storms. The high-sterned ships favoured by humans had little style to them but were effective and their cargo capacity was huge, perfect for the timber they so desired. Elven traders needed greater speed to get perishable goods to Balaia quickly, and their hulls and rigging had developed along a different path as a consequence.

Auum smiled.

'I could get used to sailing.'

'You're only saying that because we're sailing towards a fight.'

Auum punched Ulysan's shoulder. 'Cynic.'

They moved to the wheel deck. The skipper, Master Esteren, was standing next to his wheel hand, his view of his ship uncluttered. Auum was yet to see him smile, and a trademark frown dominated his weathered and deeply tanned face. His powerful arms were folded and he rolled with the ship without need of support, muttering corrections to the helm or barking orders to his hands that carried clear from stern to bow. His crew, plainly in awe of him, snapped to fulfil his orders with an alacrity and accuracy that Auum could only admire.

'Master Esteren,' said Auum.

'Auum,' said Esteren. 'Enjoying the view from aloft?'

'It has improved considerably of late. You need your lookout up there to give you an accurate measure because there are sails a way off to the north-west. Distant yet but we don't have time to waste.'

Esteren barely acknowledged Auum, switching his gaze along the deck.

'Selas, to the nest. Sails reported north-west. Distance, course and closing speed, please.'

'Done, skipper,' came the reply.

'The accepted term is aye, Selas. Be right or . . .'

'. . . be off. Sorry, skipper.' The lithe, small and very young *iad* streaked up the mainmast rigging and onto the iron spikes to the crow's nest.

'Auum, find me your chosen adept. We need to set up ship-to-ship communication.'

'To back up your signals?'

'No, to relay my true orders. When the time comes, all my signals are going to be lies.'

Auum smiled. 'I like that.'

'That's why I'm in charge,' said Esteren.

Selas's voice echoed down from the crow's nest.

'Ten sails. Seven points off the port bow, heading south-south-east, on a run. Our speed, five knots on a long starboard tack, closing speed approximately nine knots. Distance sixty nautical. That's all, skipper.'

'Stay up, Selas.' Esteren nodded. 'Less than seven hours to contact. Enough time to set ourselves properly and come on them in the right formation. I need that adept. Have your people rest. If this goes right it'll be over quickly enough, but even for a TaiGethen it's going to be draining. I'll call you when you need to prepare.'

'Seven hours?' said Ulysan. 'I thought we were faster than that.'

'We're close-hauled, Ulysan,' said Esteren. 'And we aren't going to get any quicker until we can turn with the wind for a return attack if we need it.'

'Thank you, skipper,' said Auum. He turned to go, but Esteren called him back.

'They outnumber us comfortably, more than two to one. My crews are going to have to perform miracles to get us where we need to be to get you aboard and fighting. That means you have to be ready to go on my word. And the adepts have to be ready to combat any magic they deploy. We're vulnerable when we're close.'

'So are they,' said Auum.

'Don't let me down.'

'Aye, skipper.'

Esteren almost smiled.

Takaar watched the enemy vessels approaching, and with them came a growing dread.

'Can you feel that?' asked Drech, standing by him near the bow.

Takaar stared at Drech and could only feel sorry for him.

'I have been feeling it for some time,' he said. 'It is the energies of the Wytch Lords. An amazing force, isn't it?'

'You admire it?'

'I respect it and I try to understand it. How else can we seek to defeat them?'

Drech looked forward. In a little less than two hours they would be in the thick of combat. Takaar could tell he was scared, although he sampled exhilaration and anticipation himself.

Until the first attack comes and you scurry below decks to cower under a tarpaulin. Were you ever a mighty warrior?

'The very best,' muttered Takaar, though the jibe had struck home.

Drech seemed not to have heard him. 'Are they on board? The Wytch Lords?'

Takaar smiled indulgently. 'No, Drech. Can you not feel how the energies are spread across the vessels? It is just as Stein said. Their shamen are conduits. There is no focus for the power, is there?'

'So they're weak,' said Drech, and the shiver that had been running through his hands calmed.

Takaar sighed

How is he in charge of training?

'I don't know,' said Takaar.

'What?' asked Drech.

You put him there.

'He was the best we had. Still is, probably.'

'You're not . . .' began Drech. 'Yniss preserve me, are you talking to me, Takaar?'

Takaar waved his hand in front of his face as if trying to deter a persistent fly.

'Of course.'

'So, are they weak?' asked Drech.

'Of course they aren't weak!' shouted Takaar. 'And if you do not marshal your adepts correctly the shamen will tear this ship to splinters!'

Drech looked over Takaar's shoulder. A few adepts were gathered there to watch the enemy approach. Drech lowered his voice.

'Most on board this ship have no experience of combat. They are already scared and they do not need to hear from you that any mistake will lead to certain death.'

Takaar shrugged. 'It is the truth.'

'Maybe it is. But as their spiritual leader you need to tell them they are strong enough to get through and that you will stand by them every moment.'

'They are strong enough.'

Drech jabbed a finger at the adepts, none of whom knew quite what to do.

'So tell them!' he snapped. 'Please.'

Takaar felt stung. 'Why are you shouting at me?'

Oh, shame, poor little Takaar being told off.

'The fight is close,' said Drech, his voice low once again. 'We have to stand together confident of victory. So tell them what they need to hear.'

Takaar wasn't sure what he meant. He'd laid it all out already. There was nothing more to say; they needed to prepare, rest if they could and focus their minds on how to build impenetrable shields against darker earth energies.

'You all know what to do,' said Takaar.

He waved them aside to make a path for him back to the base of the mainmast where Aviana was in communication with her sisters, one on each ship. He ignored the mutterings of the adepts as he passed, leaving Drech to attempt to pacify the fearful. It hardly mattered. In a short time they would either learn or they would die.

Takaar knelt by Aviana. She looked calm, her breathing was measured and her eyes were open.

'What news?' asked Takaar.

'Manoeuvres will begin in an hour. We're going to lead the second pair. Auum's ship is the lead of the first pair. The skippers need shielding from mast tip to keel on the open sides. We are to keep out of the way of the sailors, and sit beneath the rails if we cannot sit below decks. We are being advised to move now. Some of the crews need to do final drills.'

Takaar nodded. 'Then let's move you first. Captain's quarters, I think, beneath the wheel deck. Whatever happens, don't lose contact. We'll prevail, I promise you.'

Aviana nodded. 'What can I report back?'

'Acknowledge all your latest messages. We'll do all that is asked. Say that the TaiGethen are praying and applying camouflage. Tell Auum we're ready.'

Chapter 7

The earth's energy runs through us all. The Il-Aryn use it to fashion castings. The TaiGethen use it to fashion great speed of mind and body.

Takaar, Father of the Il-Aryn

The small elven fleet had split into two pairs. Esteren had taken his vessel, *Soul of Yniss*, and the *Spirit of Tual* on a long port tack. The second pair, *Gyaam's Blessing* and *Capricious* continued on the starboard tack and would pass well in front of the oncoming fleet. The timing of their return tacks, to bring them into the enemy flanks, was going to be crucial.

Auum and Ulysan were back in the crow's nest alongside Selas, who was providing a running commentary of their position relative to the enemy. They were still well to the north-west. If Auum was any judge, Selas had an extraordinary eye for distance and speed.

Auum watched the enemy, who could no doubt see them but would not know an attack was planned. After all, they would assume that the ships they could see were merchantmen giving them a wide berth. Their ships were grouped loosely into two rows and Selas estimated their spacing to be at least a hundred yards on any side. That gave the elven ships room to get among them should the humans decide that continuing at best speed was preferable to engaging.

'They'll try to close up when they realise we're attacking, but that's risky in itself,' she had told them. 'It takes a good deal of skill to sail that close without collision or losing speed, so it might work to our advantage.'

Down on deck the crew readied themselves for the tack to starboard. Teams waited by the sheets lashed to cleats running down both sides of the three-masted vessel. Esteren was running as much canvas as possible – no spar was unadorned – and the ship was a magnificent sight.

With the exception of Cleress and one other adept, who were seated right in front of the wheel, no Il-Aryn or TaiGethen were on deck, leaving the crew free to perform the manoeuvre.

'Is this going to work?' asked Auum.

'Why wouldn't it?' said Ulysan. 'Four against ten; we're going to drive each ship between two enemies and then get our people to jump across the frothing water into the teeth of shaman magic and enemy blades. What could possibly go wrong?'

'Who is it you lack faith in?' asked Selas. 'My sailors, the Il-Aryn or your warriors?'

Auum saw the mischievous glint in her eye.

'Big ships are hard to turn,' said Auum. 'And hard to shield.'

Selas smiled. 'It's not so hard, just a tack and some twitches of the wheel. Look, the *Spirit* and the *Blessing* will tack on to a reach so they'll have pace when they move across the front rank of ships. All they have to do is find the angle up between the two outside pairs.

'For us and the *Capricious,* it's a little more tricky. We'll both be close hauled and making two knots at best, so our tack timing is really important if we're to sail in between the front and rear ranks. And then to point up further into the wind to pass between the outside pairs . . . well, that's why Esteren is here. You and your Il-Aryn need to be ready, though. It's going to be tough with magic flying in from port and starboard. You won't have much time to jump the gap.'

'I'm glad you're confident,' said Auum.

'If the shields stay up, we'll be all right,' said Selas. 'It's a shame our Il-Aryn can't deal out damage, though, isn't it?'

'Today, I agree with you,' said Auum. 'Mostly, I pray to Yniss that they never work out how to kill with magic.'

'One moment,' said Selas. 'Here we go . . . Skipper! Angle closed. Speed, five knots. Distance on tack, two nautical.'

'Ready about!' roared Esteren. The bosun relayed the message. Crews snapped to attention up and down the vessel. 'Lee-ho! Helm, hard a-starboard.'

'Hard a-starboard, aye.'

Soul of Yniss began to move up into the wind. On the deck sheets were loosed and fifteen sails spilled the wind. Crew on the starboard side began hauling on their sheets, dragging sails into position to catch the breeze. Team leaders called out the hauling rhythm, their teams singing the riposte to each line.

'Not fast enough!' yelled Esteren. 'Burn the fat off your hides and pull!'

The ship's prow moved across the wind. The sound of canvas flapping rolled like thunder across the ship. Cleats slapped against wood, sheets whipped and tautened.

'Ready jib and spanker!' called Esteren.

The bosun echoed the call. Crews readied the jib and spanker sail sheets. The ship moved further on to the port tack.

'Take the wind! Steady the helm.'

'Take the wind, aye!' roared the crew.

Strong elves hauled on the sheets. At the bow the billowing jib sail tightened a little, filling with wind. At the stern the spanker flapped, its boom creaking as the crew hauled it in. The ship picked up speed, driving into the end of the tack.

'Top gallants ready!' roared Esteren. 'Take the wind!'

The sails heading the three masts moved to capture the breeze, the bosun yelling orders to trim each sail for best advantage.

'Bosun, bring the rest in,' said Esteren.

'Aye, skipper.' The bosun marched into the centre of the ship, booming out orders to bring the mainsails to bear.

'Helm, course north-west. Point up a degree. There you go, steady her.'

Esteren's voice still carried across the ship though he was standing right by his helm. Auum shook his head as the ship settled on the new tack. To his left the *Spirit of Tual* had completed her tack and was astern of them by no more than three lengths, and the gap between them was less than fifty yards.

'Wow,' said Auum.

Selas smiled. 'It's always best seeing it from up here. Skipper'll have things to say though. It's never quite good enough.'

'Good job you're up here, then,' said Ulysan.

'Just wait,' said Selas. 'If we meet the enemy half a yard astray, he'll have me scrubbing the head the rest of the way to Balaia.'

'How long to contact?' asked Auum.

'Less than half an hour,' said Selas.

'Selas!' Esteren's voice seemed to howl up the mast and rattle through the crow's nest. Selas started and her face coloured. 'Halt the chatter. Position, speed, distance.'

'Aye, skipper.' Selas gazed forward briefly. 'North-west plus one point to the wind, closing speed seven knots. Distance, two nautical.'

'Send your guests down. There is work to do.'

Selas smiled at Auum.

'You heard him.'

Ulysan laughed. 'Everyone did.'

'Let's go,' said Auum. 'Fighting to be done. See you up here at dusk, Selas.'

'It will be an honour to witness the sunset with you.'

Back on deck, Ulysan called the TaiGethen and Il-Aryn to their positions. Up in the crow's nest, Selas was calling the moves made by the enemy fleet. Auum joined Esteren at the helm.

'They aren't breaking,' said Esteren. 'Either they're inexperienced or they're expecting to break us with heavily concentrated magic.'

'I think we can assume it's the latter,' said Auum.

'The Il-Aryn had better know what they're doing or this is going to be a very short battle.'

'Drech says that they do,' said Auum. 'I trust him.'

Esteren nodded and stared at the enemy vessels, on which they were coming up quickly. 'Helm, two points west.'

'Two points west, aye,' said the helm.

'Cleress, let me have the positions of your sisters,' said Esteren, his voice gentle, almost reverential.

Cleress was silent for a moment, her Il-Aryn minder crouched by her, whispering encouragement. Auum saw her eyes flitting about beneath their lids.

'*Blessing* and *Capricious* on target. TaiGethen ready. Il-Aryn standing by. Takaar warns of shaman casting range . . . shield early . . . fighters should keep low. Stein will cast to the centre of fleet. *Blessing* turn across imminent.'

'Message, Cleress, please,' said Esteren. '*Blessing* and *Spirit* free to turn at will. Free to engage at will. Relay Takaar's advice as orders from me. *Capricious* to turn on my signal.'

Cleress indicated understanding.

'Ready your people, Auum. Signals! Run the flags for fleet to come about. Quickly as you like. Helm, steady as she goes, but let's not crash into anyone, eh?'

'Aye, skipper.'

'Crew! Prepare to repel borders. Stretcher crews stand by. Fire teams, stand by.'

The bosun's orders reverberated from stern to bowsprit. Auum's heart rate increased and his body energised in anticipation of the fight. He could see figures running around on the decks of the enemy ships, which still ploughed forward, but even to Auum's untrained eye it was clear they would not escape the closing elven vessels. Selas reported they were closing up, and her estimations and calculations of angle and speed had been extraordinarily accurate.

Auum trotted down the main deck. As on all four elven ships, the TaiGethen were split five cells each to port and starboard, ready to board both of the ships they passed between. In a line between the TaiGethen stood twenty Il-Aryn. The other twenty were hidden but ready to respond to the call. The Il-Aryn leader on board was a Gyalan *iad* Auum had not seen before they put to sea but had since impressed him.

'Istani, any problems?'

'No time for problems,' she replied, nodding at the enemy looming large ahead. 'We're ready.'

'Trust us,' said Auum. 'Don't second-think. You must protect the ships because should we fail, you can outrun them back to Calaius.'

'We won't let you down.'

'Yniss bless you.'

'Gyal kiss you with blessed rain,' returned Istani.

'Tais,' called Auum. 'We pray.'

Stein could feel the weight of the Wytch Lords' power swilling through the shamen gathered on the enemy vessels. Standing next to the mizzenmast, he worried about the ability of the Il-Aryn to block what was coming, and of the TaiGethen to tackle the Wesmen. The shamen were powerful and their swordsmen strong and brutal. He could barely feel what it was the Il-Aryn said they possessed.

Yet Takaar would brook no doubts, and Drech, the one who spoke such sense and was a genuine scholar, had unstinting faith in his charges' abilities. Still, Stein refused to be caught napping. Though he'd been asked to preserve his mana stamina for a possible rearguard action, there were still things he could do and the shamen would not be able to deflect because they'd have no idea he was there until it was way too late.

The enemy were mustering but unsure of themselves. Shamen were gathered in groups on the ships he could see and the Wesmen waved weapons, shouted abuse and postured in a faintly ridiculous but typical fashion. Stein felt the Wytch Lord power intensifying. He glanced over at Takaar.

'Incoming,' said Stein. 'Imminently.'

Takaar glared at him but his face softened almost immediately. He nodded.

'Credit where it is due, you're right,' he said quietly then raised his voice. 'Drech, give the order.'

'Raise the barrier,' said Drech. 'Enclose this vessel. Ix bless you for your strength, your belief and your talent. Deploy.'

The casting snapped into place with barely a pause. Stein hunched reflexively at the weight of magical power it drew. There was no mistaking what the Il-Aryn could do now, and he found himself staring, his eyes attuned to the mana spectrum.

'Gods drowning, what *is* that?'

An ovoid covered the ship above and below the waterline. He could see it because he could both sense it and because it sharpened the focus of everything beyond it. Stein fought to understand what he was seeing. Lines of mana ran through the casting but in a way a lace might secure a boot rather than as the base fabric. It appeared to be made of little other than air and perhaps water but had an aura of incredible strength – that of the stormy sea and of the tempest's energy. It shimmered occasionally as if reaffirming its shape and integrity, the Il-Aryn who had cast it sitting perfectly still, line astern, arms folded into their laps and their heads resting on their chests.

Takaar was walking towards him, his arms spread and a beatific smile on his face.

'It is a wonder, isn't it?'

'It is,' said Stein. 'Will it work? What have you made here?'

The front row of Wesmen ships was past them, leaving the nearest enemy vessels in the second row less than a hundred yards away. The elven skipper pointed up a little into the wind, aiming for the gap between the first pair of ships. TaiGethen crouched beneath the port and starboard rails, waiting for the order to attack. They had no ropes and no grapples, but having seen what the Il-Aryn had done, Stein ceased to be concerned about their ability.

'We draw on nature's power. We manipulate the elements. There is nothing stronger than nature because even when we are all dust, it will endure. We have rendered the air about this ship and the skin of water encasing the hull solid as deep mountain stone. No power can break it.'

Eighty yards. The TaiGethen were praying. The intensity of the Wytch Lord magic was painful in Stein's skull. He prayed Takaar was right.

'But can I cast anything out of it?'

'I don't see why not,' said Takaar. 'It's a repulsion field on the outside only. You could push your hand through it.'

Takaar paused and giggled like a child. Sixty yards. Stein prepared.

'Oh yes, that's almost the best part,' Takaar said, apparently to someone else. 'Shall we tell him?'

Stein wasn't really listening; his concentration was focused solely on his casting, which in comparison to the Il-Aryn's was a work in stately progress towards a less spectacular goal.

Takaar was still talking. 'Don't tell anyone else, but from the outside the barrier is opaque, like water cascading down glass. They can't see through it.'

Forty yards.

'Really?' Stein almost lost the shape of his spell. 'That's very good. Very good indeed.'

Wytch Lord magic spat across the shortening gap from both sides as the elven ship moved smoothly between the enemy vessels, turning a few degrees into the wind. Black lines traced across the barrier, which rippled like a millpond pierced by a stone. Stein clung to his casting while the energies thrummed and fought all around him. On the deck adepts grunted and shivered. Drech urged them to strength.

Twenty yards. The enemy ship in Stein's vision was huge. He felt as if walls were closing on them from both sides and he could hear the shouts and taunts of Wesmen as if they were surrounded. The TaiGethen tensed. Stein looked beyond the stern of the onrushing Wesman ship. The flank of the central vessel, the ship the elves could not board on their first pass, was just in range. Stein cast, seeing his orb fly in an arc towards his chosen enemy. The skipper of the elven ship turned a few more points north, leaving them broadside on to the enemy on both sides and almost in irons.

The two enemy vessels moved past them, one trailing the other by about half a length. Shaman magic tore at the shield, and the Il-Aryn fought to keep their casting sound. From the rails left and right the Wesmen howled promises of death. The TaiGethen leaped to oblige them.

Chapter 8

Of all the great errors an adept can make, the greatest is assuming a power on a par with my own will grow.

Takaar, Father of the Il-Aryn

Auum had seen *Gyaam's Blessing* turn east towards them and sail across the bows of the front rank of enemy vessels. Just astern of them, *Spirit* mirrored the move, ploughing west across the light swell and triggering a belated reaction from the enemy.

Esteren sailed astern and out of range of the front rank before pointing up a few degrees into the wind to come between their target vessels. They closed fast. The sounds of the ocean, gulls and sails were joined by the roars of the Wesmen crowding the rails of their ships. The Il-Aryn's casting snapped into place. A weight settled on Auum's shoulders and he breathed deeply to ease it.

Wytch Lord black fire crashed into the barrier, spitting and fizzing, seeking a weakness to exploit. The barrier bowed and rippled, and the Il-Aryn gritted their teeth. The ships closed; walls of timber bristling with sharpened steel in the hands of powerful warriors.

'Know your landing!' called Auum. 'Steel is death! Fight hard, move fast. Remember: over there we have no defence against the black fire.'

'Ready, Auum!' called Esteren. 'Coming up five more points.'

The ship turned. Sails began to luff, spilling wind as Esteren moved as close to the wind as he dared. The gaps between the three vessels closed dramatically but were still too far for any human to jump. Not so a TaiGethen. The *Soul of Yniss* lost way.

'Now!' yelled Esteren. 'I can't hold her here.'

'Tais, with me.'

Auum led – surging up from a crouch, bouncing on the rail and launching himself towards the enemy ship. He locked on to his landing point on the upper hull just below the main deck. As he arrowed his body and flew in head first, feeling arrows whip by, a bright yellow light surged across the sky ahead of him. It was an orb of flame, human magic, and it detonated against the hull of the central enemy ship. Stein was casting.

'Bless you, my friend,' said Auum.

He landed, gripped instantly and propelled himself up using all the power his arms could muster. He rose across the eye line of the Wesman warriors, thumped his feet down on the rail and took off again instantly, turning a half twist in the air, drawing his twin swords and landing on the deck.

TaiGethen thudded down in a line on either side of him on the crowded deck, Ulysan was immediately to his right and Ollem, his third, was on his left. Auum didn't wait for the Wesmen to turn. He hacked a blade into the neck of one warrior and drove his second into the lower back of another just below the laces that secured his leather chest plate.

Wesman bodies fell along the starboard rail. Others plunged screaming into the sea. The survivors were turning to face them now. Others flooded across the deck from other parts of the ship.

'Get among them,' called Auum. 'Ulysan, Ollem, with me. Head aft.'

Without clear targets at close quarters, the shamen concentrated their fire on the *Soul of Yniss* as she moved away at her best speed to the north, aiming to come about once she'd reached clear water. Auum glanced over at the shield, opaque and alien-looking. It wasn't as solid as before. Most of the enemy fire was concentrated on the top of the shield where it closed over the mainmast, and ruptures appeared sporadically. They closed quickly but were deflating the defence little by little.

Wesman shouts, orders and abuse rolled all around them. Weapons clashed, jaqruis mourned across short spaces and blood sprayed over sailcloth. Auum ran past a cell forming up to take on a large band of Wesmen closing from both sides of the mainmast.

'Duele, head forward and get to the shamen. They're doing too much damage to the Il-Aryn barrier.'

'Yes, my Arch.'

Duele surged into the attack, swaying left to evade a powerful thrust to his head and jabbing his right-hand blade into the neck of his attacker, his left into the midriff of a second. Auum ran on, his Tai at his shoulders. The space was closing ahead of them.

'He's good, that Duele,' said Ulysan.

'One day he'll run with us,' said Auum. 'When he matures. Give it a century or two. Let's get to it.'

The Tai ahead was under pressure from quick and strong attackers. Auum saw the elf barely block an overhead blow and stumble back. The Wesman went in for the kill, but a blade from the right caught him in the side and he fell into his comrades, blood sluicing from the wound.

'Hassek, overhead in three,' called Auum. 'Tai with me.'

Auum ran on two paces, planted his right foot and jumped, turning a roll over Hassek's Tai and the attacking Wesmen. The moment his feet touched the deck he spun and slashed both his blades into the back of the nearest enemy, then ran on into a moment's clear space.

Crewmen were running from them back towards the wheel deck. At the helm the captain was barking orders and warnings. Other crewmen were headed up into the rigging.

'Beware above,' said Auum.

'Got it,' said Ulysan.

'Ollem, stay right. Watch the shamen, they have fast hands.'

'Yes, my Arch.'

Auum saw the Wesmen form a line at the head of the wheel deck, crowding the two short flights of steps. Eight of them protected their shamen, whose fire was still playing over the *Soul*'s barrier, tearing greater and greater holes in its fabric. Auum sheathed his left blade and pulled a jaqrui from its pouch, throwing it backhand.

The blade whispered away and up, taking a slight deflection off the deck rail and whipping past its target's defence. It chopped into the base of his nose, slicing deep into the upper jawbone. The Wesman shrieked, his head snapping back, his sword dropping from his hands and his body toppling.

Ulysan took the left stairs and Ollem the right. Auum ran up the stair rail next to his fledgling Tai, sword in both hands. The Wesmen didn't flinch. Auum beat back a swipe to his head and snapped a kick into the face of his attacker before bringing his sword down at an angle to carve deep into his neck.

Next to him Ollem batted away two strikes, ducked a third and jabbed up into the groin of his nearest foe. Auum leaped from the rail, drawing his second blade again. The Wesmen had backed up a pace and closed ranks. Auum could see the shamen behind them and, beyond them, the wheel and the skipper.

Ulysan launched a ferocious attack on his end of the line. He dropped, swept the legs from one before he even registered the move, buried a blade in his neck, bounced to his feet and swiped his blades across in front of him, taking another in the head and chest.

Three left and still they would not flee, not that there was any-where to run. The centre of the trio came at Auum, bringing the others with him. Auum crossed his blades in front of his face and at arm's length to catch the heavy overhead blow from the Wesman's axe. He felt the power in the man's arms and saw the fury in his face.

Auum heaved the axe up, shifted quickly to the right and aimed a kick into the man's knee, smashing the joint backwards. The warrior crumpled, trying to strike a blow as he fell. Auum moved beyond the wild swipe and stabbed him through his heart.

Ollem and Ulysan finished their work and the Tai ran on. It was just a handful of paces to the group of seven shamen, whose fire swept away from the *Soul* and towards the onrushing TaiGethen.

'Jaqrui, jaqrui!' yelled Auum.

He dropped both blades and dragged out his jaqruis, hurling them hard at the shamen. One caught the edge of a line of black fire and was knocked up and away to tear through the canvas above their heads. The second lodged in the base of his target's neck. Blood spurted from the wound and the shaman clutched at himself, his fire dying with him. Auum saw Ulysan's jaqruis take out two more.

Auum pitched himself to the deck, rolling low. Turning he saw the jaqruis still in Ollem's hands. The whelp had sheathed his swords first, losing precious time. He got the blades away but a line of fire drilled into his chest above his heart, setting his leather jerkin aflame.

'Ollem down!' shouted Auum as he completed his roll, stood and lashed a kick into the shaman's head, knocking him senseless and quenching his fire. Ollem gasped and fell. Ulysan flew over Auum's head and thumped down in the midst of them. It was unsophisticated but very effective.

Ulysan was up the next instant, his feet and hands moving faster than any of them could follow. Auum ran around him to the crew-men standing at the wheel, who saw him coming. The helmsman let go of the wheel and scrabbled backwards to the aft rail. The captain, like his warriors, showed no fear and took the wheel himself.

Auum knocked him down with a straight punch to his mouth and nose. He glared at the helmsman. 'Only way is to jump,' he said in halting human.

He stood astride the captain. The man, his face bloodied and his nose flattened, stared at Auum through eyes confused by the blow to his head.

'Who are you?' he managed.

'I am Auum.' He took a jaqrui from its pouch and sliced the captain's neck open.

The helmsman had jumped and would drown in the sea. Auum turned from the captain's body and took the bobbing wheel. He turned it hard to starboard, towards the central ship of the rear line, which was already burning under the force of Stein's spell. He wedged the captain's body under the wheel, locking the rudder.

He trotted over to where Ulysan knelt with Ollem. The youngster was both moving and talking.

'How do you feel?' asked Ulysan.

'I'll live,' said Ollem, coughing. 'The heat . . . Thank you, Auum.'

'You were lucky. We'll get Stein to take a look at you. Can you still fight?' asked Auum.

'I can.'

'Good,' said Auum. 'Fast hands, Ollem.'

'Yes, my Arch.'

Auum stood. The fight on the ship was all but done. He could see Duele at the prow, looking for more targets, but the body of one TaiGethen lay on the deck. Auum cursed.

'Let's clear up and get overboard. Much to do and the day is waning.'

Capricious moved steadily between her two enemies, one of which was beset by TaiGethen. The other was unchallenged for now. The distance to her had been too great for the TaiGethen to risk. The skipper would come around for another pass.

The shaman casting was relentless, scouring the barrier for weaknesses. Black fire spat through with increasing regularity, and Drech's voice, calm at the outset, was strained as he fought to keep his adepts together.

Stein could sense the barrier beginning to weaken in several places and the shamen could sense it too. Their fire was moving steadily towards the mana lacing the construct, and where the two forces met the Wytch Lord power was the greater.

'Takaar, that barrier is going to fail.'

Takaar stared at him as if he'd just recommended suicide.

'How little you know,' he snapped. 'There is nothing they can do to pierce it.' He giggled into his hands and whispered to his other self, casting a sidelong glance at Stein, who clung resolutely to his temper.

'They are picking at the mana strands, Takaar. You only have to look.'

'We have them defended.'

'You do not!' spat Stein. 'Look, damn you.'

Takaar drew himself up and advanced on Stein. 'You forget yourself, human. I am Ta—'

'Save it,' said Stein and he turned away. 'Drech! Look to your mana stitching!'

'You will not undermine me!' howled Takaar.

Drech had heard him, Stein was certain of it. He felt a change in the focus through the barrier. He rounded on Takaar, finding him but a pace away.

'I'm trying to save your life. All our lives.'

'I am the voice on this vessel,' said Takaar, so furious his face was colouring and his whole body shook. 'How dare you speak for me?'

Stein made to grab his collar, but Takaar moved impossibly fast. Stein felt his hand being swept aside and himself falling, registering that his legs had been taken from under him only when his backside struck the deck hard. Takaar pounced on him, knees either side of his chest, his hands around Stein's throat. He was smiling, and Stein felt a chill throughout his body alongside the trembling beat of his heart.

'Not just Il-Aryn but TaiGethen too,' said Takaar, increasing the pressure on his throat. He smirked. 'Silly human thinks to lay a hand on me.'

'Takaar.' Stein gulped. 'Don't. We need each other.'

'I think that time has passed.'

Takaar's hands gripped tighter. Stein had his hands on the elf's wrists but Takaar was strong and his madness only made him stronger. Stein began to choke, praying Drech or someone could see what was happening. Nothing else was going to save him.

A scream rent the air. Black fire cascaded through a great tear in the barrier, which collapsed in on itself, dumping freezing water across the deck. Takaar's head snapped round and he was gone as fast as he had struck. Stein sat up. The Il-Aryn were sprawled on the deck or stumbling around dazed. One had blood pouring from her ears and she screamed again, her voice taken up by others.

'Get it back!' roared Takaar from somewhere, his voice desperate and high. 'Get! It! Back!'

'Too late,' murmured Stein.

Black fire lashed the ship from the fingertips of a dozen hands. Stein dived for the questionable sanctuary that was the base of the mainmast, shuddering at the thought that he'd seen all this before and it hadn't ended well. Jagged like lightning, the fire bit into rigging, sail and timber. Fingers of magic tore at the hull, ripping into timbers and shattering them, tearing off great splinters and hurling them up into the sky.

Fire laced the deck, spitting holes and slicing through yards, sheets and stays. Above him sailcloth burned. Black streaks pounded into the great trunk of the mainmast. Stein felt it shudder and creak above him, a snapping noise sounded deep within it.

All around him elves were diving for whatever cover they could find. Il-Aryn, crew and TaiGethen alike fled, and for far too many it was hopeless. Javelins of hateful magic buried in chest, face and gut, throwing their victims around like dolls. He saw a TaiGethen pinioned to the rail, fire blazing from his eyes, his body jerking and smouldering before the power was done with him and he fell into the water below.

'Got to do something,' muttered Stein, though he knew a spell would draw their fire to him like moths.

He could hear the Wytch Lord magic smashing beneath him, tearing the ship apart. *Capricious* was heeled over now and the unmistakeable sound of rushing water added to the screams, the crackle of flames and the splintering of wood. From above flame rained down as the sails disintegrated. And, with a decisive crack, the mainmast broke and fell to port.

Stein hurried around the base, finding himself in the firing line.

'Get overboard!' someone shouted. 'Abandon ship! Abandon ship.'

'Not yet.' Stein prepared quickly, his mind focused while his body prepared for the death strike of enemy fire that must surely come. 'Have some of this!'

Stein stood, spread his hands as wide as he could and cast. Ice borne on a hurricane howled from his fingertips, over the heads of desperate and dying elves, across the sea and into the heart of the enemy vessel. Timbers, sails and faces blackened under the onslaught of the super-cooled storm. Frost rimed mast and spars. It gathered in waves across the deck. And it killed. The thought of that was so good Stein didn't want it to stop.

Wesmen and their so recently triumphant shamen had their shouts of victory frozen in their throats. Their limbs seized, their hearts became frost and the blood in their veins was stilled in an instant. The black fire shut off but for one shaman in the stern, who turned his focus from the ship's hull to the lone mage.

Stein saw it coming and dived aside. Dread magic spat across the deck where he'd been standing.

'Whoa!'

He rolled and came to his feet, scrabbling to find a little more cover, though precious little was left. Waves were breaking over the starboard rail as the vessel heeled over. She wallowed, and the bodies of elves shifted in time with the ocean.

'Time to go.'

Stein raced for the bow, pulling together a final casting on the run. It was difficult to concentrate. The shaman had him in his sights and the black fire was closing fast. Deck timbers split behind him. The ashes of sails floated about his head. Fire raged over the jib sail, which flapped glowing edges, spraying hot canvas across his vision.

Stein prayed he had enough of the casting together to make sense and dived over the bow rail. Wings of Shade sprouted from his shoulder blades, wisps at first but strengthening as he poured everything he had left into them. He powered into a climb, feeling his feet trace the wave tips before he spun into a full ascent, gaining height so quickly it stole his breath.

Well beyond the reach of Wytch Lord magic, Stein levelled and circled, making a lazy descent to survey the state of the fight. He tried to take in as much as he could, anything that might be of use to those who needed to know.

Behind the rear line of the enemy, the *Soul of Yniss* was in clear water and executing a turn that would bring her on to a run back through the carnage. The rear line itself was in total chaos. In the centre the ship he'd fired earlier was going nowhere. The sails had burned away and the masts were aflame. One was down and the deck and hull were awash with fire. She would sink inside the hour.

Immediately to her port side, another enemy vessel was on a collision course with her. Every sail was full and she looked a picture of serenity. All that was missing was any movement on her deck or her rigging. Stein took a breath. These TaiGethen were something else when they got to work. It was much the same story with the remaining vessels in the back line. Some fighting was still going on, but the black fire had been silenced. Around the dead vessels the water was full of elves swimming hard for their next targets, making progress through the water that a dolphin would respect. Well, perhaps not quite, but that was the story he was going to tell when he got back to Julatsa.

At the head of the enemy fleet things were not quite so clear cut. The central vessel of the front five, which they'd dubbed the flagship whether it was or not, was continuing unchallenged, just as they'd planned, knowing they could catch it with their superior speed. But the vessel on its port side was also intact, meaning the *Spirit of Tual* had failed to get her TaiGethen close enough to board.

Out on the flanks both enemy ships were under attack and wilting, though black fire continued to arc out from each. And as Stein closed in a little, he saw TaiGethen in the sea and swarming up the hull of the remaining vessel. The enemy had seen them but he gave them no chance.

Stein dropped further, on his way towards the *Soul* to report to Esteren. On his way past he saw that the *Spirit* had been forced into a tack to starboard, which was leading her out of the fight. She'd been supposed to come about into a run to chase down the flagship, but there had been no space for that turn. And across to the other flank, the *Gyaam's Blessing* had not made sufficient headway east and could not block the flagship, leaving her free to make her way south. It would all cost time unless they could think of another plan.

Stein swooped down over the heads of TaiGethen powering through the swell. Auum was leading them, his body flickering through the water, leaving barely a ripple in his wake. Stein turned and tracked him for a moment before dropping down to hover above him.

'Auum,' he called.

'Stein,' said Auum, not looking up, nor slowing to listen. 'What's our status?'

Stein filled him in. 'We'll be a long while chasing her down, that's all.'

'I hear you,' said Auum. 'Leave it to us.'

'You're supposed to be boarding the *Blessing*,' said Stein.

'Not any more.' Auum glanced at him for a moment. 'Where's Takaar?'

'In the water if he's alive. Drech too.'

'Find them and save them both. Though it pains me to say it, we need Takaar.'

'He tried to kill me just now.'

Auum smiled. 'Then that's something else you and I share. Go.'

Curious to know what Auum meant, Stein flew away towards the foundering wreck of *Capricious*, unsure if he hoped to find Takaar alive or not.

Chapter 9

The energies of Ix run through all things and each has its own unique signature. It is one thing to understand this and quite another to use it, for the strands of energy are dense and intertwined, even in the simplest of Yniss's creations.

Takaar, Father of the Il-Aryn

Ollem was struggling. Though his heart hadn't been pierced by the black fire, his ribs, flesh and muscles were bruised and burned, and he was having increasing difficulty keeping up the pace. Auum could tell his breathing was laboured whenever the swell allowed him to see. Ulysan was swimming close behind him, the worry plain on his face. The water was cold. Ollem wasn't going to last.

Ahead, the two remaining enemy ships were making good speed, but the fit TaiGethen would catch them soon enough. They had to prevent the shamen getting a message back to the Wytch Lords. Stein had been certain the shamen could not send word to Ystormun, but he would eventually check in and would then know he was under attack.

The elves had to land somewhere hidden and unopposed, or the fight might be lost on the shores of Balaia. Auum took another look at Ollem and his decision was made. He circled an arm above his head and trod water, waiting for his people to gather about him. Twenty-nine including himself bobbed in the water. Ulysan had a hand on Ollem's back. The only fatality had come from Duele's cell and he wore the fact like a cloak of stone. It gave Auum an idea.

'We have to up our speed,' said Auum. 'Ollem, I'm sorry but you have to get to a ship. The *Blessing* is closest. But you won't go alone. For any of you who know you can swim no faster and then fight, there is no shame. Do not die for pride. Iriess, you will go with Ollem.'

Iriess thought to protest but Auum held her gaze until she nodded.

Auum continued: 'Duele, you will fight with Ulysan and me.'

Duele smiled through the pain of losing one of his own. 'The honour is too great,' he said.

'Don't be daft,' said Ulysan, his smile as broad as Duele's. 'A taste of your future, perhaps.'

'Shut up, Ulysan,' said Auum. 'Tais, let us swim hard and fight harder. Keep low in the water. We'll take the flagship stern to bow.'

Stein took a closer look at the enemy vessels in the second row. The one they'd attacked had surviving crew and at least one shaman on board. It was sailing away after the flagship, still under control. None of the others showed any signs of life.

To his left, *Capricious* was all but gone. She was lying on her side with water bubbling and frothing around her. Too many would go down with her but he couldn't worry about what that meant to their efforts in Balaia. Instead, Stein searched the flotsam for survivors. He was heartened to find a significant knot of them on or around the stripped-clean mizzenmast.

Both Drech and Takaar were among them along with the latter's Senserii guard, masked elves who made Stein very nervous. Drech was full of energy and spirited words. Takaar was plainly lost within himself, staring at the wreck of the ship as if he expected to wake from his delusion of invulnerability at any moment.

Stein flew low over them, telling them he'd be back, an idea sparking in his head. He turned and flew back towards the enemy ship taken by *Capricious*'s complement of TaiGethen.

'There they are,' he shouted into the wind.

It was a sight to truly gladden his heart. TaiGethen warriors, perhaps fifteen of them, were swimming to the side of a longboat on which five wounded elves were seated while eight others pulled on oars. They'd lost two, which was a shame but not a disaster by any means. Stein called a warning of his approach and landed lightly on the bow, resting his feet but not too much weight.

'You've more to pick up,' he said. 'The other side of the wreck. Takaar is with them.'

'We thought as much,' said a voice from the water to his left. Stein looked down at the elf, fighting briefly to remember his name. Grafyrre, that was it; one whom Auum held in the highest regard. 'We're heading to pick up survivors and get on board the *Soul*.'

'Perfect,' said Stein. 'She's coming about now. I'll spot survivors for you. Most can swim; some you'll need to pick out of the water.'

'Takaar?' asked Grafyrre.

'Still alive. Drech too and a good number of your people.' Stein dropped onto the bow seat and dismissed his wings. He turned and looked forward, waiting until they had cleared the sinking wreck and given him clear sight of his target before he began to cast. 'Keep her steady if you can. There's a little thing I need to do.'

Even before he had completed the shape and cast his spell of rapacious flame and heat, he was imagining the screams of the burning shaman and how satisfying it would be to destroy the last of those who had broken *Capricious*.

The body shuddered and grasped at the bow rail to steady itself. Slowly Ystormun gained control. He found the legs and made the body stand. He found the arms and adjusted the grip on the rail to lever himself upright. The view gradually melted into focus, giving him a view of glorious clear water ahead and Calaius on the horizon.

But then the hearing cleared from its muted roar and he could hear anxiety in every command and a harsh edge to the shouts of Wesman warriors. And when the sense of smell finally came to him, the stench was of magic and fire. Ystormun shook the head – his head – but nothing changed.

Gasping in a breath, he turned, looked back down the ship and wasn't sure what to stare at first. Way back now, he could see two of his vessels on fire. Others sat dead in the water, sails limp. Another was sailing off into the east and the open ocean to nowhere. Only one other of his ships was still with him, and chasing them were two, no three, elven cutters.

A howl of alarm dragged his gaze from the disaster in the distance. He saw elves swarming over the stern. Like rats, or perhaps it was monkeys, they came. Ystormun cursed: *TaiGethen. What in all the hells were they doing here? How in all the hells could they possibly be here?*

But here they were. They engulfed the wheel deck, executing captain and helmsman and murdering shamen in mere moments. The ship began to turn to the east, the wheel set over hard. And on they came, vaulting the rail, hurling their damned jaqruis as well as themselves at the defending Wesmen.

And however courageous the tribesmen might be, they had little chance. The elves were so *fast*. Perhaps his memory had dimmed over the centuries, but he didn't remember this speed.

Ystormun moved. He raced to the forecastle rail and bellowed down to the main deck, 'Defence! Shamen get up here and prepare. I want two lines of warriors in front of us now and I want elvish eyes smoking before we crest another wave. Move!'

Shamen and Wesmen scrabbled to obey, knowing instantly who was in possession of the body. In an instant nine shamen had joined him with Wesmen guarding the stairs.

'Get line of sight down the ship. One rank. Cast on my word,' said Ystormun.

The wave of TaiGethen washed around the mainmast. Ystormun saw a Wesman begin to raise his blade to defend himself, but a sword pierced his gut and a foot crushed his windpipe so quickly he didn't manage to cry out when he fell. TaiGethen ran along the rails, slashing sheets and lanyards. Sails flapped lazily.

'Ready!' called Ystormun. 'Cast.'

He heard a mourning sound repeating over and over. The air was full of flashing metal. He threw himself to the ground behind his shamen who screamed and jerked as dozens of crescent blades thudded home. Blood sprayed in all directions and a body fell on top of him, its owner trying to pull the jaqrui from his forehead though his brain was oozing around it.

Ystormun shovelled the twitching body off him and stood, preparing to cast, determined to take at least one of them before this body was slain. He was greeted by the sight of a single elf leaping high over the last of the Wesmen, turning a somersault and landing directly in front of him, blades poised.

Ystormun stared, his casting forgotten.

'You,' he gasped.

The TaiGethen's eyes widened slightly but his mouth twitched up in the shadow of a smile.

'Yeah,' said Auum. 'Me.'

The edges of his blades were so cold.

The *Soul of Yniss* had joined *Gyaam's Blessing* in the pursuit of the one remaining enemy ship still sailing south. Drech with the rest of the survivors of *Capricious* had come alongside the fast-moving elven vessel and clambered up rigging thrown over the starboard rail. Lines had been secured to the longboat and it had been hauled up the side, complete with its injured passengers.

Ahead, the enemy flagship was wallowing, sails flapping in the breeze as it gradually came into the wind. TaiGethen were in longboats heading back to them. Others were going back through the enemy vessels. Each one was to be scoured and stripped of anything useful. *Spirit of Tual* had been tasked to stand on station to take any cargo on board.

Drech was standing in the prow of the *Soul* with a strangely calm and thoughtful Takaar. Stein was aft, reporting to Esteren, and was intent on sleep, having spent every mote of spell-casting stamina he possessed. Drech didn't blame him for keeping his distance from the Il-Aryn's finest but most flawed practitioner. The enemy ship before them was under full sail and they would not catch her before nightfall. Drech felt the tension across the ship.

'Can we not impel a wind to speed us up?' asked Drech. 'Surely we can find something in the paths of Ix that governs the heavens.'

'Wind is too chaotic,' said Takaar. 'Harnessing it would take more skill than we possess. We've barely touched research on the powers that rush above our heads.'

'Over six hundred years of study, research and practice and we have done no more than scratch the bark of a single tree in the forest of our potential.'

Drech smiled at his own metaphor. Takaar was staring at him, a smile on his face that made Drech nervous.

'Now there is something we might try. It should work, even at this range because there is nothing to block its path, and no other fuel directly ahead as long as the impression is cast directly outwards. I wonder if any would mind if I tried. I would need your help of course, your strength and your focus; mine alone will not be enough, but together we can do it. I doubt we'd even need any of the others. The poor souls are exhausted anyway. Better they rest in case we need the shield again. The Ixii and Gyalans possess such ability but their stamina is so much less than that of the Ynissul, don't you think? So we must attempt this. Nothing to lose and so much time to gain. Another day, even. What do you say? Will you help me? Shall we try? Just think how much it would advance our knowledge if I was proved correct, and I very much think I am. Another step taken. Another notch in the tree of understanding.'

Drech was desperately trying to follow what Takaar was saying. The elf was staring at him, eyes teetering on the brink of a sharp descent into the pit of his madness, unless it was tears that threatened.

'How much of that were you saying directly to me?' he asked carefully.

Fury shot across Takaar's expression, but he forced a faint smile and nodded.

'All of it,' he said, his stare intensifying. 'All of it.'

'And what are we going to attempt?'

Takaar's smile became conspiratorial. He took Drech's arm and turned him to follow his gaze to the enemy ship.

'We're going to make it sink.'

'From this distance?'

'You doubt me?'

Drech thought about that for a moment.

'No, not at all.' He gestured ahead. 'Lead on.'

'Let yourself see the energies of Ix,' said Takaar, closing his eyes.

The first joy of the Il-Aryn was the moment the lines of energy that travelled the earth and everything living on it or under it became visible. Until you made sense of it, the scene was nothing more than the heaviest of rainforest deluges travelling in every direction. But slowly every adept could unpick sets of threads from the flood because, as Takaar first preached, every individual plant and animal has a different density of energy. Wood has energy of a deeper density than a liana but not as deep as stone. A panther's energies are less dense than those of an elf. The energies of the core elements of earth, air, fire and water have signature flows and enormous strength to set them apart from any individual creature or plant.

Takaar's next breakthrough was to understand that single energy lines almost always represented combinations. For instance, water is the most common element of all and is critical to the make-up of every living thing. Drech had found the idea that he was mostly water absurd, but Takaar had created some demonstrations that persuaded him otherwise.

And there was the third joy: understanding the innate ability to manipulate the energies to produce something different. That had been central to unlocking the potential of the Il-Aryn as a magical force. It had given them a basis for learning and research and the

development of a range of castings and constructions. There was no
end to it that Drech could see, and that was a thrilling thought.

Drech saw the thundering energy lines that made up the ocean and
took time to wonder at the way they clashed and spat at each other
but never broke apart and how, despite the apparent chaos, there
was an order to the sea that was only truly challenged by the actions
of the wind.

Ahead was their target, picked out in ten and more differing pulses
of energy density. Water of course was the ship's greatest constituent,
but the complexities that made up wood, and the simple ones representing the sail canvas and indeed the rigging ropes were there for
the skilled adept to see.

'Now then, let's see how far we can push ourselves,' said Takaar.

'What do you plan to do, take out a mast or something?' joked
Drech.

'I think we can do an awful lot better than that. A shame most of
them won't see this, but we can reprise it another time.'

'See what?' asked Drech, excitement edging his mind.

'Lend me your strength. Keep the flow steady. No spikes, because
I'm going to try something a little reckless.'

'You do surprise me.'

'Concentrate!'

Drech did as Takaar asked. He placed his hands on Takaar's
shoulders to make the transfer more solid and fed his mind's energy
into Takaar's body for him to use in bolstering his own. Takaar
accepted the gift with a grunt and set to work. Drech watched him
and quickly saw what he was attempting.

Every impulse within him bade him pull away and shout at Takaar
to try something else, because what he was doing, if it went astray
and fed back through the elemental lines, would kill them both
instantly. But he resisted. Takaar had never been wrong. He clung
to that thought while Takaar teased at the water energies across the
divide between the two ships.

Drech was watching elven magic's greatest practitioner at work,
and he never ceased to wonder at the combination of delicacy and
strength of will that Takaar brought to bear. It was artistry, and
no one could ever hope to better him. Takaar was channelling the
unbridled force of elemental water through himself, using himself as
a stopper in a bottle, keeping the raw destructive power inside and

releasing only that which he required to do his work. No wonder he had need of Drech's energy.

Drech watched him tease out strand after strand and gather them as if they were threads caught in his fist. And when Drech was sure he had enough, Takaar carried on, never once faltering but whispering words to himself that gave him the confidence to continue.

When at last he was done, Takaar gave a little laugh. 'So. Let's see what we have learned today,' he said.

With his mind he jerked the strands aside. For an instant, ephemeral and terrifying, nothing happened. Then water cascaded from the air around the target's hull and fell to the sea in a myriad drops. The hull was reduced to dust scattered across the water. Drech caught the merest glimpse of cargo, furnishings and men tumbling towards the water when the ship's deck, deprived of support, slapped down on the surface.

Takaar roared with laughter.

'Look what I've done! Look!'

Drech stared. For a few moments the hull-less deck slid on, and then the weight of the mast, sails and superstructure defeated it and it tipped onto its side, balanced by the sailcloth and mast timbers before beginning to settle.

'Yniss preserve us!' yelled Drech, and his voice bounced across the ocean to their floundering and confused enemies in the water. 'I see it and only because you did it before my eyes do I believe it.'

Drech turned to call anyone he could to come to the rail and look, only to find himself pressed by Stein and every one of the Il-Aryn, all drawn by the power Takaar had employed. Everyone was charging forward to see for themselves. Well, nearly everyone. Takaar was leaning on Drech's shoulder, utterly spent.

'What did you do?' asked Stein, gesturing weakly towards the remains of the enemy ship.

Takaar, exhausted but drunk on his success, leaned forward and placed a finger on Stein's chest, tapping it gently as he spoke.

'Remove water from any of us, a ship, an elf . . . or a human, and all that remains is dust,' he said.

The bell at the helm rang and Esteren's voice rang out.

'Ready to bring us about, heading north by north-west,' he ordered. 'Stand by. Selas, get up to the forward nest. I don't want to collide with any wreckage. Bosun, you are not in position. Let's come around, wait for our passengers and head on. Tell Takaar he is not to employ that casting on any of my timbers, under any circumstances, or he'll feel my boot in his arse.'

Esteren's chuckle was as loud as his voice.

'Good work, everyone. Now let's get north.'

Chapter 10

It is a strange thing indeed to speak face to face with those whose names and deeds are noted in our history books.

Stein, Mage of Julatsa

It was full night and calm had returned to the diminished elven fleet. Only topsails, jibs and spankers were running to keep speed low and manoeuvrability high for the skeleton crews during the hours of darkness. The first mate of the *Soul of Yniss* doubled as the helm. The crow's nests were empty.

Services had already been held for the lost, and as they drifted across the waves, dirges and prayers for those to be committed to the sea and Shorth's embrace would continue until first light. Combined with the creaking of ships' timbers, the rush of the sea, the ripple of sailcloth and the lonely call of stray gulls, the elven voices lent a surreal quality to the darkness.

In the captain's cabin of the *Soul of Yniss*, on a rug woven in a likeness of the stone apron of the temple at Aryndeneth, sat Auum, Ulysan, Esteren, Takaar, Drech and Stein. They had been served a herb and boar broth and now had plates of fruit, sweet leaves and steaming broad-based mugs of earthy root tea before them.

They had barely spoken a word, choosing to listen to the songs and chants, occasionally joining in or mouthing silent prayers of their own.

'We should get to it,' said Esteren. 'I don't know about you, but I require sleep before dawn.'

'We'll try not to keep you,' said Auum, a glint in his eye. 'So, Ulysan, let's go through the numbers, depressing as they are.'

Ulysan swallowed the remains of his drink and reached for the jug, talking while he poured and set the jug back down.

'We lost a single TaiGethen, *Gyaam's Blessing* lost four, *Spirit of Tual* lost two. None of us lost a single crew hand or Il-Aryn adept.

That's the good news. Obviously we lost *Capricious*. Thirty-seven crew lost including the captain. Eight TaiGethen lost. All the Senserii survived. Twenty-eight Il-Aryn lost.'

Drech hissed in a breath.

'And the wounded?' asked Auum.

'Mainly minor injuries, not a great deal to worry about. The majority were caused by the sinking of *Capricious*. They range from cuts and bruises to severe sprains, breaks, and we have two nasty sword injuries. The surgeons aren't going to lose anyone and Stein says he can speed healing along.'

Auum inclined his head to Stein, who shrugged.

'I'm sorry,' said Auum. 'Esteren, Drech, Takaar. We have all lost valued friends and comrades. To lose a ship and so many of those on board is a bitter pill, but we have kept an invasion force from our shores.'

'We all knew what we were getting into,' said Esteren. 'But thank you nonetheless.'

'A full list of names of the fallen will remain in the captain's cabin,' said Ulysan.

'Why did so many Il-Aryn die but so few TaiGethen from the same vessel?' asked Takaar, his face grey with exhaustion and knowledge of the losses he had suffered.

'And no Senserii,' said Auum sharply. 'You know the answer. Please do not try to cause a conflict where none exists.'

Takaar's face closed still further.

'Could have saved more. Should have saved more,' he muttered.

'Perhaps it's time you got some rest,' said Auum.

'Don't patronise me,' snapped Takaar. 'You want me out of the way so you can plot, is that it?'

Auum felt the aches of the day's exertions more keenly all of a sudden. He kneaded the bridge of his nose with thumb and forefinger and tried to remain calm.

'Gently,' whispered Ulysan.

Auum nodded. 'It's just that you look exhausted, as I feel. After what you did today you have every reason to be asleep already. There's nothing to plot, Takaar. We just need to go over our next moves. We don't need to be sidetracked by pointless debate about who saved whom and who didn't and why. It's done. Accept that everyone did everything they could.'

Stein cleared his throat noisily.

'It isn't pointless to the dead.'

'It is especially pointless to them,' said Esteren. 'Please, Takaar, let this rest.'

Takaar waved his hands in a shooing gesture. 'Yes, yes, brush it under the rug. Never mind the dead. Never mind if they could have been saved. Never mind who chose to live, letting others die.'

Auum sprang across the rug and pulled Takaar's face to his, hands on the mad elf's head.

'Then let's lay it out for you so you can grasp it, shall we? Because everyone but you has worked it out.' Auum's eyes bored into Takaar's, who held his gaze unflinching. 'Your ship was sunk because the barrier came down. The shamen worked out the weak point was the mana threading and concentrated all their efforts there. When Stein told you this, you chose to attack him rather than warn Drech to fortify the threading. The shamen targeted your Il-Aryn the moment the barrier was down because they were easy targets, on their knees, disoriented and tired.

'My people got as many as they could over the side, but it was too late for the rest. And your twelve Senserii rescued one elf between them: you. Perhaps you'd have done better casting your clever new trick then, rather than saving your own skin.'

Auum moved back to his place in complete silence, righting a bowl he'd knocked onto its side on his way to Takaar. He sat and drank the remainder of his infusion.

Ulysan whispered in his ear, 'Gentle, just as I advised. Well done.'

Auum suppressed a smile and looked at Takaar, who appeared stunned. He was muttering under his breath, deep in conversation with his tormentor.

'We do have some good news as regards our landing capacity,' said Esteren carefully.

Auum nodded his gratitude. 'The boats we captured were worth the effort, I take it?'

Takaar lurched to his feet.

'I think perhaps I will take my leave,' he said. 'I find my exertions have sapped my strength more than I thought. A shame the fact that I have saved the expedition a full day has gone unmarked, but these are the wounds true genius must often bear.'

Takaar shambled out. Esteren followed him, bade him restful sleep and shut the door behind him.

'Anyone who laughs is going over the side,' he said.

'What was the point of that, Auum?' demanded Drech. 'He's fragile enough as it is.'

'Not fragile enough that he won't bolster his own sense of injustice,' said Auum. 'No one calls the actions of the TaiGethen into question.'

'It's a dangerous time for him,' said Drech.

'When isn't it? Remember what I said: he's your problem, so keep him in check. Look at the power he wields. What happens if he decides to turn it on us? Stein was lucky he was physically attacked rather than turned into so much dust.' Auum shook his head and turned back to Esteren. 'When do we make landfall?'

'We've got to sail halfway round Balaia when we sight land,' said Esteren. 'So get comfortable. We'll be there in six days, at a guess.'

Auum blew out his cheeks. 'Still, no time like the present. So, skipper, talk to me about getting us on dry land. Drech, I advise you to go and look after your patient. Stein'll fill you in on our plotting.'

The wind changed direction steadily, and by the time Balaia filled the horizon cold air was funnelling across the deck, strengthening by the hour. Auum pulled his cloak tight around him and stared into the gathering twilight, wondering when they'd set foot on foreign soil.

'Warm enough?' asked Ulysan, coming to his shoulder.

'Barely,' said Auum.

'Nice cloak,' said Ulysan.

Auum knew where this was going and he smiled. 'Thank you.'

'Looks just like the one you said you wouldn't need when I was adding it to your kit.'

'There is a remarkable similarity.'

'In fact I recall you being really quite dismissive and sarcastic about it.'

'Surely you have somewhere else you need to be?'

'No, no, nothing pressing. Now you said, "The day I wear that cloak other than for ceremonial reasons is the day Gyal's tears cease and the rainforest dies." I wondered if you wanted to amend that statement at all?'

'I hadn't expected chill of this intensity,' said Auum.

'It's seven days north and it's full of humans, what *did* you expect?'

'Not this,' said Auum.

He felt low. The thrill of the fight had long since faded leaving an endless stream of nagging anxieties behind. If he was leading them to their deaths, how would he square that with Shorth? Could they really hope to free the trapped Il-Aryn with the armies of men and Wesmen clashing? And why was he really here at all? The conflict within him concerning elven magic and its place in Calaius raged on. He wished the magic gone but had to concede it occasionally had its uses. It was the question of where it would lead that worried him most.

Ulysan was staring at the dark mass of Balaia, his arms folded.

'So this is what lies beyond the mists, eh? So much for the old song. It's not up to much, is it?'

'It just feels so desolate and we've not even landed yet. Look at it. Nothing speaks to you of life, not as we see in the rainforest. Beeth be blessed, but I can barely even see any trees. Grass, mud and mountains. It's horrible.'

'Well, let's make sure we're not there long,' said Ulysan. 'Do you want to hear what Esteren said?'

'So there was a reason for you to bother me with your unique sense of humour after all. Go on.'

'He's going to head east along the coast and go round that way. It's a little longer but probably calmer, and he's worried about another attack given what you said about Ystormun having a presence on their flagship. Less chance of that if we aren't skirting Wesman lands. You are sure it was him?'

Auum nodded and shuddered. Despite having had the satisfaction of being able to gut the host body, the very notion that bastard could project himself into another was one Auum still had difficulty accepting.

'Magic. It invades every part of us. What if he can project himself into you or me?'

'You'd best ask Stein about that, but I'm guessing it's not possible. He has some special link with those shamen, according to Stein.'

'And that's the crux of it, isn't it? Stein. Not that I don't trust him, but for all that he knows, and all that he does and says, we really have no idea what we're going to face in Balaia, do we? We've set out so unprepared. He has no idea of the force that might or might not be laying siege to Julatsa, does he? His Communion can't penetrate whatever the shamen have cast around his city.'

'Exciting, eh?'

'No, not really.' Auum squeezed Ulysan's shoulder. 'Thanks for listening to my rambles.'

'You just need convincing it's worth it,' said Ulysan.

'Maybe. I don't want anyone to die on that miserable rock. And they're going to, aren't they?'

Ulysan raised his eyebrows and said nothing.

The longboats sat low in the water and offered no protection whatever against the freezing sea spray carried on the chill westerly wind that lashed across the benches. Hoods were drawn close, faces were turned away, and those on the oars pulled hard to speed them to shore.

Auum had taken first stint and now sat forward. The swell was growing, making progress steadily more difficult, but they were under no threat of being swamped, just of freezing to death before they reached the shore. Auum willed the land closer and smiled at the irony given his fear of setting foot there.

They were about half a mile away now. Esteren and the elven ships were heading back to Korina, the capital of Balaia, to trade, restock and look as innocent as possible, a much easier task now the warriors and Il-Aryn had been offloaded. Two of the quartet of sisters had stayed with the fleet, with Ephemere and Cleress joining the raiding party. Esteren would bring the ships back to the landing point as soon as he was able.

The two Il-Aryn were in another boat, as were Drech and Takaar. Much to the latter's annoyance, Stein was with Auum. Something about the human was compelling. He was fearless and strong-willed, unafraid to speak his mind, and Auum could respect that. But there was something else that made him fascinating, and Auum had just worked out what it was. He waved the mage forward and, when the human sat down, spoke immediately.

'You don't find this at all strange, do you?'

'What do you mean?' asked Stein.

'You're sitting in a boat full of TaiGethen, who remain the sworn enemies of all men, guiding a raiding party on your own country. You have no control or influence over us, just the word of a race that has no trust in yours.'

Stein shrugged. 'That's where our relative lifespans give us such different views of the world. Men did unspeakable things to the elves and we still bear that shame. But today's men weren't there, weren't even born for hundreds of years after it all came to an end. We can't change the past, only make the future one that benefits all of us.

'But you, so many of you, *were* the elves enslaved. You were caught up in the cruelty of Ystormun's plans. You suffered personally, lost so many friends and loved ones it breaks my heart. For us it's history, for you it's memories.'

'I hear you.' Auum nodded. 'And your current situation, on this freezing boat full of warrior elves?'

Stein chuckled. 'It feels completely right. I've been preparing for this all my life, as did generations before me. The honour being mine is a reason for great pride; the necessity for it a reason for great anxiety.'

Auum smiled. 'How much help do you really think we can be?'

Stein jerked a thumb over his shoulder.

'Look how much help you've been already. Ten ships and all souls aboard taken from the Wytch Lords. That's a big blow by any standards. You don't see yourselves with my eyes, and I'll tell you this. You're *fast*. Don't get me wrong, the Wesmen are good fighters, but they have no chance against you. And I don't suppose anyone has any way of combating the castings you can bring to bear either.'

'When do we tell him we were only fighting at half-speed?' said Ulysan from the oars.

Stein looked from one to the other. 'What's he talking about?'

'There is another state of combat,' said Auum, glaring at Ulysan's back.

Stein gaped. 'Even faster?'

'Yes,' said Auum.

'Why didn't you use it?'

'It's tiring. We can only use it for short periods of time before having to rest, so we couldn't risk it. In any event, it should only be employed in dire circumstances.'

'All right, but—'

'No more. That knowledge goes no further.'

'Understood.'

Auum smiled into his hood, seeing Stein champing at the bit for more.

'Time you explained what I can see on your coastline.'

Stein stared into the darkness and sighed. 'Well, I suppose I can hazard a few guesses, although I can't see too much. Dead ahead is Triverne Inlet, where we can find safe landing. The lights you can see to your left are the town of Jaden. The mountains stretching away from you to the right are the Blackthorne Mountains, which run the whole breadth of Balaia. Our legends say two land masses were thrown together by angry gods and mountains cast up where they collided. It's as good an explanation as any.

'To the west, the Wesmen have their lands and live under the thrall of the Wytch Lords. To the east are the lands of man: beautiful, green, lush and welcoming. Just a pity we can't stop squabbling about who owns what. It'll take us a couple of days to reach Julatsa when we land.'

The flotilla of longboats rowed into the inlet a short while later with Stein directing them to a shore of mud and pebbles on the eastern side. Auum felt the grating of the keel and the boat rocked left and came to a halt. He stood, feet on the wood, and stared at the ground before him.

'Yniss forgive us for what we do,' he said and stepped onto foreign soil for the first time in all his thousands of years of life.

Other boats hit the beach and elves spilled out. Kit was moved fast onto shoulders, and Stein led them up a sharp rise. Cresting it, Balaia was laid out before them in the stark colours of night. Auum took a deep breath, tasting the scents of grass, flowers and animals with the pervading odour of man covering everything.

In the immediate landscape there was little but grass growing on gentle rolling rises that led away to the south and east. There were isolated stands of trees and the occasional group of buildings of human design but not a great deal else. Auum could see the lights of Jaden and the mass of buildings that made up the town. Julatsa was too distant to see, but the smoke and dust smudging the night sky almost directly south gave away the besieged city's location.

But the dominant feature was the Blackthorne Mountains, which rose from the far side of the inlet where the land met the sea. They grew steep and impenetrable and fled away south, great sentinels of rock capped in white, dividing east from west in the most spectacular manner.

It was an extraordinary natural feature, and either side of it two peoples had grown to be such entrenched enemies that, if Stein was to be believed, only the extermination of one would satisfy the other. Or perhaps it was just humans who desired the extermination of any challenge to their assumptions of authority and ownership.

Auum looked around at his people gathered on the rise and staring out at the new land. A hundred and five TaiGethen, a hundred and thirty Il-Aryn, twelve Senserii and Takaar stood with their backs to the chill wind blowing off the mountains.

'We need a place out of the wind to rest and eat,' said Auum. 'Are these buildings I can see inhabited?'

'I'm not an expert on every farmstead, Auum,' said Stein. 'But I doubt there's anyone there at the moment. A significant Wesman force landed in the inlet for the siege, and I guess most isolated farms got burned out. Any smart farmer will have run to Jaden, which so far, has been left alone.'

'Let's start there,' said Auum, turning to face his people. 'A short walk and we hope to find a place to rest and eat. This place feels strange and smells stranger. Look to your brothers, sisters and your gods for strength. Faleen, Merrat, Grafyrre, take your cells and scout the route. We'll follow on. TaiGethen will walk the flanks and secure our rear. Il-Aryn, look to Drech for your orders but stay within the warrior corridor. Let's move.'

Chapter 11

The humans call Balaia beautiful. It is covered in coarse grass, has few trees and is blighted by a clutch of ugly cities. It has little colour, even less wildlife and is cold most of the time. Now ask me again why their minds are impenetrable.

Auum, Arch of the TaiGethen

Every step into the belly of Balaia hunched the elves' shoulders a little more. The TaiGethen were the worst affected. The sky was vast and the star field glittered down untainted by cloud or canopy. There was no cover and no prospect of cover. On board a ship an elf could go below, but here there was no hiding.

They'd come upon the trail left by the Wesmen on their way to Julatsa shortly after leaving the inlet. A churned path through the grass consisting of wheel ruts, boot and hoof prints was spread with debris. It was about ten days old and Stein had not liked the scouts' answer when he'd asked how many might have marched along it.

They were sitting at the farmstead now, or what was left of it. The Wesmen had killed those they'd found, torched it and taken any livestock. The elves had moved three bodies and laid them downwind for reclamation, tucked under some low hardy bushes. The ground was charred to bare earth, and though the fires had not taken all of the stone walls down, there was no roof on any of the buildings. No cover.

Auum had set a perimeter, placed guards at key points and brought everyone else in to rest as best they could. Fires had been lit and food prepared. Many were asleep, but Auum sat with a few of his closest. Stein was with them, a welcome guest and proving himself of good humour when tested.

'Admit it, it is always this cold, isn't it?' said Merrat.

'No, it isn't.' Stein glanced to the heavens. 'But this is autumn and the wind can be chilly. You should come here in summer and see the land then. Covered in colour, crops swaying in the warm breeze, the leaves on the trees green and—'

'You have trees?' asked Marack, her voice breathless, her expression one of wide-eyed surprise.

'Yes,' said Stein carefully.

'Do you put them away at night, perhaps?' suggested Grafyrre.

Stein smiled. 'No, they're a little big for that.'

'But perhaps you can count them all quickly, on account of there being so few of them,' said Grafyrre.

Stein laughed. 'Yes. It's something I do on a daily basis.'

'When you're done counting to eight, what do you do for the rest of the day?' asked Ulysan.

'Get my axe and cut one down to make the job easier tomorrow,' said Stein.

The elves roared with laughter. Auum clapped his hands. Takaar, who was seated surrounded by his Senserii like some visiting dignitary in hostile lands, turned his head for long enough to look down his nose at them.

'Very good,' said Auum, wiping a tear from the corner of his eye. 'Since you know all about trees, how many are there between here and Julatsa?'

Stein raised his eyebrows. 'There's not much of anything between here and Julatsa. Just loads of those beautiful rolling hills then a good deal of flat open ground. Even you can't get to the enemy unnoticed.'

'We'll find a way,' said Auum.

'What do they want?' asked Faleen.

'Who? The Wesmen or the Wytch Lords?'

'Whoever,' she said. 'Why are they at the walls of Julatsa?'

'There's a short answer and a slightly longer answer,' said Stein.

'And they're different?'

Auum looked around his group, seeing them hanging on Stein's every word. That was a first in elven history. Auum had to remind himself that Stein was an exception among humans.

'Actually, yes. Will you indulge me?'

Auum smiled. 'I think you have everyone's attention for now.'

'But don't get boring,' said Ulysan. 'No history lectures.'

'I'll do my best. The short answer is: they're there because the

Wytch Lords have ordered them to be there. Very simple and straightforward. But the Wesmen themselves have coveted the eastern lands, my lands, for hundreds if not thousands of years. The other side of the mountains is barren for the most part. The ground is rocky and living is tough.

'So they want our lands, and I don't blame them, but what they hate most is our magic. They have none themselves and they see it as the barrier to their victory over the east. The Wesmen have long desired the destruction of human magic, and the Wytch Lords are promising them that. The irony, of course, is that they are merely trading one dominant magic for another.'

'I don't think I'm following this,' said Marack. 'We've already fought these Wesmen and they are brave and organised people. They aren't savages. Why would they put themselves in the Wytch Lords' thrall?'

'At the risk of lecturing, it's not a choice that the tribal lords would have made. Their belief is in strength of arms and numbers. But there is an uneasy relationship between the tribes and their shamen. The tribes are riven with infighting, and this has been their weakness for as long as anyone can remember. Occasionally a lord will rise with the strength to lead a significant alliance, but for the most part it is the shamen who talk to each other, practise their revolting spirit religion together and seek influence beyond the spheres of their own tribes. They were easy prey for the Wytch Lords and once the shamen were seduced, forcing the Wesmen to fight for them was relatively easy, though not all have bent the knee.'

There was a silence. Auum glanced across at Takaar and knew he was listening too. There was an oddly bright expression on his face, as if he'd had some sort of revelation. Auum suddenly felt just a little bit uneasy and he could see at least Marack and Ulysan were thinking much the same.

'Seems to me we might be fighting on the wrong side,' said Auum, keeping a smile firmly on his face. 'After all, you lot losing your capacity to cast would help us out enormously, don't you think?'

Stein laughed but he shifted uncomfortably. 'Want to side with the Wytch Lords, now do you?'

'No, I want to see each of Ystormun's bones in the mouth of a separate panther but the Wesmen warriors . . . well we seem to have more in common with them than with you, don't you think?'

Stein frowned, his discomfort gone and his usual confidence returned. 'How do you work that out?'

'We've both suffered at the hands of human magic. We both find that others amongst us practise magic against our better judgement, and while we grudgingly accept it has occasional benefits, we wish magic remained a rumour.'

Stein nodded. 'It makes me sad to hear that, but I know why you feel that way.'

'You have absolutely no idea at all,' snapped Auum.

'Forgive me,' said Stein. 'Your first experience of magic was of the appalling damage it can do. But there is so much more to magic than that. Your own Il-Aryn display healing, beneficial and defensive qualities that I would die to understand, let alone wield. And Julatsan magic is based on peace, although we fight when we must.'

'I'm sorry your view is tainted. Perhaps I can persuade you otherwise while you're here.'

'Good luck with that,' said Ulysan.

'As usual, Auum sees only what he wants to see and ignores that which is uncomfortable,' said Takaar, walking into the firelight.

'Always the grand entrance, Takaar,' said Auum, feeling his muscles tighten and his mellow mood slip away. 'Aren't you tired from all that talking to yourself?'

Auum felt Ulysan grip his arm and he shook it off.

'Don't do this,' whispered Ulysan. 'You know he's trying to goad you.'

'He shouldn't even be here,' hissed Auum. 'He puts the whole expedition on edge.'

'Why won't you accept what you are?' asked Takaar, his face, his whole body imploring.

Auum folded his arms across his knees. 'I have never had any trouble doing so.'

'You cannot escape the Il-Aryn energies,' said Takaar. 'None of us can. It is what makes us.'

'Go back to your campfire and your Senserii. Long day's walk tomorrow.'

'Don't you remember, all those centuries ago, what we talked about in the forest outside Katura?'

Auum dropped his gaze. He remembered. The grief had overwhelmed him. Elyss had been murdered in front of his eyes and he had exacted revenge but not understood how. Takaar had told him.

'What does that have to do with anything?'

Auum was uncomfortable, the eyes of his people on him now.

'I told you then: every elf has the energies running through them, but not all realise this and fewer still can harness them.'

Auum shrugged. 'What of it?'

Takaar laughed. 'And still you refuse to see? Ystormun was searching for the answer with all his experiments on Garan and he failed to grasp the most basic fact. Don't be as ignorant as him.'

'Be careful where you tread,' muttered Ulysan.

'You are a faithful lieutenant, Ulysan, and his denial is your denial.'

'I'm tired, Takaar. Make your point and go away.'

Takaar smiled in the superior way he used when he felt he was imparting something of great importance to the unenlightened.

'You hate magic but you *are* magic.'

Auum blinked slowly. 'You don't get any better, do you?'

'Every elf carries the Il-Aryn with them; all are inherently magical. It is what gives us our long life. I manifest my energies as an Il-Aryn master, you manifest yours, as do all of the TaiGethen, through your speed of thought and body.'

Auum surged to his feet and marched across to Takaar.

'How dare you denigrate the gifts of my god? Our god! Yniss bestowed upon us all that we are. He blessed us with the abilities we display. This is not magic, it is faith and it is strength of body. It is belief and it is the work of centuries. We are one with the land because it is the place of our birth. No magic runs through my blood or guides my hand.'

Auum pushed Takaar hard but the mad elf did not stumble.

'You cannot deny what you are.'

'I do not,' snarled Auum. 'I am born of Yniss and that is my glory, that is who I am. Take your heresy and get out of my sight.'

He pushed Takaar again and heard the Senserii stand and fan out. The TaiGethen did the same.

Auum shook his head. 'Sit down, Gilderon. I'll not hurt him. His words do that for him. Just keep him away from me.'

'You will work it out one day,' said Takaar, apparently oblivious to Auum's anger. 'I don't expect thanks when you do.'

Auum stared at him, seeing his wild eyes flicking around, unable to settle as the battle in his mind played out yet again.

'Then you'll not be disappointed, will you?'

Auum turned his back and waved his TaiGethen to sit down, but he could not. Waving away Ulysan's offer of company, he walked out into the night to be alone.

Auum carried his mood into the morning. The first sight of the colours of Balaia in daylight had not improved his temper. The Blackthorne Mountains were an oppressive force always in the periphery of his right eye, lowering down. The grass Stein had described as beautiful on the rolling hills was a coarse knee-high pale green plant equally poor for walking through and hiding in.

There were trees dotted here and there, but their scarcity was shocking and what there were had thin trunks, small leaves and looked fit to keel over at the merest push. The dominant ground feature was the Wesmen's path driving straight for Julatsa. By mid-morning they could see the city on the horizon, though it was largely obscured by dust and smoke.

Without Communion there was no information from inside the city, but reports from Auum's scouts painted a bleak picture. Around five thousand Wesmen backed by shamen had encircled Julatsa. Stein's face was grey with worry and his appetite for food at the midday break was much diminished. Auum knew just how he felt.

'Vaart has noted cracks in the walls either side of the south-facing gates, and that's where the majority of the pressure is being exerted. Some damage is being done by the defenders but the black fire has good range,' said Ulysan.

'How long before the walls fall?' asked Auum.

Stein shook his head. 'We'll have invested magical strength in the walls and gates, but it only takes one casting to fail and the enemy to realise it. I had no idea there were so many of them.'

'Where are your allies?' asked Faleen. 'I thought your colleges were united against this enemy?'

'The greater part of our armies is engaged at Understone Pass, and of course every college must maintain enough defence for itself.'

Auum frowned. 'What and where is Understone Pass?'

'It's a tunnel through the Blackthorne Mountains about four days south of here.'

Auum sighed. 'I've heard it all now. Not only did one of your idiot mages create an apocalypse then tell your enemies about it, you've also built a tunnel through your greatest barrier.'

'It was supposed to help trade, engender trust and eventually bring peace,' said Stein.

'It is stupid in so many ways that I cannot begin to start,' said Auum. 'You built a tunnel to your enemy's lands. Rather than force them to sail or come over the mountains, which looks some task, you thought you'd give them a nice easy route. Dear Yniss as my witness, how did you ever enslave Calaius?'

'Forgive me, Auum, but this is a distraction right now,' said Faleen. 'You're saying, Stein, that we can expect no help from your allies.'

'The signs weren't promising before the siege was laid.'

'And only your city is under siege. Why?' asked Grafyrre.

Stein blew out his cheeks. 'The Wesmen want to destroy us one college at a time. They threaten the pass with enough force to ensure they cannot be ignored and, meanwhile, manage to bring thousands to my walls.'

'Solid tactic,' said Merrat.

'Until we showed up,' said Ulysan.

'What are we going to do?' asked Stein again.

'Where's Drech?' asked Auum. 'Ah, there you are. Been listening? Good. We need to make some big holes in the shaman strength. If we can that'll relieve the pressure on the walls and leave us free to get inside once we knock a path through the Wesman lines. What did you learn about the Wytch Lord magic? Can you stop it?'

'We've only had brief contact with it, but I can tell you it's sourced from somewhere beyond anything the Il-Aryn will ever use.'

'It's an inter-dimensional magic,' said Stein. 'Very hard to counteract.'

'Tak—'

'Don't mention his name,' said Auum. 'He's to have nothing to do with this.'

Drech looked over to where Takaar was speaking to many of the Il-Aryn. The adoration in their eyes made Auum shudder.

'He has the most experience,' said Drech.

'Whatever is cast has to stop them and get my TaiGethen to the Wesmen. I need someone I can trust. That's you and not him.'

Drech nodded. 'There is one thing we can do.'

'Good,' said Auum. 'Go and work on it. Stein, can the Wesmen see in the dark?'

'Not as far as I know.'

Auum chuckled. 'You don't help yourselves, do you?'

'I don't understand,' said Stein.

'What need have we of trees when we have the night?'

Chapter 12

Julatsa means enlightenment in an ancient language. The college seeks to live up to that name but must necessarily deal in the magic of destruction too. It is an uncomfortable path.

Sipharec, High Mage of Julatsa

The night was lit up by a ring of fires. The Wesmen camped where they dropped, about three hundred yards from the walls. Tribal standards were planted in the ground. Warriors ate, drank, slept and sparred. They had outer pickets, but each of these was lit by a fire too and Auum could only shake his head at the idiocy of it all. Not one of them would have any eyes for the night.

Auum had split his force into two. The smaller part, made up entirely of TaiGethen under the direction of Grafyrre, he had sent to the main gates, where they were to create a diversion to draw away as many as they could. Auum led the other force, which was to take the rear gates and hold the corridor open until Grafyrre's twenty-one made it back.

Before they launched the attack, Auum visited Takaar and the Senserii.

'Gilderon, speak with me.'

Gilderon looked to Takaar, who waved a hand impatiently. Gilderon broke from the Senserii and stalked to Auum, his ikari in his hands.

'What do you want?'

Auum spread his hands. 'You have no love for me yet I respect your loyalty as I do your prowess as a fighter. I need to ask a favour. I know you will be protecting Takaar when we move, but I also need you to protect Drech. My TaiGethen will keep the Wesmen from you, the Il-Aryn should stifle the shamen but there are always risks and we cannot afford to lose him. Will you help?'

Gilderon inclined his head.

'Thank you.'

'It is not for you.'

'Nevertheless, let's not be enemies. We were once good friends.'

'In another life, Auum. We both chose our paths and there is a chasm between them. I will do as you ask only because it is right for Takaar.'

Auum returned to the TaiGethen and relayed his intentions to Drech and Stein.

'What now?' asked Stein.

'Now we wait. Just a little bit.'

Grafyrre led his seven cells towards the Wesman camp sprawling in front of Julatsa's main gates. The gates themselves seemed remarkably undamaged given the amount of power the shamen must have brought to bear on them, but the walls to either side were looking ragged and were sagging.

'Don't lose your Tais and don't lose your heads. When the shamen start to gather themselves, get out. Don't leave anyone behind. Tais, we fight.'

The seven cells split from each other as they approached the outer pickets. Grafyrre had identified sets of fires for each one. He'd taken the most central route for himself, his cell of Ferinn and Lynees, two newly emerged TaiGethen, moving silently with him. Three Wesmen stood at the picket talking among themselves. Their fire was bright and cast a pool of light beyond which they would be able to see nothing at all.

'Go,' said Grafyrre.

He exploded from his crouched position, driving in as hard as he could. He came across the fire feet first and found his target's head with both, driving him straight back. Knife in hand, Grafyrre dropped and slit his victim's throat. He paused while his Tais completed their kills and stared ahead. They had not been seen.

Grafyrre moved in low, his chin brushing the top of the few stems of grass that had eluded the boots of the Wesmen, and headed for his next target fire. It was busy. Fourteen Wesmen lounged about it, others were asleep further away. Shamen were among them, one of them telling a story judging by the gestures he was making.

Grafyrre dropped prone and crawled over the rough ground towards a sleeping enemy. The snoring Wesman stank of spirit liquor. Grafyrre crawled up to his body, peering over his stomach at the fire. A few of the warriors had short weapons belted on, but most of their heavier blades and axes were gathered in one stand a few feet to the left of the campfire.

Grafyrre drilled a knife into the sleeper's temple, who jerked, coughed and was still. He looked to his Tai and nodded. Both signalled that they were ready. Grafyrre re-sheathed his dagger and stood, drawing his twin blades as he did. Ferinn and Lynees stood to either side of him, three painted ghosts rising from the grass.

The Wesmen became aware of them slowly, the first who saw them nudging the warrior next to him. A third was sitting with his back to them, close enough to touch. He stopped tearing at the animal bone in his hands and looked round, took in Grafyrre's camouflage, his weapons and his stance and made a grab for a weapon.

Grafyrre stamped on his wrist and chopped a blade through his shoulder. The Wesman howled and fell forward. Jaqruis sighed across the fire, striking targets in the face and throat. Ferinn and Lynees chased through after them. Ferinn lashed a kick into a Wesman nose. Lynees chopped her blade into the side of another scrambling to his feet.

Grafyrre headed right. Three shamen stared at him, their palms held up in front of their chests, mouths moving in quiet chant. Grafyrre whipped a blade across the neck of one, hacked his other into the arms of the second and landed a butt square on the bridge of the third's nose.

Ahead of him, a warrior had stood and grabbed a dagger from his belt. Grafyrre moved in, blocked a straight thrust aside and thumped a kick into the Wesman's stomach. He staggered back, winded. Grafyrre moved up a pace and thrust a blade through his heart.

Grafyrre could feel the camp coming alive around him. Shouts were going up, voices raised in alarm, and a horn sounded, urgent and anxious and cut off abruptly. He nodded.

'Good, good.'

Lynees leaped high, kicking out to either side, her feet connecting with shamen heads. She landed, her blade blurring in the firelight. Blood blew across the smoke and hissed on the fire. Grafyrre moved to join her. The Wesmen were beginning to organise themselves. A knot of eight or so was gathered under a standard, weapons bristling as they tried to cover every angle.

Shamen were running for the dubious security of their warriors.

Grafyrre led the charge at the knot by the standard. He hurled a jaqrui in first, seeing it deflect off an axe blade and spin away, its target never seeing it and alive only by good fortune.

Lynees and Ferinn were at his shoulders.

'Over the blades,' he said.

The three TaiGethen tore in, jumping high two paces from the Wesman blades. Grafyrre's front foot caught a warrior on the forehead, snapping his head back and putting him down. Grafyrre landed astride him, pierced his chest with a blade and spun to his left, fielding a fast strike on his sword. The Wesman drew back to strike again but failed to see Ferinn coming from his right. Her kick caught him in the side of the head, knocking him senseless.

Grafyrre dropped to his haunches to avoid a swipe. He bounced back up, kicked out into his target's knee and followed up with blows from both blades, seeing one blocked and the other bite deep into the Wesman's side. Lynees swept the legs from another Wesman and jabbed a blade hard into his gut. She turned a forward roll across his body, rose in the same movement and jammed her sword into the groin of another.

Horns were blaring across the Wesman camp now. Grafyrre turned to face the last of the knot of Wesmen. Behind him the standard exploded under the force of black fire.

'Get to shadow!' he called.

He rushed the Wesman, swaying outside a thrust to his midriff and hacking into the small of the tribesman's back. He grabbed the injured man around the throat and turned him into the path of two shamen. Black fire ripped into his body, seeking the elf who held him.

The Wesman screamed. Grafyrre held him upright and pushed him into the shamen, his body colliding with them on its way to the ground. Grafyrre dropped his blades, pulled a jaqrui from his belt pouch and threw. The blade mourned across the short space and thudded into a shaman's temple, knocking him down. Grafyrre ran hard at the other one, seeing him stretch out his arms to cast. He leaped above the black fire that raged from the shaman's fingertips and landed with his legs around the man's shoulders.

Grafyrre grasped his head in both hands and twisted hard. The shaman grunted and fell. Grafyrre went with the fall, rolling away, coming to his feet and tearing back in to smash a foot into the enemy's windpipe. He ran to pick up his swords and headed for the shadows beyond the ring of campfires.

Ferinn and Lynees joined him to look at their work. The camp was in uproar. TaiGethen were still among them, doing awful damage. Wesmen tried to organise themselves but had no idea where their enemy was coming from in the confusing firelight and the puddles of dark night.

To the left and the right Grafyrre could see others hurrying to join the defence. If the elves escaped unscathed it would have been the perfect attack. But now it was time to break. He had to trust that each cell leader would see the signs. Some were already moving back into the night. Howls of pain told of others still deep in the skirmish.

Grafyrre heard the crackle of black fire and saw fingers of it pick at the ground where elven feet had run. He tracked back to the source and saw a defended group of shamen looking for targets.

'Let's get them and get out,' he said. 'Tai, with me.'

Auum watched the concerted movement away from the main gates and nodded his approval. Stein had long since flown into the college to seek assistance and Auum hoped he could muster some cover at the city walls by the rear gates.

'Time to go,' he said. 'Let's keep the pace high. TaiGethen to the flanks. Drech, stay near Takaar and the Senserii. Il-Aryn, don't cast unless you must; you'll only attract attention. Take Drech's lead. Let's go.'

The run was about half a mile. Though a good number of Wesmen had answered the horn calls, hundreds had stayed put, warriors and shamen both. Auum moved off, Ulysan and Duele with him, spread to cover the front. The Senserii with Takaar and Drech among them ran immediately behind, and the rest of the Il-Aryn came in their wake, TaiGethen running a defence around them.

At the outer pickets the TaiGethen moved to take out the guards, leaving Auum clear space in which to run. They gathered momentum. Two cells ran wide either side of Auum as they approached the first fires.

'Keep it up, don't get stalled.' Auum drew a jaqrui and cocked it ready. 'Tai, break on my word.'

Auum watched Wesmen rushing in ahead of them. Horns sounded close and more were readying themselves on both flanks. Auum glanced behind him. Gilderon watched everything and missed nothing. There was no one Auum trusted more to make the right decision every time in a fight.

Auum threw his jaqrui. The crescent blade keened across the thirty-yard space and lodged in a Wesman chest. The warrior coughed blood and pitched forward. Others roared and charged.

'Break!' ordered Auum.

With his Tai on his flanks, Auum cruised to a sprint, drawing both blades from their back scabbards and cycling them in his hands. The line of Wesmen ahead was two deep and seven wide. Behind them and off to both sides, shamen were readying. He trusted Drech to sense them as he said he could.

Auum charged directly at the centre of the defence, where axe-wielding warriors blocked his path. He ran hard, dropped to his knees and slid across damp grass, his blades held out to either side. He felt them bite into legs even as the axes swung over his head. Auum relaxed his arms, sliding past his targets before coming to his feet. He didn't pause, running on at the back line, hearing Ulysan and Duele finishing what he'd started.

The TaiGethen were among the Wesmen, who did not know which way to strike. Auum faced three, two with long swords and one with an axe. Blood dripped from his blades where he held them, one high across his face and one low across his legs. He waited for a heartbeat, hearing the fight going on around him.

The three rushed him and Auum watched them come. The axe came overhead and he stepped aside, hacking his left blade in at waist height. From the right a long sword was thrust at his heart, and he battered the blow aside, opening up his body and bringing his left blade across and into the exposed flank of his enemy.

The second swordsman had been blocked by the axe man. He backed off behind his comrade but the pause was his undoing. Auum spun to his left, jumped high and thudded his right blade into the warrior's shoulder. The Wesman screamed and dropped his blade.

Auum was in space. Shamen were either side guarded by nervous warriors. The elven column was coming on; Senserii now headed it, their *ikari* at the ready. The shamen were readying to cast and Auum prayed Drech knew what he was doing as he headed out to the right, his Tai with him. Warriors barred the way to the shamen. Simultaneously, a large group of Wesmen ran at the head of the elven advance. They had no idea what they were running into. Auum almost pitied them.

Shamen stood and cast. Auum threw himself to the ground and rolled. Black fire erupted from fingertips, but the moment it appeared, a modulating green light encased the shamen's hands, extinguishing the fire. It was momentary but enough to disrupt them.

Auum came back to his feet and charged at his enemies.

Safe behind his Senserii, Takaar felt serene but also fragile and useless.

Look at everyone doing their part while you cower behind your minders.

'Auum said I may not cast.'

And you listen to him, don't you? The mighty Auum. See Drech, see what he has your pupils doing? Did you even know that was possible?

'We can all develop our own castings,' muttered Takaar, but he stared at Drech, not three paces to his left behind two ranks of Senserii, marching confidently along with a smile on his face.

He should have shared the secret with you.

'Yes, he should have,' said Takaar.

That's the way of the Il-Aryn, is it not?

'Yes, it is,' said Takaar and a tear threatened.

Just worth mentioning. Probably just an oversight in all the excitement.

Wesman warriors struck the forward quartet of Senserii, who had spread to give themselves room to use their bladed staffs. Takaar felt a thrill course through him and it eased his anger. The Senserii did not break stride. Gilderon jabbed out with his staff, piercing a Wesman above his heart. He brought the staff back, holding it as he would a quarterstaff in two hands. His movement confused the onrushing warriors. The right end licked out and sliced an enemy face from forehead to chin. The left deflected a heavy downward strike and, faster than the Wesman could follow, the blade was in his eye, turned and ripped clear.

The elves ran on. Takaar could see TaiGethen on their flanks. Horns echoed against the blank dark of the city walls, which loomed large, filling the horizon. Lights burned on the walls, and he could see men and elves on the ramparts and inside the fire-blackened gatehouse.

Ahead, a large force of Wesmen was gathering just outside spell range of the city. Others moved to join them and more ran into the flanks of the column, where they met the steel, fists and feet of the TaiGethen. At their rear, though, Takaar sensed trouble. Shamen were gathering. He could feel the Wytch Lord power there.

Takaar looked to his right. Drech was walking at an even pace, his eyes closed and his mind showing him the way through the streams of energy. Takaar tracked them for a moment, seeing his focus ahead, managing the concentration of his Il-Aryn. He had no idea what was behind. Takaar turned and pushed back through the column.

What are you doing?

'Disobeying Auum and saving his precious TaiGethen.'

Senserii fell into place next to him, and they moved quickly down the line past the Il-Aryn casting their distraction constructs at the hands of the shamen. At the rear the TaiGethen knew what was coming and had spread out to defend against it. Three cells ranged against a muster of fifty or more warriors.

Takaar stood behind them and let his mind sample the energy lines. Every moment isolated the group further from the main column. Takaar concentrated on what was below his feet. Earth and rock dominated and a clay layer separated the two. This was no time for finesse. The shamen were coming, fifty yards away and closing quickly. The TaiGethen prepared to attack.

'Faleen, trust me,' said Takaar. 'Too many of them.'

Takaar felt for the line of force running through the clay layer. It was sluggish and easy to grab. He let the power of the land flood him, teasing out strand after strand to dance before him.

Takaar spread his hands, palms up. He took the power of the land across his shoulders, forced his arms up over his head, and a wall of mud and clay thirty yards wide and ten high erupted from the ground. Takaar staggered under the weight of it and felt the steadying hand of a Senserii on his back. He shifted his focus, drying the clay and hardening the barrier, moving the water aside and letting it fall on the enemy behind.

He dropped his arms by his side and drew in a shuddering breath.

'Now I suggest we all run,' he said.

Auum tore into the flank of the Wesman force, hacking left and right with his blades, fighting power with power. An enemy axe clashed against his right blade, sending sparks into the night, its edge opening a shallow cut on Auum's cheek. Ulysan ducked a wild swipe and buried a blade in a Wesman gut, slicing it clear and spilling entrails across the ground.

Duele flew in at head height with his blades cocked in front of his face, left leg outstretched to connect with a Wesman chest. He landed behind the warrior line and in front of the shamen readying to cast their fire. Auum drove his shoulder into the warrior in front of him and rammed a blade into the top of his thigh. The tribesman went over, grabbing at Auum and pulling him down too.

Black fire slashed overhead. Il-Aryn castings responded, but their effect was diluted now. Auum heard an elven scream behind him. He rolled away from the Wesman, breaking his grip. Ignoring him, Auum drew a jaqrui and threw at the shamen, seeing it take the fingers from both hands of one on its way to jut from the skull of another.

'Get the shamen!' roared Auum.

Duele was already among them. His blades were in their scabbards and his fists and feet snapped out, breaking concentration, buying time for support to arrive. Auum saw Ulysan down a warrior with a sword pommel to the chin. The big TaiGethen moved forward. In front of him shamen moved the focus of their fire. Auum wanted to shout in warning but it would do no good.

Ulysan struck the head from one, but the other, standing two paces behind, was too far away. But the shaman didn't get the chance to strike his killing blow. The black fire died on his fingertips as he clawed at the ikari jutting from his chest. Auum turned. The Senserii swept over the remains of the Wesman defence, which broke and scattered before them.

Auum nodded his thanks to Gilderon, who did not acknowledge him, stooping to twist his staff before dragging the blade clear.

'Reform!' called Auum.

The column came together and hurried on towards the opening gates. Horsemen galloped out followed by archers and swordsmen to form a corridor. The horsemen swept either side of the elven column, clearing Wesmen from their flanks. Spells arced out over their heads, crashing into the ground behind. Walls of fire erupted from the ground alongside them. Black fire fizzed and crackled. Auum saw a horseman taken from his mount, an axe in his back. Another flailed at the fire unpicking his chest.

'Move! Run!' shouted Auum. 'Men are dying for us. Go, go!'

Auum ran down the column, urging them on. The Senserii made

the gates, turning to stand and usher the Il-Aryn inside. Auum ran beside Drech.

'What happened? Your castings stopped working.'

'They drew on more power,' said Drech. He looked exhausted. 'So much to learn.'

'You saved many.'

'And lost some.'

'It was unavoidable,' said Auum.

He gripped Drech's shoulder and rushed him through the guard and into the city before letting him go. Beyond the gates the night was ablaze. Horsemen thundered back into the city. Volleys of arrows and more spells covered their retreat. The last of the elves ran in, Auum seeing one of his TaiGethen in the arms of another, bleeding from a wound to the head. Takaar was carried in on the back of one of his Senserii.

Ulysan limped up to Auum, blood coming from a wound in his calf. Auum sheathed his blades.

'That could have been worse,' said Ulysan.

'What happened to you?'

'Stray arrow,' said Ulysan. 'Not deep.'

'Get it seen to.'

Auum paused and drew breath. Now they were inside, the elves had stopped, as much cowed by the alien atmosphere of the city as they were fatigued by the run. Many were sitting by the side of the cobbled street, while people were emerging from tall houses to see who had come to their aid. Horsemen milled about, and from further up the street of tight-packed buildings he heard shouting.

Auum pushed through the crowd and a smile broke on his face.

'I see you made it,' he said.

Stein shook his hand. 'Did you like the welcome committee?'

'Just what we needed.'

'Bring your people to the college. We can billet them all there, get the wounded seen to and work out what's next. This isn't going to go unchallenged by the Wytch Lords.'

Chapter 13

How can they live like this? Their houses loom over them like cruel masters, their streets throng with people packed so tight you cannot draw breath and their food is bland and colourless. Small wonder their faces look so grey.

Auum, Arch of the TaiGethen

They had reached the city with fewer casualties than Auum feared. Three Il-Aryn were dead, another five were wounded but responding. One TaiGethen had fallen and another three had severe wounds. Auum did not expect them to survive the night despite the ministrations of Julatsa's keenest mages.

Grafyrre had arrived with his full complement of raiders about two hours later. They'd crawled their way to the walls and scaled them, surprising a defender or two before heading for the college and some hard-earned rest.

The college itself was dominated by its tower, the building that housed the growing Heart of Julatsa, the very centre of Julatsan magic. Auum felt burdened by the atmosphere within the building and knew it to be the pressure of the magical focus created by the Heart.

After a bath and the application of balms to ease a few muscle aches and to soothe the cut on his face, Auum had been led to a large circular chamber high up in the tower itself. From there he could see the city from the balcony that encircled the chamber. It was about half the size of Ysundeneth and felt cramped. Everything was forced within the walls, buildings rose three or four storeys high and the hubbub of noise was ceaseless.

The walls and guard towers were manned by swordsmen, archers and mages, a powerful defence against the attacking Wesmen, and yet within the atmosphere was anxious. Presumably food supplies would be getting short before too long, and there was always the fear of that which you could hear but not see.

The arrival of the elves had caused quite a stir and had, he was told, lifted the spirits of the entire city. The apparent ease with which they had broken through the enemy ranks had encouraged the populace to believe that victory was possible. But Auum did not like the role in which he and his small band of raiders were being cast. They were not here as saviours of the human race.

That thought remained with him when he was invited to sit at a long oval table with elves and men, most dressed in lavish robes that presumably signified some sort of status within the college and city. There were senior soldiers present too. Auum sat flanked by Stein and Drech on one side, Takaar on the other. Ulysan was on a chair behind him and Gilderon sat behind Takaar.

Twenty people in all were at the meeting, and the round of introductions made Auum's head spin. High mage, mayor, elder council, general of the militia, general of the college army . . . and an Il-Aryn *iad* called Kerela who had achieved high office. She was someone Auum needed to speak to in private. The meeting took place in a mixture of elvish and human, with translators at the ears of any struggling to understand one or the other.

'First of all my apologies for keeping you from your beds or for dragging you from them,' said the High Mage, Sipharec. He was a middle-aged man, clean-shaven, tall and slender to the point of being gaunt. His eyes were a powerful bright blue but there was something behind them, a sadness. 'But what we have to discuss cannot wait until dawn when the Wesmen resume their efforts to knock down our walls. Walls which we have defended for more than ten days without help from any on the outside, until now. Auum, Drech, Takaar and all your people, welcome, and thank you for giving us fresh hope. Stein, I doubted you could succeed. I am sorry.'

Stein shrugged. 'It was without doubt a fool's errand, but this fool is a lucky one.'

'Auum, I know you have questions,' said Sipharec in very good elvish. 'Perhaps you can start the debate.'

Auum inclined his head. 'My questions are simple enough, but there is a great deal I don't understand and I will not commit my people to a conflict I do not understand. We're here; we have secured our mages, and I am content with that. We share a common enemy and I am content with that too. But I am concerned and confused by

the alliance you have with the other colleges and I am most concerned by what will happen in this country when the Wytch Lords
are defeated.'

Sipharec frowned. 'I'm not sure I understand your concern. With
the Wytch Lords gone, we'll have peace here and will begin to grow
again as colleges. Julatsa will seek to strengthen its bonds with the
elves and build a deterrent against any other Wesman incursion. It's
a dream as we sit here, but not something that should give rise to
concerns, is it?'

'I'll make it plainer,' said Auum. 'The Wytch Lords are invading
because they want to secure Dawnthief, the spell that seals the
stupidity of human magical research for ever. What happens to that
spell when the Wytch Lords are defeated?'

Sipharec's glare at Stein was sharp and poisonous.

'The search will continue,' said the High Mage evenly. 'The spell
cannot be allowed to fall into the wrong hands.'

Auum sighed and felt the weight of magic rest more heavily on his
soul than ever.

'Those who seek to own this spell are, by dint of their desire, the
wrong hands,' said Auum. 'Tell me, what would you do with it,
should you find it?'

Sipharec smiled indulgently. 'Keep it away from those who would
research it further and who would use it as a rod of power.'

'And these people you fear, they represent, who is it . . . Xetesk
and Dordover? They will fight you for it. You do see that? The end of
one war will be the prelude to another as you stab each other in the
back for something no one should own. And ownership risks us all.
The innocent of Calaius and Balaia will live only at the whim of a
group of mages. No one who owns this spell could resist its charms
for ever. No elf can tolerate this.'

Auum stared squarely at Kerela. The *iad* met his gaze but could
not hold it.

'Something to say, Kerela?'

'You misunderstand the motives of this college,' she said.

'Do I? I know you are the only college under siege and hence, to
my mind, the college the Wytch Lords feel poses them the most risk.
Why is that?'

'No, no, no.' The bass voice belonged to the college's general,
Harild. He was an old man but his eyes sparkled with vitality and his
body had not withered. 'Two things have combined to bring the

Wesmen to our walls, and neither is our progress in finding Dawn-thief. First, we are the closest college for invasion forces coming around the Blackthornes from the north. Second, we have elves here, and the Wytch Lords reserve a special hatred for the elves. Can't think why.'

Harild raised his eyebrows and Auum almost smiled.

'That doesn't explain your desire to own Dawnthief. According to Stein, no one knows where this thing is, is that right?'

'Yes,' said Kerela. 'Septern's Manse was destroyed utterly when the Wesmen attacked it seeking Dawnthief. We assume the secrets are there, but they remain hidden from us.'

'Then surely it is in the right place now – out of reach of all. Am I being naive to suggest that if you really want to progress, you must agree not to seek it and make this location off limits. Guard it if you have to. If no one owns the spell, no one can use it, and I for one will sleep more easily.'

'It's a lovely plan, but Xetesk will never stop searching. They are terrified of others, particularly Dordover, finding it first.'

'Forgive me,' said Sipharec. 'But is this pertinent to our current situation?'

'Tell me,' said Auum, ignoring Sipharec. 'Which college has the largest army?'

General Harild shrugged. 'Xetesk, easily. Why?'

'And yet they haven't managed to send even a token force to your aid? Not a solitary mage?'

Sipharec spread his hands. 'They have an invasion of their own to deal with.'

'How wide can this pass be if it takes three colleges to repel an invasion there?' Auum looked around the table and was dismayed at what he saw in the expressions on all their faces.

Only Stein could see where he was leading. 'Understone Pass will take a large cart and team very comfortably,' he said.

Auum shrugged. 'Allies, you say? Seems to me they are sacrificing you. Once you're out of the game it's one less hand grasping for the spell, isn't it?'

He was right and they knew it, though none of them would admit it. Sipharec exchanged glances with both Kerela and Harild.

'So where does that leave you? Will you help us?' asked Sipharec.

'The Wytch Lords must be destroyed or they will destroy Calaius. This is where the strength to defeat them lies. But I will not leave us at greater risk in the aftermath of their defeat. I will not fight alongside Xetesk; their true motives are plain enough. And you'll have to decide where you line up. If I learn we are being used to further anyone's claims to Dawnthief, I will withdraw every elven warrior and Il-Aryn and return to Calaius. Take our chances there.'

Takaar cleared his throat. He'd been fidgeting ever since the meeting had begun. Auum tensed but said nothing.

'If I may speak,' said Takaar.

Kerela favoured him with a warm smile. 'The chamber is yours.'

'Thank you.'

Takaar stood and walked around the table as he spoke, stopping to rest a friendly hand on a shoulder or refill a wine or water cup. He didn't get too near Auum and repeatedly worried at his left arm with the fingernails of his right hand. Auum determined to relax and watch the performance, let him say what he felt he must. Either his instability would trip him up or his supreme arrogance would undermine him.

'We do not all think as Auum thinks. Auum is a warrior. He is the finest ever to grace the TaiGethen and so the finest ever to set foot in your country. He understands speed and strength of arms. He knows a hundred ways to kill you with foot, fist and blade. But he doesn't understand magic. He has no conception of the power a union of magics can generate. The Wytch Lords fear a union of elven and human magic, and that is why they are outside these walls. Not to fight alongside Xetesk is patently absurd. Only together can we defeat them.

'And while Auum's TaiGethen are a blessing in every fight, they are not critical. My Il-Aryn are. They answer to me and I will bring them to your aid.'

Drech stood, slapping the table. 'You do not command the Il-Aryn,' he said. 'I do.'

Takaar's face was stone for a moment before his lips twitched and he muttered words in ancient elvish, presumably to his tormentor. A smile slid across his expression but the fury in his eyes was raw and unchecked. Auum sat back, satisfied that the lucidity of Takaar's speech was about to be comprehensively undone.

'You are an administrator,' said Takaar, moving steadily around the table towards Drech. Auum could see Kerela was desperate to intervene but at a loss as to how. 'You organise the timetable of lectures and the menu in the refectory. You are no leader, you are no commander. You are no visionary. Who do they look to when they need inspiration or spiritual help? Not you, Drech, never you. You are closed; I am open.'

'It really is amazing how little you see, perched in your hut at the top of the hill,' said Drech. 'We all admire your insight and your teachings. You are the one who understands most about the energies of the Il-Aryn. And while you can impress the young, wrap them in the stories you weave, they would not follow you into a stream to go for a paddle. They boarded ship because I asked them to. You are here because they love you, as they would a charming but infirm grandparent. But they do not follow you. You lost that honour on Hausolis and you will never get it back.'

Auum felt the crushing weight of magic across his back and shoulders. Tension filled the chamber. Kerela was out of her chair and running around the table towards Takaar.

Drech was staring at Takaar, fear on his face. Takaar pushed a hand towards him and he flew back, crashing into Ulysan, who caught him before he fell to the floor.

'Takaar, no!' screamed Kerela.

'We shall see where the strength really lies,' spat Takaar, continuing his march around the table.

Drech was scrambling to his feet, his hands held out in front of him, desperately trying to form something to protect himself.

'This chamber will not see magic cast,' roared Sipharec.

'Takaar, stop!' said Kerela, laying a hand on his arm.

Takaar stared at her and Auum saw her courage wither. She stumbled back a pace, and Auum surged from his chair and onto the table, heading for Takaar.

'Gilderon!' he called. 'Help me.'

Takaar had eyes only for Drech. He stopped, appeared to be gathering something in his hands and then slowly began to close them into fists. Drech clutched at his head and shrieked. Auum dived across the table and took Takaar about the chest and shoulders, bearing him onto the floor to slide into a wall.

Drech's agonised cries ceased. Auum looked into Takaar's eyes and punched him on the chin, rapping his head against the stone floor and knocking him unconscious. He felt a hand on his shoulder pulling him up.

'Get off him!' hissed Gilderon.

Auum spun as he stood. 'You were too slow, Gilderon. You failed him. Don't let it happen again.'

'You do not touch him,' said Gilderon.

'The next time he threatens an elf I'll do more than touch him. Get him out of here and keep him calm. See that he behaves.'

Gilderon stared at Auum, the muscles in his face at war as he debated deep inside whether to obey. He put a hand on Auum's chest and pushed him away from Takaar, who was groaning and muttering on the floor. Gilderon stooped and picked him up, placing him over one shoulder. He turned and strode from the chamber.

Auum ignored the Julatsans and Kerela, who stared at him, demanding answers. Drech was sitting up, rubbing at his temples while Ulysan held a cup of water for him.

'How are you?' Auum asked, kneeling by the Il-Aryn master and noting the tremors running through his body.

'I'll live,' said Drech, but the eyes he turned to Auum betrayed his fear.

'What did he do this time?' asked Auum.

'He's so fast,' said Drech, half to himself. 'Impossibly fast. He made the air hard as stone to push me over. And he was trying to drag the blood from my brain. He's dangerous, Auum.'

'I warned you. Whatever he is to his beloved students, his ego cannot handle the merest bruise. If you challenge him, he reacts like a child. He cannot contain his emotions.'

'I'm sorry,' said Drech. 'I thought this would focus him, give him a role he could play and be content with. His talents are so great and he has apparently shared so little. Just look what he can do when he puts his mind to it.'

'I saw the ship destroyed and I heard about the clay wall. But I saw this too. He acts on pure impulse. None of us can afford that. If you can't control him, he'll have to go. I'll see the Senserii get him to Korina,' said Auum.

Drech reached out a hand and Ulysan pulled him to his feet.

'I'll speak to the Il-Aryn. Tell them Takaar needs rest and help. I'm sure I can make them understand.'

Auum took Drech's face in his hands and kissed his forehead.

'I'm sorry it came to this. I'm sorry you couldn't control him. No one can.'

'Still, it makes you part of the exclusive club of those Takaar has tried to kill,' said Stein.

Drech almost smiled. 'I'd rather not be a member.'

Sipharec cleared his throat. 'I think you owe the council an explanation.'

'We cannot afford to lose Takaar,' said Kerela. 'His powers could change the course of any battle.'

'You can't afford to pay the price of those powers,' said Auum. 'You've seen the precipice he flirts with. It is like that with every breath he takes. He might destroy a thousand enemies in one moment and murder the finest of us the next. He must go.'

'And what of us?' asked Sipharec. 'What of Julatsa and the war against the Wytch Lords?'

'Well I don't know about you, but to my mind the only way to get Takaar out of here and away to Korina is to break this siege. It's one thing getting in and quite another getting out. Tomorrow we fight.'

Chapter 14

Clarity from confusion, light from darkness, focus from fog. The Il-Aryn mind is conflicted. The more conflicted, the greater the potential. Mine is the most conflicted of all. Rarely do I wish it was not so.

Takaar, Father of the Il-Aryn

'I said what needed to be said.'

And did what needed doing?

Takaar, sitting on the side of his bed, dropped his head to his chest.

'I should not have lost my temper.'

And with it whatever authority you thought you had.

'I still have that! The Il-Aryn will not desert me.'

The Senserii will not let you leave your room. And they are supposed to do your bidding without question.

'Gilderon will not betray me,' said Takaar.

But you are not on the walls. You have no influence.

Takaar listened to the world beyond his luxurious bedchamber. The dull thump of spells and the crackling sound of black fire picking at the city walls dominated the hubbub of anxious ordinary people that filtered through his windows. Out there plans were being made.

'They will come to me when they need my advice. They cannot do without it.'

Remind me. When was the last time Auum asked for your advice? Or Drech?

There was a knock on his door.

'Come,' said Takaar.

The door opened and Kerela walked in. 'Please excuse the intrusion.'

'Kerela, your presence is a blessing. Tell me, how goes the training of our people?'

'I must tell you something.'

'It can wait.' Takaar held up a hand. 'Sit with me. Tell me of your successes.'

Kerela nodded and sat on the bed next to Takaar. 'We lost some, but we knew we would. The mana bowl is a dangerous place, and some could not open their minds to the human magic despite its similarity to ours. But you were right. Even those with limited Il-Aryn ability have found strength in the lore and magical structures of the Julatsan approach. Some have turned from the Il-Aryn and I for one will never leave here. This is my home, as it is to hundreds of those you sent here.'

Takaar smiled. 'You are my greatest triumph. Don't let Auum dominate you. Follow your heart's desires. Fight alongside Xetesk. Ally with anyone to break the Wytch Lords. They must not threaten Herendeneth; we're vulnerable there.'

'What about Dawnthief? Surely Auum was right: we must leave the spell hidden.'

'From Xetesk, yes. But from me or you or the good souls of this college? No. Research makes us stronger and in that spell lies the sum of all magical knowledge for those capable of unpicking its secrets.'

'Then you must not let them send you away. We'll need you when this is done.'

Told you. Your authority is long gone.

Takaar picked at his arm, and the cacophony in his head meant he had trouble framing his next words.

'S-send me away?'

'Auum wants you to go to Korina to your ships. Drech has sanctioned it.'

Drech.

'Drech!'

Betrayer.

'Betrayer!'

'Takaar?'

Takaar turned to Kerela and managed a smile though his hands were iron and he desired so much to indulge his rage. The cacophony would not die down.

'Kerela, I am sorry. Those who once loved me are starting to desert me. You remain faithful, don't you?'

'Always,' said Kerela. 'But they are determined you should go. I will petition Sipharec to give you sanctuary here.'

'The Senserii will not let me be put on a cart and carried away like some chattel.'

Kerela's voice was a whisper. 'I don't think they will stand against Auum and Drech. Their greatest desire is to see you safe.'

'I won't hide here. I must join the fight and, when it is done, join the search.'

'Patience. Please, Takaar.'

You have none of that.

'I have none of that.'

Mages at the base of the city wall and behind the gates expended huge energy investing the stone and timbers with more and more strength. Arrows flew in volleys from the ramparts and castings kept the Wesmen back whenever it looked as if an assault might be imminent. But outside, on the trampled ground, the shamen stood in large groups protected by their warriors and out of range of spell and arrow, launching attack after attack on Julatsa's defences.

Harild had explained that they had sent raiding parties to their deaths in pursuit of the shamen. The black fire ate through magical shields, and the Wesman warriors were quick and brutal. And so the stage was set and the end of the play was no mystery. Julatsa's walls or gates would be breached. Not today and probably not tomorrow or the next day, but it was only a matter of time.

'Still no word from Xetesk or the other colleges?' said Auum.

Harild shook his head. 'Our latest messengers say they are fully committed in the defence of Understone Pass. No aid is coming.'

They were standing in the main gatehouse. Fire picked at the great timber doors below and dislodged stone from wide areas surrounding the great hinges and braces either side. Shamen had tried to attack the gatehouse itself but Il-Aryn magic had turned the fire away.

'You should have flown mages out under cover of darkness,' said Ulysan. 'Come at them from the rear.'

'We discussed it but the shamen can sense the use of mana; it's like they can smell a casting just like they can with your Il-Aryn. Trying it would have been suicide.'

'But this is the time to attack, isn't it?' said Auum. 'At night they're scattered throughout the camp. Right now they're gathered in five clear groups. Strong in magic but vulnerable to attack if we can get close enough.'

'Aye, but there's the problem,' said Harild.

'Hmm,' said Auum. 'Where's Drech?'

'Back at the college talking to the Il-Aryn and any of the Julatsan elves not on the walls. Why, got an idea?'

Auum looked back at the nearest shaman team plastering the walls with their black fire. There had to be close to fifty of them, closely guarded by two hundred Wesman warriors taunting the defenders, exhorting them to come out and fight.

'I have, but the timing is going to be critical. I'm going to need every TaiGethen warrior ready and able to use their emergent speed. I'm going to need the Il-Aryn too, and the Julatsan mages and your cavalry.'

'Auum?' said Ulysan.

'We'll break them one group at a time.'

In the middle of the afternoon they were set. Auum had settled on sixty TaiGethen to go out, leaving twelve full cells plus the wounded inside the city as back-up. A hundred Il-Aryn prepared themselves for a single casting while the remaining twenty-seven would spot for weaknesses. Every elven Julatsan adept had volunteered to fly out, and Auum had let Kerela choose seventy of them. Eighty cavalrymen were mounted and ready.

'Get this wrong and a lot of us will die,' said Auum.

'They know this casting,' said Drech, still doubting. 'It's inconceivable that Ystormun hasn't informed them about the weakness.'

'I'm counting on it,' said Auum. He turned to his TaiGethen, every one painted and ready. Prayers had been spoken and souls commended to Shorth. 'Thrynn, Faleen, Hassek, Grafyrre, Merrat, Nyann, Merke, Vaart, Marack, Nokhe, Hohan, Oryaal. All of you survived Katura. We are veterans of battle, our brothers and sisters are not. Lead your cells but lead the others also. Die old, not today.

'Harild, watch for the moment. I trust you and your cavalry.'

Harild nodded but his doubt was there, plain to see. 'How can you get to them? I don't understand.'

'Trust me and look to your role. If you're late, the blood that flows will be of elves and the men of Julatsa.'

'We won't fail them.'

Auum nodded. 'Drech, ready your Il-Aryn. TaiGethen, form up.'

They were all mustered at the main gates, which still shuddered under the impact of Wytch Lord magic. Auum took a breath to ease the constriction in his chest as Drech and his Il-Aryn drew on the earth's energies to form their grand casting. Just as on the ship, it came into place quickly, a shimmering barrier of air made solid. Auum could not deny the bitter taste in his mouth at the necessity. He didn't think he would ever reconcile himself fully to the use of magic.

'Open the gates!' called Harild.

Auum could hear cheers from the Wesmen as the gates were hauled open, screeching and protesting against their winches and hinges. Black fire rattled hard against the timbers, the fingers seeking targets within the city, but Drech moved his barrier into place and the sudden quiet from the spell attack was distracting.

'Forward!' ordered Auum. 'Drech, just hold it as long as you can and then get back inside.'

The TaiGethen moved behind the barrier, which Drech and his people held steady while the black fire moved quickly to its apex, picking away at the mana strands that bound it and were its weakness. Auum could hear free Il-Aryn shouting out warnings and he fancied he could feel the casters fighting to strengthen weak spots.

Beyond the barrier Auum could see Wesman warriors forming up to either side of the shamen, unable to see through the barrier but correctly identifying its intent. They began to advance, careful not to cross into their shamen's line of sight. The shamen were positioned some hundred yards from the gates and dead ahead of them. Auum and the TaiGethen had moved twenty slow yards forward when the warning came from Drech.

'We're losing it.'

The barrier was twisting and shimmering violently. Shaman fire ripped at it in more places than Auum could count and holes were appearing through which the fire spat.

'TaiGethen, be ready.' Auum moved forward another three paces, seeing Wesmen advancing steadily, warily. 'Drech, now! Tais, scatter!'

The barrier disappeared, and for a heartbeat the shaman magic was gone too. Auum let the power of Yniss flood him and the earth beneath his feet cushion him, and he ran. The TaiGethen broke apart, sprinting away hard at multiple angles designed to confuse and distract their enemy.

Auum saw and heard it all so clearly. The growing surprise on the faces of the enemy warriors combined with the confusion of the shamen about where to send their fire. There were mages in flight, soaring high above the battlefield, heading out behind the enemy camps. And when the shamen finally began to target the TaiGethen, the sound of hooves was music to Auum's ears.

Auum seared across the ground, his Tais around him, racing past the Wesmen and ignoring the targets they represented. Black fire laced out in multiple directions, seeking elven bodies. But while the fire travelled at extreme speed, the minds and the hands of the shamen did not.

Auum saw black tendrils swinging towards him. He slithered to a halt and started down a different line. He rolled beneath one tendril, leaped between two others and moved in. Beside him a line of fire caught a TaiGethen in the flank, spinning him out of control to sprawl on the ground.

Auum could see their eyes now, the desperation on their faces and the feverish playing of their foul casting in front of them as they tried to bring down elves they could barely see. But the closer the TaiGethen got, the greater the risk they ran despite their speed. He had to trust to luck and believe that his Tais would make the right moves.

Auum was ten paces from the shamen when the fire caught him. He slid low beneath a blitz of fire tendrils and rolled, his body outstretched. He gathered himself and leaped high, meaning to land in their midst, but the line of black fire caught his left arm, spinning him fast and off balance. It burned through his shoulder and down into his hand. He could smell his seared flesh, and his shirt smouldered and glowed orange where the fire struck.

Still moving under the shetharyn, he crashed into the shamen, tumbling and turning, trying to get his feet beneath him while the burning consumed his arm. Gasping in a breath, Auum came to a halt sprawled on top of a shaman, his eyes looking up into a sky filled with moving bodies. There was shouting and he heard the hiss of blades leaving scabbards.

Black fire crackled all around him. He rolled again, his feet finding the ground, and rose, right fist already lashing out at any body in his vision, his left arm hanging useless by his side. TaiGethen crashed into the shamen in numbers, deflecting their attention from him.

A dagger came at him from his left. He spun and kicked it from the shaman's hand, leaned in hard and butted him in the forehead. He drew a blade and whirled a complete circle, forcing space to open up. Fighting was going on all around him. He heard the detonation of spells ahead of him and the thundering of hooves behind.

Auum focused as well as he could, weaving his sword in front of him and trying to sense what was at his back. He moved towards a shaman. He was wearing a broad necklace of animal bones; the skin that showed beneath cloak and clothes was heavily tattooed, and there was an expression of pure malice on his weathered flat-featured face.

Auum struck forward, and the shaman danced back. He clapped his hands together and the black fire capered between his palms. He opened them to strike at Auum, who dropped to his haunches and swept out a foot, tripping his enemy and sending him back a couple of paces, his magic gone.

Auum rushed forward. In the press of shamen battling for their lives against the blurring TaiGethen he didn't see the knife blade that tore into his left arm, redoubling the pain. The blow rocked him sideways. Instinct took over. Auum kicked out to the side and high, feeling his boot connect with a face. Simultaneously, he threw his blade. It spun end over end and buried itself to the hilt in the shaman's chest, splintering his bone necklace.

Auum dropped to the ground, on his haunches again. A dagger blade whipped over his head. He turned quickly, dragging a jaqrui from its pouch and flicking it out and up, seeing the blade lodge deep in the thigh of his target. Behind him a scream split the air. Auum forced himself back to his feet to grab back his blade. In front of him a shaman stood for a moment, confusion on his face while his brain dribbled from his split skull.

Ulysan was at his side. Auum felt himself picked up and rushed back in the direction of the city walls. He saw other TaiGethen bodies smouldering on the ground but the shamen were gone, massacred.

Harild's cavalry galloped past, sending Wesmen to their deaths or running blindly away. Spells crashed down from the mages sent to the back of the enemy lines. Drech and his Il-Aryn moved back onto the battlefield, creating a safe corridor against further black fire.

Ulysan slowed, giving them a sight of the battlefield before they ducked back through the barriers. Wesmen were gathering in defence to their left. Ahead of the gates, the enemy were gone. Bodies crowded the ground. There was cheering from the walls. TaiGethen moved across the area, helping the wounded away and carrying the bodies of their dead.

The cavalry made one more sweep and galloped back through the gates. Through his misted eyes Auum could see more shamen moving up behind their warrior guards. The taunting had ceased. They had landed a significant blow but Auum counted seven TaiGethen bodies being carried away. Too many. If they were to break the siege, they needed to adapt their tactics.

'Come on, let's get you seen to,' said Ulysan.

Auum looked into his face. He was bleeding from a cut to his cheek but his eyes were alive with excitement. 'You seem to make a habit of carrying me bleeding from battlefields.'

'Well I did it once seven hundred years ago. That's hardly statistically significant.'

'It hurts,' said Auum.

'Looks like it.'

Ulysan supported Auum, and the two old friends moved as quickly as they could back within the barrier and on into the city. Auum waited until the last of the elves was back and Harild ordered the gates closed. The cavalry had already trotted away to their stables, leaving the big open space behind the gates full of victorious but grieving elves.

'Get the wounded back to the college,' said Auum. 'We need them treated and ready for the next strike. Pray for your friends who have fallen. Drech, your Il-Aryn should rest. Your work was exemplary, thank you.'

Drech walked over to Auum, waving his people back towards the gates.'We'll meet at dusk in the refectory. Congratulations.'

'Thank you.'

'It appears you are not quite as fast as you think you are.'

'Not now,' breathed Ulysan.

Auum felt himself tense and his arm begin to ache horribly. He leaned on Ulysan to turn himself. There was Takaar, striding up to them with his Senserii in close attendance. Drech watched him come with suspicion and weary anxiety written all over his face. The remaining TaiGethen looked on, but Auum held up a hand to put them at ease.

'We've cleared a path for you. Best you leave now before the Wesmen close it again. It's a good few days' walk to Korina. Cleress has been in contact with her sisters and they're expecting you. Gilderon, the quartermaster of the city will find you travel rations.'

'I only seek to help and yet you snub me at every turn,' said Takaar, appearing genuinely hurt. 'I could have saved you from that wound. And it looks bad. I can treat it.'

'Touch me and I'll break your arm,' said Auum. 'You tried to kill Stein on the way here and you tried to kill Drech last night. You're like a child, but you have dreadful powers and you're prepared to use them on anyone, even those who try to help you. You are not the elf you believe yourself to be and you never will be again.'

Takaar nodded and put his hands over his face. His shoulders began to shake and his body shuddered with sobs. When he looked back at Auum, tears streaked his face and his eyes were imploring and full of contrition.

'I know and I am sorry,' he said, sniffing hard and breathing deeply to calm himself. 'Drech, I cannot forgive myself, but I hope you can forgive me. Auum, all I ask is a chance to prove myself. I can turn the Wytch Lord fire against the shamen who cast it. I've worked out how. Let me show you.'

'Be careful,' whispered Ulysan.

Auum had been teetering on the verge of reaching out to Takaar, so genuinely sorry the elf appeared to be, but drew back.

'You've had so many chances and occasionally you have done something truly remarkable. But the next time you blink, that voice in your head tells you to walk another path and I cannot risk that, not here. This is hostile territory and I have no confidence in you.'

Takaar's eyes narrowed just a little.

'I must be given another chance. You cannot be victorious without me. I. Am. Takaar.' He looked briefly to his right. 'There. Did I say that right?'

'Go back to the ships,' said Auum. 'Pass your wisdom to the Il-Aryn through the sisters. Rest and recover.'

'I do not need to recover!' screamed Takaar. 'I need to be here. Without me you'll all die.'

'I'm prepared to take that chance.'

'I am not!'

Takaar's eyes darkened. He stretched his arm towards Drech, who gasped and struggled. Takaar opened his fist and Drech shuddered once, violently, and made a strangled noise in his throat. His eyes flooded with blood and exploded, showering steaming red droplets across Takaar's face and the cobbled street. Blood coursed from Drech's ears, his skull collapsed and he crumpled to the ground.

'Now you need me!' shouted Takaar, his face covered in gore and his eyes glittering with euphoria. 'Now I am indispensable! Now I alone control the Il-Aryn!'

Auum felt nausea clog his throat.

'Murderer!'

Auum couldn't move but Ulysan did. The big TaiGethen pounced, bearing Takaar backwards onto the ground, snatching a jaqrui from his pouch and holding it against Takaar's throat. Takaar keened like an injured animal, begging to be set free, and Gilderon pressed an ikari blade to Ulysan's temple as the Senserii came to the ready. All around Auum, TaiGethen drew their blades in response.

'Release him,' said Gilderon. A trickle of blood ran from Ulysan's temple.

'Auum?'

Auum walked forward staring into Gilderon's eyes. Twenty Tai-Gethen moved with him. Silence spread as the work of the city surrounding them ceased.

'Back off, Gilderon. Harm him and the Senserii die right here and right now.'

Gilderon glowered. He did not move his ikari.

'You are not capable of taking me,' he said. 'Call Ulysan off or I will kill him.'

'Auum?'

'Stay where you are. Gilderon knows you can kill Takaar before he can twitch. Don't you, Gilderon?'

'I do not need you, Auum,' said Takaar. 'Drech is gone; that is my gift to you. He would have undermined you. But I won't. I will go because you need me out in the field. We must find Dawnthief. Bring it into our bosoms and make it the weapon that defeats the Wytch Lords.'

'Time for you to keep your mouth shut,' said Auum. 'Your life is forfeit, murderer.'

'I must be allowed to go. I can divine it. Just think what that would mean. A force for good in the right hands.'

'You are not the right hands,' snapped Auum. He was feeling faint with the pain in his arm. The burning would not die and blood dripped down his arm from the knife wound. 'How can you remain loyal to him, Gilderon?'

'We believe in him. He found us and he saved us. We owe him our lives. Tell Ulysan to release him.'

'He is a murderer, as just witnessed by you. I cannot let him go.' Auum studied Gilderon's face. 'You do understand that, don't you?'

Auum felt what he assumed was shock begin to descend on him. The vision of Drech's death played out in his mind, overlaid by Takaar's continuous babble. In front of him the Senserii were unmoved and his TaiGethen likewise. He had to find a way to end the stand-off before he lost the strength to stand. He looked down at Takaar. The elf was muttering to himself, in conversation with his tormentor. Time and again he named Dawnthief and the search he thought only he could undertake with any hope of success.

'You cannot keep him here, you must see that. We will take him,' said Gilderon. 'But you must let him get up and leave with dignity.'

'Dignity? Look what he did to Drech! Was that dignity or respect for another? He should leave in chains if he leaves here at all.'

Auum laid a hand on Ulysan's shoulder, and the big elf relaxed and got up. Auum knelt and dragged Takaar to his feet with his good hand clamped on the collar of his shirt.

'What did you just do?' Auum screamed into Takaar's face. 'On a whim you killed the best you ever trained. Why did you do it? How could you do it?'

Takaar's face dripped with sympathy for the ignorant.

'He didn't believe in me,' he said.

'What?' Auum gaped. 'I don't believe in you. Are you going to kill me too?'

'Is that what you'd like?'

Auum pushed him away to stumble into Gilderon's arms.

'Raise your hand to me and I will cut it off.'

'This must end,' said Gilderon.

Auum clutched his left shoulder, clamping his hand hard over the wound. His whole arm throbbed and he felt so tired. Dealing with Takaar was always such a drain. Every moment he was within Takaar's sphere was a moment in which anything could go wrong. And now he had murdered his best student in cold blood. For nothing.

He should be put to death, but the blood that would flow when the Senserii attacked wasn't worth it. Yet Takaar left alive was a horrible risk. He was capable of reappearing at any time, and what he chose to do could make the difference between defeat and victory.

'You'll take him to Korina?' asked Auum.

Gilderon nodded. 'Directly.'

'He must not be allowed to go anywhere near the search area for Dawnthief. Yniss knows, he might just find it and hand it straight to the Wytch Lords.'

'It will never fall into their hands,' muttered Takaar. 'I can hide it. Bring it home.'

'On that condition, I will let him go with you,' said Auum.

Gilderon nodded again. 'Agreed.'

Auum stepped back. He looked up to the gatehouse.

'Ulysan, get up there. Tell me what you see.'

Ulysan ran up the stone stairs and stared out.

'They're taking away their dead and they aren't moving back in. I can see a large gathering away to the left. My guess it'll either be a big push or a withdrawal.'

'Get him away now,' said Auum. 'Keep your Senserii safe and return to the fight. We need you but not him. I never want to lay eyes on him again.'

Gilderon bowed and held his ikari horizontally across his body. 'Die old, not today.'

The gates were opened and the Senserii ran out with Takaar trotting in their midst, still chattering and gesticulating to himself. Auum climbed slowly up to the gatehouse and stood by Ulysan.

'This is a disaster,' he said. 'What are we doing here?'

'Trying to survive.'

'This whole journey was a mistake, Ulysan. I can feel it deep within me. I don't think any of us will be going home.'

'You don't believe that. Get Takaar out of your system. Remember he's insane; don't let him get to you.'

'Is he really mad? Or just a manipulative bastard cursed with power he is all too happy to use to further his ends.'

'It doesn't matter now. We've wounds to dress and our dead to grieve for. Turn your back. Forget about him.'

'I'm incapable of doing at least one of those things.'

Chapter 15

The Wytch Lords' power derives from their union. It breeds their immortality and their strength. Break the cadre, break the Wytch Lords.

Bynaar, Circle Seven Master of Xetesk

Ystormun howled in the mind of his host body, driving the shaman to his knees.

'You will not retreat. You will never retreat! How dare you speak your fear? Victory is close if only you have the wit to grasp it.'

'My lord,' managed the shaman, his hands pushed into the ground to keep himself from sprawling face down in the mud. The tribal lords and their elder shamen were gathered about him, fearing to touch him in case they should suffer similar pain. 'You cannot combat their speed. We touched so few and they killed so many of us.'

'Where were your guards? Did they stand or did they run?'

'You can only run from what you can see.'

'Idiot!' Ystormun fired pain into his host's mind. 'I will speak with them.'

Ystormun flowed across the shaman's mind and dragged the body to its feet. He stalked around the eight gathered before him, seeing them shrink from his gaze. He stopped before a tribal lord whose name he had to recall from the mind of his host.

'Gorsu, explain your failure.'

'Not one of my warriors turned and fled. Run down by cavalry, burned by spells and cut to ribbons by elves moving at evil speed, they stood their ground and tried to defend their charges. It was not failure, it was brave defeat.'

'Defeat is failure,' said Ystormun. 'And you will not fail again. Now you are aware of their speed, you know what to expect. At dawn you will concentrate your forces on the gates and you will break them. You will enter the city and hunt down every elf. I will have Auum's head mounted in my chambers and you will bring it to me or you will die trying. Our power will not be denied. The city falls tomorrow.'

'But—'

'You question me?'

Gorsu held out his hands in a placatory gesture. 'Please, no. But our efforts have so far failed to break either gates or walls. Your powers are not enough to shiver stone.'

'Then you must break them by other means. Scale the walls, shoot the mages from the ramparts. But you will not retreat. I will not suffer cowardice.' Ystormun stared at Gorsu. 'A lord who hates magic should be honoured to perish seeking its downfall.'

'I am one such,' said Gorsu.

'Then . . . ?'

'We will do as you command, Lord Ystormun.'

'Naturally.'

Ystormun left the host body and it slumped to the ground on hands and knees, retching and shuddering. Gorsu watched it convulse a few times before concluding that Ystormun was definitely elsewhere. He landed a savage kick into the shaman's gut, spinning him onto his back, clutching at this new pain with both hands.

'If he was before me now . . .' said Gorsu.

'Then you would be cringing and begging for another breath of life,' said Jhalzan, lord of the Northern Marches.

Gorsu spun to face him. 'And you would be on your belly like the snake you are. Care to have me put you there now?'

Jhalzan stared at Gorsu with cold eyes. He didn't make a move towards a weapon.

'We are all afraid when a Wytch Lord is among us,' he said. 'Kicking young Navar is akin to kicking your horse because you fell from his back.'

'He spoke Ystormun's words.'

'But he is not Ystormun,' said Lorok, Gorsu's own elder shaman, a Wesman clad in bone and hide and tattooed so heavily it was hard to tell the age of his skin. But he was old, unnaturally so. 'And we have until first light to plan an assault. Perhaps we should pray to calm ourselves, break bread, eat meat and find a way to do as Ystormun bids.'

Gorsu looked down at Navar, who was staring at him as if waiting for the next blow.

'What was *he* doing inside you? Why is *he* here?'

'Because the elves are here and he hates the elves above all things,' said Navar, gasping for breath. 'His touch is far harsher than that of Belphamun but his mind is not guarded.'

Gorsu snarled. 'It sickens me that we are forced to do his bidding. We are Wesmen! Why do I find myself tethered to the whim of a creature with no skin?'

'Must we have this again?' asked Jhalzan. 'Without them we would all be dead by now, burned or frozen or worse. Have patience, old friend. When eastern magic is gone, we can build free of its stink. We won't need the cadre then, and there are only six of them.'

'But with such power,' said Lorok.

'Only because it comes from the fingers of every shaman,' said Jhalzan. 'How will they dominate this world when you refuse to be a conduit for them?'

Lorok said nothing, but Gorsu saw the look that passed between him and Navar. The young shaman got to his feet and brushed dust and debris from his cloak. He looked at Gorsu as if expecting an apology. Gorsu pointedly turned his back on him and looked at Julatsa's walls. They were more than forty feet high, but the Wesmen had ladders to scale them.

And would, but for the mages up there by the hundred and those elven warriors who moved so fast and fought so hard. By all accounts they were few, perhaps only a hundred, but their skills were already known to every warrior, and the stories would become taller around the fires tonight. Gorsu needed a way to combat them.

'Lorok, a question.'

Lorok came to his shoulder. 'Yes, my lord?'

'Combined casting is the only way to achieve long range, is that right?'

'Yes. The joining of so many minds lends distance and strength.'

'My problem is that we will need multiple castings as we scale the walls. How close must you be for each shaman to target individual elves or mages?'

'Well within spell range of the enemy,' said Lorok.

Gorsu shrugged. 'My warriors too. We are all throwing ourselves headlong into battle at the behest of your masters.'

'Our masters,' corrected Lorok.

'There is no one alive who is my master,' said Gorsu tersely. 'How close do you have to be to target those on the walls? We must have time to climb and space to fight when we reach the ramparts.'

Lorok looked at him blankly. 'I understand the basics of taking the walls, Lord Gorsu.'

Gorsu managed a smile. 'Of course. But the Wytch Lords have provided you with nothing but their demonic fire, and I would not send my warriors into battle without shields for those who wish them.'

'Making a shield is simple. Developing a casting to protect from magical attack is not,' said Lorok. 'Do your hide barriers deflect magical fire?'

Gorsu growled. 'Ystormun wishes us to take a college city with inferior weapons. Perhaps he should be standing with us.'

'Perhaps you should be careful what you say, Lord Gorsu.'

'Why?' Gorsu turned to face Lorok. 'Are my words being relayed to your masters then?'

Lorok shook his head. 'That is unworthy of you.'

'Is it? I am not the only tribesman wondering where the loyalties of our shamen really lie. Nor am I the only one wondering if you can really turn your backs on the power they grant you.'

'How long have I been your shaman?' asked Lorok. 'And in all that time have I given you one reason to doubt my loyalty to you and our tribe?'

Gorsu shrugged.

'Then why do you question me now? I and my brothers are going to support you tomorrow and many of us will lose our lives doing so. We are proud Wesmen, we are the shepherds of your spirits. It saddens me that you're suspicious of us.'

'The world has changed, Lorok. I do not feel master of my own destiny, and that makes me suspicious. Your masters have ordered us to mount an attack that is ill judged and unnecessary. Should we win we will be weakened, and should we lose we will rot, and Ystormun and Belphamun will merely look for more fodder. This is not our way.'

'It is our only chance to break human magic,' said Lorok.

'We will never break it,' said Gorsu, and he felt a shameful pang of hopelessness.

'Never speak such words,' hissed Lorok.

'The truth is inconvenient, is it?' Gorsu turned away from Lorok.

'My Lords Jhalzan and Hafeez, my cook fire is hot and the stew is strong; the drink is stronger still. Join me and let's plot our victory.'

Gorsu glanced back at Lorok.

'And you know what you must do. See that your brothers are ready.'

Auum flexed his left hand and sensed the weakness in his arm. He felt lost and alone. The Wesmen might have been bruised but they had not fallen back, and tomorrow would bring another battle. More TaiGethen would die, and Auum needed to run with them, even if he couldn't hold a blade.

Doubts crowded his mind. He needed Drech but Drech was gone. Takaar too. That should have pleased him, but he could not shake the feeling that he had made the wrong decision. Stein and Ulysan had no such worries, but Takaar was out there beyond any sort of control and, for all Gilderon's assurances, would do exactly as he pleased.

'We had the right to kill him and we didn't,' he said. 'Why not?'

'Because he's Takaar,' said Ulysan.

Auum turned sharply from his vantage point on the highest balcony of the Julatsan college tower. It gave him a view across the calm city all the way to the furthest Wesmen campfires. Dawn was only a couple of hours away, and Auum had long since given up on sleep.

'It comes to something when I can't hear your heavy boots,' said Auum. 'Is that why we showed him mercy?'

Ulysan shrugged. 'Why else? Deep down I still hope that he'll come back to us and be the elf he once was. Stupid I know, but it's what I've always hoped.'

'I loved him,' said Auum, feeling suddenly on the edge of tears and cursing himself for the weakness. 'I so wanted him to see past his guilt and his paranoia, but he can't, can he? You aren't stupid, Ulysan. We all wish for the same and we're all disappointed so often, aren't we?'

'But your hope hasn't died, has it?'

Auum shook his head. 'No, curse him. And try as I might to hate him, I can't maintain it. I can't dismiss him.'

'So stop wasting your energies on Takaar. Concentrate on our real enemies.'

'I do, and I fear their magic. Even under the shetharyn I was hurt, and we lost seven. *Seven.* Their black fire is an indiscriminate power and its touch is so harsh. We can't play such a game of chance again, and I can't see another way to take the fight to them.' Auum walked back into the antechamber and sat on a bench. 'And if they choose not to attack us, what then? Yniss preserve me, I wish we'd never left Calaius.'

Ulysan followed and sat next to him. For a time the two of them stared at the tapestries and paintings hung around the room. They were dour images of the building of Julatsa and the council in session.

'You know we had no choice.'

'I tell you something else: if I ever see Calaius again, I will deny I was ever here. And should I ever decide to board ship to this barren, stinking country again, you have my permission to kill me.'

Auum felt so confused. In the rainforest it was all so clear, yet here where you could see everything laid out, it was all obscured. He put his face in his hands.

'If we break the siege, what then? I can't agree to fight alongside Xetesk.'

'Stein says it's our best chance of success.'

'I know the numbers, but in my soul it feels wrong. The Wytch Lords were spawned from the type of mage that now inhabits Xetesk, weren't they?'

'That was hundreds of years ago. In the lifetimes of men that's an eternity,' said Ulysan.

'Then why do I feel we are being dragged in the wrong direction? I don't like not knowing what's ahead.'

'I think we have to trust Stein and Kerela and the other Julatsans.'

'Why?' Auum rubbed at his left arm. 'Stein maybe but the rest . . . well . . . You know what I think.'

'Let's take this a day at a time,' said Ulysan. 'We're nowhere if we can't break the Wesmen here.'

Auum felt a fractional release of tension.

'Any ideas on that front? We have to think of something different.'

'Just one,' said Ulysan. 'Think about it the other way to today's battles. We need to get our mages and Il-Aryn close enough to threaten the shamen, because we know we can take the fighters. The question is, whose casters have the greater range?'

The door to the antechamber opened. A soldier, out of breath and red in the face, came in.

'My Lord Auum, General Harild wants you on the walls at the main gates,' he said in stilted but passable elvish.

'I am no lord,' said Auum, smiling at the young human.

'Why didn't he get a mage to relay a message?' asked Ulysan.

The soldier blushed scarlet. 'I asked to come. I wanted to meet you, speak to you in your language.'

Auum felt an unexpected rush of warmth and took the soldier's hand, shaking it as was the human custom before kissing his forehead.

'Well done, although I can't imagine why you should want to meet me.'

If it was possible, the soldier's red cheeks reddened further. 'You are Auum. Your freeing of Calaius is famous. And I saw you fight out there. Can I learn to be that fast?'

Auum laughed and stepped back. 'What's your name?'

'Tilman,' he said. 'My family's mostly farmers.'

'Well, Tilman, your elvish is impressive and you can improve upon it until your dying day. But our speed is given to us by Yniss and no human will ever be so blessed. I admire your ambition, though.' Auum winked at Ulysan. 'That's two humans I like now.'

'What's going on out there?' asked Ulysan. 'Why are we needed on the walls?'

'The Wesmen are gathering. It's a change of plan for them. They have brought, um . . . I don't know the word . . . to climb the walls.'

'Ladders?' said Auum. 'Good. That spares me a few awkward decisions, doesn't it?'

'I suppose,' said Ulysan. 'But unless they've chosen to sacrifice themselves in an ocean of mage fire, they must have thought of some way to protect their warriors during the assault.'

'Well, there's only one way to find out. Lead on, Tilman. I want to know more about you before the spells start to fly.'

Chapter 16

No one can understand the joy of the shetharyn who has not experienced its touch. To lose it once found would be to die.

Faleen, TaiGethen

A network of mages linked by a Communion casting was positioned all around Julatsa's walls to warn of forces approaching from any direction. Down in the city the emergency plan had been put into operation, taking vulnerable members of the population inside the college grounds, organising fire and stretcher teams and setting up ambushes at key points in the tight streets.

Harild's college army and the militia were on the walls or behind the gates. Hundreds of bows and thousands of arrows were ready, as they had been every day of the siege. The cavalry were on standby to charge the gates should they be breached or to hasten a rout should the Wesmen be beaten back.

Auum had split the remaining thirty-one TaiGethen cells between three points along the walls to match the concentrations of Wesmen warriors mustering on the open ground below. The Il-Aryn and college mages were in casting groups spread along the walls and around thirty of them stood behind the gates ready to launch orbs.

Auum stood in the gatehouse with Harild, Stein and Ulysan. His left arm ached terribly but at least he could use it to balance himself, if not to hold a weapon or close his fist to punch. It would have to do. He stared at the gathering enemy forces and shook his head.

'Unless they've got a new trick, I can't see any way they'll avoid a slaughter on the approach. How do they even propose to get a single foothold on the walls?'

The warriors were singing and chanting. Auum had counted sixty wooden ladders, all wide enough to allow three abreast. A large proportion of the Wesmen carried hide shields and those who didn't had bows. Spread among them were the shamen no longer in large groups but in ones, twos and threes. They were a powerful force but were about to attack into a storm of human magic.

'The shamen must be planning something,' said Ulysan. 'Have you seen them spread out like this before?'

'No,' said Harild.

'It makes them more difficult to target.'

'But they have to be our focus,' said Harild. 'Without the shamen, the Wesmen are totally exposed.'

'And there's really nothing elsewhere around the walls?' asked Auum.

'No. It's so empty I was thinking of sending the cavalry out through the rear gates.'

Auum nodded. 'And why did you decide against it?'

'Because there's too much open ground to east or west coming around the walls and into view. Too much time for the shamen to target them. We're better keeping them here as a shock force or perhaps as a diversion.'

'Agreed,' said Auum.

He stared at the enemy again. The chanting beyond the gates ceased. Four thousand and more Wesmen faced the city in silence, their shamen moving among them, laying hands on them, muttering prayers and invoking their spirits for victory. The silence was unnerving. Auum could feel the tension rise inside the city. Everyone knew the time had come.

'Keep your heads down when you see the shamen preparing,' said Harild, his voice booming out. 'Get the message along the walls. Get the spotters up in the sky. Make this day glorious.'

'No parley flag,' said Ulysan.

'They don't want us to surrender; they want us dead,' said Auum. 'Stay on my left. I'm weak there.'

'I shall be like glue,' said Ulysan.

'Perhaps not quite that close,' said Auum.

The Wesmen howled like wild dogs and rushed across the open space of a hundred yards and more, scattering into ladder teams flanked by archers. Shields were held out against the inevitable rain of spells and arrows. The shamen ran among the warriors.

'Archers. Loose at will!' roared Harild.

Arrows whipped away but not enough, not nearly enough. Auum looked along the walls. He could see shock on the faces of mages, Il-Aryn and bowmen alike. Only the TaiGethen displayed no fear.

'Stein,' said Auum, 'get among your people to the right. They're waiting too long. I'll do the same left. Come on, Ulysan.'

Auum ran from the gatehouse, jumped down the steps to the ramparts, where Ollem was waiting for him, and sprinted along behind the nervous defenders. He heard another order from Harild. There was a brief pressure of human magical power across his shoulders before a volley of bright yellow orbs of fire soared out from behind the gates, trailing smoke and plunging into the ground just in front of the foremost Wesmen.

The multiple detonations ripped up the ground and scattered fire in every direction, slowing the advance of the enemy centre, but they flooded forward undaunted elsewhere across the line, howling and roaring.

Now was when they missed Drech. The Il-Aryn were leaderless under their reluctant figurehead Ephemere, whose voice was quiet and had no carry. To the right of the gatehouse, Auum didn't even know the name of the nominated leader.

'Deploy the barrier,' ordered Auum. 'Keep their fire from our rampart.'

More arrows flicked out, meeting a wall of shields with only a few finding gaps. A couple of warriors fell. A second volley of orbs drove into the ground outside the gates. This time they struck flesh, wood and leather. Wesmen were hurled backwards and sideways, wreathed in fire. Ladders were reduced to ash.

'More!' yelled Auum. 'Target the ladders. Cast! Cast!'

Beside him three mages were standing and preparing. Below, the Wesmen were scant yards from the wall. Ladders were raised ready to be laid against the stone. Arrows flew thick from the walls while Wesmen archers knelt, nocked shafts and fired.

'Down!'

Wesmen arrows struck home, punching mages and human archers from the walls.

'Get fire on the archers!' Auum stood. 'Look for the shamen.'

Along his section of the wall, his TaiGethen were marshalling those around them as best they could. The mages next to Auum cast, and a wall of flame sixty feet long sprang up in the midst of the advancing line. Wesmen dived in all directions, some wrapped in flame and screaming. More and more spells were flying down from the walls now. Wesman shields raised in defence were frozen by gales of super-cooled air. Flechettes of ice sliced into unprotected flesh and ripped through leather armour.

But still they came. Ladders thudded against the wall in ten places . . . fifteen. Julatsan defenders fired down on the climbers while the TaiGethen stood ready to receive them. The second Wesman line slowed twenty yards from the walls. Shields were raised and, in among them, there was quick movement.

'Shamen preparing!' yelled Auum, but his warning was a moment too late. 'Where's my barrier? Get down!'

Hands stretched beyond the shields sent black fire from every fingertip. The tendrils scoured the top of the ramparts. Mage, Il-Aryn, TaiGethen and soldier alike were caught in the storm. Fire wormed into bodies and faces, searing and drilling deep, piercing hearts and ripping open stomachs. Wherever it struck flesh, the fire fed greedily. Defenders fell by the dozen, some dead before they hit the ground.

Auum rose and drew a blade, holding it in his right hand. Ulysan moved ahead of him, Ollem behind. Wesman warriors reached the tops of ladders. Axes swung and more defenders fell. The TaiGethen surged into the attack. Spells showered out into the attackers, driving the second line back a few paces.

Auum had almost reached the head of a ladder. It vibrated with the movement of climbers on its rungs. The first Wesman over the top hacked his axe into the head of a soldier too slow to bring his blade to bear. In front of Auum, Ulysan thrust his blade into the Wesman's chest and he fell.

Another two appeared and, between them, an archer with an arrow nocked. He released, Auum swayed right and the arrow fizzed past him. Behind him, Ollem grunted and Auum turned to see him drop to his knees, the shaft jutting from his neck. Blood was flooding down his jacket.

'Ollem!'

'Fight,' said Ollem, his voice thick with blood. 'I'll be all right.'

Auum swung back. Ulysan evaded an axe, ducking under the blade and rising fast. Ulysan's blades sliced into the Wesman's gut and face and he tumbled forward. Auum stepped up and jabbed his blade into the archer's face, tipping him back off the ladder. The other warrior thrust his sword at Auum's body. Auum jumped back and left, coming in again hard, back-handing his blade into the neck of the enemy.

Still they came. Shaman fire laced across the top of the walls again, driving defenders back and leaving the way clear for yet more ladders and Wesmen. Auum wanted to roar for his barrier again but it was obvious why it wasn't going to happen. TaiGethen defending the Il-Aryn were moving them back away from immediate threat and indeed some were being directed to ladders to the ground to leave more space for fighting.

Auum glanced at Ollem and thought to call for help, but the young TaiGethen was still and his chest had stopped rising. Auum felt a hot anger settle on him.

'He never had a chance,' muttered Auum. 'Too young, too strong to die like this . . .'

'Auum!' screamed Ulysan.

Auum snapped round. Ulysan was fighting two Wesmen. The rampart seemed to be full of them. A blade was swinging towards Auum's head. He used his anger and the threat alike. The axe head slowed before his eyes. He rocked back on his heels, simultaneously bringing his blade to ready.

The look of triumph in the Wesman's eyes faded. The blade moved past Auum and on to collide with a crenellation. Auum moved forward, pushed the warrior's head back with his weaker left hand and rammed his blade into his throat.

Auum dragged the blade clear, stepped over the falling body and headed for the ladder. A Wesman archer released a shaft, taking a soldier further along the wall through the shoulder. Auum grabbed his bow and pulled hard, heaving the Wesman onto the rampart, then stamped down on the back of his neck, moved on and buried his blade in the flank of another axe man, pushing the body over the wall, where it fell as a warning among his comrades.

Auum reached Ulysan, dropping out of the shetharyn. Ulysan ripped a blade into the gut of a warrior and heaved his body over the wall. Either side of them TaiGethen and Julatsan soldiers fought to clear the walls of Wesmen and defend the mages.

Spells were still firing out from behind the gates but elsewhere both arrow fire and castings were desultory. The shamen's black fire played across the crenellations, daring the defenders to expose themselves to fire down.

'We've got to force the shamen back,' said Auum, ducking as a finger of black fire flickered on the stone a pace from where he stood. 'Suggestions?'

More Wesmen ascended the ladder, flanked by shaman fire. Ulysan round-housed the first, catching him on the side of the head and clattering him into the next. Black fire reached for the big TaiGethen, who dropped to his haunches, the tendrils clutching above his head. Both Wesmen fell.

'Get the mages onto the ground and casting blind over the walls,' said Ulysan.

Arrows flicked over the ramparts. Defenders responded, firing blind from behind crenellations. The Wesmen were relentless, though. Thirty yards to the left they'd established a bridgehead and were forcing the defenders back. Auum saw soldiers fall and Faleen lead her Tai into the breach.

'It'll take too long. Got to create a diversion.'

The two elves stared at each other. 'Cavalry.'

'Hold!' yelled Auum to any who would hear him. Hassek nodded his assent and took his Tai directly to a new ladder laid against the walls.

Auum ran back towards the gatehouse, ducking arrows and black fire and forcing his way through knots of fighting. He climbed the stairs three at a time and took a breath when he ducked through the door. Dead littered the gatehouse. Eyes were burned out, arrows stuck from chests and throats. Harild was crouched below the lip of the wall, glancing over and ducking back, roaring orders lost in the tumult. Black fire chased Auum and Ulysan down next to him alongside two aides, both of whom were too terrified to be of any use.

'Can't stop the Wytch fire,' growled Harild.

'How's the right holding?'

'Holding is all they're doing, Auum. I'm sending mages down but it's confused. They have no lines of communication. Stein is somewhere down there but I've lost my Communion mage. One shaman gives them ten fingers of fire at this range. They're murdering us.'

'We have to distract them,' said Auum. 'Get your cavalry in the saddle. Ride out through the centre and don't stop. Then circle wide so you can hit the rear.'

'They'll pick the riders right out of their saddles. It's suicide.'

'No, it isn't. Cast left and right as the gates open. Ride hard for open ground.'

'What about your precious Il-Aryn?'

Auum was stung. 'I don't know why they haven't cast.'

'Perfect.'

'But the TaiGethen will not leave the cavalry defenceless. We're going out too.'

Harild frowned. 'Through the gates?'

'No,' said Auum. 'Look to your cavalry. We'll be ready.'

'Now?'

'Now.' Auum stared at Harild. 'You are brave beyond duty. A third human I actually like.'

Harild smiled. 'Well, then this whole mess is worth the pain. You'll be ready?'

'Before you,' said Ulysan.

They watched Harild reach safety on the rampart steps down to the ground. Auum sent Ulysan to the right-hand door of the gatehouse, and he reported back a mirror image of Auum's view of the left.

'The TaiGethen are spread too thin and we've lost some. The Wesmen are attacking on a wide front. We're barely holding them back. Mages are heading for the ladders, Il-Aryn too.'

Auum leaned out of the back of the gatehouse. Ephemere was down there looking lost and frightened.

'Ephemere! Ephemere!' Belatedly, she looked up. 'Report to Harild. Gather your Il-Aryn. Get a barrier up when the gates open.'

'The gates?' she said, her voice barely carrying.

'Just do it. Do something! For the love of Yniss, we need you.' Auum turned back to Ulysan. 'Get out to the right. Have as many ready as you can. Wait for the castings and the cavalry before we move.'

'And who's going to save your sorry hide?'

Auum laughed. 'I'll run with Graf, you with Merrat. See you out there and may Yniss save you for greater tasks.'

'Like saving your sorry hide.'

'Precisely. Go.'

Auum leaped down to the rampart, feeling exposed without Ulysan by his side. He had been a constant presence for over eight hundred years and a friend for thousands. Ulysan was an extension of Auum – utterly indispensable.

He pushed the weakness from his mind and headed along the rampart, sword in his right hand. The Wesmen were attacking on a front almost two hundred yards wide. From the gatehouse he'd seen almost thirty ladders. Where the TaiGethen cells fought, the Wesmen could not gain a foothold but at four other points they were making solid ground and the Julatsan soldiers were beginning to wither under their onslaught. Fighting with their backs against a drop of thirty feet should they slip, they were losing ground steadily.

Auum spared a quick glance below. The cavalry was mounting up. Horses stamped and snorted, sweat flecked flanks and leaked from beneath saddles. Metal rang echoes against the gates, a counterpoint to the shaman magic picking at the timbers.

Auum had to make the end of the rampart before the gates opened in order to alert his Tais to the new plan – two hundred yards through packed fighting. He had one blade, one damaged arm, two feet and no Ulysan. He took a deep breath.

'This is going to be interesting.'

Auum sought the shetharyn. It was there but he would not be able to hold it for long. He hefted his blade, leaned forward to hide himself from arrow and magic as best he could and ran hard alongside the crenellations, wishing he'd hurt his right arm instead.

Ahead, Thrynn's Tai fought well: no Wesman had gained the rampart. Auum shot into their midst and smashed his sword into the skull of a warrior on the ladder. He paused, ducking behind the wall.

'We're going over. Follow the cavalry, use your speed. Trust in Yniss.'

Auum blurred away. Ahead the rampart was blocked. Two soldiers were falling back, one stood firm in a wide stance. Auum dropped and slid between his legs, rising and jamming his blade into the groin of a Wesman. He pulled it clear, thrust it into the chest of the warrior in front of him and leaped high, dragging his blade clear and turning a forward roll in the air over the heads of the fight. Auum landed, ran on two paces, jumped with legs outstretched and hammered both feet into the head of an enemy archer. He rode the falling body, and straight-punched another with his left hand, knocking him on to Hassek's blade. Auum delivered the same message on his way past. Dimly, he heard the gates begin to crank open. He sped on, watching the fight unfold before his eyes: every blow, every spray of blood, every pace and every scream of fear or pain. Auum jumped clear over Marack's head, yelled his message and landed with his legs around the neck of a Wesman on the wall. Auum flexed his back, dragging the axe man down to the parapet floor, leaping clear as he struck the timbers. He powered on, forcing his way along the wall at a crouch, now sliding on his back through a press of legs. His blade was running with blood, his passage spreading confusion among attacker and Julatsan soldier alike. His left arm ached and he felt fresh blood oozing from the wound in his shoulder. Almost there. He jumped high, spinning horizontally to take him over a press of Wesmen and landing crouched behind them in a breath of space. He jabbed his blade backwards into the calf of one, turned and sliced through the hamstrings of another. Delivered the same message to Vaart's Tai. Auum raced along the rampart behind two more cells, angling his body out over the drop and forcing himself to even greater speed. Same message. He powered on, his eyes picking the clearest route, his sword now fending off bodies as he passed. Duck, slide, sprint, jump. He felt his breath shorten as fatigue began to take hold. Grafyrre's Tai was ahead and the ladder in front of them was clear, the ground below littered with Wesmen bodies. The timbers were slick with blood and the stink of it made his eyes water. Auum ran in hard and dropped out of the shetharyn. He was out of breath and put his hands on his knees.

'Yniss preserve me, but that was good,' he said.

Grafyrre turned to him, his expression questioning. Auum opened his mouth to speak but felt the weight of Il-Aryn magic behind him and the dull glow of a barrier. Hooves thundered on cobbles.

'Never mind,' he said. 'Just follow me.'

Chapter 17

Septern's talents were so far beyond those of any other mage he must have been blessed by all the gods of man.

Kerela, Julatsan Mage Council

Gorsu could scarcely believe it. They were going to win, against all the odds, and not even the elves or the bastard eastern magic could stop them. From the ground the warriors swarming the ladders were roared on by their comrades who crowded at the bases for their turn. Many had died, many would still die, but Gorsu could see the gaps appearing in the defensive lines and the spaces his tribesmen were creating.

The shamen among the reserve line had done terrible damage but, more importantly, they had forced archer and mage alike from the walls to cower elsewhere, leaving the way clear for the assault. The early morning sun was shining on the Wesmen and although he hated Ystormun and his filthy cadre, Gorsu couldn't deny he was looking forward to the glory they would bestow upon him when the day was done.

Julatsa had nothing left. A few arrows flew over the walls from the ground behind but they fell short. Spells still hit the ground in front of the gate, but the Wesmen had long since cleared the strike zone so now their only effect was to deplete the casters' stamina. It was no surprise when the spells stopped falling.

Gorsu ordered more warriors to the foot of the ladders, ready to ascend. He wanted more pressure on the Julatsans, more space – enough to get the shamen up there to fire down into the streets. Then it would only be a matter of time. He turned to Lorok.

'Your shamen have proved themselves this morning.'

'I'm astonished you ever doubted they would.'

'I doubt the courage of all but my own warriors.'

A sound from his left caught Gorsu's attention. Julatsa's gates were opening, cogs grinding and hinges shrieking in protest. Simultaneously, a brief commotion stirred through the struggle up on the walls ahead of him. It travelled left to right. He saw warriors fall.

New human castings fired out from behind the gatehouse, angling left and right, slamming into the ground just before his reserve lines, sending up walls of fire and spattering flame across as yet unscorched ground. An opaque barrier snapped into place in front of the gates as they rattled open. It was a fresh if utterly unsubtle tactic. Gorsu added his voice to the stream of orders turning shaman fire on the barrier. Hafeez was bellowing for his tribesmen to form up ready to take on whatever came through.

The weight of black fire directed at the ramparts was diminished but that shouldn't matter. This was a desperate counter-attack, and once beaten back it would leave them even closer to victory. Gorsu waited for a heartbeat and felt a moment of calm, like the fading of a breeze, before cavalrymen galloped through the barrier, backed by casting after casting crashing down on their flanks.

'Get men behind them; attack the gates!' roared Gorsu. 'Hafeez, get men—'

Gorsu caught a change in the movement on the walls in the corner of his eye. He swung round and his breath caught in his throat. They were jumping off. Forty feet, surely a death fall. He stood and stared. It was . . . it was beautiful. They soared out, arms spread to balance themselves. Thirty of them at least, diving headlong, tucking their bodies into tight forward rolls and landing on the ground as if they'd stepped from the bottom tread of a flight of stairs.

And then they ran. Dear spirits, they ran, and he could barely see them any more.

'Incoming!' Gorsu screamed, drawing his long sword and racing into the middle of his reserve lines. 'Protect the shamen. Turn your fire, damn you all, turn your fire!'

Gorsu heard an eerie keening sound and dozens of his warriors and shamen fell, ugly blades stuck in their faces, chests, stomachs and limbs. Blood fountained in the air and a head bounced and rolled on the packed ground. The elves were among them, just like before, only this time the shamen could not get clear sight.

They were like blurs across the ground, impossible to track. He saw the glint of blades, saw elven bodies fly through the air and saw his people being slaughtered.

'There are only thirty of them,' he muttered. But his warriors were packed too close together, desperate for defensive compactness when they needed exactly the opposite. 'Space! Give yourself room to swing! Keep them back; hack at the air, or anywhere!'

Gorsu pushed into the lines, his blade in two hands. He swung it in front of him as an elf surged at him. The edge carved into empty air and Gorsu felt his hair move and a breath of wind over his head. He swung round. The elf landed, struck one blade into the throat of a shaman and carved his other into a tribesman's shoulder.

Black fire traced across the ground and played into the air, as much a risk to his people as it was to the elves.

'Find your targets!' he roared, spinning round in a tight circle. 'We can take them!'

Cavalry ploughed into the Wesman lines to his left and thundered on towards the warriors turning from the ladders to join the fight. Wytch fire took three riders from their saddles before elves killed the shamen. It was chaos. Up on the walls his warriors were being beaten back now that there were no more climbing to join them.

Arrows started falling again, picking off shaman and warrior alike. Gorsu looked for Hafeez in time to see him fence away a jab to his midriff but miss the second strike to his face. The lord crumpled, his nose and right eye split open, his lower jaw smashed.

'Form a circle,' howled Gorsu into the tumult engulfing him, hoping some would hear. 'I want order!'

But he wasn't going to get it. They were attacked by so few but the enemy seemed to be everywhere and his forces were too close to the walls. Arrows were raining down more steadily now. Gorsu sought a target, anything to give him and his people hope. There was one elven body on the ground but surely a hundred of his warriors.

There: running into a knot of warriors and shamen but slow compared to the rest. He was close enough and he was clearly wounded. Gorsu could see an arm hanging limp, blood staining a bandage near his shoulder. Other elves flowed around him, carving destruction, but he was weak.

Gorsu howled a battle cry and raced in. One blow could turn the tide, especially if he struck it. One blow and they could rally. Gorsu heard the thundering of hooves again and dived to the right, rolling away from the charge that battered into his forces, scattering his warriors in all directions.

He rose and ran on. The damaged elf struck a killing blow and turned half away from Gorsu, who raised his sword and swung it hard. Only at the last did the elf sense him and turn, catching the blow on his blade and deflecting it, but at the cost of his balance. He fell.

Gorsu drew back for the killing blow. He felt something to his right. He faltered and turned his head. Another elf stood there where a pulse ago there had been empty space.

'How can you be there?' whispered Gorsu. 'How can you be so fast?'

Gorsu saw the blade chop into his neck. He felt it slice all the way through. He stood just for a moment then his head rolled back and he felt himself falling.

Dimly, he heard elven voices issuing orders.

Ulysan pulled Auum to his feet.

'Yniss spared you, then,' said Auum.

'That he did.'

Auum glanced up at the walls. They were filling with mages and archers once more. Harild's cavalry had driven great holes in the enemy lines and the Wesmen were in tatters.

'Time to finish it. Break back to the walls!'

Elves sprinted from the enemy. Up on the walls it was the signal they were waiting for. As the Wesmen tried to gather themselves, a devastating volley of spells and arrows engulfed them, scattering them across the field, driving them back. Beyond the reach of the castings, cavalry drove in, wheeled and returned, reinforcing the rout.

Inside, Auum sat with his back to the wall, feeling the pounding of hooves and spells vibrate through his body. He felt exhausted.

'I wonder how many we lost,' he said.

Ulysan squatted beside him. He was cut on both arms; there was a slash in his jacket and a livid bruise developing on his forehead.

'Pray to Shorth it is not too many, but we have to expect losses. Even under the shetharyn, we are still vulnerable to a lucky blow and to their black fire. We're both evidence of that.'

'So little time to rest,' said Auum. 'We've got to move on in a couple of days, join the main fight as, apparently, we must. I have no desire to stay in this stinking country one moment longer than I have to.'

Ulysan smiled. 'But you were never here, right?'

'And don't you forget it. Come on, time to grieve for the fallen. Help me up, would you?'

*

Takaar could sense the extraordinary density of magic long before they came to the shattered remains of the Septern Manse. At first they'd tracked a group of Wesman warriors and shamen but they'd overtaken them when it was clear they were heading for the same destination.

They'd increased their speed, making light work of the easy terrain and sleeping for only a few hours a night. The Senserii were still with him, despite his determination to visit the Manse, because they were *his* people. They were the only ones who still believed in him and trusted him.

And it confuses me every day that they do so.

'You know nothing of loyalty,' muttered Takaar as he followed Gilderon through some dense scrub, hoping to get a view of the Manse from a rise.

Your version of it, involving running out on your people and killing your most devoted student? No.

'I will not return to ancient history and I will not explain myself again. Not to you.'

Two of the Senserii had scouted the ground around the Manse earlier that morning, and Gilderon had recommended they lie low until nightfall, given the human presence in and around the ruins. But now night was full and the cloud cover darkened the sky to a pitch that humans would find very difficult.

Takaar could see the glow of campfires long before they had crawled to the edge of the brush to look down on the Septern Manse. His eyes adjusted quickly to the scene of light and deep dark and he took in the blasted buildings and chattering humans while he breathed the strong scent of magic, past and present.

There was precious little of the Manse left. One or two of the outbuildings appeared largely intact but they were of no consequence – stores and stables, nothing more. The surviving footprint of the Manse gave a good impression of its scale. It must have been an impressive structure. At its centre a quartet of chimney stacks still stood proud, supported by the remains of dividing walls and a single door frame. Elsewhere, scarred brick and stone occasionally rose up a storey and in a couple of areas even supported a broken roof timber, but mostly the Manse had been blasted to its foundations.

Kerela had given him the impression that Wytch Lord magic had caused the destruction, but that was inaccurate. A Wesman attack may have triggered the devastation, but the remnants of the energy lines suggested that every single casting that had detonated was from the inside out.

'He made this all happen,' breathed Takaar.

And wouldn't it be wonderful to know exactly how.

'It would but I think it rather unlikely we'll learn it here.'

'Takaar?'

Gilderon was staring at him. Takaar held up a hand.

'Just thinking aloud,' he said.

Gilderon nodded, as he always did. Takaar always wanted to say he was talking to his tormentor, as Gilderon knew he was. But he never did.

It's because you're ashamed of me. That hurts.

'What is our next move?' asked Gilderon. 'We can't stay here. Auum will expect news of our arrival in Korina soon enough.'

'Auum be damned,' hissed Takaar. He looked down at the five campfires and counted around forty people gathered about them, pottering among the ruins with lanterns or buzzing around the extensive stores stacked near four rows of tents which could easily contain other humans. 'When will the Wesman force reach here?'

'Two days at the speed we witnessed. They are fit and strong,' said Gilderon.

'You like them, don't you?'

Gilderon frowned and shook his head. 'I respect them as fighters and in one respect I agree with Auum. We have more in common with them than with our chosen allies.'

'Magic has changed all that,' said Takaar shortly.

'Magic is changing everything.'

Do I detect dissension?

'You detect nothing,' said Takaar and he searched Gilderon's face for betrayal.

'Takaar? We can't stay here,' repeated Gilderon.

'How many Wesmen were in that raiding party, do you think?'

'Fifty warriors and nine shamen,' said Gilderon. 'A significant number. But that's not why we can't stay here.'

Gilderon gestured at the humans in front of the Manse.

'These are our allies,' said Takaar.

'Are you so sure of that?'

'Why are you questioning me so much all of a sudden?' asked

Takaar. He looked into Gilderon's eyes again but saw only loyalty there. 'Seems like Auum has turned your head too.'

Gilderon tensed. 'Auum has no influence over me. But he has raised proper suspicions concerning those who seek the spell.'

'Gilderon,' said Takaar gently. 'Auum's views on magic are based entirely on ignorance. Surely you believe that magic is the greatest force for good in this world or you wouldn't be with me. Finding and understanding Dawnthief can only enhance that force, don't you see?'

Your patronising tone is coming along very well. Have you noticed just what a skilled fighter Gilderon is?

Takaar saw the doubt in Gilderon's eyes and felt those of all the Senserii on him.

'It bothers you all, does it?' he asked.

'We are not schooled in magic. We respect its power for good, but we also fear its destructive potential. We believe there are some things better left hidden.'

Takaar nodded, feeling sympathy for the lesser intellect. 'I understand. And yet you still agreed to come to this place.'

Gilderon shrugged. 'We can report the current situation to Auum and Julatsa when we reach Korina.'

'We're going to do much better than that,' said Takaar. 'Those men down there are our allies against the Wytch Lords. It is our duty to warn them that the Wesmen are coming and in what strength.'

'I must caution against that. If Auum is right and Xetesk does not believe itself an ally of Julatsa—'

'He is not right,' snapped Takaar. 'And we will warn these people before they are attacked.'

Takaar stood and walked through the remaining brush, striding down the slope towards the campfires. He marched into the midst of the camp, causing consternation. Men scrambled to their feet, orders and warnings were shouted.

Beyond the tents Takaar saw around thirty men stand as one. Each was huge, hefting an axe in one hand and a long sword in the other. Like the Senserii they wore masks on their faces, though these were full face and looked like leather rather than cloth, with holes cut for mouth, eyes and nostrils.

Gilderon hissed for Takaar to stop. He took heed, finding himself in a wide circle of nervous humans with the Senserii forming up beside him. They watched the masked men approach. There was something inhuman about them: the energies that surrounded them appeared to link them together, almost as if they were tethered. He frowned.

'Please,' said Takaar in the human language taught him by Garan all those years ago. 'We are allies here and we want the same thing. I can help you. I am Takaar.'

His announcement was greeted with total silence. The masked men were standing just behind a group of mages, whose energies gave them away. There was no immediate threat of violence but equally there was no doubting the threat of the tethered warriors.

One of the mages walked towards Takaar. He was a tall man, imposing with broad shoulders and a barrel chest. He was dressed in a heavy cloak over a leather jacket and trousers. His black boots crunched across fire ash.

'I am sure your name resonates powerfully where you come from – Julatsa, I presume – but it means nothing to me.'

Hard to believe isn't it? Someone, here in the middle of nowhere, doesn't know who you are.

Takaar smiled in what he hoped was a benign fashion.

'I am the father of the Il-Aryn,' he said. 'The father of elven magic.'

That's it, play the modesty card.

'Ah yes. Your magic is so fragile most elven adepts come to Julatsa to learn.'

Takaar's smile became brittle like his temper. 'Don't insult what you don't understand.'

The mage held up his hands.

'I suppose it was powerful enough to evade our patrols,' he conceded.

'That has more to do with being quiet than being powerful,' said Takaar. 'Your guards spend too much time looking in and not out. Please, let's not start with suspicion. I am here to help.'

The mage's smile was thin. Takaar had hoped to be offered a place at the campfire but no move was made.

He doesn't like you. He doesn't believe you.

'He doesn't know me,' muttered Takaar.

'I'm sorry. I didn't hear that,' said the mage.

Not knowing you is normally when they like you best, isn't it?

'Nothing,' said Takaar, once again talking in Balaian. 'Thinking out loud.'

Another mage wandered from the group a few yards back. Takaar noticed the masked men begin to fan out, Gilderon noted it too and his Senserii responded.

'I presume you left Julatsa before the siege was laid,' said the newcomer in decent elvish.

'No,' said Takaar.

'Yes,' said Gilderon simultaneously.

'Well it can hardly be both,' said the newcomer.

Takaar glared at Gilderon, who met his gaze squarely.

'Your naivety will get you killed one day,' said the Senserii.

'Your role is to fight not to speak,' said Takaar.

'It is to defend you,' corrected Gilderon. 'Which is what I do with my every breath.'

The mage had rocked back on his heels and folded his arms.

'Whenever you're ready, perhaps you could answer my question,' he said. 'I'll be blunt. This is a difficult situation. This site is barred to any but Xeteskian researchers and security. We need to know more about you so we can decide what to do with you.'

Oops.

Takaar gestured Gilderon back with a wave of his hand.

His tormentor noted the tightening of the skin around the Senserii's eyes.

Such conflict in such a faithful servant. Drech was faithful too, wasn't he?

Takaar spread his hands. 'I apologise for our interruption. We are not Julatsan though we have come from the college. Our TaiGethen forged us a path through the siege and no doubt by now have broken it completely, allowing Julatsa forces to join those of Xetesk and the other colleges in the fight to defeat the Wytch Lords.'

The mage swore and clicked his fingers. Another, clearly junior, mage ran up.

'Get word to Bynaar. Julatsan forces will be heading south along the Blackthornes towards Understone Pass. And tell him we need greater strength here as a matter of extreme urgency.' He turned to Takaar. 'Just when exactly do you think the siege would have been broken?'

'Well now, let me see,' said Takaar, scratching his head and ignoring the hissed warning from Gilderon. 'We travelled here in five days, running up to fifty miles a day. Auum would be leading more raids on the enemy the day after we left so let's say it's three days since the siege was broken. You probably had a few spies in place.'

The pair of mages in front of Takaar stared at him with poorly disguised dislike.

'I thought we had,' one of them muttered.

'Enough, Koryl.' He turned a cynical sneer on Takaar. 'You expect us to believe you ran fifty miles a day? Or indeed anything you have told me so far?'

Takaar shrugged. He was starting to feel uncomfortable and the itch was growing in his forearms again. The mage's words were making echoing sounds in his head and he could hear them all laughing. He wasn't sure what to say in response.

'Yes,' he said. 'Why not?'

'It doesn't matter, not really. What matters is that you are allied with Julatsa.'

'We are all allies here,' said Takaar.

Not even you can still believe that.

'In the search for Dawnthief there can be no alliances. But I thank you for your information. You really should have listened to your masked friend.'

'You're dismissing us?' Takaar was getting confused. 'I'm Takaar. We have to work together.'

The mage shook his head and began to back away with Koryl. 'I know who you are. No, we don't have to work together and no, I am not dismissing you. I'm killing you. Protectors, now!'

Chapter 18

There are no more Senserii because the scriptures allow for no more. Only a fool challenges the word of Yniss.

Lysael, High Priest of Yniss

Gilderon moved and the Senserii moved with him. Each knew his place in the circle enclosing Takaar. The mages melted back, some of them preparing castings. The Protectors ran forward, each one hefting his weapons easily. They outnumbered the Senserii two to one.

Gilderon twirled his staff, adding to the whistling sound of his brothers' staffs, the blades at either end glittering in the firelight.

'Takaar, please, a barrier.'

'Why would they attack us? We came to warn them!'

'Takaar,' insisted Gilderon. 'Focus.'

The Protectors surged in, each man working seamlessly with those to either side.

'Defend and assess!' called Gilderon.

An axe swept in head high. Gilderon's ikari deflected the heavy blow, his body adapting to the impact. A sword thrust to the stomach followed it. Gilderon moved his staff fast in front of him, knocking it past his left flank. The Protector did not stumble. A third blow came from another Protector. Gilderon ducked, then jumped high to avoid the follow-up.

There was no pause. Gilderon found himself assailed by three. His ikari blocked, turned and caught blows. No time to look at any but his flanking brothers, who were coping though the onslaught was heavy and relentless. These men would not tire quickly.

'Takaar!' he shouted, snapping his staff left across his face and then right across his torso, clearing two blows. 'A barrier.'

'They can't cast,' said Takaar vaguely. 'They have nothing left. We need to talk, not fight. I'll speak to them.'

'Stand fast,' said Gilderon. He caught a massive double overhead strike on his staff, holding it at arm's length in front of his face. 'Cast. If you want to live, cast.'

'Of course I want to live. I have never contemplated death.'

Gilderon ignored him. 'Senserii, engage to kill. Put them down.'

Gilderon ducked a swinging axe, levelled his staff and jabbed it forward, catching a protector in the midriff. He moved a pace back to free the blade. Blows came in from left and right. Gilderon rolled, his staff horizontal across his body. The blows struck the ground behind him.

The injured Protector loomed above him. Gilderon switched his staff to the vertical, jabbed a blade into the ground and swung round it, thumping his feet hard into the Protector's chest. The man fell back. Gilderon followed him, plucking his staff clear of the ground and whipping the bloodied blade into the Protector's right eye slit.

The Protector collapsed back, making no sound. Gilderon dragged the blade clear, spun on his heels and fended away blows to both flanks. He struck out left, feeling the blade skewer muscle and hearing a grunt from his target. He struck right, low and fast, the blade slicing into the thigh of another.

In the moment's pause he stepped back, reforming the circle. He spun again, his staff across his chest. Two Protectors came at him. One delivered a blow wide left without looking, deflecting another Senserii staff as it arrowed towards its target. The Protector's other weapon came at him incredibly quickly. Gilderon fenced it away, feeling a whip of air pass his ear. He circled his staff above his head and brought it down two-handed towards the same Protector's skull. The axe from the other knocked his blow aside.

They were good, very good.

'How many down!' he called. 'I'm listening.'

'Four enemies,' came the reply between the clash and spark of weapons, the thud of blade on mud and the whispering of feet over the ground. 'Silasin is wounded.'

'Keep strong, Yniss is our guide,' said Gilderon.

Three Protectors bore down on him. Their blows came in a flurry, well directed and with great power. Gilderon weaved his ikari in front of him. An axe slid away left, two swords cracked into the centre of his staff, driving him briefly to his haunches. He snapped the staff to the vertical to fend off another axe and bent his back almost to the horizontal to evade a third axe. He spun left and the last sword bit into the ground.

'There are too many of them,' muttered Gilderon.

He straightened to field the next assault. Next to him Silasin was struggling. He had a deep cut on one leg which was pumping out blood and one eye had been closed by a heavy punch from a sword pommel.

'It's like fighting a six-armed man!' called Helodian behind him.

And it was. Protectors moved forward, driving the Senserii back. Gilderon jabbed, his thrust batted away by the flat of an axe.

'Hold firm,' shouted Gilderon. 'They will tire, we will not. Takaar, you have to do something!'

But Gilderon could see they weren't going to tire quickly enough. Beyond them mages were ready to cast. Unless something changed, they wouldn't be needed.

Takaar was sitting on the ground. He rubbed his chin and wiped at an eye.

'This noise is intolerable,' he said, wondering why there was such a clashing and shouting all around him. He looked up and saw the Senserii surrounding him. 'I can hardly hear myself think.'

Normally, that would be a good thing.

'I don't understand what you mean.'

I mean that you not thinking is normally the best state, but at the moment it might prove disastrous.

There was a change in the tone of his tormentor's voice. Less of the strident proclamations or whispered words of warning about all the betrayals around him and almost, well . . .

'Are you scared?' asked Takaar, smiling to himself. 'You are, aren't you?'

When presented with the real possibility of death, I find that I wish to cling on to life for the moment.

'Are you going to die?'

All that you dreamed of when you heard about Dawnthief is about to disappear. Your Senserii are not able to hold these Protectors for long. You aren't looking, I am. If you want to find the spell and do what must be done then you need to help them. Gilderon has been calling on you.

'He does not believe in me.'

But he still wants to protect you. Now do something.

Now that he came to think about it, he did recall Gilderon saying a few things, but in all the noise he hadn't really heard them. And there was a strange tenor to the calls of the Senserii as they worked their ikari. They were getting closer to Takaar and he didn't really want anyone near him at the moment.

Well then . . .

'Hush. Let me think.'

Takaar looked up into the dark sky, into which smoke and glowing embers spiralled. There was a flood of energy all around them too and he luxuriated in it for a moment. It was the human magical aura, and when it was focused, as now, it was a truly glorious sight.

Dark blue shapes revolved and modulated in the hands or over the heads of the Xeteskian mages. Bold spheres, rotating helixes, spiked geometric shapes . . . all beautiful in their way but shot through with vicious power. But it was the human warriors who really caught his eye. They were sheathed in mana, tendrils of the energy binding one to another. A thick cord of it sprang from the back of each man's neck too, joined in the sky above them and twisted into a great pulsing rope that trailed away out of sight to the west.

'Amazing,' said Takaar. 'An element of such glorious strength and versatility.'

It was quite at odds with the core energies of the Il-Aryn but it was an element nonetheless. On Calaius it had always seemed a random, fleeting force. Here, moulded by humans, it was a thing of enormous power. Takaar smiled; so much the better because elements could be isolated and therefore they could also be excluded.

'What an opportunity for experimentation,' said Takaar.

Dimly, he heard a cry of pain and another shout from Gilderon. The clashing of weapons closed on him further and he felt uncomfortable. He needed them all to go away. He should probably help make that happen.

Do it.

Takaar did it.

Gilderon was breathing hard. His balance was still forward but he was being driven back by the relentless heavy strikes from the Protectors. They were an extraordinary force. One on one, elves would prevail, but here, with their superior numbers, they were more or less unstoppable.

'Keep yourselves tight,' called Gilderon. 'Silasin, speak. Are you secure?'

Sword strokes battered against his staff. Gilderon blocked and

turned them away as well as he could. The weight of each blow
sapped his strength and he could no longer get close enough to strike
back. Not without leaving Silasin exposed. He knew other Protectors
had been downed, and while no other Senserii was wounded yet,
they were losing this fight. Mistakes would happen as fatigue set in.

'My leg is heavy, 'said Silasin. 'I'm weakening.'

'Teralion, defend Silasin's left. I have his right,' said Gilderon.
'Takaar, please, help us.'

The Protectors stepped up as one man, crowding the space. A rain
of blows fell. Gilderon swayed left, deflecting an axe down into the
mud as swords came at Silasin. Gilderon punched one aside with the
tip of his staff before catching an axe full on the shaft.

Teralion swept his staff over Silasin's head, just catching the top
of a sword, which glanced off a bladed tip. Meanwhile Silasin was
driven to his knees by a trio of blows aimed at his head. Teralion
moved his staff in front of him to block axe and sword sweeps and
Silasin tried to stand and force himself some space.

Gilderon moved half a pace towards him, seeing his injured leg
trembling and ready to give. As one, the Protectors pressed their
advantage. Both Gilderon and Teralion were forced to defend themselves, and while they could not aid Silasin two Protectors attacked
him in concert, one slicing down and forcing him to block high, the
other swinging an axe at his midriff. Silasin's bad leg conspired
against him. He couldn't rock back in time and the axe sliced cleanly
through his gut, spilling his entrails across the ground. Silasin
screamed and fell.

'Close up!' ordered Gilderon. *'Takaar!'*

The suddenness with which the situation transformed took Gilderon's breath away. He felt a change in the air, a cessation of
movement and a fall in temperature, or that was how it seemed to
him. There was a brief silence before the mages beyond the ring of
Protectors shouted. He couldn't understand the language but their
emotions transcended words, and they were panic and alarm.

In front of him the Protectors had stopped. Confusion was evident
in the stances they took. One or two seemed unbalanced, taking
paces back or to the side. Weapons dropped, and the eyes that stared
at him through narrow slits held loss. This chance could be gone in a
heartbeat.

'Attack!' called Gilderon.

He surged forward, slashing the end of his ikari across the throat of the Protector in front of him. The man's weapons dropped from his hands and he clutched at his neck, sagging to the ground, his shouts drowned in his blood. The Senserii had followed his lead and thirteen more Protectors were dead. The rest broke from their confusion, raised their weapons and moved back to ready.

But they were just men alone now. Whatever Takaar had taken from them made them vulnerable and they knew it. Gilderon moved left, smashed his staff into a Protector's chin and sliced a blade into his chest, cutting through his leather armour and deep into flesh and muscle.

The Protector grunted. His weapons moved fast in his defence. Gilderon ducked a flailing axe blade and swayed inside the follow-up sword thrust. The Protector pulled back. Gilderon feinted to smack the body of his staff into the enemy's chin again but instead swung his weapon about and jabbed a blade up under his chin to skewer his tongue to the roof of his mouth.

No longer did Gilderon have to worry about the attacks of men seemingly able to strike without looking. Takaar's casting had been devastating, and after their initial attack the Senserii now fought one on one. Confidence energised them. Their enemies retained all of their power and speed but not their ungodly reaction time.

Gilderon switched his grip and reversed a blade into the cheek of a Protector, ripping his mask. The man fell back, the rawness of his face revealed, and the Senserii's curiosity overcame him. He moved up fast, cracking his staff into the back of the Protector's legs, dropping him to his knees.

Gilderon moved in close, hands at the top of his staff and sliced through the straps securing the mask. It fell to the ground. The Protector turned a momentary hate-filled glare on him, showing him the sores and weals on his face, before his eyes bulged in terror and he roared his fear, snatched up the mask and ran. The fight was won.

The mages and researchers had gathered in three loose groups, the former trying desperately to cast. The fleeing Protector, yelling something unintelligible at the sky, burst through one group, scattering men in all directions, and carried on running until, quite suddenly, he fell to the ground screaming, his hands clutching at his chest until his body slowly ceased to thrash.

Undefended, transfixed by the scene and unable to believe what they had witnessed, the mages and researchers stood mute. Some were clearly contemplating running, but, at a nod from Gilderon, the

Senserii surrounded them. It was a loose corral, fourteen elves hemming in forty humans, but the blood and bodies of the Protectors were ample deterrent against any escape attempt.

'Takaar,' said Gilderon, trotting over to where the mad master sat cross-legged, deep in his casting. 'We have them.'

Chapter 19

There is no doubt that the Protectors are a calling of the most potent warriors, rightly feared by their enemies. But the nature of their enthralment and the bargains struck to give them their inhuman skills tell you all you need to know about the moral position of Xetesk.

Sipharec, High Mage of Julatsa

Takaar raised his head. The beauty of the dome he'd created rested in its absence of chaos. Even the air was still as if the breeze could not penetrate, or more likely the mana was a catalyst for the other elements.

Fascinating.

Gilderon's interruption was unwelcome.

Quite the opposite. It means that you have been saved and, happily, so have I.

'What would you have me do with them?' asked Gilderon.

Takaar curled his lip and bit back a comment.

That was an uncharitable thought, even for you.

'But I must release the casting. I can't move it with me; it's simply too complex.'

'Any who attempt to cast will be killed. We'll stand close,' said Gilderon.

A sound solution.

'Demonstrate your intent and ability to them. Pick anyone. None of them is pure, none deserves life.'

'Your wish,' said Gilderon. Takaar saw him making hand gestures to one of the others. 'We're ready.'

Takaar stood. He felt oddly powerful, a little giddy with it. He stared at the humans, who were being herded into a single tighter group. He saw one of the Senserii, Teralion, standing two paces to the left of a powerfully built mage whose face radiated fury and humiliation.

'I am about to release the casting that has so easily defeated you. Perhaps you shouldn't have scoffed at my offers of help.' Takaar found his heart beating very hard and his breathing became shallow and gasping. 'We should have been allies and now we are enemies. Some of you will think to cast. Gilderon will demonstrate why that is unwise.'

Your grip is slipping. Can you hold on any longer? The tension is unbearable.

Gilderon nodded once. Teralion's staff jabbed up into his target's skull at the occipital bone. The mage collapsed, his spasmodic twitching mercifully brief. A chorus of muttered swearing ran around the corralled humans.

'The Senserii are among the finest fighters the elves possess. I leave your casting decisions to you.'

Takaar dismissed the spell. Every human eye was on the body of the unfortunate mage. Takaar walked towards them as steadily as he could though he was feeling a pain in his head and a stabbing behind his eyes that distracted him.

Going . . . going . . .

'Be quiet!' hissed Takaar.

Takaar searched the faces, seeing fear, anger and belligerence in equal measure. He pointed at the mage who had so belittled him without even knowing him.

'I will talk to you. Leave the group,' he said in elvish, knowing the mage understood him. 'Gilderon, watch the rest.'

The mage, despite protests from his friends, walked through the circle of Senserii.

'You have no idea of the mistake you have just made, do you?' he said in Balaian loud enough for his people to hear.

'What's your name?' asked Takaar.

'Pryfors. A name that resonates in Xetesk and beyond. I am one of this country's premier research masters.'

Takaar shrugged. 'You haven't found anything here though, have you?'

Good question.

'Thank you.'

Credit where it is due.

'Please, I am trying to talk to Pryfors.'

I'll do my best to remain silent but you know how tricky that can be.

Takaar chuckled and felt the tension ease in his head and chest. Pryfors was staring at him.

'Who are you talking to?'

'No one,' said Takaar.

I beg your pardon?

'Well, you know what I mean.'

No, I don't.

'No, I don't,' said Pryfors.

Takaar blinked. 'Why am I talking to you? Do you know anything?'

Pryfors glanced round at his colleagues, and when he turned back there was a new lightness in his expression.

'Look, it's been a long day and an even longer night. People have died, and none of us wants more killing, right?'

'In a war people have to die,' said Takaar, unsure where Pryfors was going.

The mage breathed in deeply and deliberately.

'They do, but, as you said, we need not be enemies. We have to defeat the Wytch Lords because they threaten both man and elf.'

'I know this already,' said Takaar, he clutched for the giddy power he had experienced so recently but found tiredness and confusion instead. 'They occupied my country, you know. The memories are so fresh.'

Pryfors stared at him. 'That was seven *hundred* years ago.'

'I am immortal,' said Takaar, then he smiled. 'But not invulnerable.'

Brilliant.

'What do you want to know?' asked Pryfors. 'My people are scared, they are tired and they have seen one of their friends murdered in front of them.'

'It was you who chose this fight,' spat Takaar.

Pryfors recoiled and put up his hands. 'And it was a mistake. I acknowledge that.'

'People never listen to me, not to what I really say. They make assumptions and they judge me. Always wrongly. Only Garan understood me.'

They were still standing only a few paces from the prisoners and their Senserii guard. Takaar thought to move away but Gilderon's slight gesture bade him stay put.

He just wants to hear what the mage says.

'He has earned that right,' said Takaar.

'Who, Garan?'

'No, Gilderon. Garan died hundreds of years ago, didn't he?'

'I have no idea,' said Pryfors. He shifted on his feet and bit his lip. 'Just ask your questions.'

Takaar regarded Pryfors and frowned. He had so many questions but could not recall a single one. No, wait. Something Kerela had alluded to . . .

'Where are the researchers from the other colleges?'

Pryfors smiled indulgently, or perhaps it was in relief.

'Only Xetesk possesses the ability to uncover the whereabouts of Dawnthief. Representatives of other colleges were here of course but all have . . . withdrawn.'

Takaar raised his eyebrows. 'How odd. I spoke at length to the council in Julatsa and they were sure they had a team here. Elves and men alike. Talented mages.'

Pryfors' smile faltered slightly. 'There has been a recent change in circumstances.'

Takaar shook his head, trying to release the pressure suddenly present in his skull. His tormentor's voice was drowned out by a clamour in his mind. He tried to focus on Pryfors' face if only to dull the noise inside him.

'A change,' he managed.

Pryfors nodded. 'Let me explain. Dawnthief is a spell that requires the most extreme care. We are all aware of its devastating potential and this ruin is ample example of the lengths our enemies will go to gain it for themselves. Xetesk is the only college strong enough to properly protect the spell, research it and ensure it remains inert.'

'The Wesmen did not do this,' muttered Takaar.

'I beg your pardon?'

Takaar wondered again why he was talking to this man. He didn't seem to know terribly much.

'Septern guarded his lands. The Wesmen triggered his castings. Follow the latent energy trails. It should be obvious to one so talented.'

Pryfors stiffened. 'Your eyes are keen.'

'And my ears are sharp.' Takaar tripped Pryfors and followed him down, putting a knife to his throat. 'I am uncomfortable with liars. I don't like being uncomfortable.'

Pryfors did not hide his fear. Takaar had a hand on his neck and a knee on his stomach. He tried to push Takaar away but quietened quickly, surprised by the elf's strength. The Senserii levelled their ikari at the prisoners to quell their disquiet.

'Please. Whatever you want,' gasped Pryfors. 'What do you want?'

That really is a good question.

'Just be quiet.'

'All right, whatever you want.'

'Not you!' spat Takaar. 'Why don't you know when I'm not talking to you?'

Takaar sighed extravagantly, his sense of frustration intense, eclipsing his pain and his fatigue.

'Please,' said Pryfors again.

'I hate to be wrong, it makes me very angry, but I'm wondering something. Auum said you wanted Dawnthief for yourselves to gain dominance. He said you didn't send forces to Julatsa because you would be happy if Julatsa fell to the Wytch Lords and Wesmen. I disagreed with him. You will tell me the truth.'

'All right, all right. We have no love for Julatsa but we also have no hatred of elves. We know we have to live together.'

Takaar pushed the knife into Pryfors' skin. Blood leaked and Pryfors whimpered.

'One more chance. I have made errors more costly in terms of lives than you could possibly match. I am forgiving. I am Takaar.'

Pryfors' words came out in a rush. 'The Julatsan team here was too close to an answer. We couldn't let them discover the spell. They would not share their information and they would not back away. We had our orders and the Protectors can be commanded from great distance. I'm sorry their team had to be killed but they brought it on themselves. And then the Wesmen laid their siege. Julatsa is not the all-embracing peaceful college it claims to be; the Julatsans are dangerous and aggressive. They would challenge us after the Wytch Lords are defeated. So yes, we decided not to come to Julatsa's aid . . . they would have done the same.'

Takaar stood up. Pryfors lay where he was for a moment before getting slowly to his feet. Takaar shoved him back towards the rest of them.

'I understand your anger at the death of the elves in the Julatsan team,' said Pryfors. 'We can make recompense to your nation and their families. We can—'

'Have you understood nothing?' shouted Takaar. His head was hot, his fingers were tingling and his grip on his knife was painful. 'I was wrong and Auum was right. How could you let that happen?'

'All I did was tell you the truth.'

'And I do not like it,' said Takaar.

Someone was hiding something from you. Maybe even Gilderon. He must have known.

Takaar shot a glance at Gilderon, whose expression was hidden behind his filthy cloth mask.

'We are not your enemies. We are the power in this country. Side with us.'

Pryfors was back inside the ring of Senserii. His people were frightened. Takaar strode up to him, the reality of the situation suddenly obvious like a rush of Gyal's tears on dry ground.

'There is only one power in this country, and it is the magic of the Il-Aryn. You'll see. I can sense so much that you cannot. No matter how you search you'll never find the spell because it isn't here. Not physically. I can find it though. I've travelled the dimensions before and I will research and understand all that Septern wrote. I will be the one to hold the power, I shall return myself to my rightful position and the elves shall be the masters. Then it won't matter that Auum was right because we won't need Auum, will we? He and his precious TaiGethen can be consigned to history. I was born for this moment. Yniss blessed me with the gift of the Il-Aryn so I possessed the skills to unlock the great secrets.

'This is my destiny.'

That is your best yet. Over eight hundred years we've been together and you have exceeded even my expectations.

They were all staring at Pryfors and he was relating to them what Takaar had just said. Some of them managed to laugh but mostly they switched their stares to Takaar. The Senserii had eyes only for their prisoners but there was a tension in their stances which was at odds with their nature.

'You're raving,' said Pryfors.

'I am fulfilling my purpose.'

'You don't understand. You are not a lore scholar. You can never unlock Dawnthief. You could never cast it.'

Takaar smiled. 'I am immortal. I can learn.'

'Let me help you,' said Pryfors, brightening.

'I do my best work alone,' said Takaar.

What, testing poisons out on yourself that didn't ever quite kill you?

Takaar ignored the voice. A sense of calm was descending on him. The path was laid. Here, in this place, he would do his greatest work, even greater than creating the harmony. It would define man and elf anew, place them in their rightful positions.

There was just one minor unpleasantness to deal with. Takaar stood as if deep in thought while he constructed the dome once more and put it back in place. Consternation fled through the prisoners, those that felt the touch of magic anyway.

'Gilderon, flethar kon aryn bleen.' *Make the earth red.*

Takaar turned his back. Pryfors' desperate cries were the first to be silenced.

When Gilderon sought out Takaar later, he was sifting through the ruins of the Manse, drawing lines on the ground and scratching marks on a piece of tree bark. Gilderon and the Senserii had moved the bodies downwind, laid out for reclamation by whatever beasts roamed Balaia. The Protectors had been accorded particular respect, their weapons cleaned and laid with them.

They had prayed then, long and fervently, seeking a means of escape from their confusion, or rather seeking confirmation that their decision was blessed by Yniss and the pantheon of elven gods. They had cleaned their ikari and their masks, using the Xeteskians' ample supply of water. They had freed the humans' horses to roam wherever they willed and set up a rolling guard about the perimeter, allowing six at a time to sleep.

'The Protector who ran looked as if he died of fright,' said Gilderon.

Takaar's shrug was the merest acknowledgement of his words.

'All are laid out for reclamation.'

'You should have left them where they were,' said Takaar.

'They were courageous warriors who deserved respect. This fight was not of their choosing and we Senserii know more about that than anyone.'

Takaar paused in his drawings, which looked to Gilderon like the map of energy lines Takaar had carved in the temple at Aryndeneth. He turned his head to consider Gilderon.

'Perhaps you are more insightful than you let on,' said Takaar.

'There was something else within the rope of mana that secured them to whatever place it was rooted. Something living.'

'Oh, I see.'

'Of course you don't,' said Takaar, and his smile held no kindness. 'Is there more you wish to tell me?'

'We have brought you as far as we can,' said Gilderon, and a weight lifted from his shoulders, letting him breathe in the fresh air as if for the first time. 'We will leave at dawn. We will find the Wesmen reading party. They won't bother you, but you know more will be coming from Xetesk.'

'So you choose to betray me too,' said Takaar, his eyes dead in his skull and his hands itching at his forearms. 'Just like Auum. Just like Drech.'

Gilderon tensed. 'I am faster than Drech.'

'I will not kill you, Gilderon, even though you would not be fast enough.'

'We must all choose our paths, Takaar. This search for the spell is the wrong one. Auum and our brother and sister elves are walking into a trap – heading, at your instigation, to join Xeteskian forces who want them dead. We have to warn them. We have to fight with them.'

Takaar sighed. 'I suppose it was inevitable that you wouldn't understand. Why would you? Only I can see the truth. You'll be too late, you know.'

Gilderon inclined his head. 'We have to try.'

Takaar turned back to his drawing and marks. He was muttering, talking to his other self.

'Will you find it?' asked Gilderon, curious in spite of himself.

Takaar said nothing, didn't even appear to have heard the question.

'Takaar?'

Chapter 20

*When does an invested wall become more magic than stone? Is
there a point at which the density of magic within stone becomes
great enough to weaken it? I feel we should find out.*

Hethyne, Research Mage, Julatsa

While Julatsa had breathing space in which to resupply, rebuild and
refocus after the siege was broken, the threat of another major attack
on the college was ever present. They planned to set up a series of
mage-led watches along the northern coast and of course at Triverne
Inlet to provide early warning. But it was the knock-on effect of the
siege that was most keenly damaging to Auum's expectations. The
Julatsan city council refused to allow any of its militia to leave in
support of the other three colleges in retaliation for the support
withheld from Julatsa in its darkest hour, while the college decided
to keep most of its mages at home, citing an unacceptable risk to its
heart stone should the Wesmen return.

When the numbers were totalled the expeditionary force was
pitiful, made worthy of the name only by Auum's TaiGethen and
the Il-Aryn, now under the reluctant command of a sour-faced
Ynissul teacher named Rith. She had spent a day denouncing her
own leadership skills when her name was put forward, but the fact
remained that she was the most experienced and most respected
practitioner still alive.

Harild had lent the force some cavalry to act as guides and escorts
for the journey, but they were under orders to return before any fight.
And very few of the elven mages Takaar had been so determined to
come and rescue had chosen to travel, which left the TaiGethen's
Arch questioning his elves' role here once again. Stein had demanded
to go with them, which had been the single blessing, but they left the
city with fifty cavalry, just eighty-two TaiGethen, one hundred and

four Il-Aryn, and a mere seventy-eight Julatsan-trained elves of the four hundred or so Auum had been persuaded to rescue.

Supply wagons rattled along at the rear of the column where the Il-Aryn had also chosen to walk or jog. If there was one thing Auum could thank Takaar for it was his insistence that his adepts were fit. A hangover from his TaiGethen days in Auum's opinion, though Rith had assured him in her dry humourless tones that it had everything to do with casting stamina and nothing to do with anything else.

Not one of the Julatsan mage council had seen them off, all distracted by some turn of events elsewhere. It was a fact not lost on Auum and he quizzed Stein about it, jogging beside his horse as they travelled across the easy ground west towards the Blackthorne Mountains.

'They lost contact with their team at the Septern Manse a few days ago. Apparently Lystern have the same problem. We don't know about the other two colleges.'

'And they're surprised, are they?' said Auum. 'Remind me why we're going to join Xetesk again, would you? Sounds like they're more likely to kill us than welcome us.'

'You're not seriously suggesting that our researchers have been murdered, are you?'

'I think they have to consider it. And what are they planning to do about it? Send more to die, or make more pointless entreaties to Xetesk – out of whom they will get no information whatever?'

Stein shook his head, chuckling. 'How long have you been here? Ten days or so, is it? And you seem to know more about the workings of Xetesk than most will absorb in a lifetime. I think your suggestions of murder and the abandonment of Julatsa are off target, but the general attitude of our Xeteskian friends? You're spot on.'

Auum shrugged. 'They are the human face of the Wytch Lords. I had a hundred and fifty years to understand exactly how their minds worked. Ystormun might have been forced out when the sundering came, but he and his band of bastards left behind plenty of malevolence, and it all rests in Xetesk, doesn't it?'

'They are not as black as you paint them,' said Stein.

Auum increased his pace and ran to the head of the column, which snaked its way towards the chill of the Blackthorne Mountains dominating the horizon. The bleak grey peaks, capped with what Stein said was snow and ice, were imposing, pressing down on the tiny elves and humans travelling into their shadow. Calaius had mountains, but these were of a different scale altogether.

Their aim was to track along the foothills all the way down to Understone Pass, where they would join the fight. Auum was puzzled that the power of human magic had not already forced the Wesmen back, but he needed to see the battle for himself if he was to employ his people to their best advantage.

Stein was adamant that they wouldn't encounter Wesmen along their route, and so far there were no signs of any enemy activity. Farms and hamlets were undamaged; the land was pristine, and when the question was asked, livestock was all accounted for.

It took Auum a little while to work out why this worried him. Had he been commanding Wesmen forces he would have sent significant numbers this way, hidden from all the college cities, to outflank the pass defenders. Something just wasn't right and he wasn't about to blame a lack of tactical acumen on the part of the Wytch Lords. Auum had learned through bitter experience never to underestimate Ystormun.

Ulysan was heading the column with Duele, who had been co-opted back into Auum's cell with the fall of poor Ollem on the walls of Julatsa. They'd lost too many up there and on the field afterwards: twelve in all from across the spectrum of experience and representing four full cells. It left them light.

TaiGethen ran the flanks and rear and also provided scouts ahead and on the points. Ulysan was chatting to Duele as the two ran, Ulysan in his easy loping stride, Duele with his soft feet which seemed almost to float a hair above the ground. His was an extraordinary skill in waiting and Auum prayed that he lived to see it realised.

'Come to see the real excitement, have you?' said Ulysan when Auum fell in alongside him.

'I can't take their denials any longer,' said Auum. 'Even Stein is blinkered when it comes to Xetesk.'

'Then we must look after ourselves,' said Duele.

'I'll speak when we stop for the night,' said Auum. 'Some among us are following blindly, and I don't like that.'

'I hear you,' said Ulysan.

'So, where are we?' asked Auum, gazing out at the landscape ahead.

'Well, there are the mountains,' said Ulysan, pointing. 'In case you hadn't spotted them.'

'I was really down until I came to speak to you and now I've improved to suicidal,' said Auum. 'If you want to run with another cell, Duele, I fully understand.'

'The thought will never enter my mind,' said Duele.

'I'm still working on his sense of humour,' said Ulysan.

'I shall pray fervently to Yniss that it doesn't turn out like yours.'

'I am hurt, my Arch,' said Ulysan, placing a hand on his chest.

'Just tell me what I'm looking at,' said Auum. 'I know you studied the maps.'

Ulysan smiled. 'No learning is ever wasted. Right, we're heading south-west at the moment and we'll encounter the River Tri where it rises at the base of Triverne Lake, probably by nightfall if we push on. Quite a beautiful spot, I'm told. We can cross at the shallows there and then hug the mountains. From here you can see the lake sparkle against the mountains when the sun hits it right – that'll give you an idea of distance.

'It's about six days to Understone from here, I'd say. The terrain is very easy. Our only problem is staying hidden if we feel the need; that's another reason to stay close to the mountains. This way keeps us as far from all the colleges as possible too. That's it really. No significant landmarks I haven't mentioned, no trees and precious few people because the land in the lee of the mountains isn't good for farming.'

'Escape routes once we're past Xetesk on the way to Understone?'

'We want to hope it doesn't come to that,' said Ulysan. 'If we're closed off from behind then we're effectively trapped.'

'Is that likely?' asked Duele.

Auum raised his eyebrows. 'It depends who you ask.'

'Right,' said Ulysan. 'Everyone else says it isn't; Auum says it is.'

Duele fell silent but Auum could see there was conflict within him.

'It's always best to speak,' said Ulysan, seeing the same thing. 'Silence only breeds resentment.'

Duele took a breath and glanced at them both.

'There is much uncertainty and fear,' he said carefully as if voicing the words was somehow heretical. 'Among the Il-Aryn certainly but also within the newer emerged TaiGethen. It's distracting. We should be united, and I feel we aren't. It is difficult to be surrounded with such differing opinions.'

Auum's first reaction was of disappointment, but a moment later he smiled.

'Uncertainty is the hallmark of this venture,' he said. 'And I am asking much of the inexperienced . . . I'll speak to everyone later.'

And he did. On the banks of Triverne Lake, with the cook fires throwing a warming glow into a chilly night and the lapping of the water on the shore a relaxing influence, Auum spoke to whoever would hear him, human or elf.

'It is terribly hard to see those you know – those you love – die beside you. I cannot promise you that it will get any easier because it doesn't. Those who fight to save Calaius must bear that burden. I ask that Yniss bless you all for being here and showing your faith in our gods and in me. I am humbled by your courage and your strength, particularly those of you who have just had your first taste of the fight. The experience of violence and death are shocking, yet here you sit, willing to do it all over again even though you worry that you are afraid.

'Don't worry. Fear is healthy; believe me, the fearless die quickly. Let your fear make you cautious and lead you to the right decisions; don't let it cripple you and make you easy prey.

'Are we on the right path? Yniss knows none of us can be sure, but we do know the Wytch Lords must be defeated. So I'm asking you to fight alongside Xetesk even though every fibre of my being screams that it is wrong. I'm doing it because there is no other choice. At Understone Pass we can strike, together, at Ystormun's twisted heart. I know you don't want human allies. Neither do I, but this is reality. We are not enough on our own.'

Auum led a prayer and invited questions. He saw Stein talking to a couple of cavalrymen.

'They were wondering why you're here at all if you mistrust us so much.'

'It's a good question,' said Auum. 'We're here because the Wytch Lords have to be defeated and we can't do it back home. So here we are to see it done. It doesn't mean we have to like it, or like humans – with some notable exceptions.'

Stein passed on Auum's response and the cavalrymen both nodded their understanding.

'Anything further?' asked Auum. 'Then let's eat and sleep. Yniss bless you all and keep you safe until dawn.'

*

Auum slept little that night, wondering if he should have kept his council. But he needed eyes. Not just TaiGethen and Il-Aryn but those of the Julatsans travelling with them. As the next day's travel got under way beneath a deep grey sky, a chill wind blew off the mountains, surprising the elves, who donned cloaks while the humans did not. He could see groups of the cavalry deep in conversation as they rode and their gesturing and pointing told its own story about the impact of his words.

Stein trotted up to him while he was running with Merrat's cell, discussing possible tactics.

'You caused quite a stir last night,' said Stein.

'Good.'

Stein blew out his cheeks. 'Yes, but I had to give one or two a history lesson to stop them riding back to Julatsa.'

'I'm not apologising for being careful,' said Auum.

'I'm not asking you to. I just thought you should know that some have their sympathies elsewhere.'

'Nor am I apologising for being careful with my choice of allies. Got friends in Xetesk, have they?'

'Yes, some of them probably do. We don't just wall ourselves in and talk in hushed tones, you know. There is more similarity than difference between all four colleges.'

'Then perhaps I shouldn't trust you either?'

Stein laughed. 'I asked for that, didn't I?'

Auum looked up at him and thought to reinforce his point, but there was nothing to distrust about this particular human. Stein smiled broadly and spoke again, pointing along the shore of Triverne Lake.

'And you said there were no trees here. Just look at that. Beautiful, isn't it?'

Auum looked and saw an area of woodland about two miles away hugging the shore for some considerable distance and stretching away a hundred yards or so towards the foothills. Nyann's cell, the duty scouts this morning, were closing on it already. He hoped they enjoyed themselves beneath the patchy canopy.

'That, human, is like a drop in the vast ocean that is the Calaian rainforest. It is a single footprint left by Yniss. I could count those trees before we arrived at the first. It would take you a lifetime to count those in our forest.'

Auum was possessed of a sudden longing to be back beneath Beeth's canopy, sheltering from Gyal's tears and glorying in Tual's creatures and all the great creation of Yniss. It was godless, this human land. It had no soul.

'One day I'd like to come and try,' said Stein. 'But before that I'll take you to our great forests when this is done . . . Grethern and Greythorne. They are places to lose yourself.'

Auum smiled. 'I look forward to it.'

'How many forests do you have?'

'Just the one,' said Auum.

'Oh,' said Stein, the smile on his face wider than ever. 'We have two.'

Auum laughed and punched him lightly on the thigh. The two of them continued on in a companionable silence until Auum moved forward at a call from Grafyrre, who was running the head of the column with his cell. Auum had to confess that Triverne Lake was a place of beauty, set against the steep climbs of the Blackthorne Mountains. The lake was a vivid pure blue lapping on gentle shores, the vegetation surrounding it was lush and verdant and the wildlife, birds in particular, was plentiful.

They were less than a mile from the woodland and Auum intended to take a break just so that he and the TaiGethen could rest under the cover of green leaves, no matter how thin they were in comparison with the rainforest.

'Do we have a problem, Graf?'

'I doubt it but your orders were to alert you should our scouts not check in, and they haven't done so since entering the woodland.'

'Got their backs to the broadest trunks already or lying on the ground gazing up at the leaves, I expect,' said Auum, doubting every word as he said it.

He looked to the south-east, knowing that Xetesk sprang from the ground down there somewhere, a stain tainted with the black of the Wytch Lords. If someone had alerted Xetesk to the movement of the elves and Julatsans, could they have had the time to conceal themselves in the woods? It was unlikely.

'Even so,' said Auum. 'We will approach with caution, halt the column beyond the range of any spell and send in another cell. Just in case.'

They moved up to around two hundred yards from the first trees. There was still no trace of Nyann but nor was there any sign of an enemy. The shadows in the forest were deep but not impenetrable, certainly not to the elven eye. Auum was getting a cold feeling crawling up his legs and into his back and belly. He shook his head, unable to believe that he was afraid of a forest.

'Nyann!' he called, then, 'Hassek, take your cell in. Silent and cautious.'

Hassek and his Tai hurried across the open ground towards the woodland. He hadn't covered half the distance when there was movement in the fringe. Auum saw Hassek slow and stop. He raised a hand. Relief flushed through Auum, turning quickly to anger at Nyann's failure to report. He saw her standing near the wide trunk of a tree and Hassek moved on.

'What's going on?' asked Stein, walking his horse up.

'Nothing much,' said Auum. 'Although . . .'

Nyann fell forward, face down in the dirt. There had been a man standing behind her, holding her upright.

Stein hunched in his saddle as if ducking something.

'Gods drowning, it feels like . . .' he said, then he swore and shouted. 'Scatter! Ambush!'

Wards exploded in the middle and rear of the column. Auum had moved the moment Stein shouted, wrapping an arm around Ulysan and bundling him forward as fast as he could. He felt himself picked up and thrown by the pressure of a ward detonating behind him. Heat washed across him, and he and Ulysan were sent tumbling across the grass.

Auum rolled and got to his feet in time to see dozens of explosive spells ripping into the column. Flames roared skywards. Horses and riders were cast into the air and supply wagons disintegrated before his eyes. Elves and men were consumed by fire, turned to ash by the extraordinary heat, and survivors scrambled away, dragging the wounded with them. Burning bodies littered the ground. Man, elf and beast screamed in agony or terror.

Auum ran back towards the carnage. Mages flew overhead, fifty at least, coming down to land about two hundred yards behind them and immediately marching towards them, preparing new castings. Auum glanced behind him. No sign of Nyann or her cell now, just a line of enemy soldiers backed by yet more mages. There were cavalry there too.

'Dear Yniss preserve us, we're trapped,' he whispered. 'How could they have possibly got here so quickly, have laid so complete a trap?'

'Doesn't matter,' said Ulysan. 'We've got to get our people away from here, up into the foothills – anywhere.'

Auum gagged as the stench of burning flesh caught in his throat. TaiGethen, Il-Aryn and human lay dead together. He ran through the mess, shouting for anyone who could hear him to get away towards the mountains. There were so many bodies, so many dead and dying.

He saw a few cavalry still mounted, and among them, mercifully, Stein. He was organising an escape of sorts, though where they could all go to evade more castings was difficult to see. The terrain to the west became very difficult within a few hundred yards. It was strewn with boulders, set with scree slopes and sharp inclines, but if they could get over the first rises, they might just have a chance.

'We've got to buy some time,' said Auum. He ran into the midst of the escapees, conscious that at any moment new spells would start to fall. 'TaiGethen, to me!'

He didn't wait to see who was with him, there was no time for that. He prayed enough had survived and ran at the mages who had flown in behind them. Ulysan was at his shoulder. Duele was there too, all three of them saved by being at the head of the column. There were others too, he could hear their footfalls.

Ahead the mages had seen them.

'Wait until they cast,' called Auum. 'Let's make ourselves targets. Watch out for ice coming head on and use the shetharyn to evade.'

Auum ran as hard as he could, closing the gap to fifty yards. The mages had stopped and orders were called across their lines. Hands were outstretched and castings surged out. Orbs of deep blue fire shot flat across the open ground, and frost turned the grass black on a wide arc racing towards them.

'Speed!' yelled Auum.

He dropped into the shetharyn. All at once the paths of the orbs became slow and their impact points obvious. The frost was propelled on a hurricane of dread cold air, washing across the ground up to a height of about eight feet. Auum whipped forward, sensing his Tai following his instincts. Grafyrre was ahead of him, Vaart too, all sprinting headlong towards the frost, knowing the orbs would strike well behind them now.

Auum increased his speed. The leading edge of the cold was a handful of paces away and he could feel the ice blowing ahead of it. He ran forward two more paces and jumped, pushing off with his left foot and flattening his body as he reached the apex of his leap. His arms were stretched out like a bird's wings and the hurricane scoured the ground below him.

Auum cleared it, bringing his legs under him and landing in a crouch, the frozen grass crunching underfoot. He sprinted on, jaqrui in hand. Fear replaced the smugness of the mage line. Some tried to form new castings but others were already backing away.

'Jaqrui!' called Auum.

Thirteen crescent blades whistled away. They struck torsos, chopped deep into arms held up in defence and bit into thighs. One, Ulysan's he thought, clipped the top of a mage's head clean off, spraying brain and gore in all directions.

Auum, his teeth bared, drew his blades and attacked. He knew anger fuelled him, and he dropped out of the shetharyn to conserve his strength. His blades hacked into the body of the first mage he reached. He paced on, placing a roundhouse kick in the side of another's head and a blade through his gut. Auum lashed a cut into the face of a third, drove a blade into the throat of a fourth and roared like a panther as he dragged it clear.

TaiGethen were flying in around him, delivering death without mercy.

'Keep one alive!' called Auum.

It was done so fast. A handful managed to cast Wings of Shade and take off again, heading back to the woodland, but more than forty were dead or dying. Auum spat on the face of one who still clung to life.

'You kill without honour and you die the same way,' he said, and drove his blade into the man's heart.

'Auum!' He turned. Ulysan had a mage by the scruff of the neck. He looked terrified. Blood trickled down his face from a cut on his forehead and his front teeth had been knocked out. His lips were burst and his nose skewed at an unnatural angle. 'Good, bring him. Tais, with me.'

Auum began to run hard back towards the ambush site, where the fighting was fierce. The remains of the cavalry were charging at a line of soldiers and archers. Enemy cavalry were gathered and wheeling to strike again too. More TaiGethen had formed a defensive perimeter in front of what looked like a painfully small number of survivors. The enemy were close enough to launch castings, but, as he watched, Auum saw orbs flash against protective shields, both the yellow of Julatsa and the brown of the Il-Aryn.

Cavalry clashed with cavalry on the open ground. Auum felt the force of it vibrating through the ground from where he was running a couple of hundred yards adrift of the survivors. He could see more and more men coming from the trees. There had to be five hundred of them with considerable magical support. This confrontation was ultimately only going to go one way.

Auum ran past the charred remains of so many good elves and up to the group of survivors, which was halfway up the first rise into the foothills. Merrat was there with Stein. More spells fell on the shields, which flared in response.

'Merrat.'

'Auum, we're in trouble. We've got injured and dying here and we can't go back around the lake. We'll be too slow and there are too many men down there. They'll pick us off.'

'What are our numbers?'

Merrat's eyes were full of tears. 'I dread to make a count. We've lost well over a hundred and fifty. More won't survive the day, if any of us do.'

Auum looked to Stein. He had a long burn down the side of his grey, frightened face and one arm was cradled in the other.

'We should have listened to you,' he said, his voice faint with his pain.

'It doesn't matter now. We have to get into the hills. I'll take the TaiGethen down to face the cavalry and buy you time. I'll seek you out later. But you have to find a place up there to hide.'

Stein nodded. 'I'll do what I can. Do you want mage support?'

'No. Take them with you. Keep our people shielded and get someone in the air looking for a path. Go.'

Ulysan came trotting up with the prisoner.

'What do you want to do with him?'

'Merrat, I think he's yours. Keep him alive if you can. Go with Stein – have your cell scout a path.'

Merrat nodded and took the shivering mage from Ulysan, staring at him with cold eyes.

There was a heavy detonation from the direction of the woodland. Auum spun about. The Julatsan cavalry was broken: he saw ten horses on the ground, only another eight or so still standing and half of those galloping away from the spell that had crashed into them. The enemy cavalry wheeled and came again, but this time straight at the main group of survivors.

'Tais to me!' shouted Auum. 'Merrat, Stein, go!'

Julatsan spells soared out over the heads of the TaiGethen, striking the enemy cavalry. Mages and soldiers were moving out of the woodland and spells fizzed across shields. Auum swore and ran hard down the slope, TaiGethen to either side of him. He took a quick glance, counting thirty or so. He prayed that was not all he had left.

The horsemen came on, looking to skirt the attacking TaiGethen. Simultaneously, enemy mages were preparing new castings and continuing their advance behind a line of swordsmen.

'Speed!' called Auum. 'Get among the horsemen.'

Auum switched into the shetharyn and powered towards the group of forty or so cavalry, which was on a curving gallop towards the flank of the group gathering itself to head into the foothills of the Blackthorne Mountains. Where a running man might look to Auum as if he was wading through mud, a horse still had some pace. Even so, the cavalry would not reach the survivors.

Auum felt a thrill across his body as he turned into a tight curving run. He could hear the steady fall of horses' hooves on the ground and feel them through the soles of his feet each time they kissed the earth. He was aware of men and mages behind him, loosing arrows and spells, but none would touch him or his TaiGethen.

With Ulysan vying for the lead until Duele scorched past them both, Auum closed on the cavalry fast. Grafyrre's and Faleen's cells were both in close attendance.

'Spread through them,' called Auum. 'Let's make this quick.'

Auum surged up, passing Duele, who laughed and drew a blade. One of the riders looked round to see the thirty elves gaining on them with every stride. His mouth dropped open. He yelled something incomprehensible and slammed his spurs into his horse's flanks.

He was too late, far too late. Auum ran between two horses, his blades in his hands, and stabbed up into the waist of each rider. One fell outwards, the other in. Auum didn't wait to see if they were dead, either the fall or other TaiGethen would finish them. The riderless horses turned aside, already slowing but still following their kin. Auum moved on.

Next to him Duele vaulted onto the back of a horse, grabbed its rider by the head and cut his throat, casting the body down and to the right. Then he stood in the saddle and launched himself full length at another. Auum watched him take the man clean out of his saddle.

Auum's next targets had swords drawn and ready, their attention on him, not ahead. Both leaned out of their saddles, waiting for him to attack, and Auum steadied his pace. Ulysan came to the side of one and sliced through the rider's girth strap, barely nicking the horse's flank. The man plunged to the ground, his sword snapping in the earth and his head staved in by the rear hoof of his comrade's mount.

Auum switched to the other side of the second horse, seeing Ulysan duck left after another target. The rider saw him and tried to bring his blade across to strike. It was a half-hearted blow which Auum blocked with his left-hand blade, then he dragged the man off his horse, hurdling the body as it crashed to the ground.

The front rank of cavalry, ten strong, was further ahead. Beyond them Auum could see the Il-Aryn lined up, some of them anyway, their hands linked and their heads bowed. The horsemen closed on them quickly; the TaiGethen would only just reach them in time. The captain raised his sword, urging his men on for the final gallop. All had blades cocked overhead in an identical position, ready to sweep down as they broke across the Il-Aryn.

Some fifteen strides before they would be hit, the Il-Aryn raised their heads as one. The air quality changed, became heavy and thick, or so it felt. Auum dropped out of the shetharyn, seeing many of his TaiGethen do the same. There was a gleam in the air, like a line of horizontal light. It flashed towards the cavalry, sweeping over the horses' heads and straight through their riders.

Auum blinked, making sure he had seen it right. Every man had dropped from his saddle, leaving the horses to slow naturally. There was a mist of blood in the air. Several severed arms thudded to the ground, thumping dully into the mud and grass to land among the sliced parts of skulls and whole heads that had pattered down.

Auum shook his head and turned back to the woodland and the advancing foot soldiers.

'Tais to me,' he called.

The TaiGethen gathered around him. Ahead of them the enemy had halted, perhaps not understanding what they had seen but knowing for certain that they had just witnessed forty cavalry on galloping horses slaughtered by elven warriors and magic.

'Spread out and advance,' said Auum.

In front of them were more than three hundred men and mages, and there were more in the shadows. Auum could see some of them looking past his warriors to the rise. Auum glanced behind him and saw the Il-Aryn moving up, flanked by more TaiGethen. There were Julatsan mages shadowing them from the air.

Outnumbered by ten to one and more, the TaiGethen had no realistic chance, but the humans had lost the stomach for the fight, for now at least. They had lost their cavalry cover and, worse, they could see Julatsan riders rounding up their horses, no doubt to use against them.

On a word from their commander, they melted back into the forest.

'That'll do,' said Auum. 'Let's go.'

Chapter 21

In time, and sooner than you think, all elven adepts will train in Julatsa because the skill of the Il-Aryn relies in too great a measure on an elf who, in my opinion, will not be capable of working much longer.

Kerela, Julatsan Mage Council

Kerela was uncomfortable under Communion with anyone from Xetesk, but Bynaar was a particularly difficult contact. She had agreed to take the communication only because Sipharec was unwell and confined to his bed.

'You have done well,' said Bynaar, pausing very slightly before his last word. 'You harboured hidden strengths, I understand.'

Something about his mind, or the way he delivered his thoughts, made her squirm where she sat in a deep chair in her chambers.

'It pays to build relationships. The elves of Calaius were always likely to help us when they heard Balaia was in trouble.'

'I had no idea they were so altruistic,' said Bynaar.

'They understand the threat the Wytch Lords pose to us all,' said Kerela.

'Yes . . .' Bynaar paused. 'Your native elven magic . . . It is an unusual style. I would be fascinated to read the lore one day, or have one of your practitioners explain some of the finer points to me.'

'I can imagine they'll be falling all over themselves to be the chosen one,' said Kerela.

'I should imagine,' said Bynaar, her sarcasm going straight over his head.

Kerela scratched at an itch on her abdomen; it was another symptom of Communion.

'You were about to brief me on the progress of the war,' said Kerela.

There was another pause.

'Understone Pass is holding firm even though the Wytch Lords bring more of their power to bear every day. We have reports of Wesman parties all across Balaia, mostly scouting, but they do damage by their very presence, and none of us has the spare capacity to send out hunters, do we?'

'We do not.'

'Tell me, Kerela, how sure are you of successfully holding off another Wesman assault?'

'Alone, you mean?' she asked sharply.

'We are fully committed both at home and at the pass,' blustered Bynaar. 'Your tone is not appreciated.'

'Neither was your lack of support. It was lucky the TaiGethen came when they did.'

'Quite. But they are gone now, are they not?'

'Heading to the pass to join the fight, yes. Just as we promised.'

'Good . . . good. So, your strength in Julatsa, is it enough without them?'

'Our walls are being repaired; we can invest strength back in them, and we still have a considerable force of mages and militia. But should the Wesmen come again in greater numbers, we would be tested. Why, do you have information?'

Another pause, this one so long that Kerela wondered if he'd fallen asleep.

'We grow ever more concerned that the invasion will change its focus and our coastlines will be beset. You are at most immediate risk if that happens. Our information is patchy but it points to you needing to stay where you are and keep your college safe while we try to stave off anything that comes at us from the south in addition to defending the pass. Difficult days, Kerela.'

'Surely they will bypass you if they can and head straight for the Manse? I always wondered why those who attacked us didn't simply go there and make it their own.'

'That is why we must be mindful of such an attack,' said Bynaar. 'Remember how much the Wytch Lords want Dawnthief. The Wesmen are never happier when than trying to destroy magic, no?'

She could imagine him chuckling to himself about that one.

'You have been in recent contact with your team at the Manse, I take it?'

'My dear lady, it is a daily occurrence, as you must know,' he said a little too quickly.

'Then you know of the problems we have had contacting our own representatives there. Lystern have the same issues. Strange that your people are still communicating when ours cannot.'

His silence was cold. 'Your implication is beneath contempt.'

'Then prove to me that they are still at the Manse. Still alive.'

'I would not lower myself to do any such thing. Your team, your problem.'

'And there I was thinking we were all working together. Last time we spoke to our people, they felt close to a breakthrough. Funny how we heard nothing more, isn't it?'

'It is not something I can explain, nor feel duty bound to investigate. Now is that all?'

'No, it is not. You told me our Il-Aryn had an unusual style. How could you possibly know that all the way from Xetesk?'

'Don't be naive. It is no concern of mine that you have no people embedded here. We have not made the same error. Give my regards to Sipharec. May he recover quickly.'

The contact was broken and Kerela's relief was instant and wonderful. She drank off a goblet of heavy red wine.

'Lying bastard,' she said.

There was a knock on her door.

'Yes?' she called. One of the Communion chamber mages poked her head around the door. 'Yniss bless you, Syvra, you look tired. What is it? Bynaar has gone, if you wanted him.'

'No, but thank you. I'll pass that on. We have another who wants to speak to you rather urgently. Can I give him permission to Commune with you?'

'Who is he and is he one of ours?'

'Yes, and he would not give his name. His lore is Julatsan, he is genuine.'

'Then yes, have him contact me.'

Kerela settled back in her chair, awaiting the intrusion of Communion contact. When it came, all her growing suspicions were realised.

It was Stein.

Auum couldn't muster any anger, consumed as he was by an overwhelming sadness. He had looked about him once the survivor group had got as far up into the foothills as they could for the day and had shaken his head at the truly pitiful band they had become.

Forty-three TaiGethen were still able to fight, plus a further seven seriously wounded, burned or with limbs broken or blown off entirely. At least four of them would not survive, even with castings. Seventy-eight Il-Aryn had survived but fourteen carried injuries and eight of those were unlikely to survive. The Julatsan cavalry was entirely gone, barring one young man whom Auum was delighted to see smile: Tilman. He had burns on his face and hands but he was not broken, and castings would heal him. Finally, just twenty-nine Julatsan-trained elves were walking. Another twelve were alive but struggling. Most of them would die.

It was an appalling result; thirty-two TaiGethen dead, murdered by magic; twenty-six Il-Aryn gone in mere instants, helpless against a greater power; thirty-seven Julatsan elves immolated or dismembered by castings they themselves studied but had failed to detect; forty-nine cavalrymen downed by spell or blade.

No one had escaped completely unscathed, and in addition to those who would not last the night there were others who could not survive the journey Auum was planning. That was another reason he was calm; it finally all made some sort of sense. But there were a few loose ends.

Stein and Merrat had been with the Xeteskian mage all the way to this chill, fireless campsite on the banks of a narrow stream that almost certainly fed Triverne Lake. His name, Auum had been told, was Ryol. He was a young man of very average proportions barring his face, which was swollen from his wounds.

He had not been treated unkindly during his captivity. In fact he had not been treated at all. He had his own water and scraps of food, which no one had seen fit to take away, nor had he been spoken to at all other than to find out his name.

Ryol had tried to ask questions about his likely fate and had promised, so Stein said, to tell them anything as long as they didn't kill him. No one had responded and that silence had worked its way into the core of his will. When Auum finally walked over to question him, he was sitting on a flat rock staring at the water in the dark, seeing it sparkle in the starlight.

Stein translated Auum's questions and Ryol's responses.

'Nyann,' said Auum. 'Hassek. Vaart. Iriess. Jerren. Some of them were my friends for thousands of years. They were all on their way to join your people and fight a common enemy. You murdered them without honour. So you will answer my questions truthfully because there is no limit to the pain I can inflict on you in the name of Shorth and I already know you have no stomach for it.'

Ryol shuddered and held up his hands.

'Just give me a chance to answer. Please.'

'It is more than you gave my friends,' said Auum. 'That must make me merciful. Why would you kill us rather than let us fight with you?'

'We . . . we didn't need you at the pass.'

'That is no answer; you should have just sent us where we *were* needed. Surely the pass is the focal point of the battle?'

Ryol's eyes gave away his torment as he balanced betrayal against his own imagined pain.

'We were ordered to attack. The pass is forbidden to you.'

'To the elves?' asked Auum. Ryol hesitated and Auum made the connection. 'No. To anyone from Julatsa?'

Ryol shrugged, unwilling to speak the words. Stein drew in a sharp breath.

'Why?' he asked.

'I don't know,' said Ryol.

Auum pounced on him, bearing him to the ground flat on his back and placing a knife to his throat. Ryol whimpered and tried to back away into the stream but Auum held him firmly.

'Speak. I can bleed you very slowly.'

'Just rumours,' said Ryol, his eyes on Stein, seeking mercy. He would find none there. 'I heard . . . I'm just a mage – they don't tell me anything.'

'Tell us what you've heard.' Auum did not release the mage but withdrew the knife. 'Whether you live or die is in your hands.'

He waited while Ryol drew breath, a little colour returning to his cheeks.

'There was a story that Julatsa was close to getting Dawnthief. Everyone knows the Circle Seven wouldn't like that, right?'

'Who are the Circle Seven?' asked Auum.

'The rulers of Xetesk,' said Stein. 'Not the most pleasant of men.'

'Continue,' said Auum.

'So they decided to take Julatsa out of the race,' said Ryol. 'Or so I heard. I mean, this attack does back that up, right? You do believe me, don't you?'

'How long have you been here?' asked Auum.

'Since before the siege was laid at Julatsa. We had orders to stop any Julatsan force. We knew you were coming – we had word.'

Auum stared into Ryol's eyes and saw the desperation haunting them. He let the young mage sit up.

'Don't as much as twitch,' said Auum before turning to Stein. 'What do you think?'

'Well it explains the loss of contact at the Manse. You?'

'Why stop there?' said Auum. 'It's just like I said. They want Julatsa gone.'

'That's a big step. Killing a team at the Manse is low, but destroying a whole college? A whole city?' Stein was shaking his head.

Auum turned back to Ryol. 'Is the battle at Understone Pass really so fierce it takes up all of your forces?'

Ryol smiled and Stein punched him square on his broken nose. Ryol squealed and fell back, clutching his face as fresh blood poured from his nostrils.

'Funny, is it?' shouted Stein. 'Hundreds of my people died because your masters deem us surplus to their requirements! Do you think I'd worry too much at seeing one more Xeteskian perish?'

Auum raised his hands to Stein for calm.

'What did you just say?' he asked. Stein translated. Auum nodded. 'You see, Ryol, I may not hate you but my friend here does. Answer my question or I may not stop him punching you again. And again and again.'

Ryol mumbled, blood dribbling down his face, 'Seems to me you can stop anyone you choose.'

'Choice is something I have and you have not. Answer. What's happening at the pass?'

Auum could see Ryol weighing up how much his answer might cost both him and his college. Auum could respect his loyalty, however strained it was by his current predicament.

'You'll let me go? Really?'

Auum shrugged. 'We should really stake you out with your entrails about you for the beasts to feast on. That's what would happen on Calaius to one who murdered so many elves. But you . . . well, mercy is probably the right course. I can see you did not do this by choice.'

'I'm sorry so many of your people have died today.'

'Thank you,' said Auum. 'That makes a difference. Now, the pass.'

'There is no battle there,' said Ryol in lowered tones. He wiped away the blood dripping from his nose onto his lips. 'The Wesmen are inside and we are outside. No blow has been struck and no spell cast there for at least fifteen days.'

'It's a stand-off?' asked Auum.

Ryol shook his head, keen to speak now. 'No, there is an agreement. I don't know what it means other than that no blood has been spilt in the pass for a long time. Can I go now?'

Auum was looking at Stein. Even as he was translating for Auum, his eyes were widening as if he was receiving some great wisdom.

'It all makes sense now,' said Stein. 'How so many Wesmen could have been at our gates so quickly.'

Stein had to stop. He put a hand to his mouth and sat down on a slab of rock, his feet on the edge of the stream. He stared at Ryol.

'His college has made a pact with the Wesmen, with the Wytch Lords. Dear Gods burning, we should have listened to you, Auum, though it's worse than even you think. Xetesk wasn't just *allowing* the Wesmen to attack us, the Circle Seven *sent* them to our gates.'

'And this is all about Dawnthief?' asked Auum.

'What else can it be?'

'Then why stop at Julatsa? Xetesk has freed the Wesmen and the shamen to attack not just you but the other colleges too. That'll leave Xetesk and the Wytch Lords in a straight fight – winner takes Dawnthief and Balaia along with it. I told you we were allied to the wrong side.'

'I've got to . . . What do you mean by that?'

'Later,' said Auum. 'I think our friend has had enough of our questions.'

Stein nodded vaguely. His hand was trembling when he raised it to scratch his forehead. He looked pale, haunted even.

'I must speak to Sipharec. They have to warn Lystern and Dordover what is happening. They're going to come back, aren't they? The Wesmen.'

'I think that's the plan. Right, Ryol, on your feet.'

Stein was still translating but Ryol seemed to understand anyway. 'Thank you,' he said. 'Thank you.'

'You fulfilled your part of the bargain,' said Auum. 'Now on your way. Don't look back and don't even think to cast. My elves are quiet and they kill faster than you can work a spell.'

'Of course,' gushed Ryol. 'I would never . . . I mean—'

'Go.'

Ryol could not believe his luck. He turned and began to jog away, thought better of it and walked instead. With a glance at Stein, Auum paced silently up behind him, drew a sword from its scabbard and chopped it hard and double-handed into Ryol's neck, beheading him. His body flopped to the ground and his head bounced into the stream with a heavy splash.

'Fuck!' yelled Stein. 'Auum, what have you done?'

Auum turned back, wiping his blade on the dead man's jacket before resheathing it. Stein was staring alternately at him and Ryol's headless corpse, gesturing uselessly.

'You said you were going to show him mercy!'

'That is mercy,' said Auum. 'He deserved a far more painful death. He killed my people, he showed no honour and he betrayed his own to save his life. Shorth will judge him. Now I will speak to my people. I need you with me, Stein. We have our countries to save.'

Chapter 22

After all we went through it was astounding to discover there were five more like Ystormun and that he was by no means the worst of them.

Auum, Arch of the TaiGethen

Ystormun strode across the rotunda, desperate to reach his rooms and rest. But he was not quick enough. Giriamun and Weyamun spotted him from across the great chamber. They were seated in two of the six ornate but terribly uncomfortable thrones built for the ceremonies of obedience and the swearing of loyalty from the Wesmen lords at the heart of the temple of Parve, but they pushed aside the advisors and slaves attending them in order to stand. Giriamun called his name.

His tone was laced with such malice that the mortals in the rotunda scattered, seeking refuge from whatever was to be unleashed about them. Ystormun paused mid-stride and held his head high, though he wanted nothing more than to let it fall to his chest, such was his weariness.

Instead he turned and walked towards them, steadily and with pride in his bearing. Weyamun chose simply to glare but Giriamun was allowing mana to crackle across his face and down his cloaked arms to spit from his fingertips.

'Very impressive,' said Ystormun. 'Do you have some new slave you wish to amaze with your little show?'

'With your every move, meddling in tasks not appointed to you, you weaken us further,' said Giriamun, shutting off the mana stream. 'And you do not even show us the respect of admitting your failures.'

'I think the real sadness is that you were so absent from your duties that you did not notice my attempts to advance our cause until now.'

'Absent?' roared Weyamun. Chill fled around the rotunda. There were mortals screaming nearby. 'Your hold on your position in the cadre is wafer thin, Ystormun. Our tasks took us to the brokering of a deal that will all but hand us Dawnthief on a plate. Meanwhile, you were stealing my forces and failing utterly to break Julatsa. Not only that; hundreds of your precious elven enemies escaped and you have no idea where they are.'

'That is an interesting take on events, Weyamun, but I would expect little more from one as feeble-minded as you. You were a very long time negotiating something that will leave our ground forces scattered across Balaia and vulnerable to Xetesk the moment they choose to betray us – which of course they will and sooner than we think to betray them. It is a fool's pact that we did not need to accept.'

'Preposterous!' spluttered Giriamun.

'It is nothing of the kind, and you will see, in the coming days, that my actions with Julatsa were wise indeed. Significant numbers of our forces remain alive. Many elves died, many mages and many of the TaiGethen too, though I admit Auum still eludes me. But he will perish trying to join a fight without ever realising he is siding with his enemies.'

'Only you could pretend that the breaking of a siege laid very skilfully by me is a victory,' said Weyamun. 'You have cost me hundreds of men.'

'They are weak and prey to another attack,' said Ystormun, waving a hand dismissively. 'And the elves are dispersed.'

'Oh yes, we know that,' snapped Giriamun. 'My latest labourers and researchers heading for the Dawnthief site encountered some of your elves. I was with my host at the time. And how fascinating to see them, even so very briefly, in action with their oh-so-effective staff weapons. None of my party will be breaking the earth after that encounter.'

Ystormun smiled. 'The Xeteskians will continue their work and we will take Dawnthief when we want it. You should not have wasted your forces so casually.'

'The Xeteskians will not continue anything, at least not for the time being,' said Giriamun. 'Those elves were coming from the direction of the Dawnthief site. Bynaar assures us that since the elves were captured there he has lost all contact with his team. You can see what this means, I'm sure.'

Ystormun paused and not for the first time had to respect some of the elves he had encountered. Giriamun had described the Senserii's weapons, which meant that Takaar was at the Manse and, knowing his fascination, probably working there. Ystormun was almost tempted to pay him a visit.

'Nothing you have said undermines my position,' said Ystormun. 'And if you will hear me at the full cadre meeting later, I will apprise you of all I have achieved on our behalf, and of my current plans.'

Weyamun sneered. 'Your words are meaningless, Ystormun. The cadre meeting will be very interesting but it has little to do with your plots and schemes. You can talk about them all you like. We, on the other hand, will be discussing your censure and removal from authority.'

'That is not in your gift,' snarled Ystormun. 'Nor would you dare.'

'Then come and watch us,' said Giriamun. 'There will be fine wine too.'

Ystormun watched them stalk away. No doubt they would rest in the knowledge of their imminent victory. But much could happen before nightfall. The days were very long here.

Stein sat and listened to Auum, as he seemed to have done a few times recently. There was something so compelling in the way he spoke. It was clear he had great wells of emotion inside, and his anger was cold and deadly, but everything he said came straight from his heart and he had no time for tact and diplomacy, no time for the niceties of others' feelings.

This time Stein was sitting with Tilman, who was completely in awe of Auum and something of a miracle himself, being the only survivor of the cavalry contingent. Stein had termed it luck; Tilman had told him it was faith in the elves that had saved him. That didn't make any sense, but if Tilman believed it, who was Stein to contradict him? Anyway, Stein was glad of his company, youthful and excited as it was; after all, he was the only other human here and Stein had tired of being the sole human on the voyage to Balaia.

The prayers for the dead had been protracted and emotional. Each fallen elf had been named and the lamentations had been long and tearful.

'What's he saying now?' asked Tilman, whose elvish was decent but not capable of deciphering either prayers or lamentations.

'Auum is inviting others to speak on behalf of the fallen. I don't think anyone wishes to speak at this time. Normally, they'd do this

at the reclamation ceremony, but they can't hold one this time. No
bodies, you see. That has hurt them.'

There was more prayer and then a short chant led by Ulysan.
Auum drank water from a skin and began to speak again.

'The death of every elf and Julatsan man today is on my head. I
led you into a trap because I believed we had to fight with Xetesk.
Instead they tried to kill us all. Remember that lesson, elves of
Calaius. The men of Xetesk will betray you. Those men of Julatsa
who stand with us will not. They died side by side with us, and those
who sit with us are brothers who you will look to as you would any
of your kin.

'I do not deserve your trust after today, but if I have it, then I
believe our path is clear at last. Will you trust me one more time?'

A chorus of assent ran around the elves. Auum nodded his
blessings and thanks.

'We were right to fight the Wytch Lords because I will not suffer
them to set foot on Calaius ever again. Our mistake was to choose to
fight alongside the armies of man. There is another way, and we must
take it or we will all die in this soulless, godless land. Will you hear
me?'

Every TaiGethen stood to pledge their faith and loyalty. The
others were slightly less enthusiastic, but Stein couldn't imagine a
world in which they would choose to travel anywhere without their
extraordinary warrior guard and its charismatic leader.

'What does he mean?' asked Tilman. 'Why shouldn't he fight with
us?'

'I think he means Xetesk, but it comes to the same thing. I'm more
concerned about the other path he's going to propose. Something he
said a while ago . . . I do hope he doesn't act on it.'

Auum took a breath. 'The Wesmen seek to destroy human magic.
Their warriors have no love of the Wytch Lords' power wielded by
their shamen –' Stein went cold all over '– though they understand its
necessity in defeating man just as I understand the necessity of elven
magic in combat. What we face is an alliance of Xetesk and Wytch
Lord power determined to destroy us along with Julatsa. We have to
break that alliance and we will do it by turning the Wesmen away
from the Wytch Lords. We will deprive the Wytch Lords of their
army and the means to deliver their magic; once they are weakened
they can be destroyed.

'I won't tell you this is going to be easy, because it isn't. All the courage and faith that you have ever shown will be needed and will be tested further. It is hostile country and a hard climb over the mountains to get there. But if we stay here we will not survive. Xetesk is too powerful and its armies can not be turned.

'Come with me. Walk with me and Yniss will walk with us.' Auum paused. 'But think first. Challenge me if you wish. We must be as one, on this mission, or we will all fail.'

There was a silence until Stein stood.

'May I speak?' he said.

Auum smiled. 'You are our brother, so it is your right. And I'd have been disappointed if you didn't have strong views.'

'I just want you to understand the enormity of your plan. And I want to ask you: why not join an alliance of the other three colleges against Xetesk and the Wytch Lords?'

'Because it won't work,' said Auum. 'Remember Xetesk was not alone in failing to help you. No one came, and that surely means they are all in this conspiracy one way or another – at least until Xetesk chooses to cut them loose. Besides, do you really think such an alliance could take on both Xetesk and the Wytch Lords?'

'We have to try, don't we?'

Auum shook his head. 'Julatsa needs to marshal all its strength just to survive. You wanted to tell us something else?'

'You know nothing about the Wesmen or their country. They are a disparate tribal people. That the Wytch Lords have brought so many tribes together is impressive in itself, though I shudder to think of the threats and promises they will have made. You can cross the mountains right here – and you'll understand why we built a tunnel when you do – but how will you find anyone? Who do you plan to speak to?

'I don't want to pour cold water on your plan, but you're going in blind to try and persuade people you've already fought to turn against their incredibly powerful masters. You think humans are difficult to deal with? We are simple compared to the Wesmen. I'm sorry, Auum, but I can't see how you can succeed.'

Auum spread his hands. 'There is always a way. Surely not all the tribes have fallen under their control? Surely they all hate Xetesk with a passion we can share? Our own threads still bicker, much as their tribes will. We can use that, encourage them to dream of independence. We did, and we beat Ystormun.'

'This is not just Ystormun. This is all of them, all six Wytch Lords, and it is their land. The powers they have the other side of those mountains are so much greater than anything you've seen here. You must understand the reality of where you are and of who and what you are up against.'

'Those we seek, we find,' Auum said simply. Stein could see that he didn't grasp the difficulties.

'Very well. Who are you seeking?'

Auum smiled. 'That's where you come in. Don't pretend you have no information on Wesman allegiances and the locations of their tribes.'

Stein looked down at Tilman, who was staring at Auum as if he was a god walking the earth.

'I thought I'd explained my doubts. Are you still so confident I'll come with you?'

'You can't leave Tilman alone. Besides, I'm right: this is our only chance and you know it. If you ally with Lystern and Dordover you'll bring Xetesk, the Wesmen and the Wytch Lords against you, and you'll be swept away before them. My way gives us some hope – small, but we'll have a chance.' Auum gestured at Tilman. 'I guarantee he's coming with us. Where do you stand?'

Stein knew he had no choice. 'I brought you here, Auum. I'll stand by you until the day you leave.'

'You are a good man, Stein, and there are precious few of you.'

'We'll have to agree to differ there. I know a whole host of good men and women.'

Auum shrugged and made to turn away. A new thought spun him back.

'You can speak the Wesmen language, can't you?'

'It is among my skills, though it's not to the same level as my elvish.'

'Good.' Auum smiled again, and this time there was genuine warmth and humour in it. 'Because if you can't we might have trouble getting our message across.'

Sipharec was sleeping, but Kerela couldn't rest with all she had heard bubbling inside her. It wasn't late so she walked through the college to the library, knowing who she would find there, absorbing knowledge as he had done all his life.

The library was vast, built on three levels with books and parchments on shelves to all four sides. During the day light came in through great glass panes set in the roof and each night lanterns were set on each of twenty reading tables, casting enough illumination to read by in comfort.

It reeked of history, and Kerela, like so many of those allowed access, spent more time here than anywhere else, often just staring at the accumulated wisdom on show. The only discordant note were the stacks of crates by the rear entrance hall, ready to store the priceless works should the city walls fall.

Harild was sitting in a leather reading chair, a clay flask of wine and a full goblet on a table next to him. He looked younger, Kerela thought, as if the recent combat had allowed him to taste his youth again and the flavour yet lingered.

'May I disturb you?' she asked, her voice a whisper though they were the only two in the cavernous building. She put her hands on the back of a chair opposite him. 'I wouldn't ask, but I have news I can scarcely believe and I must speak to someone.'

Harild was known to hate interruption when he was reading in the evenings, but when he raised his head from the book, a work on the economics of magical research if Kerela recognised the script, his face was soft with a smile.

'Please sit, Kerela. No elf can ever be considered an intrusion.'

Kerela smiled though her heart was heavy with Stein's report. She pulled out the chair and sat down. Harild gestured to the wine and she shook her head.

'I see I have something else to thank Auum for,' she said.

Harild's ambivalence towards the elves in his college and city was well known, but it had thawed almost to the point of gushing during the few days of fighting.

'I am a soldier and I needed another soldier to fully reveal the strength of the elven heart. My apologies that it took me so long to see your true colours. I'm proud you are part of this college.'

Kerela blushed.

'I don't know what to say,' she managed.

Harild cleared his throat and his voice returned to a measure of its usual gruffness.

'Tell me what you've heard and who from. Leave nothing out.'

Kerela recounted her Communion with Stein. Harild did not interrupt, but as the news unfolded he closed his book and sat back, his eyes occasionally seeming to mist up. He placed his hands on the table, and every now and then they tightened on the edge, whitening his knuckles before he forced himself to relax.

Kerela watched Harild's face first go grey and then age ten years before clearing and tautening. She could see him working through possibilities and plans and coming to the same conclusions she had. When she was done she found she was shaking and reached across to Harild's goblet. She took a long swallow. He nodded and was silent for a while.

'When will Sipharec be available to discuss this?' he asked, his voice hoarse and quiet.

'He's exhausted,' said Kerela. 'I think he's sicker than he's admitting. We can't afford to wait. There are some things we can't make decisions about without the whole council, but you're in charge of the army. What should we do?'

'It is sadly evident that this whole conflict has ceased to be about defeating the Wytch Lords and has become a race for Dawnthief. I have no doubt that any alliance with Xetesk is only ever temporary, but to hope it fails before we are attacked again is naive in the extreme.'

Harild paused and refilled his goblet. He offered it to Kerela, who shook her head. He drained it and refilled it again.

'One is enough.'

'Good though, isn't it?'

'Very,' she said.

'We already have scouts and lookouts watching the sea for Wesman ships. There is little more we can do there, and we do not have enough men to launch attacks on any approaching invasion force. So we have to concentrate on our defences, as we already are, and on one other area.

'We must make the Septern Manse ours. We should send a large force of soldiers and mages there; seed the place with more wards than we've ever laid; make sure that any force that comes to take it pays the highest of prices. And while we're there, work to solve this magical riddle for ourselves.'

Kerela felt her pulse quicken. 'You're suggesting triggering conflict at the Manse.'

'It has already been triggered. We know Xetesk's true leanings, and they know that we know. Do you think they won't move to re-inforce their position? We have to get there first, clear out whoever's there and make it ours. Ownership of that place is key to this fight right now.'

'Doesn't it weaken us here? We have to protect our city and people.'

'And what better way than diverting enemy forces elsewhere? Look, we know Xetesk has murdered our team there and probably Lystern's too. Dordover wasn't even represented because of its foolish trust in Xetesk. We can retake it if we act now. Call a council meeting, make the decision. And remember, we can always recall our forces.'

Kerela found herself excited at the prospect of action.

'I'll call the meeting. At least we won't be sitting inside our walls wondering when the end will come; we'll be out there taunting it.'

'That's the spirit, and there's more to discuss. Let me find you a goblet and we'll finish this flask together, eh?'

Chapter 23

Are the Blackthorne Mountains impassable? Not if you're an eagle.

Ancient saying, unattributed

Auum woke to a bleak morning. When he opened his eyes, all he could see were the towering peaks of the Blackthorne Mountains and he wondered what madness had possessed him to think they could climb them at all, let alone at the speed they needed to.

'It always looks worse from a prone position,' said Ulysan.

Auum took the proffered hand and let himself be hauled upright. He brushed himself down and stretched away a few aches left from his uncomfortable bed on the rough grass. All around him people were waking up. TaiGethen stretched, prayed and practised some moves; mages and Il-Aryn sighed or frowned, unhappy to have opened their eyes to this reality.

'How are we doing?' asked Auum.

'Not so well,' said Ulysan. 'Come and see.'

Walking across a slight slope towards the stream edge where they had tried to make the wounded more comfortable, Auum saw Julatsan elves in the sky, monitoring the forest for enemies. Ahead, he saw bodies being laid out for reclamation while others were being tended, healed with spells as far as that was possible and given water and food.

Auum sent a silent prayer to Shorth as he walked among the bodies, each one a further blow to his will. He had known some would die, but they had fought so hard to live that he had allowed himself false hope. Five TaiGethen had gone to Shorth's embrace along with eight Il-Aryn and ten Julatsan elves. He could hear crying and whispered laments for the dead.

Faleen was kneeling over the body of one of her Tai, the youngster Illyan. His head was scorched black and red and he had been blinded by fire. His injuries had been so severe the only help the mages could give him was relief from pain. Auum put his hand on her shoulder and she looked round, gripping it with one of hers. It was burned and blistered on the back too. Her eyes were moist, though she had known this was coming.

'He never once cried out, never asked for anything but a little water. Look at what happened to him; he didn't even have the chance to defend himself. This isn't right, Auum.'

'Have you slept?'

She shook her head and smiled. 'No, I stayed with him, describing what I could see and remembering the rainforest with him. He said he could smell banyan and panther, and he died just as the sun crested the horizon. I think he could sense it, he was waiting for it. Yniss bless him but he was so good, so quick.'

'He and all of our fallen will be avenged, and those enemy souls we send to Shorth will suffer eternal torment for their crimes. You're with me, aren't you, Faleen? I need you.'

Faleen nodded and stood, Auum helping her to her feet.

'What do you need me to do?'

'Stay with him if you want to,' said Auum.

'No, he's gone, and we need to move. I have spoken all the prayers. He is with Shorth now.'

'Yniss makes you strong, Faleen. We need to organise the wounded and get them away from here, back to Julatsa. We saved a team of horses and a cart, so they can ride in that. We also spared a couple of cavalry horses for those able to ride but the rest were bled out overnight. Marack and Thrynn's Tais are butchering them for our journey.

'Can you oversee the wounded? Take whoever you need and get them to the cart and away. Every moment they are here makes me more nervous. If the humans attack, we won't be able to save them.'

'Consider it done,' said Faleen.

Auum embraced her then trotted away with Ulysan to find Stein. He was speaking to Grafyrre and the two of them were staring up at the mountains. They had an hour or so's walk into the steepening foothills before the first true mountain slope would have to be tackled.

'You have a route?' asked Auum.

'It doesn't look too taxing,' said Ulysan.

Both Grafyrre and Stein eyed him coldly before Grafyrre spoke.

'It's a difficult ascent for the first part. There'll be handholds for a TaiGethen and mages can fly but as for the Il-Aryn . . .'

'We'll just have to help them through it,' said Auum.

'How much warm clothing do you have?' asked Stein. 'It's going to be very cold up there.'

'Mother Ulysan made us all bring cloaks,' said Auum.

'And how wise I am,' he said.

'Occasionally you score a hit,' said Grafyrre. 'We're going to need as much clothing as we can carry in our packs along with the horsemeat and water. The dead don't need their clothes or boots, Auum.'

Auum nodded. 'Do what you must.'

'Really cold,' said Stein. 'So cold you cannot grip with your fingers or speak because the muscles in your mouth refuse to frame words. It's a cold that gets into your bones and makes you shiver so violently you fall over. You will be so cold that if you can't find shelter, it will kill you.'

'So what's your point?' said Ulysan, that boyish smile on his face.

'What's the coldest you've ever been? I wonder. Beyond castings, I'd wager you've never seen ice and certainly not snow. I guess you've never even seen a frost, and we get those here from time to time and run to our fires and warm our toes. Up there it is forty times colder and there will be no fires. You have to know this because the cold will make your people start to stray in their minds, and you have to keep them focused or they will die.'

'Do you think we can do this?' asked Auum.

'Anything is possible and mages can cast warmth up to a point. I know elves are sturdy and determined. But this will be beyond your experience and you must be wary of it. The cold can kill. One slip and you're done.'

'Thank you, Stein. I'll speak to everyone individually when we are on our way. Graf, get the old heads to make sure no one leaves any clothing behind, all right?'

Grafyrre nodded. Auum took another suspicious glance at the blank mountain slopes before tracking away a mile or so with Ulysan to take a look back at the woodland. He could see the glow of fires within and smoke rising above the trees and dispersing into the sky.

'What will they do?' asked Ulysan.

'They were here to kill us. They're still here, so I'd be surprised if they didn't come for us again.'

'We should ready ourselves then.'

'Not this time, Ulysan. We can't afford to lose any more people. We have to focus on getting away.'

'What's up?' asked Ulysan.

'What do you mean?'

'Well you can't sit still. You're biting your lip, fidgeting and curling your toes inside your boots. It's like you're impersonating Takaar.'

'Am I? Sorry, I had no idea.'

'So, tell Mother Ulysan what's on your mind.'

Auum sighed out a breath. 'Stein's right. This is madness.'

'That's not quite what he said.'

'It's what he meant, and he knows this country. It's just . . .' Auum trailed off, fighting for the words while he fought a wave of hope-lessness. 'Time is against us. We are so few and we have so far to go. It's so hard to see a path to victory and Yniss knows my prayers are fervent. I can't think straight in this wilderness, and I need you to tell me when I'm going wrong. Like now. Am I wrong?'

Auum sat with his legs stretched downslope. Ulysan dropped to a crouch next to him.

'You're not wrong. Very recent history reminds us that you are never wrong. We don't have any other choice if we aren't going to turn tail and run home.'

'That would only put off the inevitable. But I question what difference we can make.' Auum sighed again and cursed himself for it. 'We've lost so many.'

'Fifty TaiGethen and a few ClawBound won a battle against six thousand men and mages.'

'In the rainforest.'

'Mainly at Katura. Using open spaces and buildings. We can do it again.'

Auum smiled up at Ulysan. 'Do you ever despair?'

'Only of your despair,' said Ulysan. 'And now you're going to tell me what's really got you stirred up this morning. It's him, isn't it?'

Auum chuckled and pushed a hand through his hair.

'Will you get out of my head? How can you know that?'

'Because it's nearly always about him. You don't know whether to embrace him or kill him, do you? And you wish he was here. Admit it.'

Auum shrugged. 'I can't forgive what he did to Drech. Not ever. But, you know . . . the things he can do are so extraordinary and when he directs them properly . . . I'll never be able to forget what he did to that ship. But I hate what he has become. I hate *him* so much of the time. His madness, his ego and his arrogance, though they are probably all one and the same thing. The fact is, we need him. Do you think he knows that?'

Ulysan laughed. 'He's always known it. But look, if you need him don't let your personal feelings get in the way. Ephemere and Cleress both survived the attack yesterday. Have them contact their sisters at Korina. Get him back here by land or sea. The Senserii will see him safely to us, and you never know, he might turn up in time to save us all.'

'And wouldn't he absolutely love that?'

Auum cringed just imagining the posturing that would follow.

'He'd have earned it in my eyes,' said Ulysan.

'He'd never stop letting you know it.'

The two old friends were silent for a time. Auum ran through everything in his mind a hundred times in those few moments: the moment he had found Takaar and the days that followed, the rise from the pit of his madness to something almost elven once again, his unpredictability, his genius and his weakness of meeting criticism with the most hideous violence. And the ship, the ship rendered to dust in the middle of the sea. A power greater than even the Wytch Lords, surely.

'All right. Get either of them to contact the ships. We can only try.'

Auum's eye was drawn to a line of elves moving slowly to his left, heading to the cart. Four were mounted on horses and the rest limped along, either supported by the uninjured or helping those worse off than they were. It was a sad sight.

'Get back to the camp, Ulysan, make sure they're all ready to go. I'll see this lot off. And Ulysan? Bless you for everything you are. I couldn't do this without you.'

Ulysan, normally so free with a quip, merely nodded and ran back towards the mountains. Auum felt in need of a run himself. He pushed himself hard, sprinting across the steep slope, over another shallow rise and onto the open ground, tearing across the earth to the wounded. It felt good. The air in his lungs was chill and fresh, the water on his right calmed his spirit and the blood thundering through his body energised him.

He slid to a halt next to Faleen, who was helping one of the two wounded TaiGethen along.

'Very impressive,' she said. 'Who was that for, us or the eyes in the woods?'

'For none of you. It feels good, Faleen. I'll race you back.' Auum put his arm around the wounded warrior, and the two of them shared the burden. 'How are you feeling, Hanyss?'

'I'll live, my Arch,' he said, his face taut with the pain of his broken leg, which had been lashed to his other as a makeshift splint. 'I'm sorry to be deserting you. I failed us.'

'No one caught in the fires of magic hidden beneath his feet has failed us. It is an evil force that skulks in the dark like a thief, waiting to snatch life from heroes like you,' said Auum. 'And you dodged that fate. You will recover and one day you and I will run the rainforest together.'

Auum could feel Hanyss swell with pride at the thought. He held his body more firmly and his face cleared a little.

'There is always joy on the horizon,' said Faleen, and she looked across him at Auum and mouthed, *Well done*. 'Come on, not far now.'

The first of the wounded had reached the wagon and were being helped on board. Two horses were taken around to the front to be hitched, their riders helped to dismount. Hanyss and Ynsiell, the other injured TaiGethen, were loaded on board. Food and water was attached to the many hooks on the sides.

Auum stood back to allow the rest on board and glanced back towards the wood. Men were pouring out of it at a run. There were mages in the sky ahead of lines of soldiers, archers and more spell casters.

He wiped a hand across his mouth. The Julatsan fliers had seen the attackers so the camp would be warned.

'Faleen, we have to go now. Get the rest on board and get this cart moving. Keep your pace up, don't stop and don't look back. Tais, with me. Run hard.'

Auum led the four who had helped the injured to the wagon, though they pressed him hard for the lead. The humans were no match for the speed of the TaiGethen, but the ground was hard up to the steeper foothills and not all the elves had such pace. Auum watched the elven mages in the air. There were three of them, trying to keep back four humans.

The humans separated, one flying close to the ground, another going high and the other pair closing up and heading directly at the Julatsan elves. The trio of elves split to counter them, with one diving on her foe from directly above. A shout sounded but it was too late: the elf thumped into the human's back with both feet. His wings guttered and died, and he ploughed into the grass twenty feet below while the elf soared skywards, arrows chasing her higher.

She barrelled up, just missing another enemy, who had the wit to furl his wings and drop away in time. The humans backed off and the elves returned to their circling. Auum ran harder, Faleen right on his shoulder now and the others crowding behind.

They tore up a shallow slope, leaped across to the next and ran down towards the stream where the gradient was easiest and led them straight into the camp. Elves were still milling about despite the cajoling of Ulysan, Grafyrre and Merrat. The TaiGethen were all ready, though: faces were painted, weapons clean and sharp, packs were on backs loaded with clothes and food.

'No time to fill your waterskins,' he shouted as he ran past Il-Aryn at the stream. 'Get your packs and get moving. My warriors are about to become sitting targets waiting for you. Move!'

He ran on, finding Ulysan by the barking of his voice.

'Where's Stein?' he said.

Ulysan pointed while chastising a Julatsan elf who was still strapping on his boots. Auum clapped him on the shoulder and ran on.

He found Stein. 'I need your mages in the air finding us the best route up the mountain.'

'Right.' Stein turned away. 'Julatsa. Wings! Let's go. Best path required.'

One of the trio of spotter mages already in the air swooped down to hover in front of Auum.

'They're closing fast,' she said. 'Bow range shortly and spell range moments after that. We need to clear out now; their mages saw us and they know where to strike.'

'Thank you,' said Auum. 'Good move out there, by the way.'

'Plenty more where that came from,' she said and shot back into the sky, pausing to point in a wide arc to indicate the angle of the human advance.

Auum waved then clapped his hands.

'Get running. Ulysan is leading. Go, go!'

Finally they were pouring away, running along beside the stream until the ground became loose shale and they had to divert to a grassier slope. Auum glanced up into the sky, expecting to see it misting with arrows at any moment. Letting his gaze drop, he almost jumped out of his skin. There, with his back to the slope the humans would fire over, was a hunched figure.

'Tilman. You can't still be here. Your boot! Get your boot on!'

Tilman raised his head. His face was blotched and there were tears on his cheeks.

'I can't,' he wailed. 'It hurts too much. I'm so sorry, Auum.'

Auum ran to him and dropped to one knee, pushing Tilman's hands away from their grip around his ankle. Auum put his hands on it and could feel the mass of swelling up into his calf and down across his foot.

'Yniss preserve us,' breathed Auum, glancing up to see his people disappearing out of sight behind a scree slope. 'Why didn't you say something?'

Tilman wiped his nose and eyes on a sleeve and managed to compose himself a little.

'Because you'd have sent me home and I didn't want to go.'

Auum felt a vibration through the earth – the enemy were close. He weighed up his options; it didn't take long.

'We've got to move fast. Can you put any weight on this?' Auum already knew the answer.

'It was all right at first – it just felt odd – but it just got worse and worse and this morning I couldn't stand on it. You'll have to leave me here.'

'Don't be ridiculous. Now listen carefully. You haven't broken it, which is lucky, but it's dislocated. Not good.'

'So I'd have been going home,' said Tilman.

'Rather than being peppered with arrows at any moment, yes,' said Auum, feeling tension build across his shoulders as the vibrations increased. 'Look, there's something I need to do. It'll make you scream, but that's better than screaming every time you put your foot down.'

'You can make the pain go away?'

'No, it'll still hurt like a panther bite but it will help. Brace yourself.' Auum positioned his hands on Tilman's foot and ankle, hearing the boy wince. 'On three. One, two . . .'

Auum pressured the ankle and turned the foot back to its correct position, feeling bone grate on bone and sinew and ligament protest. Tilman screamed and clutched Auum's body, dry-retching and shuddering. Auum gave him a moment and then moved him back to lie on the grass.

'Now we really have to go,' he said. He grabbed Tilman's boot and gave it to the youth. 'Hold this. Don't drop it, you'll need it later.'

He took Tilman's free hand and dragged him up onto his good leg. He stooped and picked up Tilman's pack and slung it over one shoulder. Arrows came flooding over the rise, falling against the opposite slope. Auum blew out his cheeks.

'Come on and try not to make too much noise.'

'Why did you have to do that now?' wheezed Tilman.

They moved off, Auum hurrying Tilman along, taking the weight off his bad leg for now, letting the human hop but keeping the pace quick.

'Because now you can put your foot down without risk of breaking bones or crippling yourself. Your mages can fix you properly later.'

Auum got them to the stream and followed the elves' tracks. They were out of sight, but the humans had come up faster than he thought and so they would have to move faster too. Another volley of arrows rushed across the space. Auum ducked reflexively, hearing shafts strike water and stone behind him.

There was a movement in the air, a pressing on his back and shoulders.

'Down!'

Auum threw them both to the ground. Tilman yelped as orbs of fire, deep blue shot through with yellow, cruised over the rise and slammed into the recently vacated campsite. Up in the sky, elven mages were keeping the Xeteskian spotters well back but soon they wouldn't need them anyway.

Auum dragged Tilman back to his feet. The first Xeteskian crested the rise, saw the pair and shouted.

'Move!' said Auum. 'You're going to have to use that foot – it's faster that way. Brace yourself.'

'Three,' said Tilman putting his ruined ankle down and gasping at the pain.

Auum smiled. 'Good on you, young human.'

Even the fleeting weight Tilman could put on his left leg was enough to almost double their speed. They made it around the scree slope and Auum saw a sharp climb before him, up to a narrow pass between two hills. The last elves were just passing through, disappearing from sight some two hundred yards away. One stood there, looking back down the pass.

Seeing them, he started to run back down the slope. Auum waved him to go back.

'Ulysan, no! Get the rest of them away!' he shouted.

Ulysan wasn't hearing him. Auum and Tilman made their best speed towards him, the young human beginning to struggle as the pain from his ankle spread up his leg and through his back. Auum could feel his body tightening with every step. Tilman stumbled more than he trotted, and Auum shouldered more and more of his weight as his strength failed.

More spells detonated behind them, cracking off the shale slopes and showering them with dust and splinters of stone. Ulysan was still running down the slope but he was looking beyond Auum, who saw his eyes widen.

'Move faster!' called the big TaiGethen.

'Only so fast we can go,' said Auum, practically lifting Tilman off the ground. 'He's not as light as he looks.'

'Sorry,' mumbled Tilman.

Arrows rattled into the stone around them and the slope behind. Auum hunched again.

'That was too close. Ulysan, how far away are they?'

'Not far enough,' said Ulysan running up to him and taking Tilman's other arm around his shoulder, the boot still held in a death grip in the youth's hand. 'Run.'

They ran up the steep slope towards temporary safety. Spells smashed into the ground not ten feet behind them, the shock waves throwing them all forward to sprawl on the ground. More arrows fizzed in, one clipping Ulysan's ear and drawing blood.

Auum rolled back onto his feet and spared a glance downslope. The sky seemed full of mages, elven and human, dodging around one another, the ground covered with humans, less than fifty yards distant.

'We're in trouble,' he said.

'You noticed,' said Ulysan. 'Let's get him up.'

And then Stein was hovering above them with another mage.

'Get out of here, we've got him,' he said.

With that, he and the elven flier swooped, grabbed Tilman by the arms and lifted him clear and fast into the sky. Auum and Ulysan looked at one another in relief.

'Speed,' said Auum.

Chapter 24

What's the difference? Well, a mage uses mana to construct the shapes of spells, drawing it into himself to mould it. An Il-Aryn has all his energy laid out before him and has to adapt and harness what he sees to create the desired result. Hence the Il-Aryn is far more limited in scope.

Kerela, Julatsan Mage Council

By the time they reached the lower slopes of the mountains they had put a good distance between themselves and the chasing pack but the race was not yet won. Auum looked at what lay before them and took a deep breath.

The incline of flat granite they were moving up grew steadily steeper over the course of about three hundred yards before rearing into the sky, a wall of bleak stone broken by cracks, outcrops and occasional narrow ledges. Clumps of vegetation clung on here and there and gliding birds climbed tall thermal updraughts, their cries echoing on the wind blowing across the base of the climb.

Grafyrre, Merrat, Merke and Marack were in a group pointing out potential routes up the wall. Auum sighed, awed by the sheer scale of it. Comparing this rock face to the cliffs at Verendii Tual was like comparing a banyan to a balsa tree.

Stein and the elven mage had lain Tilman against the mountainside and the elf was assessing his injury and preparing a casting. Auum trotted up with Ulysan to crouch beside him.

'Still with us?'

Tilman managed a vague smile. His face was covered in sweat and his colour was a sick-looking grey.

'Thank you,' he said.

'You may be a fool, but you are a courageous fool,' said Auum. 'What can you do for him?'

The elven mage laid his hands on Tilman's ankle and cast. Tilman

relaxed and his breathing became more regular, some colour returning to his cheeks.

'I can take the pain away,' said the mage. 'But until we have time
to probe the extent of the damage, I don't know. It's not horrible in
there, but without magical assistance he isn't going to be walking for
fifteen to twenty days.'

'We're about to climb a mountain,' said Auum. 'And we aren't
leaving him here.'

'We'll take him up,' said Stein. 'Look, Auum, what you did for
him . . . a human . . . it means a huge amount, and, um . . .'

'I think he's trying to ask you why you risked your life to save a
mere human rather than leave him to become cinders and an archery
target,' said Ulysan.

'Thanks, Ulysan. Where would I be without your insight?'

'Lost and alone, skipper.'

'Sometimes an attractive prospect,' said Auum. He turned to Stein.
'I would do the same for anyone who would lay down his life for an
elf. It's the TaiGethen way.'

Oryaal was running up the slope towards them, the veteran warrior indicating behind him.

'They're on to us. Spotter mages have got close enough to identify
our position, and the mages and archers are moving up. There's a
good ambush point—'

'No more fighting,' said Auum. 'How long before they are in
range?'

'They're moving slowly because they know we've stopped, and
that makes them nervous, but they can be on us in a quarter-hour or
less once they know we're climbing.'

Auum hissed a breath over his teeth. With this many elves unused
to climbing that was too short a time.

'Then we've rested here for too long. Ulysan, let's get our best
climbers on the face now. We need six routes, if we can find them. I'll
speak to the Il-Aryn. All Julatsan elves should be in the air, helping
the climbers. Stein, you have your first charge already. Have your
mages try and identify the likely fallers and help them however you
can. How high is the first rest point?'

Stein grimaced. 'A long way. Three hundred yards at least, but
once we're there the incline is dramatically shallower and we'll be
able to walk. It's a narrow edge but doable, taking us far past the
snow line.'

'All right. We've got a few little ledges on the way up if we're desperate. Let's go.'

Ulysan moved off, calling for Merrat, Grafyrre, Merke, Marack, Thrynn and Hohan. Auum trotted to the gathered and nervous-looking Il-Aryn.

'None of you will fall,' said Auum when he had their attention, 'because the TaiGethen will not let you. Follow your leader. Use the same hand- and footholds they do. Be afraid because that will make you careful. Stretch your bodies when you must and grip hard; jam your feet into those cracks hard. Know you can do this. You are all fit and strong because that is the way Takaar made you.

'If you are struggling, cry out and we will help. The Julatsan elves will be around you. Have faith in Yniss, faith in yourselves and faith in all of us. I believe in you, or you wouldn't be here now. Let's go. Ulysan will assign you to your teams of TaiGethen.'

Auum watched them go and prayed to Yniss that none of them slipped. And so the climb began. Marack and Merke moved smoothly up the first thirty feet or so to a point where they could assess the next segment. The going was a little harder for Grafyrre and Merrat, who were climbing to either side of the first pair. Hohan and Thrynn were to Merrat's right and moving well enough.

There was now space on the wall and Ulysan cajoled the first Il-Aryn to start. He bit his lip and looked behind him, seeing Oryaal back at the lookout point. Up in the sky the Xeteskian mages couldn't fail to see what was happening.

'We need to move faster,' said Auum, coming to Ulysan's side.

Three TaiGethen were moving up after the first six Il-Aryn. The routes were close enough to be bridged by expert climbers, meaning each TaiGethen could shadow two Il-Aryn, but it still looked thin.

'Do you want another route?' asked Ulysan. 'Next six, on the climb. Follow your friends – you'll have arrows at your back in no time. Up you go.'

'No, just push them harder. We're spread thin enough as it is.'

'If they can get close enough for castings then we're helpless.'

'I know,' said Auum. He looked up. 'Marack, move on up. All of you, careful and quick.'

Auum's heart was beating hard. There was a human expression Stein had used once, something about a rock and a hard place. It made perfect sense now. He couldn't get the image from his head: of them all spread across the mountainside while the Xeteskians fired spell after spell at their backs, sending burning corpses down to disintegrate on impact. He shook his head. Someone was calling his name.

'They're advancing!' shouted Oryaal. 'You've got to climb faster.'

Auum looked back at the wall. Less than half his people were on it and none of them was out of spell range yet. They'd missed something, they must have done . . .

'Stein!' yelled Auum, hearing the name rattle off the mountainside. 'Stein!'

Stein heard his name called and flew back down from his vantage point on a small ledge where Tilman sat a few hundred feet above Hohan. Elves were swarming up the rock face but so many were still on the ground waiting to start the climb. He could see the Xeteskians running up the last shallow slopes before the mountain proper.

For a while Stein couldn't see Auum. In his browns and dark greens and with his painted face, he was difficult to spot, but eventually he saw him waving and flew down to him.

'They're very close,' he said.

'We have to delay them, slow them somehow,' said Auum. 'We need an arc of wards, maybe two arcs if you have time, placed to keep them back out of casting range.'

'The spotters will see us doing it – there'll be no surprise.'

'I don't care; I just need them cautious. Dead is a bonus.'

'Got it,' said Stein.

He flashed back up into the sky, cursing himself for not thinking of this before. He moved fast among his adepts, calling them to him and leading them back to the ground, where he ordered the placing of wards – alarms, fire and smoke, anything quick but hard to divine placed in an arc two hundred or so yards distant from the wall and its increasingly desperate climbers.

All the while he had half an eye on where Auum stood with another TaiGethen watching the humans advance. As soon as the mages had finished one casting, Stein had them move forward ten paces and lay another. He'd love to have laid three arcs but time was pressing and their stamina finite. They'd need all their strength for flight.

Halfway through the second arc, Auum and the other ducked as arrows flicked off rocks nearby to scatter and skip across the stone.

'Keep your heads down and finish your castings!' called Stein. 'Back in the air when you're done.'

Stein knelt on the ground and invested the space before him with a wall of flame, small in stature but effective enough. He set the modulating shape half in and half out of the stone, seeing the flashes of white amid the yellow of the spikes and sphere. Not perfect, but it would last more than long enough before it dissipated naturally.

Calling wings to his back, he rose into the sky, waving at a nearby Xeteskian spotter mage being prevented from disrupting their castings by the threat of three TaiGethen patrolling the casters, jaqruis in hands.

'Should keep you busy,' called Stein.

'You're all dead, Julatsan. Either on the walls or up in the cold. Where on earth do you think you're going?'

'What is it to you, traitor? You know the Wytch Lords normally incinerate those with whom they reach agreements. I'll be able to hear your screams from the top of the mountain.'

A quick glance down showed him Auum and . . . Oryaal, that was it, gathered in the arms of two mages each and carried over the arcs of wards before being dropped and haring back towards the rock wall. More than two thirds were now on the climb. He rose a little higher and saw the trail-finders making good progress, but their charges, unsurprisingly, were far slower.

His mages were beginning to gather near the slowest, helping them find their holds and urging them to greater effort. None had slipped so far but it was surely only a matter of time. On the ground Auum was waving more Il-Aryn on to the wall interspersed with Tai-Gethen, forcing them into ever closer formation. They made a broad target.

Stein swung about. The Xeteskians were on the approach to the mountain. They had slowed just as Auum had hoped and their spotter mages were hovering above the arcs of wards. He calculated how long it would take them to identify and mark each ward, then find a path through the trigger points, and for a blissful moment he thought that they might escape unmolested.

But the enemy were not done. They had upwards of eighty mages at their disposal, and while half at least fell to divining and marking wards, the rest took wing and flew for the wall. Stein swore and filled his lungs.

'Incoming!' he roared. 'Defend the wall! Here they come.'

Stein flitted up, yelling his message again. His mages began to turn and the enemy were on them, targeting those highest up the rock face. The air was full of wings and men. Elven mages screeched and attacked, their native ferocity lending them strength.

Stein plunged on a Xeteskian mage diving to pluck an Il-Aryn from the wall. He feathered his wings against his body and careered down, crashing into the mage's legs just as he laid a hand on the Il-Aryn's shoulder. The Xeteskian spun away from the wall but he'd snagged the adept's clothes, and the unfortunate elf scrabbled futilely for grip before dropping screaming to the ground seventy feet down.

Stein roared his frustration and pounced on the struggling mage again, feet first into the centre of his back. The Xeteskian's wings, already guttering, flickered and died. He fell close to his victim. Stein turned away and looked for another target. The mountainside echoed with cries and warnings, screams and pleading.

TaiGethen climbers were getting as close to their charges as they could and hung out at extraordinary angles, blade in hand, fighting to keep the enemy back. He spotted a figure climbing hard on the periphery, moving as if he was climbing a ladder, so swiftly did he ascend: Auum. And the one behind him had to be Ulysan.

Stein saw one of his mages spiralling up in a perverse embrace with a Xeteskian. Each looked for the punch that would break the other's concentration. The elf threw back her head and plunged her bared teeth into the neck of the human. Blood spurted out, the man shrieked and tried to drag her head off him. She raked her fingers down his face and through his eyes and he dropped, still shrieking, from the sky. The elf spat out a mouthful of flesh, exulted and searched for another target.

Stein heard a flurry behind him and shot up sharply. A Xeteskian mage grabbed for him, missing him by a hair, and carried on, aiming for the wall, which was dotted with the colours of man and elf, like some frenzied flocking of birds. Stein flew a tight spiral down, chasing him in as the mage flew straight at a TaiGethen fencing off another attacker and leaving her flank undefended.

'Your right! Incoming,' called Stein, flying in harder, knowing he couldn't get there in time.

The TaiGethen kicked out at her first target, forcing him to back away hard on wings that flickered and steadied. Belatedly she sensed the threat and began to turn. The mage surged in, his hands out-stretched. A shape tight to the rock face flashed past Stein and dropped onto the mage. There was a flash of steel and the mage's wings vanished.

The human dropped and the TaiGethen used his corpse to push himself back against the wall. He scrabbled for purchase, seeking a handhold, but there was none. Stein flew down hard and flattened him against the wall, arresting his descent as much as he could. The elf found a handhold and gripped it hard with his fingertips.

'You hadn't thought that last part through, had you?' said Stein.

'No,' admitted Auum. 'Though I don't think the fall would have actually killed me. You can let go now, I'm safe.'

Stein boomed a laugh and shot back up into the sky, seeking his next target. It presented itself immediately. Six Xeteskians flying in a tight formation blew through a line of Julatsans, sending one down wingless and the others to spiral away while they fought to maintain their castings. They rushed the wall, colliding with Il-Aryn and TaiGethen alike, dislodging three or four.

Stein called any to him that could hear him and flew in hard behind them. The enemy pushed off from the wall and turned for another attack. Il-Aryn were screaming, one hung from the hand of a TaiGethen warrior herself hanging from a precarious fingerhold. They were more than eighty feet from the ground and the Il-Aryn was crying for aid fit to burst his lungs.

Stein stormed in, seeing another two Julatsan elves on the way. The Xeteskians barrelled in. Stein got between them and the helpless climbers. He kicked out and flailed his fists, trying to connect with anything and finding precious little there. His momentum took him past so he stood on the air, angled his wings acutely and turned back in.

The two elves arrowed in feet first, driving three of the enemy back. Stein got among the others, a fist connecting satisfyingly with a jaw. He took a blow to his side and twisted over, the sick feeling of his wings passing through another's casting crossing his mind.

Then arms were about him, clogging his wings with a stream of mana. Stein felt his casting begin to fail. He kicked back, attempted to get his own counter-stream going and writhed in the grip of his enemy, trying to turn. From the left, towards the wall, he heard a mourning sound.

The mage's grip relaxed and Stein pushed away and turned, his wings strengthening. The Xeteskian was pawing at a jaqrui jutting from the back of his head. He whimpered and then plunged to the ground. Stain looked to the wall. Auum was leaning out from a crack into which his hand was jammed.

Stein nodded and headed up. He could hear Auum shouting, his orders travelling up and down the wall.

'Get them moving. We're out of time.'

Stein turned yet again and saw he was right. The Xeteskian mages had all but finished their work on the ground. The enemy were peeling away from the fight in the air, heading out to prepare on the ground. He spun one more time, seeing the Il-Aryn begin to move, but it was horribly slow. Half of them were barely twenty feet from the ground and had no hope of getting high enough.

But he could save them, some of them anyway.

Chapter 25

At one time every human mage practised a form of the One magic. But by the time Septern died, he was already the last of them. That just left the Il-Aryn, and their numbers were never huge.

Kerela, Julatsan Mage Council

Takaar could sense it but he could not divine any way to access it, though he was convinced he was standing on the doorway. He had sensed these sorts of energies before, three thousand and more years ago on Hausolis when he had triggered the gateway to Calaius. It had been a mystery to him then and it remained frustratingly so now.

Down there, because it felt like 'down', was a small room in a wholly different dimension to Balaia. Enormous energy swirled and played within its tight boundaries, the merest tendrils of which leaked up through the doorway. Takaar had traced its outlines in the dust and could sense residual human magical force lingering there. They had come close, the Julatsans, far closer than the Xeteskians, who had been looking in entirely the wrong place.

'If only I had known you.' Takaar knelt on the opening and let his tears fall in the dust. 'Such dreams we could have shared. We were only separated by a stretch of water yet had no knowledge of one another. The two greatest minds in magic ignorant of the greatest gift either of them could possess – each other.'

It's good to see your opinion of yourself hasn't suffered at all even though every one of your followers has deserted you.

'It is a tragedy that has blighted the history of man and elf,' said Takaar, stroking the hidden doorway and smearing his tears across the dust. 'Together, we could have done such great things.'

Made something even more devastating than Dawnthief, you mean?

'Like the rest of them, you don't understand. A meeting of such minds could have solved so many problems, proved the existence of our gods, cured disease, brought comfort to every soul living here and on Calaius.'

Such modest ambitions.

'Stop your mewling complaints!' thundered Takaar. He stood and clutched at his head. His blood roared around his skull. 'Get out of me! What use have I for you? Seeking to bring me down all the time, criticising even my dreams. You are hated, despised. Get out! I want nothing more to do with you.'

But I am you.

'NO! Without you I could soar. Live free of pain and doubt. I could realise my dreams, surpass them and become the elf I was destined to be. An elf whose name is revered throughout history, whose statue stands in every temple and city. A god among elves, not merely walking with them, as one of them. And you are holding me back.'

Yet it is you, O god of elves, who cannot open a mere door.

Takaar dropped back to the ground and wept, his head in his hands and all his failures crushing his spirit. And this was surely the greatest of them all. Just a *door*, and he couldn't open it. Like a child trying for a latch beyond reach he could only stare in frustration. But a child would grow taller and the task be rendered simple, whereas this would remain impenetrable without the man who had locked it.

'There has to be a way.'

He dug at the ground with his fingers and he could see in his mind the shovels that had been used in this place, fruitlessly digging ever deeper. He laughed at their pathetic attempts and their lack of basic understanding. They could dig for miles but the door would not be revealed because it existed elsewhere. Nothing would open it.

'And you died without revealing your secrets. Took them with you because the world was not worthy of them. I would have held them for you. And I have secrets of my own that I would have shared with you because only you would understand them.'

You're so sure he died?

The tone was so gentle it made Takaar start. He frowned, having to think for a moment.

'Surely there can be no doubt of that? He either perished down there or in the inferno that took this place. And with him went so much *spirit*.'

So what will you do?

'What is there to do?'

Septern saved the world when he died. He took the secrets of Dawnthief with him, and they will never be recovered.

'But look at what was lost! All that he could have given to the world went with him.'

He made a judgement and he was proved right. We are not ready for the power that Dawnthief represents. Wars are being fought over it, even though none possess it.

'It should have brought peace,' said Takaar, weeping again, but this time he felt only sadness, not frustration. 'Why won't they understand?'

Men only see the weapon, not the knowledge that built it.

'They will never stop looking for it, will they?'

And they will never be ready to possess it.

Takaar raised his head. The day was chill but fresh and the sun was burning away thin cloud. He stood up and walked about the ruins of the Manse, following the latent energies, visualising the building as it would once have been, pulsing with life, vibrant with learning. Just like Herendeneth. The desire to return there was so strong, but it was here that the future would be decided, not in the classrooms he had built.

You want to be remembered?

'Revered not reviled. There is no path to the former.'

Self-pity has weakened you so much?

'I don't understand.'

You can stop this war. You can turn it; you can weaken the Wytch Lords.

'Still trying to get me to kill myself?'

I have never stopped, well maybe once or twice I desired life over your death, but that isn't the point. I know the likely cost, but it is for you to decide. Scratch in the mud here or become the elf you say you want to be in life or death.

'But all my knowledge, all I have learned but not yet passed on . . .'

Septern made his choice. You will have to make yours.

'Get them up, get them up!' shouted Stein. 'Mages to me! Faster! Move like bloody lightning.'

Every moment he expected the dull impact, the flash of heat or ice and the end of his life in a brief screaming agony, even though he knew the enemy were not quite ready to cast yet.

'Pair off!' he called. 'Lowest first, never mind the TaiGethen. Parilas, with me.'

Stein and Parilas swooped down to the lowest and slowest Il-Aryn.

'We're picking you off one by one. Be ready, don't struggle and don't tense up. We won't drop you, I promise.'

The pair hovered behind an Il-Aryn, picked her off by her wrists and climbed hard, the wall rushing by in front of them. Up they climbed to the point where the incline became far shallower and the elves could sit above any casting, safe until they set off again.

They dropped the mage a few feet to the bare rock and flew back down, passing more mage pairs flying rescue missions. He saw the TaiGethen urging the highest climbers to greater efforts, practically pushing some of them up and out of range. Out on the approach the wards had all been divined and enough made safe. The Xeteskians were streaming through a single point and fanning out immediately they were inside the arcs.

'One more trip!' he called to Parilas.

The elven mage nodded his head and they powered down again. The Xeteskians were all but ready now; Stein could feel mana streams intensifying as they were drawn into multiple constructs. The remaining few Il-Aryn were scrambling up in panic now and arrows were starting to flick off the mountain.

Stein and Parilas reached their target and hauled him unceremoniously off the wall, surging up at prodigious speed. He was dropped safely next to his people. Others had made the entire climb and with them came most of the TaiGethen.

'We need to try one more,' said Parilas.

'One more,' agreed Stein.

They plunged down the wall. Mage pairs were still diving below them, grabbing Il-Aryn and darting back up into the sky. At a shout from the Xeteskian commander, the archers fell back. Moments later, the castings arced out.

Stein and Parilas drove their wings forward hard, braking their descents. Orbs of fire, at least thirty of them, crashed into the wall about forty feet up, each one amplifying the power of the last. A great wave of flame washed up the side of the mountain. It travelled at horrific speed, consuming a mage pair and their Il-Aryn passenger, turning them to ash in its wake. More were on the wall and would be taken.

Up it rolled, a hundred feet, two hundred feet, three—

'Tilman,' breathed Stein, then he shouted. 'Tilman!'

Stein broke from Parilas and powered towards the ledge where he had left the boy thinking he was safe. But the fire wave would wash over his perch and he was helpless to move. Stein shot across the mountain, the heat travelling above the wave making everything hazy in front of him. It threatened to choke the air from him and vaporise the wings at his back, but he would not turn from his promise to keep the boy safe.

Stein was forced higher as the wave ascended. He looked down towards the ledge and saw it engulfed in fire just before the casting lost its force and began to fall back. He screamed his sorrow and anger, and his guilt rose in his throat, erupting as anguished cries.

Stein braked, staring at the ledge, unable to deny the image of poor Tilman wailing for help while his death roared up to steal him from the mountain. He rose slowly, but then he saw a figure moving carefully up the wall, crabbing left to where the incline began to ease.

He flew in to see if he could help, and as he closed in, the warmth flooded back into his heart. There was Auum, climbing with all the confidence of a TaiGethen born to the trees and with the strength and agility a man could only achieve in his dreams. And on his back, arms around his neck and with that one boot still in his hand, was Tilman.

Stein flew in close, his relief momentarily robbing him of words. Tilman noticed him and turned his head.

'It was getting a little warm waiting for you so I hitched a ride with Auum.'

'A wise choice,' said Stein. 'Thank you, Auum.'

'I didn't spend all that time saving his life on the ground just to let them cook him on the ledge,' said Auum a little breathlessly. 'How did we do?'

'We couldn't save everyone,' said Stein. 'I'm sorry.'

'Why didn't we fly them up earlier?' asked Tilman.

'Because the Xeteskian fliers would have picked us off. We'd have lost twice the number,' said Stein.

Auum nodded. 'Come on. Let's get to level ground and see who we've got left.'

The truth was that it could have been much worse. For all Stein's guilt at not saving everyone, had he not risked his life and asked his fliers to do the same, the fifty Il-Aryn who were safe and well on the gentle slope leading to the ridge would have numbered thirty or less. They'd lost fourteen mages along with three Julatsan elves. It was a cause for sadness, for prayer and lamentation but, given their parlous position, not a disaster.

Auum sat with Ulysan and Grafyrre while others of the TaiGethen moved among the Il-Aryn, offering congratulations and seeing they were comfortable enough on their perch. They had their backs to the ridge and were looking out over Balaia.

'How high up are we?' asked Ulysan

'About nine hundred feet,' said Auum. 'We've barely scratched this mountain.'

'Feels colder already, doesn't it?' said Grafyrre.

He was right. There was a wind blowing from the west, and it brought with it the chill air of the mountain peaks and the snow and ice Stein had promised them. It was a gusting breeze, picking at hair and clothing. Auum was not looking forward to walking into its teeth.

'Do you think it'll look any better the higher up we go?' asked Ulysan. 'I mean, look at it; it's so empty.'

Auum smiled. There was so much open ground, which undulated pleasantly enough and was all the shades of green and brown you could wish for, but it was so *plain*. There were trees, there was even a sizeable forest dead ahead, though in comparison to the glory of Calaius perhaps three drops in the sea. But it was a forest none-theless.

But what dominated Auum's attention way beyond the far shores of Triverne Lake were four great smudges on the land, one of which partly obscured the forest they could see.

'I wonder if those are—' he began.

'They are,' said Stein wandering up behind them. 'Those are our beloved colleges, wreathed in the fog of human existence. From left to right: Julatsa, Dordover, Lystern, Xetesk, the latter conveniently the closest to Understone Pass.'

'How far is Xetesk from the pass?' asked Grafyrre.

'About a day's ride. It's thirty-five or forty miles. Just a morning trot for the TaiGethen. Whoa! What the hell do they want?'

A trio of Xeteskian mages had appeared above the rock wall and were flying towards them at a gentle pace, high enough to avoid jaqrui and spell. Coming closer, they waved a white piece of cloth. Stein looked at Auum.

'What do you think?'

'Don't ask him,' said Ulysan. 'He beheaded the last man who offered him a parley.'

'The beheading was some time after the parley and he was trying to kill me,' said Auum.

'Just saying,' said Ulysan.

'So . . . ?' said Stein.

'They can talk to you if they want,' said Auum. 'I have nothing to say to those bastards. Just remind them I'm faster than any casting they might think to unleash. Do you want to talk to them?'

Stein shrugged. 'A little taunting never hurts.'

Stein walked a little downslope, waiting some forty yards from the edge of the wall for the Xeteskians to land. The three men were all young and strong, landing and walking with an arrogant air. Skullcaps were tight about their heads, and their cloaks were identically trimmed black with silver stitching – junior mages.

'Nice place you've got here,' said the central one, walking slightly ahead of the others.

'What do you want?' asked Stein. 'I have no time for chat.'

'We've come to offer you custody and safe passage to Xetesk, where you will be treated with respect until the conflict is resolved.'

Stein glanced behind him. Auum, Ulysan and Grafyrre were all standing and much of the group was bunched up behind them, wanting to hear.

'I am long since past believing the words of any representative of Xetesk. I'm sorry you've wasted your time.'

'You will all die up here,' said the second of them, his tone sneering.

'We take a different view, but thank you for your concern. Is there anything else?'

'Your water is finite, your food too and your cover non-existent. Unless you're planning to build houses up here and plant crops, we will outlast you, and our offer will not stand when you come crawling back down the wall,' said the first.

'The place has lovely views, don't you think?' said Stein. 'From here we'll be able to see the Wesman hordes swarm about your college when the Wytch Lords betray your perverse alliance. It is you who have little time, if you ask me. We'll take our chances here.'

'You must agree to our terms,' said the third. 'It is your only chance to live.'

'Ah, of course, you were told to leave none of us alive, weren't you? No one to tell the tale of your betrayal. That bird has flown, my friends, but don't worry. Julatsa has no intention of attacking you. We will bide our time until the war is done and the reckoning starts.'

'We will win the war,' said the first.

'Well, we'll see, won't we? Now let me be clear: we are not going to surrender to you.'

'Then starve on your mountainside,' said the first.

All three took wing and flew away, and Stein roared with laughter. By the time he'd walked back to Auum, he had the ear of every elf.

'They think we are staying here until they go,' he said. 'They think we're going to try and wait them out. Oh, they are so predictable.'

'Will they attack again?' asked Grafyrre.

'Not up here,' said Stein. 'They're blustering now. They'll watch us go, and our departure will light a lantern in the dim recesses of their minds, but by the time they realise what we're doing it will already be too late.'

'That reminds me, Ulysan,' said Auum. 'Did Ephemere contact the ships?'

'She did, and Takaar isn't there, at least, not yet.'

Stein saw Auum frown.

'It isn't that far, not for running elves. Unless he's dead, he has to have made it, unless . . . Stein, draw me a line from Julatsa to Korina and tell me what you pass close to on the way.'

Stein knew what he was talking about, what Takaar desired.

'The Septern Manse is the most notable landmark.'

Auum chuckled. 'That mad old bastard, I never really doubted he'd persuade Gilderon to make a detour. I wonder what havoc he's wreaked there, him and his Senserii.'

'But is he still there now, do you think?' mused Ulysan.

'One thing I promise you,' said Auum, 'he won't be heading for the ships.'

'And probably won't be rushing to our aid either,' said Ulysan.

Auum shrugged. 'We've got this far.'

'So we have,' said Stein. 'And now it's time to get going. It's a long slow walk to the next resting place, and we don't want to be on that ridge in the dark.'

'Doesn't bother us,' said Ulysan.

Stein rolled his eyes.

'All right then, *I* don't want to be on the ridge in the dark. Come on, I'm bored with the view anyway.'

Chapter 26

You have experienced nothing until you have experienced bone-aching cold.

Auum, Arch of the TaiGethen

All of their good humour had been eroded to nothing by early afternoon. Stopping for food had been even more unpleasant than continuing to walk, though progress had become so slow they barely seemed to be moving forward at all. It was a single line of misery, picked at by increasingly strong winds and showered by wind-blown ice on the whim of whatever god ruled these mountains.

In all his thousands of years Auum had never felt himself so unprepared for anything. And they had begun in such high spirits, despite the losses on the climb and those killed by magic the previous day. The incline was easy, the ridge was narrow but not so uneven as to present a real risk for the careful walker, and the sun had broken through the clouds to provide some warmth despite the gusting wind.

Auum had chatted to Stein at the head of the line, the human pointing out the names of peaks they could see piercing the sky to the north and south. They were to be in the mountains for two days, more if they were unlucky in the paths they chose, but Auum had not been unhappy at the prospect. The scale of the range was staggering and the beauty matched it. There were white-capped peaks, ice slopes, vertiginous cliffs and chasms that surely led straight to the bowels of the earth. It was breathtaking.

It was not until shortly before midday that Auum felt the first stirring of unease. The clouds had covered the sun and the temperature had fallen sharply. With the clouds had come an icy wind straight out of the west and into their faces, driving the temperature down still further. They had been showered in snow from the high peaks ahead before a chill rain had soaked them to shivers.

The stop for food just after midday had been a miserable affair.

Mages spaced throughout the line had melted snow in pans for a hot drink and they had boiled horsemeat to make a thoroughly un-appetising meal. The meat was tough and tasted like Xeteskian revenge for their escape.

Auum had moved up and down the line trying to keep their spirits up, but it was difficult to do when, despite the cloak about his body and the shirt tied across his mouth and nose, he was absolutely freezing. He rubbed his hands together, not daring to put them in his pockets in case of a fall, and with every step he stamped his feet to try and keep the circulation going. His boots were made for the rainforest and, durable as they were, they were not built for warmth.

Their clothing was woefully inadequate. Worse, their bodies had adapted over generations to the heat, humidity and occasional gentle chill of the rainforest and were unable to cope with the cutting cold. Auum found it hard to draw a full breath and was not alone in feeling a growing sense of anxiety that the next time he inhaled, he might get nothing.

The Julatsan elves were able to generate some heat, which they could share with embraces that were all too short, but they had to maintain their stamina for walking, heating water and food and to fly if they must.

The further they climbed, the harsher the wind became. The white of snow and ice hurt their eyes; the savage cold numbed their faces and froze their hands and feet, and when it became a gusting gale, most of them were forced to move on all fours, their already aching hands having to clutch at stunningly cold rock through the snow.

Auum was doggedly staying upright, and Stein, who had demon-strated remarkable resistance to the cold, was right behind him. Ulysan, who was the fittest of them all, carried Tilman on his back and had to be in trouble physically. He only ever smiled when Auum looked down the line at him. Yniss bless him, thought Auum, the moment he ceases to smile we are all in desperate straits.

'How far to the next face?' shouted Auum, turning his head so his words were not whipped away by the wind.

Stein squinted ahead and his frown deepened. He could not hide his concern and it was only having Auum ahead of him which stopped him setting a faster pace. Night would fall quickly here, and they could not afford to be exposed when it did, or most of them would not survive until dawn.

'At this pace, I don't know. I can't send fliers up, it's too windy and the updraughts here are horrible to negotiate.'

'Have you been up here before?' asked Auum.

'Often,' said Stein. 'I've walked this ridge before, but it never seemed so long and I always chose a fine day in the middle of summer when the snow is a mere memory at this height.'

'What is there at the end of the ridge?'

'Shelter of a sort. There's an overhang and a rock shelf facing east so we can be out of the worst of the wind. Going to have to huddle close together tonight.'

'Why didn't you tell me it would be like this?'

'I did, Auum. Didn't change anything, though, did it?'

Auum shook his head. 'And what happens after that? Where do we go next?'

Stein had the good grace to look a little sheepish as he replied. 'I've never gone any further. The path to Wesman territory has never appealed.'

'But your fliers . . .' said Auum, feeling suddenly vulnerable and utterly responsible for those he had talked into coming up here.

'They haven't been able to scout routes because of the wind. We need it to drop.'

Auum felt a different sort of chill. 'You're saying there may not be a way on and down?'

'That's the way of the Blackthornes, and it's a good job too or the Wesmen could march armies over them.'

'And what if we can't find a route?'

Stein shrugged. 'Then we will have to turn back.'

Auum put his face to the wind once again and pushed on a little bit faster.

'That is not going to happen,' he muttered, then he roared at the blank face of the mountains ahead of him. 'Do you hear me? You will not beat me! As Yniss is my witness and my god, you will not stand in my way!'

The mountains said nothing but the wind blew harder, throwing his words back in his face, taunting him with the promise of more ice. Auum flexed his hands and pressed them into his armpits. It made no difference. He wondered if he'd ever be able to feel them again.

*

They had run far and fast, across hill and through valley past farm-stead and hamlet by night and by day only to find this. Gilderon knelt in the midst of the ash and wept for the fallen while his Senserii spread through the carnage, trying to understand what had happened and how many had perished.

That all the dead here were elven was not in doubt. The weapons and buckles that had survived the inferno were unmistakable. Here and there some bones remained, but of the flesh and blood there was nothing at all. There were also bolts from cartwheels and part of one axle too.

'This can't be all of them,' he whispered. 'Yniss forgive me but I must pray that Auum at least has survived.'

'Gilderon.'

'Helodian,' said Gilderon, looking up. 'Speak.'

'This was not their last stand. We found tracks leading into the foothills and Teralion has found bodies laid out for reclamation. The tracks head on towards the mountains. Cordolan is following them. It is clear a good number survived, though the ground makes it impossible to count how many.'

Gilderon felt a measure of relief. 'There's something else?'

'Yes, there are cart and horse tracks heading away from here back towards Julatsa. Four horses, two pulling the cart, which was well laden, hopefully with survivors. The age of the tracks means we only just missed them. I put us less than a day behind any survivors.'

Gilderon saw a movement out of the corner of his eye and stood, gazing towards nearby woodlands. A shape shot out of them, soaring high into the sky. Another followed. More figures moved out on foot.

'We've been seen,' he said. 'Senserii, at the ready.'

'Humans,' said Helodian. 'Murderers. Tracks lead to and from the wood and into the foothills. They did this.'

'They are fighting a war much like those at the Manse, assuming they are of the same college. What was its name?'

'Xetesk,' said Helodian.

The mages on wings came closer, hovering about twenty feet in the air and the same distance away. One said something Gilderon couldn't understand though its tone suggested it was a question. Gilderon was silent and the mage repeated the question, this time in a more strident tone.

Gilderon pointed at him. 'Xetesk?' he asked.

The mage nodded. Gilderon hefted his staff and threw it in one

smooth motion. The weapon flew straight, its blade catching a glint
of sunlight before it struck the mage's chest and he fell to the ground
with a gasp. The other mage shot skywards and backwards shouting,
presumably, for help.

Gilderon ran to the fallen mage, who was lying on his back. The
ikari had fallen from his body. Gilderon picked it up. He spoke
knowing the human couldn't understand him.

'You are guilty before the eyes of Shorth for the elves you killed
here. Shorth is a god of great mercy, but not for you. I send you to
him and your pleadings will not avail you.'

Gilderon jabbed his ikari blade into the mage's eye, piercing his
brain and killing him instantly. He pulled it clear and wiped the gore
on the mage's clothing. Looking up, he saw the humans massing and
coming at them hard.

'We can't take them all,' he said. 'Where is Cordolan?'

Helodian pointed at a figure sprinting down the side of a low hill,
heading towards them on a wide angle to avoid the human advance.
Gilderon nodded.

'Good. Let's lose them. Senserii, we will run till dusk.'

And at dusk, hidden in a small copse, they chose their path and
reaffirmed their faith and loyalty. Cordolan spoke first.

'The survivors went up the walls. Some didn't make it. There are
bodies, burned and broken, abandoned to rot at the base of the
mountain. But some must have escaped or why are the humans here
still?'

Gilderon nodded. 'Helodian, you are ill at ease. Speak.'

'What we saw today . . . the ash and the strength of the human
forces still at the site . . . we can't defeat that sort of force alone. We
don't know how many of Auum's people have survived and we can't
follow them over the mountain. We are many things but we are not
climbers.'

Gilderon nodded. 'I understand. And are we all feeling the same
unease, as if our path has been muddied and we must seek a new one
if we are to help in this fight?'

Every mouth issued words of assent.

'Then I can offer you comfort,' said Gilderon. 'We need answers,
so it is the cart and horses we have to find. We'll pick up their tracks
in the morning, though I assume they are returning to Julatsa. Then
we'll know how many are still travelling in the mountains, and
finally we must make obeisance to our master and seek forgiveness

for our lack of loyalty and attention. We deserted him and we must make recompense for our error.'

Their faces brightened and he smiled, pleased they all wanted what he had desired ever since they had left Takaar.

The Senserii slept and Gilderon kept watch. The words were easy but the task was not. Easy to say they would seek Takaar's forgiveness. But he was not as he had once been, and his reaction, when they returned, might not be one they would survive. Still, they had to try. They needed him and he needed them. Gilderon prayed he did, anyway.

They made it to the overhang with night almost full, and it was clear the weather would kill some during the night. It had closed in yet further and the snow fell in a thick mass of flakes that clung to the clothes and skin, blown on a mourning, howling wind that carried the voice of their deaths.

Hands were frozen, cut and blistered, boots were torn, and inside feet were ice and ankles swollen. Their faces, despite the coverings, were raw with the constant attrition of ice and wind, and their eyes were pained by the bright white, the only part of them wanting the blessed dark of night.

Auum tried as best he could to get the weakest of them into the centre of the group and pack others in around them to give them some warmth, but the cold seeped up through the stone on which they sat and the wind blew more snow around the sides of the wall at their backs.

They had eaten a joyless meal, a rough stew of horsemeat and some roots gathered on the way past the lake a couple of days before. For some eating was an ordeal in itself, and they had to be spoon-fed so they wouldn't spill it on their already sodden, freezing clothes.

Auum tried to ignore the fact that he was shivering so hard he couldn't sit down. He could barely open his mouth to talk and had taken only a few swallows of the stew, seeing others needing more sustenance than he did. It was probably an error with the cold penetrating through to his bones and on into his heart and soul. Stein had told them it would be cold, but this was a level of pain beyond anything he could have conceived.

'Something to tell your children about,' said Ulysan.

He was still managing to smile despite the obvious discomfort of carrying Tilman for the day. He looked utterly spent but still refused to sit down and had checked on everyone else, all one hundred and twenty of them, exactly as both Auum and Stein had.

'I'll have to write it down before I freeze to death,' said Auum, a new shiver racking his body so hard it made him grunt. 'Trouble is, my fingers are frozen and I couldn't hold a quill.'

'Nor do we have bark or parchment, but it was a sound plan other than that.'

Auum cast his eyes over his people. Julatsan elves were moving among the tight-packed bodies, doing what they could with warmth and healing, but it was like using a fruit knife to fell a banyan. He and Ulysan were standing at the outer edge, a few yards from a sheer drop into a chasm. Auum wondered how many bodies they might be rolling into it come morning. Perhaps there would be none left to chant the lamentations.

Auum felt a keen anger bite and it warmed his soul a little. He let it grow, take form and substance in his mind, and he realised where his anger stemmed from. He turned to the quiet huddled group, most of whom had their faces buried in their arms and their knees dragged right up, trying to eke out a modicum of comfort.

'This cannot be it,' he said loudly enough to cut across the whine of the wind. 'This cannot be all we can do. It is going to get colder and colder as the night deepens, and how many of you, with your nerveless hands and your soaking clothes, think you are going to survive? I'm not certain I will.

'The TaiGethen cannot fight this. We cannot make fires from nothing. So what has your wonderful magic got to offer, my Il-Aryn and Julatsan friends? Conjure me a log and some kindling. Conjure me a timber shelter. Do *something*.'

Stein stood. His lips were swollen and his face was raw and red.

'I understand your frustration, but we are few and we cannot expend all of our strength. I could have my mages warm the stone, but the cold runs deep and the warmth will be stolen before it can be of use because we are so exposed here. We have to conserve our energy.'

'For what? If we don't do something, most of us will not be alive to benefit from your precious stamina come dawn.' Auum stared at the faces of TaiGethen and Il-Aryn around him and saw either determination or surrender. He picked out Rith. 'And you, what can you do? Takaar's teaching of seven hundred years cannot be so feeble that you cannot warm yourselves, surely?'

'We can't make heat out of ice,' said Rith. 'It doesn't work that way. We don't channel mana like a Julatsan, we use the energies around us to forge what we can. We adapt what we have; we cannot create something from nothing. I'm sorry.'

'*Sorry?*' Auum spat out the word. 'Is that it? Just as on the walls of Julatsa when the pressure was on and you found you could do nothing? Takaar's precious Il-Aryn, the new power among the elves . . . Yniss save us and Ix abandon you, but on this evidence I never had anything to worry about, did I?'

Rith could not hold his stare. He saw her shudder violently as she dropped her head, and he wasn't sure if it was the cold or the onset of tears. Auum spread his arms.

'We have suffered to bring you here. TaiGethen saved you by the lake, we saved you on the wall and we kept you alive to get here. Now it is your turn. Don't you dare look away from me, Rith.'

Her gaze returned and there was fire in it at least.

'We did not ask for this! We did not want war and we did not want to freeze to death on a mountainside, but you forced us here, gave us no choice but to go with you. You brought us here and now we are spent and we have no hope.'

'None of us wanted war,' snapped Auum. 'But it is what we have. Either here and now, or in our lands in the days to come. I choose to fight here and I will die here if I must, but it will be by sword thrust or black fire, not because of a lack of elven spirit.'

Rith shrugged her shoulders, the shudders in her body so violent they made the gesture painful. 'We cannot draw heat from ice. I am sorry.'

'I do not believe you. I refuse to believe you! I have seen Takaar sink a ship. I have seen you create barriers that beat off Wytch Lord magic, and only yesterday you made the air sharp enough to behead our enemies travelling at a gallop. And you are telling me you cannot create something to keep the damn snow off my back?'

Rith's mouth fell open and she looked at him as if he were a fresh warm morning.

'We've been thinking about this all wrong,' she said. 'Give me a moment. Il-Aryn, gather round, I have an idea.'

Rith began to speak and Auum turned away, uninterested in the mechanics of whatever she thought she might do as long as she did it quickly. He felt a nudge at his elbow and Stein was standing there. He had a bowl in one hand and, as Auum watched, he played a flame from his palm beneath it until its contents steamed. He handed it over and produced a spoon from his cloak.

'Here. You didn't eat enough. Admirable but stupid. If you die all hope will be lost.'

'You don't feel pressure, do you, Auum?' said Ulysan.

Auum thought to refuse, but his stomach saw sense and he began to scoop the warm stew into his mouth, having trouble holding the spoon in his unresponsive fingers.

'I think,' he said, 'the quality of Ulysan's jokes has reached a point where all hope is already lost.'

'I wonder what they're doing,' said Ulysan.

'Saving all our lives, I trust,' said Auum.

'Is it that bad?' asked Ulysan.

'I know how I feel and I know how much I can take. It's night, and the temperature is falling like a stone down that chasm. If we cannot get warm, we're all going to die right here.' Auum stabbed a finger at Stein. 'And if that happens, don't you dare let anyone who can escape die too or I'll haunt you from Shorth's embrace.'

'To leave you would be to betray you.'

Auum gave Ulysan his empty bowl and pulled Stein into an embrace which the human found uncomfortable but which Auum would not let him break. Eventually, he released him, kissing his forehead.

Ulysan raised his eyebrows. 'Some honour,' he said.

'If all humans were like you, our races would have been friends for a thousand years. What a waste.' Auum stepped away and looked back to Rith. 'Now then, how are they getting on? I wonder. Even though I'm freezing and I consider you my brother, Stein, I won't embrace you again. Your clothes absolutely stink.'

Chapter 27

You never know what is lurking in the dark recesses of the flesh.
Sipharec, High Mage of Julatsa

Kerela was scared and she was tired but she knew there would be precious little sleep for her. Sipharec was dying and his passing would make her high mage, a position for which she suddenly felt herself entirely inadequate. She knew she would have the support of Harild and that meant a great deal, but her first task, should Sipharec pass during the night, would be to preside over a war with Xetesk and the Wytch Lords.

She shuddered as she entered her rooms. The great balcony doors had been left open and the curtains were blowing in the chill night air. It was somehow fitting, the cold matching her mood. Sipharec . . . who would have thought it?

Not a cancer, which is what he had assumed, but a failure of his heart and liver. As if they'd had enough and were shutting down. There was nothing magic could do but ease the pain. The poor man was so angry and bitter he would not see his job through that he had not left his rooms since he had fallen ill just a few days ago.

Kerela's mind was tumbling with anxiety so much that she failed to notice the figure sitting on the end of her bed until she had closed the doors and turned back into the room. She stifled a cry and placed a hand on her thudding heart, relaxing when she saw who it was.

'Most people make an appointment,' she said. 'How did you get in here? You're exiled.'

'No ward or wall can keep me from where I must be,' said Takaar. 'And I must be here.'

He was filthy from the trail, his hair unkempt and with dirt staining his clothes and face. He had a hollow look in his eyes as if he hadn't slept in days and a pinch to his cheeks told of a lack of food. But those eyes were alive with his madness barely in check, and Kerela was acutely aware of how dangerous he could be.

'Where have you been?' she asked.

He smiled, and his voice dropped to a whisper so quiet she had to lean in to hear him.

'I have been to the Septern Manse.'

The smile on his face was childlike. Kerela gasped and sat down on the bed next to him.

'What did you see? Tell me, were our team there?'

Takaar shook his head and Kerela sagged, though she had known in her heart that they'd been killed. Friends of hers, people beloved by the college, had been in that party – peaceful people, talented people.

'Only Xeteskians were there. And fighters with masks, strong and quick but dark of soul.'

'Protectors,' breathed Kerela. 'They sent Protectors. We never stood a chance.'

'There is no one there now.' Takaar smiled but there was no glory in his tone when he spoke his next words. 'Because I am a better mage than they and the Senserii are better fighters.'

Kerela knew she shouldn't but she hugged Takaar. He tensed and she let him go at once but couldn't keep the smile from her face.

'I shouldn't feel good that they are dead but I can't help it,' she said.

Takaar shrugged. 'They killed your people and you are an elf. Never be ashamed of your heritage.'

'Harild will be delighted. He's sent a force down there to take the Manse and make it ours.'

Takaar hadn't appeared to be listening but he frowned. 'Why?'

'So that when this is done, Julatsa can own Dawnthief.'

Takaar was distracted, squeezing his eyes shut and then opening them as wide as he could and staring around the room.

'You're wasting your time,' said Takaar. 'You should call them back. No one will ever secure Dawnthief.'

'That's some statement,' said Kerela, suppressing a laugh. 'How do you know?'

Takaar stared at her as if she was stupid.

'Because I am a better mage.'

'You're going to have to offer more than that if I'm to change our agreed defence tactics.'

'I know what you told me,' said Takaar after a pause. He looked to his right. 'She'll understand. Eventually, they all understand.'

Kerela felt a frisson of nerves. This was the first time she'd seen him engage with his other self, and it was deeply unsettling. She waited, not knowing what else to do and being reluctant to interrupt. She became acutely aware of her vulnerability. No one knew he was here and she was alone with him, the elf who had turned Drech's head to ash.

'Don't press me!' Takaar snapped. Kerela jumped and moved a little further away along the edge of the bed. Takaar turned a terribly fragile smile on her. 'I'm sorry, I startled you.'

'It's all right,' she said, her heart thundering in her chest.

'See what you've done,' hissed Takaar.

Kerela took in a long trembling breath. 'I don't think—'

Takaar's hand shot out and took hers. His grip was gentle though his fingers and palms were rough with dirt and scratches.

'You must hear this,' said Takaar. 'Before I . . . Anyway you must hear this. Dawnthief isn't at Septern Manse. It isn't anywhere in the Balaian dimension.'

'Dimension?' Kerela knew the history of the elves and Takaar's discovery on Hausolis, but the theory had always confused her and she had left its study to others in the college. 'You're sure?'

'Of course,' said Takaar dismissively. 'I can sense the place where it must be held, where the secrets are kept. I can even draw the doorway in the mud of the manse ruins, but I cannot open it.'

'How can you be sure that no one can just because you can't?'

It was a dangerous question, and Kerela regretted it the moment she asked, but Takaar merely favoured her with a patronising smile. He patted her hand and withdrew his to itch at his right forearm, which was already red and scraped from his scratching.

'It is closed against all those without his talents. I can read the energies even though I can't unpick them to work the lock. He understood all four of your magics, didn't he?'

'That's what he always claimed. His was a boundless ego.'

'A boundless talent,' said Takaar. 'Don't belittle what he knew.'

Kerela felt Takaar tense and she swallowed hard, feeling herself begin to shiver.

'I don't. But he was never shy of telling us how great he was.'

Takaar stared at her, his expression bleak. 'And you should have listened. Maybe then he would be alive, and I could speak with him and we could do the great things together.'

'I don't—'

Takaar stood and marched across the room to the fireplace, which needed more fuel before the embers cooled. He rubbed his hands across his face, but when he turned back the fury she feared was not evident and instead there was a broad smile on his face.

'He may not be dead!'

Kerela blinked. Everyone had seen the manse. No one could have survived the conflagration. Takaar rushed back across the room, and for a moment Kerela thought he was going to drag her into an embrace but he stopped short. His eyes were alive with possibilities and his hands were shaking as he gesticulated.

'Think! He has hidden the spell in a chamber placed in another dimension. Why would he not hide there himself when his enemies closed around him? He could open doors to other places. Who knows where he is now, laughing at your pathetic attempts to find his secrets. Ha! And until humans find another mage who understands the magics of all four colleges as he does, they'll never even open the door!'

Kerela felt exhausted all over again by Takaar's sudden energy, but she could not deny his excitement was contagious and what he was saying had a certain logic to it. But there was a major flaw in his hopes.

'There is no such person,' she said. 'There never will be. Not unless Septern left instructions somewhere, to act as a key.'

Takaar snorted. 'Why would he do that? He has taken such care to remove himself from those he thinks unworthy of his secrets, why would he leave a key on a hook for anyone to find?'

'It wouldn't be a key in that sense,' said Kerela.

Takaar rolled his eyes. 'I know. You don't understand. It is a challenge, and only the mage who can solve the problem is worthy of his secrets. And it will be an elf who does it because we have the time that humans do not.'

Takaar wandered back into the centre of the room, muttering to his other self. Kerela shouldn't have been so confident in his words but there seemed no doubt he was right. Truth be told, he almost always was. Kerela rose from the bed and moved slowly towards him, desiring to hear what he was saying.

'. . . could do it. Why not me? Is the study of human magic so different? I am an immortal and dare I say it, a genius . . . You don't agree? Well, that comes as no surprise, but I must start now. Here in the library. It's a new challenge.'

Kerela reached out a hand but snatched it back when he snapped his head round in her direction. His eyes looked straight through her. He sagged visibly and half fell into a chair, tears on his cheeks.

'There is always another task to perform and it must be me, mustn't it . . . ? You're right – only I can do this – but more than that, only then will I have the time, the *peace* to do my work here.'

Takaar stared up at Kerela and there was such sadness in his face that she almost burst into tears herself.

'The great risk is that I will not come back and then both his and my secrets will be lost for ever. The choice I make is the hero's choice.'

It was a moment before Kerela realised he was addressing her directly.

'I'm sorry, Takaar, I'm not following you.'

'Dawnthief must wait. The Wytch Lords must be defeated.' He sighed, and his head dropped to his chest. His fingers fidgeted with the ties on his jacket. 'Where is Auum?'

The change of subject threw Kerela for a moment. She sat in a chair opposite him and poured two goblets of wine from the jug on the table between them. She took hers and drained it in one. Takaar did not raise his head.

'Auum went to join the fight at Understone Pass. He took the Il-Aryn and some of our mages with him. They were ambushed by Xeteskians and have fled into the mountains. Auum knows the Wytch Lords and Xetesk are in alliance and he is seeking out tribal Wesman lords in order to turn them against the Wytch Lords. It's a desperate gambit if you ask me, but he's right that if their alliance holds, they'll sweep us away.'

Takaar was nodding.

'He hates magic that much he seeks to befriend others who share his view.' Takaar raised his head and his eyes sparkled. 'But he's underestimating the hold the Wytch Lords have on the shamen. He never spoke to Garan, you see. So he doesn't know what creatures like Ystormun are capable of deep in their shrivelled souls.'

'His plan could work,' said Kerela.

'But not in the way he expects. I must find him.'

'I can help you there,' said Kerela. 'I am in contact with Stein.'

Takaar shook his head, and his eyes lost their sparkle as his mind closed around him once more.

'No. I know a way and I will bring all the help I need. Tell him I will find him. Tell him he must hold on. He cannot do this without us.'

'Us?'

Rith gathered her Il-Aryn in a tight huddle. Auum could see their distress. It was difficult for some of them to stand and every one of them shivered so hard it was unpleasant to watch. But he was no better. His teeth knocked together, his hands thrust inside his jacket would not be able to grip a sword, and he only knew his feet were still there because he stamped them hard on the ground while his strength ebbed away, stolen by the cold.

When the huddle was done, most of the Il-Aryn moved away and sat once more, their bodies twined together. Eight remained standing. Rith blew out her cheeks and looked at Auum.

'Here we go,' she said. 'Pray for us.'

Auum nodded. 'Yniss will hear you and Ix will grant you energy. You will succeed because you are who you are. I believe in you.'

Auum felt his pulse in his throat and he stilled to watch the Il-Aryn. Every eye was on them and prayers were being spoken. Whatever it was they were doing, everyone knew it represented their last chance. They were standing in a circle facing each other, their arms about each other's waists or shoulders, keeping them tight, keeping them a degree warmer. The preparations seemed to go on for ever. The snow swept under the overhang and the wind howled around the wall, accelerating the drop in temperature.

The sudden quiet took a heartbeat to register. The last snowflakes settled gently, no longer driven by the gale, which was muted, venting its fury against the barrier the Il-Aryn had built. The relief was extraordinary. Auum watched the faces of the elves begin to soften, luxuriating in the calm within. Stein, his mouth gaping comically, pushed his hands against the barrier, which glowed and pulsed a pale blue.

'What is it?' he asked. 'This is not a mana construct.'

Rith was smiling. 'It's just air, but we have made it solid. It's like the barrier against the Wytch Lords, except it need only deflect natural elements so we have stopped the movement of the air and expelled the moisture within it.'

'I can work with this,' said Stein. 'My mages can warm this shell. This makes it worth investing heat in the stone beneath us. And we should bring loose rocks to pile up wherever we have the space and warm them too. How long can you keep this up?'

'I have fifty adepts,' said Rith. 'If you can warm us, let us conserve our energy, eat and sleep, we can rotate. Then we can keep this up for ever.'

'But if you'll allow me, you need to make a small adjustment,' said Stein. Rith bridled but said nothing. 'We need ventilation or we will suffocate, and we need to dry out too. Without any vents all that moisture will hang in the air. And you will need someone on hand to create an opening for those who need to go out for . . . you know.'

Rith's expression softened and she smiled.

'We can do that.'

'This magic,' said Ulysan. 'Bloody rubbish, isn't it?'

Auum said nothing. There was nothing to say. He was still shivering and soaked but he watched the Julatsan elves begin to lay castings in the stone and on the inside wall of the barrier. Blessed warmth began to grow. He touched the barrier with his fingertips. Without it they would all have died. Magic had saved them all, it had saved him.

Auum caught Rith's eye and inclined his head in silent apology.

Chapter 28

I wish someone had told me that wanting to be in charge and being in charge were such utterly different things.

Kerela, High Mage of Julatsa

Stone had never felt so comfortable. Auum hadn't lain down until his clothes had dried out enough to give him a little comfort. Neither had he been able to settle when feeling returned to his face, hands and feet. The tingling and aching had been difficult to endure but ultimately very satisfying.

Before he rolled his damp cloak up for a pillow, he took the time to whisper words of thanks to, and say prayers for, those of the Il-Aryn currently maintaining the barrier. He lay for a while enjoying the chatter around him before sleep swept him off to the dark.

Moments later he woke to the light of a new dawn. Beyond the cocoon the snow fell thick and unrelenting, blown by the harsh wind. He shivered at the prospect of leaving the shelter. Next to him Ulysan was snoring. Auum thumped a fist on his chest and he turned away, still snoring.

'The idea is that you wake up,' said Auum.

He could smell cooking horsemeat, and there were plenty of elves already awake who were eating their fill, gazing out at the cold and smiling at their fortune.

'I know,' came Ulysan's voice muffled by his body. 'But now I can't get up because of this pain in my chest.'

'It's a sobering thought that while we have escaped death, at least for now, we have not, nor ever will, escape your jokes.'

'Did not Yniss say that some things must remain constant for us to survive?'

'No,' said Auum.

'Well he probably should have done.'

Ulysan sat up, and Tilman stirred and pushed himself up on his elbows next to him.

'How's the patient?' asked Auum.

'Me?' asked Tilman.

'No, the other human with a bad ankle,' said Ulysan.

Tilman didn't understand the big TaiGethen.

'Yes, you,' said Auum.

'I can walk,' said Tilman. 'It's still healing but the mages say that exercise will help now.'

'Looks like you're out of a job,' Auum said to Ulysan.

'Then you woke me for no reason.'

Auum clapped him on the shoulder. 'I have a much better job for you and for Merrat, Graf, Marack and Hohan for that matter.'

Ulysan stared at him, his expression bleak. 'It's pathfinding, isn't it?'

'A brisk walk in the cold never hurt anyone,' said Auum.

'Dear Yniss spare me, I wish I was Il-Aryn,' said Ulysan gloomily. 'When do we start?'

'As soon as we can borrow enough clothes to keep us warm. We need to get off this mountain.'

'Just as I was starting to enjoy it.' Ulysan glanced at Tilman. 'Can you climb?'

Tilman patted his leg.

'Bad ankle,' he explained.

Ulysan roared with laughter.

Hohan dropped the last fifteen feet back down to the ground, slipped on the ice and was caught by Marack.

He shook his head and pointed up into the blizzard. 'There's an overhang. I don't think even Ulysan could grab the edge let alone some frozen Il-Aryn,' he said. 'It's not possible, sorry.'

Auum, his hands cold despite the thick bindings of torn cloth on his palms leaving just his fingertips free for climbing, leaned back to escape the worst of the angry wind. They were running out of options. Hohan had almost fallen on one ice-covered climb; Ulysan had made good ground on a face that led to a low peak but could find no way beyond it; and Auum had attempted to cross an ice bridge only to have it crack beneath his weight. He'd been able to get back but the bridge had fallen into a chasm. Marack had climbed high but had found the wind so strong it all but lifted her from the cliff face, and she had come back without reaching the top, saying it would be impossible for the Il-Aryn to ascend.

That left Grafyrre and Merrat, who had inched out along a narrow ledge over a precipice to where the former thought he had seen a climbable fissure during a break in the weather yesterday. They'd been gone longer than Auum liked.

'They'll be fine,' said Ulysan, sensing his mood. 'They're almost as good as me.'

Auum nodded and stared in the direction they'd gone. The elves weren't far from the overhang and the warmth of the barrier, and it still gave Auum a good feeling to think of the moment it had snapped into place and he'd known that they were all going to live. But the morning's search for a route had been fruitless, and should the pair come back blank, the only remaining chance was further along the ledge beyond the crack. No one knew what lay there; only that it turned into the teeth of the gale.

'I'm going to take a look,' he shouted, leaning his head into Ulysan as the wind roared its fury yet again. 'See if I can help.'

'Leave them,' said Ulysan. 'Don't fear for them.'

Auum couldn't help it – he felt anxious and fidgety.

'It's not like you can hold a rope for them, is it?' added Marack.

Auum held up his hands. 'But what if they're in trouble?'

Ulysan raised his eyebrows. 'This is Merrat and Graf, remember? It's not Tilman and Stein out there.'

Auum cracked a smile which broadened when he saw two indistinct shapes moving towards them through the blizzard. Merrat and Grafyrre joined them on their ledge, blowing on their hands and stamping their feet.

'It is seriously cold out there,' said Merrat.

'Well it's good to have you back on this ledge in the warm with us then,' said Ulysan.

'Speak to me, Graf,' said Auum.

'It's climbable, even relatively straightforward in places,' he said.

'I sense a but,' said Auum.

Grafyrre nodded. 'It's narrow in places too. You won't get up there with a pack on your back and some of our larger individuals might struggle.'

'Surely we can tie a line of packs and let them hang below,' said Marack.

'We can work on that.'

'There's another but isn't there? What's at the top?'

'First off, it's a good long climb. We've been assessing the best routes all morning as well as scouting the next section. It's a tough ask for the mages and adepts and it's far too windy for flying,' said Merrat.

Grafyrre continued, 'There is respite at the top, though. It's a wide plateau bordered by two peaks, north and south. Easy walking, plenty of scrambling and the odd little climb though it's really exposed. It ends with an ice-covered slope down at quite a gradient. You wouldn't want to slip on it.'

Auum had a sinking feeling. 'And what's at the end?'

'We didn't get that far but we suspect it's a sheer drop,' said Merrat.

Auum turned his palms up. 'So, is it our route? It's your say. We try it, or do we go further round the ledge?'

Grafyrre and Merrat looked at each other for a few moments.

'We should take it,' said Grafyrre. 'I didn't like the look of the ledge further on and it comes right round into the gale. Anything climbable that way is going to be extremely difficult.'

'All right,' said Auum. 'Let's go and relay the good news. We'll try and solve the pack issue when we get there.'

'Who did you mean when you talked about "larger individuals"?' asked Ulysan while they were waiting for Rith's team to create a door for them to enter the dome.

Merrat threw an arm around his shoulders and patted his barrel chest.

'No one, old friend, no one in particular.'

The weather had deteriorated enough for Auum to abandon all thoughts of moving up the fissure in the mountain that day. It was a popular decision, not just because of the battering winds and snow so thick visibility was zero, but because another night meant more rest, more healing and greater strength for the day ahead.

They set off at first light the following morning. The wind had lessened slightly though the snow was still dense and cloying. The whole party had moved to the face Hohan had tried to climb the day before, and while small groups were led forward to the ledge to climb, the rest were able to enjoy another Il-Aryn shelter, though this time not heated by Julatsan elves.

TaiGethen moved above and below the inexperienced climbers,

using themselves as footrests, halting any slides and heaving up those not strong enough to brace themselves against the walls of the fissure all the way up. The narrows caused brief anxiety, but only Stein had struggled with the width so far. Most of the packs had made it up with just a few snags and tears, although some were lost. It was a small price to pay for good progress.

So it was that Auum and Ulysan along with Oryaal, Evunn, Duele and, inevitably, Tilman reached the climb with their group of seven Il-Aryn. While Ulysan explained the method and Oryaal demonstrated the route with an effortless grace the adepts would not be able to replicate, Auum stared upwards. Grafyrre had estimated seven hundred feet and it was at least that long a climb.

Auum chewed his lip, looking up at the narrowing of the walls about two thirds of the way up, while the wind whistled into the fissure and the snow bunched at his feet before being blown away, some spiralling in an updraught like ash from a fire.

Tilman proved himself a lithe climber despite his ankle, and he went up with Evunn to show the path while the Il-Aryn followed at their own pace, Duele and Oryaal behind them. The ascent was steady and without panic, and the knowledge that shelter and a hot meal waited at the top gave energy to aching muscles.

Ulysan and Auum waited at the bottom, meaning to have a race once the way was clear, but Auum could see the big TaiGethen was eyeing the ascent without his usual all-conquering confidence.

'You all right?' he asked.

Ulysan smiled. 'It's narrow.'

'You'll be fine. Just hold your breath and keep crawling.'

'You know what I'm talking about.'

'Despite what I may often say, your head isn't that big.'

Ulysan was breathing a little too fast but he still laughed.

'Let me do the jokes,' he said.

'Just as soon as we're at the top. Come on, let's get moving. Never mind the race. This wait isn't doing you any favours.'

They climbed side by side, scaling the first section with ease. Auum felt invigorated, testing himself against the mountain. Across from him Ulysan kept on glancing up and, as they approached the narrows, he began to sweat despite the cold.

'Keep it going, Ulysan,' said Auum. 'Plenty of room for your ego yet.'

Ulysan was gasping. They were forced to turn ninety degrees, their backs to one wall, hands and feet on the other, pushing up. Auum could see, far above, the last of the Il-Aryn and TaiGethen scrambling over the top and away. Faces rimmed the opening and Auum waved they were all right.

Only they weren't. The narrowing fissure forced them into an ever more upright position, never too much to prevent them from pushing and pulling their way up but tight on the torso.

'You're doing just fine,' said Auum.

Ulysan swallowed. He moved another foot or two up and his left ear brushed a tiny outcrop in the otherwise smooth wall. He overcompensated and his right ear brushed the other side. He froze.

'Auum!' he said, the fear alive in his voice.

'Just rest your head back to the left. There's room, I promise you there's room.'

Ulysan's head was an unusual shape and his ears stuck out a little, but Auum couldn't see anywhere he risked getting caught though he would get a few scrapes along the way. The big TaiGethen nodded and reached up again, leaning his head as Auum had said. He braced his feet and pushed, inching up.

Right above them the walls angled slightly to the right and closed fractionally, taking the incline off the vertical, but only by a few degrees. Auum moved into the turn, feeling the rock above his head and angling his body to give him the position to drag his legs through.

'Just follow me and do what I do,' said Auum. 'You'll be fine. It's tight but not too tight.'

Ulysan inched up and his head touched the angle in the rock, forcing him to tilt his neck. He gasped and stopped, rocking his head from side to side to convince himself there was room.

'You're nearly there. You need to push up, get your shoulders across the angle and you'll have all the space you can dream of.'

Ulysan reached forward, pulled and jerked his legs down to push himself up but didn't bend his torso to ease over the angle. His head struck the rock face above him and his shoulders jammed against the walls as he tried to turn his whole body to give his head more space to twist.

'No.' It was little more than a whimper. 'No.'

'You're all right, Ulysan,' said Auum.

'I'm not,' he said, gasping in shallow breaths. 'I'm stuck. I'm stuck! Please, Auum, I'm stuck!'

'You're not stuck. You just need to back up about a foot and reorient yourself.'

'I can't go back. Please don't make me go back.' Ulysan was starting to panic. His hands were scrabbling so hard he was drawing blood, and his feet worked at the wall, moving him nowhere. 'I can't move. Please, I can't—'

'Ulysan, take a single deep breath . . . concentrate on the air flowing in and out, good and slow.'

'I can't!' wailed Ulysan. 'No room for my chest. It's stuck fast. I can't breathe, Auum, I can't!'

Auum was in the wrong place to help. He was a body length ahead and facing up, only able to see Ulysan if he twisted his head down to look past his shoulder. He moved up as fast as he could, looking for the space and angles to turn around.

'Don't leave me!' screamed Ulysan. 'Please! Don't leave me here alone in the darkness.'

Auum edged his body around, feeling his back catch on the wall and his left ear scrape painfully against a sharp ridge. Ulysan was still screaming. Auum heaved himself about, feeling the pressure across his body as he faced vertically down. He jammed his feet, pressed his back up as hard as he could and inched across and back down towards his oldest friend.

Ulysan was still scrabbling when Auum laid his hands on the suffering TaiGethen's and stilled them.

'I'm here,' he said quietly and as calmly as he could. 'You're not alone.'

'Ellarn?' asked Ulysan, managing to turn his head just enough to meet Auum's gaze.

'No, Ulysan, it's Auum. Come back to me, Ulysan. Ellarn went a long time ago.'

'It's going to be just like before,' said Ulysan. 'Trapped in the dark, no one to hear me.'

'I heard you, Ulysan,' said Auum. 'Can you hear me?'

'I can hear you. Where are you?'

'I'm right in front of you, old friend. Do one thing for me. Breathe slow, breathe deep.'

'That's two things,' said Ulysan, and relief flushed through Auum; at least something was left to work with. 'Auum, are you there?'

'I'm here, Ulysan. I've got your hands. Did you breathe?'

'I did. I think I did.'

'Good, Ulysan. You're not lost. You're not in the dark.'

Ulysan stared at him. 'It's not dark?'

'No. Come back to me. Remember where you are. Do you remember?'

'I'm stuck . . . I'm stuck in a crack and I can't move. Auum, help me!'

Ulysan's fingers began to scrabble again and Auum tightened his grip.

'Feel that, Ulysan. That's me. I'm here with you. Yniss is here with you. You are in a crack but you aren't stuck. I want you to listen to my voice and do what I ask. Can you do that for me?'

'I can try.'

'That's all anyone can ever ask.'

'Auum? Is Ellarn dead?'

'Yes, Ulysan. Ellarn is dead and safe in Shorth's embrace.'

Ulysan wept, his cheek against the rock face and his tears frosting on his cheeks.

'But you aren't, Ulysan. And I am going to help you get out of here. You trust me, don't you?'

Ulysan tried to nod but it was little more than a twitch of his neck. 'I'm cold. It's cold in here.'

'Then let me help you. Warmth and food are close by, but you have to trust me and do as I ask.'

'Don't let me die in here.'

Auum felt shivers course up and down his body. Ulysan's quiet words tore into his soul and he had to force himself to focus on the practical or he'd be weeping too and they'd both be lost.

'I am not going to let you die. I will never let you die. Shall we get out of here?'

'Yes.'

It was a whisper of quiet affirmation, almost lost in the whistle of the wind, but it was all Auum needed to hear.

'Good, Ulysan, good. Now listen closely and we'll be warm in no time. The first thing you have to do is push yourself back to free your chest and shoulders. Just a very little, just very gently. You can do it and I'll be watching.'

'I'll fall,' said Ulysan.

'No, you won't,' said Auum. 'Brace with your back and legs and slide ever so slowly, just a little. I can tell you when to stop if you like.'

'I can't.'

'You are Ulysan. You can do anything.'

'I couldn't save Ellarn.'

Tears sprang into Auum's eyes. After so long Ulysan's pain had not died; the guilt remained, waiting to rise and bite him when he was at his most vulnerable.

'Nothing could have saved Ellarn. It wasn't your fault.'

'He was so close and I couldn't reach him.'

'I know. And I know you loved him and you will always miss him. Keep him in your heart and know he is safe. We will pray for him when we reach the top. But right now you have to move back for me, just a little bit, Ulysan. I'll keep hold of your hands, and when I squeeze, you can stop.'

Ulysan was quiet for a time and his body calmed. His breathing became a little more regular.

'Don't let me fall.'

'Never, my brother, never.'

Ulysan relaxed and his body slipped too fast. His back came away from the wall and his feet slithered on the rock. His hands jerked from Auum's grip. He screamed like a child. Auum let himself slide. He was slimmer and quicker than Ulysan, who was scrabbling to stop himself again. Auum grabbed his hands as his body angled back over the vertical.

Auum roared with pain as he jammed his feet hard, one up one down, against the walls of the fissure and pressed his back as hard as he could into the rock surface. Ulysan's weight carried them both on. Auum pushed harder, feeling his jacket snag and tear. He ground to halt with his arms and head over the drop, hanging on to Ulysan, who was dangling in space.

'Ulysan, stop swinging your legs!'

'I'm going to fall!' he cried. 'Don't let me fall.'

'I've got you,' said Auum. 'But you must stop moving. I've got you. Ulysan, look at me. Look at me!'

Auum had him, but he couldn't say for how long. His feet were dragging by fractions and he couldn't keep the pressure of his back on the wall for long with Ulysan's weight on his arms and shoulders. Ulysan was gasping in shallow breaths, still trying to get his feet on to the wall. But he'd forgotten everything he'd ever learned about climbing and all he did was weaken Auum's grip.

'Ulysan! I am your Arch and your friend. Look at me, see my eyes.'

Ulysan looked up, and Auum saw all the pain of his memories etched on his face. Tears had streaked the dust on his cheeks and his eyes were wide and terrified.

'It'll be just like before only it'll be me this time.' Ulysan wailed a cry that echoed up and down the fissure. 'It'll be me!'

'No, it won't, because I've got you. Ulysan, keep looking at me. Tell me what happened before. Did you die?'

'No,' said Ulysan, and a flicker of hope entered his eyes. 'I held on and I was saved.'

'You held on and you were saved,' said Auum, holding Ulysan's gaze. 'And you're holding on now and you'll be saved now too. Yniss is watching over us. He is saving you for greater tasks ahead.'

'Like saving your sorry hide?'

'Exactly that, and you can't do that hanging there.' Auum's feet slipped a little more and Ulysan dropped an inch. He whimpered. 'And now it's time to put you right. Are you with me?'

'I can't get my feet right.'

'That's because you're facing the wall. Turn your body out a quarter and brace a foot against each wall. I've still got you.'

'Don't let me go.'

'If I do that, you won't be able to save my sorry hide. You owe me.'

Ulysan actually smiled, and Auum thought they might get out of this alive. The big TaiGethen turned his body and Auum braced himself while Ulysan jammed his feet against the walls. The relief through Auum's arms was more welcome than he would ever admit; he'd been closer to letting go than he thought.

'You did it! You did it, Ulysan! You're halfway there.'

Auum could see the control return to his friend's body. Ulysan moved his legs to get better purchase and his arms moved reflexively.

'Good, you're ready,' said Auum. 'I'm going to let your left arm go, and you're going to get it on the wall above your left leg. Can you do that?'

'Yes,' said Ulysan.

'All right then,' said Auum. 'I'm releasing my grip in three, two, one, now.'

Ulysan's hand slapped against the rock and he pressed his palm in hard. He jerked on his right hand and Auum placed it against the rock and let go. Ulysan steadied and looked up, down at his body and the drop below, and up at Auum.

'I did it,' he breathed.

'Yes, you did. You can do anything; you're Ulysan. And now I want you to follow me into the angle and do exactly as I say when I say it. Can you do that?'

Ulysan looked up at the tightening of the walls and the slight angle to the new incline. He swallowed hard.

'Don't let me get stuck in there.'

'Follow me.' Auum began to inch backwards, watching Ulysan all the way. 'The wall is angling above your head. The moment you feel it touch, tip your head away and bend at the waist . . . now. That's it. Pause there.'

Ulysan was gasping again, his hands groping for the next grip point but his legs rock steady.

'You're doing fine, Ulysan. You're almost there. Now, move your legs up, keep your body where it is and push very gently. Reach your arms ahead and try to flatten out.'

Auum watched Ulysan come forward inch by grinding inch. His body was tight in the crack and his head rubbed the walls, his ears bending over closed.

'It's so close,' said Ulysan, a note of panic entering his voice again. 'It's getting tighter. I'm sticking, Auum.'

'No, you aren't, you're still moving. Keep coming, Ulysan. Slowly. Smooth movement, that's it. Now pull with your hands and brace your back up. That's it, you've got it. Your legs are coming round. I can see them.'

Auum crabbed a little further back, aware of his own precarious position. Above him the fissure widened again. He needed to turn before he lost the pressure of the wall on his back. Ulysan inched on. Auum could see the fear on his face, the tautness of his skin and the desperation in his eyes.

'Just a little more . . . Ulysan.'

'What?'

'You're in. Yniss preserve you, you're in! You've done it! Now come on, keep moving just like you are and come up where I am.'

'Auum.'

'What?'

'You're facing the wrong way. That's a poor way to start a race.'

'What?'

Ulysan's desire to get away from the seat of his terror gave him strength and pace on the climb that Auum could only wonder at. By the time he'd turned himself the right way, Ulysan was past him and up into the wider final section of the fissure. Auum tried to close the gap, but Ulysan was practically climbing hand over hand, his legs propelling him upwards at a reckless pace.

Auum was only too happy to let him have his head. He climbed in Ulysan's wake, feeling the ache in his muscles and the emotional fatigue draining his strength. But his relief kept him moving. He saw Ulysan crawl over the lip of the fissure and stand, looking back down, shooing away the figures that came to his side.

Auum moved up the last few feet. Hands clamped over his wrists and hauled him bodily out of the fissure and onto a freezing cold, wind-blown and snow-covered plateau. He thought there might have been a cheer, but Ulysan's embrace eclipsed it. The big TaiGethen crushed him in his arms and against his chest. His breath heaved in and sobs shook his body.

'Thank you. Dear Yniss, thank you for Auum. Thank you.'

'It's all right, Ulysan,' said Auum. 'You're safe now.'

'Safe,' said Ulysan, and the word must have sounded like blessed peace because the strength went from his legs and Auum let them both sink to the ground, still locked together. 'Safe.'

Auum didn't register for how long, but there they stayed until hands and gentle voices ushered them into the warm.

There was no desire to move further that day. They rested in the sanctuary that magic provided. Ulysan slept for the most part, and Auum watched him in case the nightmares took him. With night falling and the TaiGethen scouts returned from the ice shelf Merrat and Grafyrre had found the day before, their course was set for the morning. Stein sat down next to Auum, bringing two cups of hot broth.

'How's he doing?'

Auum's smile was fragile, his lips trembling despite his best efforts.

'I don't know,' he said, putting a hand on Ulysan's shoulder.

'He's your best climber,' said Stein. 'You don't have to tell me, but what happened in there?'

'We all have our demons,' said Auum.

Stein held up his hands. 'Then there's you too. You were down there with him the whole time and yet you're trying to pretend you aren't affected. Talk to me, Auum, let it out. The tension is radiating from you.'

Auum thought for a moment, wondering if what he wanted to say – and to a human of all people – represented betrayal.

'You will never repeat what I am going to tell you,' said Auum.

'I am your brother. I will never betray you.'

'We'll make an elf out of you yet,' said Auum. He paused to gather his thoughts. 'Ulysan was young when it happened. It was back on Hausolis, the old elven homeland. A freak set of circumstances . . . He was exploring a cave system when there was a rockfall that trapped him and Ellarn. There had been heavy rainfall too, and while they were trapped another storm struck the hills. Water poured down the tunnel they were in. It was powerful enough to loosen all the earth and rock that had trapped them. They were washed back down towards the sinkhole they'd climbed. Ulysan managed to grip on to a root and stop himself going over the edge but Ellarn was swept down. His body was never found.'

'Who was Ellarn?' Stein had to clear his throat to speak.

'He was Ulysan's younger brother. Ulysan was teaching him how to climb.'

'How did he get out?'

'I can't imagine the suffering he went through,' said Auum, wiping his eyes. 'Clinging on for hours in the dark, calling out for Ellarn but only hearing his own voice echoing back his grief. He was rescued when it was plain he and Ellarn were long overdue and in trouble.'

'Who rescued him?'

'He doesn't know,' said Auum. 'One day he'll remember.'

'How long ago was this?'

Auum blew out his cheeks. 'More than three thousand years.'

Stein gasped. 'It all came back when he thought he'd got stuck in the fissure? Such a long time to hold on to such pain.'

'Immortality has its curses.'

Chapter 29

Those who entertain the possibility of defeat will always suffer the reality.

Auum, Arch of the TaiGethen

You are making the right choice. I am certain Auum will forgive you.

Takaar had moved quickly, resting and eating sparingly, following the trail left by Auum and his ill-fated force. Word had reached Julatsa of considerable numbers of Wesmen landing on the northern and southern beaches, moving inland towards the colleges. No doubt they would skirt Xetesk in the south and lay siege to Lystern. It gave yet more impetus to his mission.

'And if Auum does not, you will get what you want: I'll be dead.'

I really can't lose.

Night was full and the shadows were deep in the gently rolling land to either side. Takaar's ears picked out all manner of sounds: animals, birds and the rustling of breeze across grass but no enemies. His eyes pierced the darkness easily though his long vision was denied him by the night. He'd stop soon, eat and rest for an hour before pushing on until dawn gave him a clearer view of his progress.

You must be very satisfied. Here you are, after all this time, running to save not only the elven race from invasion but humans from destruction too. An opportunity for redemption worth waiting a thousand years for.

'You make it sound as if I sat around wasting the intervening years. Just look at what I have achieved.'

In Il-Aryn terms a great deal. In terms of elven harmony almost nothing.

'I care nothing for that.'

Oh, but weren't you credited with its creation?

'And look where it got us. The hatred never died; it just festered in our souls. Even I accept it was a mistake. You cannot force such things on people, they have to evolve.'

You're admitting a mistake?

Takaar didn't answer. Auum's trail was going to take him across a river at the mouth of Triverne Lake. He wondered if he should follow, if the passage of a lone elf would go unnoticed if enemies were still waiting there, as Stein had claimed.

Travelling this side of the lake brought him closer to the colleges and he couldn't afford to be seen until he had reached his destination. Takaar stopped. Several figures rose and moved towards him. He had thought them a tumble of rocks, so still had they been.

Oh dear.

'I will not die here,' said Takaar, letting his mind seek the energies needed to create a killing force beneath his enemies' feet.

'You cannot cross the river. The enemy is waiting.'

Oh. Your deserters. Do you think they've come to finish the job they lacked the courage to finish at the manse?

Takaar flapped a hand at his tormentor for silence while he oscillated between anger and relief.

'Gilderon,' he said. 'Tired of your personal quest, are you? Taken to thieving on the plains of Balaia instead?'

Gilderon led the Senserii to Takaar and they knelt before him, their ikari held in their right hands and away from their bodies. Their heads remained bowed while Gilderon spoke for them.

'We seek your forgiveness. You saved us and gave us purpose yet we thought you had lost that purpose. We were wrong. We should have trusted you, had faith in you. We are sorry and wish only to serve as your guardians once more. Please hear us.'

'How did you find me?'

'We overtook a wagon carrying Auum's wounded to Julatsa. They had recent contact with Kerela, who told them the path you were travelling. Our first task was to ensure you did not cross the river. So we waited. Your safety is everything.'

That must swell your ego to previously unheard-of proportions.

'They are the lost seeking a path, just as before,' said Takaar.

They are betrayers who deserted you on the eve of a great discovery.

'I discovered nothing.'

You discovered your own purpose, which is why we are here. You needed them then and they were gone. They will do it again.

'Still your babbling,' spat Takaar. 'You sow this poison because you fear that with their aid I might actually survive.'

That is their purpose.

Before him, the Senserii had not moved. They among all elves accepted him and his tormentor and never questioned. Yet his tormentor was right: they had abandoned him in a dangerous country to go and join Auum, whom he hated above all elves. But what was he doing but making the same journey now? Takaar smiled inwardly. Who had been right and who wrong if the conclusion was identical? They awaited his mercy or his wrath and they would accept either without flinching.

Oh, how it must pain you, the agony of such decisions. Decisions such as only the gods can make and be assured they are right. You know what you have to do, what you always do to those who betray you.

'You have my forgiveness and my gratitude for admitting your error and seeing clearly to your true path, which is at my side for the greater glory of elves.'

His tormentor screamed inside him. The Senserii rose and he allowed them to kiss his hands.

You think mercy is a godlike quality and indeed it is, but it must be meted out correctly, as must punishment. And you have not done so. You will never be among gods; you do not have the wit or the wisdom!

'Mercy is always wise.'

That's an assertion you might want to save for Auum.

They would be off the mountains today and down among the foothills in Wesman lands. It didn't matter that the dangers there probably outweighed those of the snow, ice, wind and rock; elves were not born to these conditions and knowing they would soon become memories had lifted everyone's spirits.

They ate a spare breakfast at first light before readying themselves for the last leg of the journey. Rith came and sat beside Auum.

'You saved all our lives,' said Auum. 'Bless you.'

'I didn't come here to garner compliments.'

Auum chuckled. 'I'm sure you didn't. What's on your mind?'

'What happens if the Wesmen turn us down?'

Auum was surprised by the directness of her question and had to pause to gather his thoughts.

'Well, we'd be out of options. No choice but to go home, prepare and pray.'

'But you're not considering that eventuality.' Rith didn't smile. 'No, of course you're not. But even if they do listen to us and rebel, what then? Even without the shamen to aid them, who is strong enough to take on the Wytch Lords?'

'Has this been keeping you awake at night?'

'I just want to be able to reassure the Il-Aryn that we're doing the right thing.'

Auum nodded. 'It's the only thing to do, Rith. We have to believe the Wesmen don't want to be in thrall to the Wytch Lords, and if we convince them to rebel, we're most of the way there. And Ystormun and his cadre? Well, that's where our Julatsan friends come in. Human magic must defeat them. Stein says there is a way and I trust him.'

'But it doesn't solve the problem with Dawnthief.'

'No, it doesn't. But it means our people are safe in their homes, at least for now. One step at a time is all we can make.'

Rith nodded but Auum could see she was unconvinced.

'We must have faith,' said Auum. 'And belief. If you think of a better plan, don't keep it to yourself.'

At last Rith smiled. 'I won't.'

Outside the barrier the snow had abated but the wind was still high. Stein was relying on it dropping enough to allow flying as they moved down the ice shelf. It was critical that it did. Merrat had reported that the drop at the end was sheer for more than a thousand feet. The face was possible to descend but realistically only for the TaiGethen.

Auum walked with Ulysan at the rear of the group on the journey across the plateau to the ice shelf. It was a strange landscape, snow-blown and with hundreds of small rounded peaks, like fingers or capped chimneys, some no taller than an elf. They wove in and out of them, heading west under a partially blue sky and in a wind that, though still strong, was no longer gale force.

'I will not miss this cold,' said Auum.

Ulysan nodded. 'Nor I.'

Auum sighed. He'd been setting Ulysan up for the entire walk and the big TaiGethen's voice had remained flat.

'I am almost afraid to say this, but the one thing I wish for right now is to hear one of your appalling jokes.'

Ulysan shrugged. 'They'll come back.'

'Anything I can do to help?'

'Nothing you haven't already done.' Ulysan shook his head. 'You know, for a moment I was back there in that hole in the Arish complex. I could even hear the rush of water . . . and my brother's scream. I looked, but it was dark and then I saw you and you had my hands and you brought me back. I'd have fallen without you.'

'But I was there and you didn't. Don't you forget you owe me.'

Ulysan said nothing. Ahead, the group was gathering at the edge of the shelf. Before he joined them to look for himself, Auum could see the tension in many bodies, and when he saw it, he could understand why.

It was vast and a blinding white that left him wishing for cloud. Its far edge was lost in the horizon and it stretched to either side as far as he could see. The near edge behind which they stood resembled a sculptor's vision of a wave rearing in the sea before crashing in on itself. It must have been formed by the prevailing wind blowing loose snow up the incline and freezing it to ice. It was spectacular but also a distraction from the dangers beyond it.

Merrat and Grafyrre had been depressingly accurate in their assessment of the slope. It looked to Auum to be twenty degrees from the horizontal and was smooth and treacherous for the most part, punctuated sparingly by low ridges of ice like ripples caught on a frozen sea.

'Is there no other way down?' asked Rith, standing near Auum and next to Merrat.

'In all likelihood there is, but can we stay here until it's found?' replied Merrat. 'Just take it slow. It's not as bad as it looks.'

'Right!' called Auum. He hopped over the wave form and felt the shine of the ice beneath his boots. He turned a gentle half-circle and came to a stop. Balance would not be so easy for others. 'Here's the method and all who want to live should follow it.'

The group gathered, eager to hear his words, wishing to miss nothing in the wind, which Auum guessed was still too stiff for flying though it was easing. The shelf was something over half a mile wide and the time it took them to traverse it might allow the wind to drop enough for Wings of Shade. They were taking a considerable risk that it would.

'Those of you who are confident enough to walk, do so slowly and try to butt your toes against the ice ridges you find as often as you can. Do not lean back as you are more likely to fall and slide. Carry at least one knife in your hand, one in each if you have them. Should you fall, dig the blades in to stop you sliding. Don't trust to anything else. You'll gain speed fast and there is no fence at the bottom.

'Those of you who do not wish to walk, sit with your legs forward and move yourself with hands and feet. Again, knives in hands. If you have no knife, ask a TaiGethen. Stop when you're told to and wait to be lifted from the shelf. Do not be tempted to look over the edge. If you think it's difficult here, it is far harder down there by the precipice.

'Take your time. We have all day. Any questions?'

There were none.

'One more thing: the TaiGethen will walk behind the rest of you,' said Auum. There were murmurs of dissent and Auum held up his hands. 'I know how it sounds but think about it. From behind we can see you slip and slide and we can get to you and help you stop. Ahead of you, we will not see you go, only know you have fallen. Which way carries the greater risk to you and us? Yniss is with us. And now we pray.'

Auum was surprised to feel more fear on the slow, slippery walk than he had on either of the far more dangerous climbs they had undertaken. Ulysan, walking by him with knives clutched tightly in his hands, was staring at his allotted Il-Aryn with a fierce fervour.

Auum didn't blame Ulysan for the way he was dealing with the trauma he'd suffered yesterday, but he needed his friend back and he felt helpless to make it happen. He had said Ulysan needn't have any Il-Aryn to watch but he had refused. Auum prayed none of them fell.

They made steady progress. The wind blowing up the slope was helping keep the pace slow and giving people the confidence to lean forward over their feet as they walked. About half the Il-Aryn and mages had chosen to walk, and while a few had slipped and fallen early on, there had been no panic and confidence was growing gently and quietly.

Two thirds of the way to the edge, Merrat came over, moving fast, his feet sliding across the ice in gentle sweeps. Stein, who with Tilman was walking next to Auum, clapped his hands.

'Now in my country we call that ice skating,' he said.

Merrat dug in the sides of his feet and came to a walk by Auum.

'We should have ice on Calaius,' he said.

'I can live without it,' said Auum. 'Is there something on your mind?'

'Are your people being watched by others?' asked Ulysan.

'By Graf and Merke, my friend.'

'Good.'

Ulysan nodded and returned to his staring. Auum shook his head but kept his words to himself.

'What is it?' he asked Merrat instead.

'We're all so concerned with getting off the mountain that we haven't spoken about what comes next. Which way will we go? Who will we try to find? We're about to be afforded the best view of the Wesman lands we're going to get. Let's not waste it, that's all.'

'Ulysan, you coming?' asked Auum.

Ulysan shook his head. 'Someone has to stop them if they slip. Someone has to be there to grab their hands.'

'I understand,' said Auum. 'Stein, we need you. Come on, Merrat, this is your idea . . . and no skating.'

A short while later the three of them sat near the edge of the dizzying drop down to the Wesman lands, feet braced against ice ridges and knives in hand just in case. The ground below appeared full of jagged rock spears pointing up to impale them as they descended. Beyond them the ground was less wild but remained doggedly rugged, dominated by mountains and high hills in the distance and shot through by an overwhelming bleakness.

Smoke rose from the fires of several small settlements perhaps a day's walk from the base of the mountains, and smudges in the air further afield represented the smoke and dust of larger towns, perhaps even a city. Auum could see goats and cattle roaming the hills searching for grass and roots, but the mass movements of armies he had half expected to see were absent.

'So, Stein, what do I need to know?' he asked.

'All right, a few main features for you. I'll start with Parve, the seat of Wytch Lord power. It's almost straight ahead, way to the west of us. You might be able to see a dual line of low peaks. The Baravale Valley passes between them and points to Parve.'

'I can see the smoke of the city,' said Auum.

Stein looked round. 'Your eyes are really that good, are they?'

'Yes,' said Auum. 'What else?'

'Wytch Lord influence radiates out from Parve, but on the western coast there is plenty of resistance. That's too far for us to go. Do you see the lake backed by mountains to the south of Baravale? Of course you do. Well, that's Sky Lake and the Garan Mountains.'

'Garan?' asked Auum. 'That's . . . ?'

Stein smiled. 'Oh yes, of course, the army commander who became Ystormun's pet experiment in immortality.'

'Takaar said Ystormun was trying to make an elf out of Garan. He was the first human that didn't deserve to die.' Stein shuffled back half a pace from the edge. 'Your ancestor was the second.'

'Anyway, moving on.' Stein cleared his throat. 'The further east you come, the more open the tribal lords are to us, though it's a relative thing. They still hate us but they will trade with us. There's a settlement at Sky Lake and two or three further south where you might be heard.'

'Do you have any particular names in mind?'

'Well, there's Gorsu, whose tribe occupies the lands nearer Baravale, but he's bent the knee despite his avowed hatred of his masters. There are others . . . Kiriak in the south but he's weak, Lantruq of course and perhaps Sentaya. He's a vicious bastard and quite likely dead by now.'

'Why?' asked Merrat.

'The Wytch Lords aren't keen on dissension. Reportedly his shamen have access to the Wytch Lord fire but, last we knew, he was refusing to take his people from the fields and arm them.'

'We'll try him,' said Auum.

'I don't know. I'd have gone for Lantruq. Strong leader, plenty of warriors and shamen still under his control.'

'Where are his lands?' asked Merrat.

'You see the tree-covered hills south of Sky Lake? He's there.'

'He's where we go after this Sentaya,' said Auum. 'I want to make a statement to Ystormun. Show him we can take his power from him. Kill his shamen if they won't turn from him. Then we get Lantruq and we have a real force behind us.'

'It won't be that simple,' said Stein. 'What can you promise either of them?

'An end to the Wytch Lords and freedom for their people.'

'Oh come on, Auum, you can't promise that. No one can.'

Auum stared at Stein. 'I have beaten them once. I can do it again.'

'Yes, you defeated one Wytch Lord a long way from the base of his power, with the help of considerable magical talent.'

'And with us are more mages, Il-Aryn and greater talent.'

'Auum, you don't understand. You can't beat Ystormun or any Wytch Lord from a distance. My ancestor trapped him in a ring of magic and even then all he could do was diminish him. He isn't going to travel to Sky Lake; he'll just turn his shamen on us.'

'When he knows I am here, he will come.'

'You're sure about that?'

'I'm counting on it. And when one is killed – or diminished – the word will spread and the Wesmen will turn. The alliance with Xetesk will fall and we will have an end to this war. Then I can go home.'

Stein was smiling and shaking his head simultaneously.

'There is a wonderful clarity to your mind, isn't there? It never allows for the possibility of defeat.'

Auum regarded Stein, wondering if he was being mocked. He shrugged.

'Those who entertain the possibility of defeat will always suffer the reality.'

There was a silence while Stein digested his words.

'A sound philosophy.'

'Can you fly in this wind?' asked Merrat.

'It's borderline but I think so. Carrying elves down will help, I think, given the extra weight. We'll have to—'

'Spread yourselves on your bellies! Dig, don't scratch. Do it now!'

Ulysan's shouts ripped across the calm of the slope. Auum stood and spun round, Merrat with him and Stein rising more carefully. Three had fallen, one having slipped and grabbed the others to steady himself so bringing them all down. They were in an untidy heap rotating slowly and gathering speed on the slope only fifty yards from the drop.

Ulysan was chasing them, bursting through the line of now stationary walkers and shufflers and heading across the slope to try and catch them. Auum's heart was in his mouth; Ulysan was going too fast. He set off too but Merrat was ahead of him.

'My people,' he said. 'I've got this.'

He skated away, his movements fluid and his speed increasing quickly as he moved at an angle to intercept the flailing elven trio, none of whom could drive a knife into the ice to slow their progress.

'Spread yourselves out!' called Auum, setting off along the edge, his feet finding purchase hard to come by and the ice ridges cracking under his feet. 'On your bellies and use those knives!'

Merrat was closing on them fast but they were starting to panic.

They were clutching one another rather than fighting their instincts and spreading themselves as wide as they could to gain maximum friction. He saw one knife strike hard into the ice, but the blade snapped and the Il-Aryn shrieked with frustration and fear.

Fifteen yards before they reached the edge of the precipice, Merrat dived full length, catching one of them about the chest.

'Hang on to each other and spread out!' he ordered.

Instead they tried climbing over each other to reach him. Merrat stabbed hard at the ice, scoring a trench. The blade shrieked as he pushed harder, slowing them but not enough. Auum ran faster, trusting his feet, whispering a prayer to Tual to keep him upright.

'Merrat! You have to get your other knife in! You're going too fast.'

Merrat tried to turn his body. 'Hold on to my legs, let me free my arm!'

But the Il-Aryn were lost to reason. Two had hold of Merrat and the third was clutching for him, denying him the chance to save them.

'Let him go!' roared Auum. He was closing but nowhere near quickly enough. 'He has to use his other knife! Listen to me!'

The first elf's feet slipped over the precipice. He wailed and grabbed again and again at the clothing of the others while his momentum carried him further over. It was horribly slow to Auum's eyes but the end was inevitable.

'Shove them off!' cried Auum. 'Merrat, you have to stop your slide! You're going over!'

Ulysan thumped down, grabbing Merrat's knife hand and driving the blade in a little further. He was spreadeagled at right angles to Merrat and his other hand swept down with a desperate force, the knife clutched in it finding a crack and wedging hard.

'I've got you, Merrat,' said Ulysan. 'I've got you.'

'Hang on!' called Merrat as they slowed dramatically.

The two clutching Merrat gripped harder, and the one over the drop swung out lazily, his legs scrabbling at the precipice and his hands knotted in the trouser legs of another. They crunched to a halt. Auum slithered to a stop above them.

'Nobody move. Hold fast, hold your nerve and you'll live.'

Marack, Nokhe and Hohan slid down and knelt to haul the Il-Aryn back to safety. Then they moved the elf away, who was sobbing his apologies and thanking Yniss for his rescue.

'Never mind Yniss, thank Merrat,' muttered Auum.

He walked past Merrat, reaching down to squeeze his shoulder. The other two Il-Aryn were detached from Merrat, who dragged himself to his knees and brushed the ice from his jacket. Ulysan had rolled onto his back, and Auum knelt in front of him, leaning in to kiss his forehead and eyes.

'You did it, Ulysan. You saved them all from falling.'

There were tears in Ulysan's eyes, like the welling-up of memories.

'I did,' he said. 'This time I could reach them.'

Auum reached down a hand. 'But remember there are some times when you cannot.'

Ulysan took his hand and stood. Merrat pushed Auum aside and hugged the big TaiGethen.

'You saved me, brother.'

'Any time,' said Ulysan.

Auum turned to Stein, who was walking slowly towards them.

'Get us down off this mountain. I don't think my heart can take any more.'

Chapter 30

It is a horrible feeling to know the time has come when you must rely on magic in order to survive.

Auum, Arch of the TaiGethen

'How far to Sky Lake?' asked Auum.

They had descended the precipice without further incident and Auum had led long and passionate prayers of thanks for their deliverance to Yniss, Gyal and Ix. It felt wonderfully warm and calm at the base of the mountains. Auum had stared up at the snow plain where they had stood so recently, wondering what madness had led him to think it had been a good plan.

Yet here they were: depleted, drained and hungry but very much back in control. They were hidden from enemy eyes by the jagged rock formations that surrounded them, and while rocks were gathered to be heated for a thin stew made from everything they had left, most of the elves were lying down wherever they could find a spot. Auum didn't blame them one bit.

'At your pace, less than two days. But Tilman can't fly so we should make whatever progress we can this afternoon and expect to get there late the day after tomorrow. Some of yours might need a good rest now too.'

Auum glared at the trio of Il-Aryn who had so nearly cost Merrat his life. Overconfident, they had been messing about, sliding and braking until one of them had done it once too often. Rith had dismissed it as simple over-exuberance and the row that had ensued had set birds to flight.

'They'll move when I say. Apparently they have no shortage of energy to burn.'

'They almost died,' said Stein. 'I know it was their fault but—'

'So did Merrat. I will not mother them, Stein. Do you see him whining?'

Merrat was sitting with Ulysan, explaining the finer points of ice skating, or so it appeared. Ulysan was smiling again, though his eyes were still haunted. Perhaps he had something to thank those idiots for after all.

'The TaiGethen are a different breed,' said Stein.

'Yes, we are cursed with honour.'

'I . . . oh.' Stein blew out his cheeks and put a hand out to steady himself. 'It's—'

Auum grabbed him and helped him sit. 'Are you all right?'

Stein nodded. 'Communion. Wait.'

Auum watched, moving away a couple of paces, uncomfortable with the weight of magic he could feel emanating from his friend. Stein's eyes closed but beneath his lids moved as if searching for something. His mouth moved too but no sound came. He frowned, the colour leaving his face, and he bit at his lower lip hard enough to draw blood. He swallowed and his face hardened. His body relaxed and he opened his eyes, the contact broken.

'So?'

Stein looked up at him, taking a moment to focus his eyes and his thoughts.

'It's bleak news,' he said and Auum's heart fell. 'The Wesmen have landed in large numbers north of Julatsa and are marching to lay siege to the city. It's a similar picture in the south though we assume Xetesk won't be beset – mind you, this might be the Wytch Lord's gambit.'

'Not yet,' said Auum. 'They still need Xetesk to prevent the other colleges from uniting.'

'There's something else, and I'm not sure if this is good news or bad. Apparently, Takaar reappeared in Julatsa. He knows our intentions and is planning on joining us.'

Auum stared up at the mountains. 'Not if he comes that way.'

'You really want him back?'

'Not him but his power. Think what it will add to ours.'

'So long as he directs it as he needs to.'

'Put it this way: he's always managed to save himself when the need arises,' said Auum. He smiled and felt guilty for it. 'He's not going to go quietly, is he?'

'No. But there is some good news – for you anyway. Kerela reported that Takaar was at Septern Manse. The Julatsan team are dead as we feared but Takaar and the Senserii took out the Xeteskians and the place is now empty. He says Dawnthief isn't there and can't be found; it's hidden in another dimension. He says we're all wasting our time.'

'So why are we still fighting?'

'Because no one in Xetesk or Parve will believe him.'

Lord Sentaya of the Paleon tribes was sparring with his youngest son when he was called. He beckoned the eight-year-old to him, knelt and embraced him.

'You're progressing well. Remember to keep your guard up and watch your opponent's body as well as his eyes.'

'I don't have that many eyes,' said Arayan.

Sentaya laughed.

'But you will, and then you will be unbeatable like me.' He took his son's weapon with his and laid both wooden blades against the frame of his door. 'Now go and tell your mother you've earned a grain cake. And take a drink.'

'Wine?'

'Water . . . with maybe a splash of red. I'll check so don't say I said otherwise.'

The boy ran off and Sentaya felt a burst of pride. Blessed with three sons, all fit and healthy: two working the fields and commanding warriors and one who would be the best of them, even Sentaya himself. He stretched and looked to the sun, seeing it fading towards evening. He should be relaxing with his family; this was no time for business.

Sentaya growled and walked round the side of his house. The central oval around which the village was built was still busy with life. The smells of cooking and smoke drifted across him, setting his stomach to rumble in appreciation. There in front of his house stood a shepherd boy with his elder shaman, Gyarth.

'You know I hate to be disturbed when I am training my son, Gyarth.'

'My apologies, Lord Sentaya,' said Gyarth, bowing and helping the shepherd do the same. 'But this youth has news.'

'Does he have a name?'

Gyarth prodded him in the back. 'Speak.'

'I am Tiral, my lord.'

Sentaya smiled. 'Atalun's boy, good. Raise your head, lad, you need not fear me.'

Tiral looked up. 'Thank you, my lord. There are people approaching the village.'

Sentaya tensed. 'People? How many?'

'I counted more than a hundred. They were a way away from me so I could be wrong.'

'Are they Wes?'

Tiral shook his head. 'No. I thought they must be eastern men but they don't move like them.'

'Make yourself clear,' said Sentaya sharply, making the boy jump.

'They . . . they have more . . . um, grace. Like their feet kiss the ground rather than stamp it ugly like the easterners do. They'll be here before nightfall.'

Sentaya didn't understand what the boy meant but it hardly mattered. He turned to Gyarth.

'Is the fleet in?'

'Most are beached; some are still out.'

'Get them in and get everyone armed. We'll meet these . . . people outside the village. Get word to my sons. Have them stand defence. Thank you, boy, you have done me great service. Now go home and stay there. Send your father to me.'

The boy ran off.

'Are you sure he knows what he saw?' asked Sentaya.

'His story is unchanged though it makes no sense. Easterners who don't walk like easterners?' said Gyarth. 'Shall I gather my shamen?'

'How many are here?'

'Three. Most are spreading the word of our impending entry into the great battle.'

Sentaya sniffed. 'Should it ever come to pass.'

'One should not question the Wytch Lords.'

'I am Sentaya. I will never bend the knee. Leave your shamen to their tasks. Should we be attacked, you know what to do.'

When Sentaya saw the small force approaching he understood exactly what Tiral had meant. They moved as if they were part of the land on which they walked. It was hypnotic and, yes, *graceful*. He was backed by sixty of his warriors, all fresh off the boats from Sky Lake and angry that their bellies would not be filled for the time being. Gyarth was with him and Sentaya wished he wasn't. He was too quick of tongue, too far under the Wytch Lords' influence. Sentaya feared being undermined and he had warned Gyarth to keep his mouth shut.

Sentaya stood front and centre of his warriors, his arms across his chest, his cloak about his shoulders and his decorated leather breastplate secured over his clothes and furs. His shaven head was uncovered because he would not hide his face from anyone.

The strangers slowed as they approached, the failing light obscuring their features until they had come close, though they made it obvious they had no weapons in hand. Most were dressed in leather and cloth; some, the most graceful, were plainly warriors but he could not be sure about the others.

Sentaya stiffened as they resolved fully out of the gathering gloom. Walking in the centre was a man, without question a mage and therefore an enemy. But those around him gave him pause and he would not signal an attack yet. They had strange-shaped ears and eyes. Their faces were hard and cruel and their presence reeked of danger. Word had spread about these people. They had broken the siege at Julatsa. They were elves from a land far to the south, warriors to be respected and feared.

'Draw no blade,' ordered Sentaya. 'I do not believe they are here to fight us.'

Wesman hands moved from weapon hafts and an elf walking next to the mage nodded.

'An unwise strategy,' said Gyarth. 'These creatures are responsible for the deaths of Gorsu, Hafeez and many shamen and warriors.'

'You are not giving me reason to hate them. This is a war. I have lost rivals; you have lost dark strength, and I remain free. Perhaps I should be embracing them.'

'You cannot refuse the Wytch Lords for ever.'

'That is yet to be proven. I will speak with their leaders.' He regarded Gyarth, puffed up as he was with his own self-importance and borrowed power. 'Alone.'

Sentaya carried the satisfying image of Gyarth's rage with him when he walked forward. The mage and the elf detached themselves from the group and came to meet him. The elves fascinated him, at once so alien in appearance but so at home with the land, as if they were bonded to it. He chose not to begin in aggressive tones. A formal approach to the strangers was appropriate.

'I am Sentaya, lord of the Paleon tribes. These are my lands.'

'The men of Balaia know you and respect your strength in battle and your right to live free on your lands.'

It was the mage who spoke, and his dialect, if heavily accented, was accurate enough.

'Then you may speak. Those who come to challenge me die here. Those who seek trade leave satisfied. Which are you?'

The mage spoke to the elf in a curious language Sentaya could not follow at all. It was a brief exchange and the mage turned back.

'My apologies, Lord Sentaya. My brother, Auum of the Tai-Gethen, cannot speak your language and I must relate to him what is being said. I am Stein, mage of Julatsa. I know I am your enemy but I ask that you hear us. Auum has a proposal. It is for your ears only.'

Stein's eyes flicked briefly to Gyarth standing behind him. He nodded and turned to his warriors.

'Bring fire and food . . . bread and fresh meat too. Slaughter a cow. Our guests may not enter the village but that is no reason for them to starve. I will hear what they have to say before deciding their fate. No respected warrior should face death on an empty stomach, should I decide they die. You will guard me. Gyarth, with respect, you must return to the village. Your duties await you.'

'And should the creatures rise up and strike you while your warriors stand guard, unable to assist you, who will save you?'

Sentaya faced down Gyarth's humiliation and fury. 'They have not come here to kill me.'

'You are staking your life on that assumption.'

'I am staking all our lives on it.'

Sentaya turned away from his shaman, a smile on his face. He was aware Gyarth could kill him instantly but knew that he would not because his masters needed Sentaya and all the warriors at his command when the invasion through the pass was ordered.

'Sit,' said Sentaya. 'Fire and food will be brought. The rest of you must retreat to a distance equal to my own warriors. That is the condition of my parley.'

'Most acceptable,' said Stein.

He spoke briefly to Auum, who issued a simple command. His elves trotted away without a backward glance. Auum was a true leader, commanding trust and respect. He stood until Sentaya sat, then did so himself. He was deferential too. Sentaya inclined his head in welcome and the gesture was returned.

'Tell me,' said Sentaya, studying Stein and seeing in him an honesty he had not expected of any mage, although his magic remained repulsive. 'How did you get here? By boat, I presume, since the pass is closed.'

'We came across the mountains,' said Stein and, reacting to Sentaya's expression of surprise, added, 'The elves are particularly determined as well as keen climbers. Even so, we lost friends on the crossing.'

Auum placed his hand on Stein's arm and Stein related his words.

'Auum says this: it was not our choice. We were betrayed by those we sought to join in a war against you. Now we seek to join you in a war against our shared enemy.'

'Really?' said Sentaya, steepling his hands beneath his chin. 'And who is this shared enemy?'

'The Wytch Lords.'

Sentaya glanced over his shoulder to check Gyarth was gone. He saw some of his warriors approaching, carrying torches and pulling two handcarts. One was piled with wood, the other carried food and wine. Another warrior was leading a cow.

'You're so sure they are my enemy?'

Stein spoke at length then, pausing whenever a warrior laying fire or food could hear him. Mostly he related Auum's words but added his own colour. Sentaya found himself amused at some of the things Stein was compelled to say on behalf of his elven brother.

Sentaya heard about Dawnthief, the alliance and the treachery of Xetesk and the Wytch Lords. He heard of the elven warrior's personal distrust of magic, and in that they were truly kindred spirits. Auum spoke of the future, should human magic be destroyed and the Wytch Lords have no rivals in power. He painted a picture of desolation and slavery, such as the elves had already suffered at their hands. Auum's was a compelling story and his desires matched Sentaya's own for the most part even though his vision of the world beyond this war left Sentaya dissatisfied. But still the Wesman lord smiled when he spoke to Stein and he was becoming used to the pauses in conversation while Stein translated for Auum.

'He is your brother yet he despises your magic almost as much as I do. It must have taken some effort to speak his words.'

Stein's eyes sparkled with humour, and Sentaya surprised himself by feeling a vestige of warmth towards the mage.

'Auum wishes there was no magic, and I can understand his point of view though naturally I disagree with it. But he can see certain of its benefits and would admit it has saved his life on more than one occasion. That is his dilemma.'

'One I don't suffer. Auum's solution destroys the Wytch Lords and their magic but it leaves yours to blossom. That does not serve me. Make me see otherwise.'

Stein shrugged.

'There is no perfect solution. You desire our destruction and, as a result, we desire yours. The truth is that neither state will ever be achieved and we will eventually battle ourselves to a standstill. Our problem is here and now. Should the Wytch Lords win, they will dominate all who survive, and none of us wants that. Can we agree on that point?'

'We can,' said Sentaya.

His warriors had laid out bread and dried meat and a fire was blazing to his right. Racks were placed across it, the now-slaughtered cow was efficiently butchered, and large joints were spiked and laid on the racks to cook. The aromas were glorious and tempting; blood and fat spat on the flames.

'Similarly, should Xetesk win this fight then it is they who will dominate and that is similarly unwelcome.' Sentaya nodded and gestured for Stein to continue. 'The current situation, with Xetesk and the Wytch Lords using the Wesmen to destroy the other colleges, will inevitably lead to one of these outcomes. Surely it is better to have four magical colleges, each one acting as a deterrent to the others? That leaves you without your ultimate victory but it does leave you free to be lord of your lands without the fist of the Wytch Lords over you.

'It is the best of the options, and it is why we want you to turn against the Wytch Lords and help us defeat them.'

Sentaya sighed. He took a hunk of bread and a clay mug of wine and tried to pull apart Stein's logic while he ate. The mage and the elf had spoken good sense but their conclusions left him unhappy and, with his last swallow of wine, he knew why.

'How will you destroy the Wytch Lords?' he asked. 'Are they not invulnerable?'

Stein had been expecting this question and spoke quickly to Auum, who deferred to him and asked Stein to speak for them all.

'I will not lie to you, Lord Sentaya. Though we are enemies, I have the greatest respect for you and I hope that is returned in some measure.'

'In some small measure,' agreed Sentaya, and he knew beyond doubt he was not going to like what he was about to hear.

'The Wytch Lords cannot be destroyed; they can only be trapped in a place where they have no power. To achieve this requires powerful magic. We must draw one of them out and trap him, thereby critically weakening the strength of all six. Only then can we hope to defeat them. Auum believes that Ystormun's hatred of him stemming from his defeat by him in the elven homeland will be enough to bring him here should you stand with us, challenging his authority.'

Auum smiled. Sentaya dropped his food, leaned forward and grabbed Auum's collar, pulling him close and hissing into his face.

'You would bring death to all my people by inviting a Wytch Lord to my village? That is madness so bold I should slit your throat for speaking it. Tell me this is not your plan.'

Just as he had not dodged Sentaya's hands, so Auum did not resist but waited until he was pushed away. He and Stein had a quick conversation and Auum deferred to Stein again.

'Think, my lord,' said Stein. 'You will have issued a challenge to the Wytch Lords simply by speaking with us, and they will respond in a way that tells your people two things: that they respect your influence and that they fear you, Sentaya. You.

'So tell your people that Ystormun will come because he is afraid of the lord of the Paleon tribes and has been forced from his hiding place to fight. We will stand by you. Our magic will take his unholy power, and you can strike at his dark heart and eat his soul.

'And when you have defeated him, you will be the lord whose banner the free Wesmen flock to. You will rule the Wesmen.'

Sentaya took in Stein's words and there was sense in them despite the enormous risk – supposing this Auum could actually be believed and Ystormun would come to him. But should it be true and they were victorious? The cloak of lord of the Wesmen would sit well on his shoulders. A fierce smile grew on his face, but doubt remained and he looked Stein deep in the eyes.

'Should he come, can we beat him?'

'Yes, we can,' said Stein, translating for Auum. 'My ancestor did it before and we can do it again. He is alone. You will have set the trap, my lord, and he will walk into its jaws.'

Sentaya nodded. 'Many of my people will die.'

'Many of ours too,' Stein repeated Auum's words. 'But we will not flinch from it. You consider us enemies but we will fight as brothers.

Trust us and for this moment trust our magic and what it can do to defeat our common enemy.'

Sentaya's disgust and anger had given way to a controlled excitement. He looked again at Auum and his regard for the elf grew further, though he was confused. Something Stein had said earlier just didn't make sense

'Surely it is ages past that Ystormun was defeated. It is ancient lore that the shamen speak when they are relating the rise to power of the cadre. Yet you said Auum defeated him.'

Stein nodded. 'The elves are very long-lived. Auum is more than three thousand years old.'

Sentaya gasped as he stared at the elf.

'But he looks no older than me,' he hissed. 'How can that be?'

'It is a gift of their gods to be so. Auum was there when Ystormun was defeated – as was my ancestor.'

Sentaya felt as if he was reeling, so many were the revelations.

'Then your bloodline is spoken of in my legends,' said Sentaya.

'Will you join us? I know what my ancestor did. I know what Auum can do. We can beat them if we stand together.'

Sentaya wagged a finger, his mind clearing of distractions.

'You're clever, Stein, and I'm tempted, but I can see further than your words. Your magic can defeat Ystormun – I will believe you for now – but whose magic can trap them beyond the ability to strike back?'

Stein nodded gravely. 'That ability rests with Xetesk. They must be informed of our intentions.'

Sentaya spat on the ground and stood up. Auum glared at Stein, who made a placatory gesture. Sentaya was not about to wait for him to translate what had just been said.

'And now we reach the truth. You would have me fracture the fragile unity of the Wesman tribes and at the same time aid you in bringing a Xeteskian army to my lands to destroy the only power able to defend us against the filth of your magic. You want me to lay my country open to whoever would take it from me. That is why I despise magic and that is why you will ever be my enemy!'

'You have me wrong,' said Stein.

'I don't think so. Warriors!'

Wesmen all around him drew axes and blades. Instantly, the elves were on their feet. Mages began to prepare and the TaiGethen drew twin blades from scabbards on their backs. The menace emanating from them washed over Sentaya, and he was damned if it didn't make the fire flicker and the beef spit.

Auum stood and barked out a command, holding out one hand towards his people, the other towards Sentaya. The elves sheathed their blades though it hardly lessened their sense of readiness. Auum appeared in front of Sentaya so quickly, he backed away a pace. Auum spoke, and Stein, remarkably calm and assured, cleared his throat.

'Sentaya, please. You're making a mistake. We have no wish to fight you. Will you hear Auum through me?'

Sentaya stared at Auum, who stood impassive before him. He gave a curt nod. Auum began to speak and Stein translated.

'No Xeteskian army will destroy your people and occupy your lands. Julatsa, Lystern and Dordover will fight against them. So shall I and my people. Trust me. We share so much. We have suffered under the boots of the same enemies. We must not become enemies. Trust the elves.'

Sentaya's ire was blunted a little but he could not yet begin to agree to what they desired of him. He waved for his people to lower their blades.

'Even if it goes according to your plan, the easterners will have their magic and we will have no defence against it. We will always be vulnerable to their whim.'

'The elves had no magic when man invaded Calaius and enslaved my people, occupied my lands. Yet we destroyed an army of six thousand warriors and mages. We used our land as you will have to use yours. I will tell you how. I will not leave you defenceless, that is my vow.'

'You I trust, but I cannot trust him or his magic.' Sentaya sighed and rubbed his hands over his face. So much sense, so much he wanted to believe but so much danger too. He would be gambling with the entire Wesman race. 'Enough. We will not fight. We will eat instead, although we will not sit at the same table.'

Stein nodded. 'Thank you, Lord Sentaya.'

Sentaya turned his back on Stein only to see Gyarth striding towards him, a look of cold contempt on his face.

'You remain uninvited,' said Sentaya. 'We are not done yet.'

'Yes, you are,' said Gyarth.

Sentaya tensed, gripping his axe more tightly. 'What have you done?'

'I have spoken to the cadre.'

'How dare you undermine my authority! I am lord of these tribes.'

Gyarth sneered. 'There has been a shift in power. A long-overdue one. They have put up with you for too long, Sentaya, and now an army is coming to drag you before them to bend your knee or be destroyed along with these creatures. They will be here in three days.'

'Traitor!'

Sentaya raised his axe and chopped it through Gyarth's neck. The shaman's head rocked back and fell from his shoulders, taking with it Gyarth's dying expression of outrage. The body collapsed to the side. Sentaya threw the weapon to the ground next to the headless corpse. He stared at Auum.

'It looks as if I am with you whether I like it or not.'

Chapter 31

Yes, I can feel the earth energies, the magic of Ix. But I can feel the wind and the heat of the sun too. It does not mean Takaar is right about me.

                                        Auum, Arch of the TaiGethen

Ystormun tried to ignore their voices while he sorted through clothes, weapons and the texts he could not be without on the trail. His servant was waiting to pack his chosen belongings and load them onto his carriage. But the clamour in Ystormun's mind was growing louder and it stole his train of thought, making him forget what he was looking for when he pulled open drawer or wardrobe.

There were no words being howled into the centre of his skull, just the deliberately discordant chants of the cadre, growing in intensity, summoning him to the Hexerion. Ystormun leaned heavily on his desk, trying to focus on the parchments he was sorting through, seeking just one that would give him solace and strength when he faced those who had beaten him. The shame still burned within him.

The pressure grew and he slammed his fist on the desk. His servant whimpered and Ystormun spun round to face the wretch.

'Pack what I have laid out. I will finish this later.'

The Wesman, too frail to be a warrior but possessed of an organised mind, had been a long-surviving servant. His eyes saw Ystormun's pain and anger but he dared not speak of it. Ystormun didn't require him to; his expression was sympathy enough and it warmed him unexpectedly.

'All will be ready for inspection when you return.'

Ystormun, a little unsteady on his feet, managed a curt nod before walking carefully from the room towards the Hexerion. Their knowledge of his approach was signified by a change in the tone of the voices in his mind to a sneering superiority.

Entering the Hexerion, Ystormun was struck by the heat. All the fires were lit including his, despite his not having ordered it, and the smell of smoke hung heavy in the air. It was a petty act. They knew of his preference for cold; it had been that way since his return from the stultifying humidity of Calaius. He stared at them all in turn, caught their contempt and shrugged it off before pulling out his chair and sitting, his fingers knitted together and resting lightly on the table.

They had expected him to leap to his own defence and so he waited for one of them to speak and reveal his own ignorance. Perhaps it would be Weyamun or Pamun; both had trouble holding their tongues. He was a little disappointed when Belphamun spoke first. His voice was measured and calm.

'We do not appreciate being kept waiting,' said Belphamun. 'Your presence, when demanded by the cadre, must be immediate, as it would be for any of us.'

'I am not in the habit of abandoning a task half complete,' said Ystormun.

'Of course we understand that choosing travelling clothes is a task requiring the utmost in peace and concentration,' said Giriamun.

Belphamun hissed him to silence without taking his eyes from Ystormun.

'Are we not worthy of your immediate presence?' he asked.

'When we are to discuss matters that are open for debate, yes, of course,' said Ystormun.

He felt the atmosphere tighten. Eyes that had been staring dismissively past his shoulders locked on his face and he felt the pressure of their combined contempt.

'Your desire to weaken the cadre will always be a matter open to debate,' said Pamun.

'Your personal feelings are leading your mind in the weakest of fashions,' said Weyamun.

'Your decision may not be taken by you alone,' said Giriamun.

'You may not leave this temple without our express consent,' said Arumun.

'Your obsession with expunging your shame is truly pathetic,' said Belphamun.

Ystormun had known it would be this way. He let their anger roll over him and made a show of acknowledging all their criticism. They said much more but the subject matter differed little. He waited until they subsided, satisfied that they were in accord and he was the pariah outside the cadre determined to see it break. Then he spoke.

'What is most disappointing is that you fail to see that my actions will bring us closer than ever to ultimate victory. Now forgive me, but can we agree that victory, in this instance, is the clearing of the way to Dawnthief, capturing it unhindered and ensuring our dominion over the eons?'

The five gazed at him, baleful and contemptuous. One by one, and almost imperceptibly, they inclined their heads.

'Yet you, Belphamun, have chosen to make an alliance of questionable gain with our greatest rival and our keenest enemy. Xetesk is simply using us to destroy its own rivals, thereby making it stronger when it eventually turns on us.'

'Your understanding is typically myopic and flawed,' said Belphamun. 'The destruction of the colleges is key to our ambitions, and our alliance with Xetesk until we choose to break it allows us to retain great strength of arms.'

'And you, Pamun, have utterly failed in your task to bring the Paleon tribes into line. Any reserve strength surely rests in Sentaya's and Lantruq's hands, and unless I am misled it is Sentaya who has just challenged us.'

Pamun could say nothing. Ystormun smiled.

'And do I need to ask how the search for Dawnthief is progressing?'

More silence. Ystormun stood and spread his hands.

'Auum has brought the remainder of his force into our lands and positioned them somewhere we can destroy them. This is my task, and I will see it done. Their destruction removes their magic and their most capable warriors. It will remove the elves from this conflict, and it is an opportunity that must not be missed. That is why I will travel and you will not stop me.'

Belphamun's fists rattled the ancient tabletop, and lines of power spat along the cracks. The remainder of the cadre jerked their elbows or hands from the surface. The smell of burning snapped briefly in the air, dissipating almost immediately.

'You will not leave this temple,' he spat, all pretence at calm gone. Ystormun had won the argument but not the prize. 'We will gather our powers together as we have always done and strike from a position of greater strength through the shamen. That is why we have them.'

'You will not deny me this victory!' shouted Ystormun. 'It is mine and I have earned it.'

'And should you fall, what then?' asked Pamun.

Ystormun laughed straight into Pamun's face. '*Fall?* The strength of my force could defeat an army ten times the size of the one I will face. And when I appear on the battlefield, invulnerable and all-powerful in the eyes of the savages, they will run screeching to their shamen to swear loyalty and I will face a handful of elves.'

Pamun's glare was tight with malice.

'Oh yes, Pamun, I will deliver Sentaya at the same time – that's what this is about, isn't it? My victory bringing about your shame.'

Pamun stood across the table. 'No, Ystormun, this is about your petty revenge on some southern barbarians. There is nothing else in your mind. Do not dare to claim otherwise.'

Ystormun crossed his arms over his chest before sweeping them wide open. The six fires blew out, diminishing the light.

'And I will have no more of this heat. Your protestations are based on the worst of all weaknesses, fear. You fear I will be defeated and our cadre will be left vulnerable to the Xeteskians' new casting. Your lack of belief will undo you. Xetesk is locked on the other side of the mountains. I will not fall. I will not even be scratched. You would deny me glory because you fear my influence will grow. *Fear.* I had not thought to see it in you, my brothers.'

Ystormun smiled at the blow he had struck. Arumun managed to hold his gaze.

'Deny that you seek revenge.'

'I do not deny it,' said Ystormun. 'Why should I deny myself the satisfaction even as I bring this conflict to a close? I will see the terror in Auum and Takaar's eyes as I kill them. I want to see the knowledge of their failure as their last breaths leave their broken tortured bodies. I want them to know that I will be visiting the same pain on their homeland. I want to tell them so myself as the skin is flayed from their bodies.

'Your proclivities bring nothing but fleeting arousal, Arumun. Mine bring joy. Indulge in hate, it is beautiful when it is released.'

'It blinds you and will destroy us all,' said Belphamun.

'I am happy to be so pivotal to your survival.'

'We are six or we are none,' said Belphamun.

'Then do not seek to stop me, or whether I live or die, we will be none.'

*

By any measure Bynaar was well protected. He was a Circle Seven mage, not a position achieved by a lack of attention to detail. Even in his temporary accommodation in Understone, with Xeteskian forces dominating every approach and comprising the garrison, he had not neglected his personal security.

His bodyguard of Protectors ringed the house he occupied. Others patrolled the ground floor, and he had guards positioned outside his rooms on the first floor. His most trusted mages watched the garrison and the lands beyond, and he was perpetually covered by a magical shield should any rival decide to disturb his sleep by attempting to murder him.

Whenever he ate he had his own cooks prepare the food, and the castings he played over it would detect any poison. And when he slept or took to the quiet of his drawing room to rest and read, his familiar was the eyes in the back of his head.

Bynaar was irritable but in the end unconcerned by the escape of some elves into the Blackthorne Mountains. He felt their survival was unlikely and, even if they did reach Wesman lands, their capacity to inflict damage could only help Xetesk's cause.

But he could not shake off an unwelcome anxiety. His latest contact with Kerela had not gone well. The Julatsans and their cursed elven allies had been irritatingly persistent. She had accused him outright of betrayal and said some unsettling things about the Septern Manse and the movement of the most powerful of the elves. If she was right then he could cause significant problems. He could not afford to have the Wytch Lords move until he was ready.

Bynaar sat with a jug of wine in front of a dying fire as night closed in. He had much to read but had instead spent most of his time staring at the flames as they danced, rose and fell, finding comfort in their patterns.

'What an interesting creature.'

The words startled him enough to cause him to spill his wine and send his parchments tumbling to the floor. The voice was melodious, rolling the language easily and imbuing it with a unique and compelling rhythm.

Bynaar pushed himself from his chair and turned from the fire, blinking the glamour from his eyes. At least the figure by the balcony doors wasn't there to kill him or why had he chosen to speak?

Bynaar wondered if he had fallen asleep but dismissed the notion the next instant. More pressing concerns raised themselves.

His familiar was where he had left it, curled up on the back of his chair in classic feline repose. Of course it should have transformed by now and flown to the attack, but it appeared not to have noticed the intruder. It hadn't even raised its head. That was quite impossible.

The figure moved from the balcony towards the pair of luxuriously upholstered chairs in front of the fireplace. Bynaar did not move, letting his eyes track and watch the elf, who had an effortless grace and a presence that utterly dominated his. He had a wild look to his eyes but it clashed with an equally frightening intelligence. He radiated power of a sort Bynaar could sense but not penetrate.

'You must be Takaar,' he said.

'Yes,' said Takaar.

'You do understand that one word from me and your life is over.'

Takaar muttered something to himself and smiled. 'That I am in this room should tell you I do not fear that.'

'What have you done to my . . . pet?'

'Nothing.' Takaar pointed at a chair. 'May I?'

'Apparently I am powerless to stop you. Help yourself to wine.'

Takaar sat but ignored the wine. 'I had no wish to disturb its sleep so I have created a silence where it may continue to rest. It is not a cat, though, and it has energies that connect with your own. Very interesting.'

Bynaar studied him. There was no way Takaar should be able to detect the bond between a mage and his familiar. He thought for a moment, realising it was unusually quiet in the house and without, even for this time of the night.

'You've created silence for this whole room too, haven't you?'

Takaar smiled. 'Was that inference or detection?'

'I'm not about to reveal that.'

Takaar's smile vanished and he cocked an ear and tutted.

'Well I think it's clever even if you don't.'

'You think what is clever?' asked Bynaar.

Takaar stared at him for a moment. 'I wasn't addressing you.'

Bynaar didn't know how to take that so he ignored it. The elf was probably just thinking out loud. Bynaar clacked his tongue.

'So, here you are. I'm assuming I am not an assassination target so what is it you want?'

Takaar's eyes widened and a childish grin came over his face. He leaned forward, his voice barely audible.

'I want to help you win the war.'

'That's not something I expected you to say.'

'You expected me to threaten your life if you didn't call your dogs away from Julatsa's walls?' said Takaar.

'Something like that.' Against his better judgement Bynaar was curious. 'So how do you propose to accomplish this, and why would you?'

Takaar's expression changed almost every time he spoke. The impishness had gone and in its place was gravitas. It was most unsettling. Bynaar wondered if Takaar was quite all there.

'Because the elves desire the death of the Wytch Lords and because you are destroying this land in pursuit of a spell you can never recover. Knowing that, you must cancel your alliance with them and destroy the Wytch Lords now because it will be your only opportunity.'

'But that leaves us with rivals, and we don't want rivals,' said Bynaar.

Takaar's expression darkened and he stared to his right, nodding his head.

'You must not condescend to me. I am, as always, just clinging on. Sometimes I slip.'

Bynaar frowned. 'You've lost me completely. What do you mean, slip?'

'I mean,' said Takaar, now adopting the expression of a mother instructing a dim child, 'that those who choose to laugh at me and undermine me are sometimes removed. Auum says I cannot control my anger. I am starting to think he is right.'

The threat that flowed from Takaar was palpable and probably carried on lines of magical energy. Bynaar felt weakened by it.

'I meant no dishonour or disrespect. But I take it you are aware of Xetesk's intentions? We will suffer no rivals.'

Takaar's hands fidgeted in his lap. 'I don't have much time and you aren't *listening*. You have no rivals for Dawnthief because you will never find Dawnthief.'

'Why not?'

'Because Septern still has it.'

This Takaar was nothing if not surprising.

'And you know this because . . . ?'

'I am a better mage.'

Bynaar put his hands on his face and rubbed at the corners of his eyes with his index fingers. He declined the challenge and decided to approach from a different direction.

'I can accept that. You are clearly extremely talented. So tell me, how do you propose to help me defeat the Wytch Lords?'

Takaar chuckled and the humour remained in his eyes. Bynaar felt relieved and cursed himself for it.

'Our greatest warrior has travelled to the east to challenge Ystormun. Ystormun will come to the battlefield because he hates Auum with a passion that has stood the test of centuries. It will prove his downfall. I will go to him to provide the strength of magical power needed to tame the beast. You are the college with the means of caging him.'

'You're naive if you think Ystormun will leave the cadre to kill one elf. Even if he wanted to, the cadre would not allow it. Together they are a considerable power since the Sundering. With even one gone, they are severely diminished. It would hand us the . . .'

Bynaar sat back, suddenly understanding.

'Now explain to me again why Dawnthief is beyond our grasp.'

Chapter 32

The Wesmen are routinely misunderstood. How is their 'tribal savagery' any different to the posturing and fighting of our own barons and lords?

Sipharec, High Mage of Julatsa

TaiGethen scouts were several hours run out of Carusk, Sentaya's home village, covering all the approaches to gauge the size of the oncoming force and to ensure no Wesman scouts could view their defensive preparations.

While the Il-Aryn trained hard to respond to various situations with defensive castings, Stein had organised his mages to set wards across wide swathes of the countryside. Half a day out and the castings were not dense, but there were enough of them to seed doubt in the minds of the marching warriors.

Closer to the village borders and its rough stockade, the wards became more tightly packed and focused, designed to inflict the maximum damage by spreading fire or ice across many more than those unfortunate enough to trigger them. And when the damage was dealt, the remaining wards were designed to obscure the defenders until the last moment and provide opportunities for bowmen and elven mages to cast freely.

'Anyone else feel a little uncomfortable about laying wards to murder unsuspecting warriors on the march?' asked Stein.

'No,' said Auum. 'After all, we're trying to kill enemies, not allies.'

'Can Ystormun divine wards?' asked Ulysan, changing tack quickly.

'Given time I'm certain he can, but there's only him and he's careless of his fighters,' said Stein. 'He won't have the patience to wait, and anyway it's a task so far beneath him I suspect he'd rather lose warriors than step from his carriage.'

The three of them were standing outside the stockade, watching mages at work and waiting for Faleen to run in and deliver her report on the enemy. She was just a few hundred yards away now and running hard.

'There is that,' said Ulysan. 'Is someone chasing her or something?'

'Just a Wytch Lord,' said Stein.

'Not bad,' said Ulysan. 'You've still got a lot to learn, though.'

Faleen slid to a stop in front of Auum, who kissed her forehead.

'Did you enjoy the run? Come on, let's go to Sentaya. We don't want to be seen discussing your news before we've shared it with him. It's his village under attack, after all.'

'How far have you run?' asked Stein.

'I don't know how far but for about seven hours,' said Faleen.

Stein blinked. 'But you aren't even breathing heavily.'

'Our host is waiting,' said Auum.

'Nor are you sweating,' said Stein. 'Unbelievable.'

It was two days since Gyarth's beheading, and the look of disgust had not softened on Sentaya's face. He had watched the mages and Il-Aryn practising and setting wards, and seeing magic being employed on his lands and in his name was causing a major conflict within him.

No caster had been allowed within the village, and the TaiGethen were treated with suspicion, angry eyes following them wherever they went. Tilman had been admitted, but his halting knowledge of tribal Wes had made conversation very difficult. Even so, Auum and Stein knew that Sentaya was wavering, that his tribesmen were not all behind him and that there were sections of the Paleon spread around the lake and further south that wanted the intruders dead. It seemed that only Sentaya's respect for Auum kept their shaky alliance in place. Stein set alarm wards around their camp when they slept.

Sentaya met them where they would not be overheard. He nodded to Auum and pointedly ignored Stein before fixing his gaze on Faleen.

'What has she seen?' he demanded.

Faleen spoke and Stein translated. Sentaya refused to look at him.

'It's a considerable force and it will be here at first light tomorrow. I estimate nine hundred warriors and forty shamen plus their supply wagons. There's a single covered carriage pulled by a two-horse team and attended by shamen in dark red clothing. It is guarded by warriors on horseback, clearly a personal guard. Ystormun is riding in the carriage. I saw him walking among his shamen last night.'

Sentaya shook his head and regarded Auum with something akin to awe. He gave a dry chuckle.

'I had thought you were bluffing, Auum. And now it is real, isn't it? Ystormun has come. For the remainder of the day you and I will set our tactics. When night falls we will feast together in my village.' Sentaya glanced at Stein. 'All of us. For one night we will be brothers and for one day we will fight as kin.'

'It is the greatest honour you could bestow on my people,' said Auum. 'Thank you. The elven gods will bless you and keep you for greater tasks to come.'

Sentaya bowed his head. 'I must speak with my people.'

Sipharec was dead. From healthy old man to corpse in so short a time, and no magic could save him. Kerela turned from his tomb, her head bowed. She whispered prayers as she walked through the college and out into streets packed with anxiety and rising panic.

So soon after the siege had been broken, the hopes of ordinary Julatsans had been crushed. Kerela spoke to no one and acknowledged no one as she walked, though she was aware that Harild, wonderful, strong, brave Harild, had fallen into step beside her.

She had known Sipharec's death was imminent but deep inside her had hoped he would rise, heal himself and stand before them as he had done for so long. But of course he had not, and his last hours had been spent unconscious with his pain dulled by magic.

Kerela walked to the city's main gates and ascended the stairs to the gatehouse. It was still under repair as were wide sections of the ramparts. Mages were busy investing strength into the walls, and she could hear the sounds of industry echoing around the city, manufacturing arrows, blades and bows.

Kerela stared out and her heart fell. She still remembered the stark beauty of the approaches to Julatsa and the horizon where you could see the sea sparkle on clear hot days. The scent of the long grass on the gentle rolling rises lingered in her memory and the laughter of children playing in the wide open spaces sounded in her head, hollow and bleak, a dream long shrivelled and dead.

The Wesmen were still gathering, and the clamour would be ceaseless until they attacked. There were so many more of them than before: thousands with ladders and sharp blades and with their shamen already chanting and dancing to gain the favour of the spirits. They were spreading out to encircle the city and this time they were not going to besiege Julatsa; they were going to come straight for the walls.

'When will they attack?' asked Kerela.

She felt completely overwhelmed and incapable of being in charge of any kind of defence. How she longed for Sipharec, Auum, Takaar and Drech. Powerful individuals blessed with knowledge and belief. She had been born well after the liberation of Calaius. She knew nothing of war.

'No later than first light tomorrow,' said Harild. He was gazing up at the sky where the light of afternoon was on the wane. 'We've done all we can. The mages are briefed, the wards are laid outside, and we will power the grid the moment they advance. We know their tactics.'

'But we have no TaiGethen, no capability to take down their shamen.'

Harild nodded, his head moving quickly. 'I know, but our duty is to hold them at bay for as long as we can. In the meantime we must pray that Auum and Takaar do what they set out to do.'

'And if they don't? If they fail?'

'They won't.'

'But if they do?'

Harild smiled a little sadly. 'Then we must save what we can and make sure our lives come at great cost to our enemies. What else is there to do?'

Night was falling. Takaar had been waiting for a day and his patience was spent. He had called the Senserii from their hiding place in the hills above Understone Pass and now waited with them while the tortuous discussions among the Circle Seven of Xetesk went on and on. He could not settle to eat or rest. His mind was ablaze and his tormentor wouldn't leave him be. He watched Gilderon watching him, and the suspicious Xeteskian mages and soldiers guarding the pass entrance watching all of them, wondering why their master had ordered them not to be touched.

Takaar half wished they'd try. Anything was better than this dreadful waiting, and he had not unleashed his energies in what seemed an age.

A small demonstration might speed up their decision.

'Or my demise,'

Either works for me, you know that.

'I thought you were all for this venture?'

Only because it will inevitably bring about your death.

'Is that really all that drives you?'

What else is there?

'Redemption, forgiveness and acceptance.'

I've never wanted those, and I fear they are beyond the murderer of Drech in any event.

'But you said—'

Don't be naive. I will say anything to bring about your death in the manner I desire.

'I look forward to your hating my every breath for millennia to come.'

We both know that isn't going to happen.

'Your certainty fires my determination.'

'Takaar?'

Takaar looked around, coming to himself once more. He was leaning against a rock three times his height, the product of a fall centuries past. Gilderon was before him, the rest of the Senserii in relaxed defensive positions nearby.

'What is it?'

Gilderon pointed back towards Understone and moved aside so Takaar could see. 'They are coming,' he said.

Takaar smiled. Understone was emptying. Mages on horseback led a long column of mounted soldiers four abreast. Bynaar had believed him

Unless they are coming to kill you, of course.

'Not even you believe that.'

I'll grant you that one.

Takaar walked over to meet Bynaar, who was leading the mage strength himself.

'You accept my word,' said Takaar. 'I am humbled.'

Bynaar raised an eyebrow. 'Nothing is quite that simple. The Circle Seven have sanctioned this action but only following a contact with Belphamun, who made an unconscious slip that confirms all that you claimed. Ystormun is on his way to Sky Lake and is perhaps a day's travel from the other end of the pass.'

Takaar nodded.

He didn't believe you. Look at all the checks he made.

'I expected nothing else.'

'Good,' said Bynaar a little vaguely. 'Just pray that your friend Auum can hold Ystormun until we arrive.'

'He cannot,' said Takaar. 'That is my task, and it is yours to reach me in good time because even my strength is finite.'

'No, no, no,' said Bynaar. 'You are not leaving me for one moment. That would suggest trust and I have none of that. Auum must hold him, and we will cage him when we arrive.'

Takaar felt as if a spike had been driven into his head. He stared at Bynaar through eyes that burned with his pain. He screwed them shut and tried to blot out the goading from his tormentor.

'You weren't listening,' he managed through clamped jaws. His hands writhed together. 'Only I . . . My task . . .'

Burn him. He does not trust you and he will betray you. Burn him and run, and they will chase you and they will see your genius and they will cage the beast and they will understand and they will forgive and you will be accepted.

'Please,' whispered Takaar. 'Say you will let me go.'

Bynaar's words came as if from a distance, and Takaar had to strain to hear them. They did not say they would let him go. Takaar felt hot across his whole body, and the energies surged within him, seeking release, seeking the unworthy.

Drech was unworthy and he had to go. Bynaar, is he more worthy? He is an enemy and he seeks to trap you. He wants the glory and you must not let him have it. The task is yours and yours alone, as Yniss is my witness. Don't let him steal your redemption from you!

'You will not steal my redemption!' screamed Takaar.

Bynaar's horse collapsed in a heap of organs and blood, its bones turned to dust and its skin bursting under the pressure from within. Bynaar was thrown clear by the blast of air from Takaar's casting. Men nearby were yelling, their horses bucking and bolting.

Gilderon and the Senserii enveloped Takaar and moved him away in the direction of the pass. Bynaar was trying to get to his feet, knocking away the proffered hands. His face was blank with shock.

'Only I can hold him!' roared Takaar as he was hurried away. 'See how I saved you? I beat him and I saved you. He wanted me to kill you and I didn't. You can trust me now!'

'Enough,' said Gilderon. 'We need to get away from here.'

Takaar laughed. 'I *can* do it. See, Auum? See how I controlled my anger?'

Bynaar was on his feet. Soldiers and mages were backing away from Takaar, their eyes flicking towards the boneless remains of the horse. None wanted to suffer the same fate. The tormentor was silent, beaten for now, but he would be back. He always came back. Takaar saw the Xeteskians begin to focus on him again.

'Helodian, Teralion, bring him,' said Gilderon. 'Run hard.'

Bynaar saw the Senserii sprint away. He watched their leader slice his bladed staff through the face of one soldier foolish enough to get in their way and then pivot on that same staff and crash his feet into the chest of a second. Then they were running for the pass and the Wesmen who lay within. And they were *fast*.

'Let them go!' he ordered, though none had moved to chase them. 'Stand down.'

Bynaar wiped the blood and mess from his cloak and riding clothes. He looked at the remains of his horse and tried to imagine the casting which had done it. He failed. Just flesh and skin and innards . . . The animal had no skeleton, no bones of any kind. How it had been done was beyond Bynaar entirely. He chuckled.

'My Lord Bynaar?'

'You know something, Pirys?' he said to the young student who stood before him. 'I'm wondering if I misjudged him.'

'He tried to kill you,' said Pirys.

'He tried equally hard not to. And for that I should be glad.'

'We're not going in, I take it.'

Bynaar barked a short laugh.

'On the contrary. My reputation in the Circle Seven is at stake and Takaar is about to clear the pass for us. It would be rude not to take advantage of that.'

Pirys stared at the black hole of the pass entrance. He licked his lips nervously.

'Then may I have your orders, my lord?'

Bynaar ticked them off on his fingers.

'Get me some fresh clothes, get me a horse and get this column ready to move. We've got a Wytch Lord to catch.'

Chapter 33

But I feel the energies of magic so keenly in my soul. Surely it is a test of my faith. I will not fail.

Auum, Arch of the TaiGethen

As soon as they were around the first long bend and out of sight of the Xeteskians, Takaar had been freed to run with them. Gilderon was shaking. The moments between Takaar's perceived slights and the seemingly inevitable retribution were becoming shorter and shorter. Where it had been days in the festering while his damned other self got to work on the increasingly small rational part of his mind, now . . . Well, this latest outburst spoke eloquently enough to his state of mind.

The only mercy was that Takaar had retained enough to inflict that cruellest of deaths on the horse not the man. Gilderon wondered if they had chosen to rededicate themselves to Takaar prematurely, though the next moment he was certain their decision had been right. After all, who else was capable of seeing Takaar to his target? The question now was whether he chose to do as he planned or do something utterly beyond reason.

Helodian had sprinted on ahead to a spot illuminated by the dim light of lanterns. The smell of woodsmoke filtered along the pass, which was about fifteen feet high and wide enough for a carriage and horses flanked by riders. It was an astonishing feat of construction.

Takaar ran beside Gilderon. His face was clear and calm and he was focused on the path ahead as if what he had just said and done was no more than a dim nightmare from centuries past. Gilderon had been with Takaar for so many hundreds of years and thought he'd seen all there was, but for the first time Takaar actually scared him, and he was forced to consider what he would do if the once-great elf lost the last vestiges of his control.

Helodian came trotting back.

'Significant presence four hundred yards ahead. Once this gentle left turn has straightened, we'll have eyes on them. They'll see us for the last thirty yards or so in their lantern light.'

'How many?' asked Gilderon, slowing them all down.

'Twenty that I can see backed by eight or nine of their shamen. They've built a barricade that may well be hiding many more. Our advantage is that the pass is tight and we can fill it and wear them down.'

'No,' said Takaar. 'Your advantage is that you have me. You have battles to come; I shall deal with them.'

Gilderon stopped them as soon as he could see the lanterns and the warriors leaning on spears or resting against the walls or the wood of their eight-foot-tall barricade. The shamen were in a group around a fire, talking and gesticulating. As he watched, an opening in the barricade was unbolted and he caught a glimpse of a great deal more Wesmen behind it.

'We can deal with this, Takaar,' he said. 'Our role is to protect you.'

'The shamen will kill you before you get within ten yards. Don't question me.'

That last was said as if from another mouth. Gilderon was about to protest further but Takaar was clearly wrestling with himself and his expression was of ill-controlled impulse.

'Show them mercy,' was all he could manage.

Takaar moved off along the dark passage towards the Wesman lantern light. Gilderon pitied them, hearing one side of Takaar's conversation.

'Fire can only be drawn from the fuel already there. It is not enough . . . You are showing your ignorance as always. To use the air is terribly draining . . . Now you're thinking. The raw material surrounds us and we have only to prod in the right place.'

Unconsciously the Senserii had drawn back from Takaar and had moved together, unsettled by the energies he was beginning to marshal. Inside the tight confines of the pass Ix's power felt multiplied, and it roared through their bodies on its way to do whatever Takaar required.

Takaar was walking forward steadily, his head twitching from side to side as if seeking something minute, his hands trembling and his fingers jerking, closing and opening while he teased at his target. Fifty yards from the barricade and deep in shadow he stopped.

'It will be loud,' he said. 'Cover your ears.'

Takaar moved off quickly, his hands outstretched in front of his face, palms away from him. Gilderon led the Senserii forward at a run. Ahead, the Wesmen began to make out dim shapes in the gloom beyond the light of their lanterns and fire. Warriors plucked weapons from where they rested and the shamen were ready to cast should they prove to be enemies.

The first effect of Takaar's spell was a series of dull cracks from up ahead. Takaar's fingers wiggled in what would have been comic fashion in other circumstances but to Gilderon, it only made what came next all the more terrifying. The shamen moved to cast. Warriors lined up to give them cover.

They should all have been running.

Takaar, not breaking stride, drew his arms back, jabbed them forward hard and closed his fists. The roof above the Wesmen collapsed, smashing their bodies into the ground and extinguishing the fire and lanterns. The noise ripped into Gilderon's head despite the hands clamped over his ears and he roared a curse as much at the sight as the sound.

Down and down came the rock, splintering the barricade. Through the clouds of dust and debris thrown up into the pass Gilderon saw Wesmen turning to run. It was impossible to hear their screams but they must have been loud until shut off by the torrent of mountain battering their bodies, bursting their skulls and crushing their limbs from their twitching corpses.

Takaar walked on, repeating his gestures. More boulders came thundering down. Smears of black appeared briefly on the walls before being eclipsed by the dust, which billowed down the pass towards the Senserii. Gilderon held his breath and turned away while the force of it rolled over him impelled by a gust of Ix-inspired wind, buffeting his body and tearing at his clothes.

He could barely see Takaar a few feet ahead of him. The mad elf circled his hands and pushed, adding more power to the wind, which now blew away from them, whipping up the dust into spirals and driving it away from the scene of his atrocity so all could view what he had wrought.

Immediately the air was clear, Takaar set off again, his hands cocked, ready to cause another rockfall. Gilderon stared for a heartbeat at the awful devastation and ran in front of him, turning and grabbing his arms.

'Enough!' he shouted. 'Enough! Look what you've done! Yniss spare us from the wrath of Shorth, look what you've *done*.'

Takaar's gaze, lost in the energies he manipulated, darted around Gilderon before settling on his face. He tried to move his arms but Gilderon held on tight, this time heedless of the risk he might be running.

'Enough,' he repeated. 'You've killed them. You've killed them *all*.'

Takaar's body relaxed, and the weight of energies dissipated, leaving a quiet broken by the rumbling of echoes. Gilderon looked to his Senserii.

'Go among them. If any live, speed their passing and pray for their souls.' His voice cracked and he stared back at Takaar. 'No one should die like that.'

Gilderon walked with Takaar, who seemed in a daze. Whether he had any notion of what he had just done was questionable. They picked their way through the rubble and debris, which reached halfway up to the roof in places. Gilderon looked up at it, fearful of another fall.

'Did you know that even the most solid of rock has tiny fractures? All I had to do was make them bigger.' Takaar's smile was ephemeral. 'Simple, really.'

'You can never do this again,' whispered Gilderon. 'It is not right. Yniss cannot countenance this.'

'Where the rock is hard for a horse to pass I will make it dust. We must leave a path,' said Takaar.

The Senserii knelt and rose as they searched. Nowhere did they find a living Wesman. Gilderon swallowed. They walked past a bloodied hand on the ground, fingers open. The arm disappeared beneath a fall of rock which must have crushed the body flat. Something was caught in the dead fingers.

Takaar knelt down and picked it up. In his hands lay a child's doll in the likeness of a warrior. He held it up to Gilderon before his face crumpled, and he wailed for the lost, for what he had done and for who he had become.

Dawn on the day that would decide the fate of Balaia, Calaius and the Wesmen was chill and grey and entirely fitting. The feast of the night before had often been tense and the atmosphere occasionally aggressive, but Auum had enjoyed it nonetheless. He'd spent most of the evening with Sentaya and Tilman, putting together a series of commands they could all understand.

Stein had suffered almost constant abuse and sported a livid bruise on one cheek as testament to the only punch thrown. Sentaya had reacted furiously to it, halting the feast to reaffirm the nature of the alliance that would last until the battle was done. The offender had almost managed to pass Stein a cup of broth as a gesture of reconciliation but somehow it had fallen on his feet instead.

Stein might have taken renewed offence at the second affront but instead had chosen to tip back his head and laugh. Auum smiled at the memory. Stein was a fine diplomat, and there were probably a few Wesman warriors lined up behind the stockade this morning wondering quite why they hated all man's magic so much.

Close to midnight the sound of many hundreds of voices singing had broken the mood in the village, and Stein, of course, had suggested a final event to boost the confidence of the Wesmen doomed to face their Wytch Lord-backed rivals at sunrise. A series of races and tasks of agility had been organised along with sparring and wrestling.

Grudgingly Auum had agreed to the notion, but the TaiGethen had won every challenge, their use of shetharyn drawing gasps and the laughter of the disbelieving in equal measure.

'I ask you, do you wish to face any TaiGethen seeking your throat?' Sentaya had roared, and following the cacophonous negative, he had jabbed a finger in the direction of the approaching enemy. 'Neither do they!'

And so it came to this: Wesman Lord, TaiGethen warrior and eastern mage standing side by side. Auum stood between the other two, just in case. They had not exactly clasped hands on the alliance, but Auum had caught them speaking to each other as the feast broke up. Sentaya might have been smiling. Then again it might have been a panther's grin; he had a very fierce face.

The three stood at the head of their forces outside the stockade which they hoped would provide brief but vital shelter when the time came. The ranks were lined up as bait for the enemy massing about three hundred yards distant. Ystormun's men had already encountered the first of Stein's wards, which had slowed their advance dramatically. Neither Ystormun nor his shamen were divining them, just as Stein had predicted.

'They might as well run headlong for all the good it'll do them,' muttered Stein. 'Going tiptoe across them makes you just as dead.'

'I'll be right behind you when you trot out and let them know,' said Ulysan.

'Are all your Communion minds open?' asked Auum.

'Yes.' Stein indicated Sentaya's outbuildings. 'He wouldn't let us in the house but the cattle don't mind us. A quick shout and you can have your cells on their way in.'

Auum nodded and sent a prayer to Tual to bless his hidden teams with sure feet and swift strikes. The indefatigable Faleen was heading three cells positioned in the deep reeds bordering the lake about a mile north of the enemy. Merrat and Merke's cells were waiting in a belt of woodland less than two miles to the east.

Auum watched Sentaya's face as the tribal banners became clearer and the shamen's garb stood out among the furs and leather of their warrior flock. Sentaya had about a hundred and fifty blades at his disposal, drawn from his village and from a cluster of small settlements around the southern end of the lake. His two elder sons commanded a third each as did he. All wore tribal marks on their faces, blue lines on their cheeks and white diagonals on their foreheads.

'It'll make us easy for your TaiGethen to spot when the lines are broken,' Sentaya had said.

Sentaya was uncomfortable standing and waiting, and even more so at the notion of hiding inside his stockade when the spells started to fall. He knew it made sense, but it went against every instinct and felt like cowardice. Worse, he would be inside his stockade as the battle was joined because magic was being employed on his behalf. Auum understood his turmoil.

'What do you know of them?' asked Auum, nodding his head at the enemy.

Stein, as always, translated. Sentaya spat between his feet before he spoke.

'I see banners from the Heconn, the Kistoi, the Rekine and the Calamet. Worthy fighters but they darkened the soul of all Wesmen when they bent the knee to grasp power they thought they could own. There is plenty of reason to hate them.'

Sentaya paused and scanned the undulating rock-strewn ground across which they were coming. A ward detonated to the left. Fire roared into the air, carrying two bodies with it. The screams were brief. Warriors paused but were ordered on, and the dead were left where they fell. Sentaya closed his eyes briefly and muttered what Auum understood to be a prayer of forgiveness.

'Is what we are doing any different to the black fire the shamen will use to try and kill you?' asked Auum.

Sentaya stared at him but did not reply. Instead he focused back on the enemy.

'We must be wary of the shamen. These are not village holy men. So many of those claiming the robes are little more than vessels for Wytch Lord magic. They are not steeped in the spirits and have never studied or lived as they are required to. They are deep in the ways of the spirits and the Wytch Lords, though, shamen schooled inside Parve's temples. Dangerous and powerful, able to channel far more effectively.'

Auum felt a moment of anxiety though he had to expect Ystormun would have brought the best that he could, the most loyal.

'Have we had word of Takaar's progress yet?' he asked Stein.

'Nothing. We know he's trying to get here but no more.' Stein turned a slightly nervous smile on Auum. 'Don't worry. We can send his spirit to cower in his temple and give Sentaya all he needs to ally the mass of Wesmen against the Wytch Lords. We'll win this.'

'You really believe that?'

'You're my brother, Auum, but if I didn't believe it, I wouldn't be standing here with a sworn enemy while facing one of Balaia's most powerful creatures.'

'You're scared?' asked Auum.

'Terrified,' said Stein. 'This is a Wytch Lord in his own lands. He will draw directly on the power residing in his temple. The Ystormun you saw in Calaius was a child by comparison.'

In front of them the Wesman army stopped on a single command. They were in loose formation, wary of traps. They spread further to the left towards the lake and to the right, meaning to attack the village on three sides. Ystormun also knew they would clear the wards for his shamen in the process. Archers were among the axe and sword carriers. The shamen were clustered in groups of eight and positioned some thirty yards behind the warriors.

They were silent. A carriage rolled up onto a rise more than a hundred yards behind the broad single line. It was guarded by shamen and warriors.

'Ready?' asked Auum.

'Always,' said Sentaya, using an elven word he'd been taught the night before.

'Die old, not today,' said Auum. 'Stein, get the strike teams running.'

A call began at the far right of the Wesman line and rippled all the way along it, setting birds to flight and the hairs standing on Auum's arms. It was a call for strength and courage.

'It's the coronyl,' said Sentaya.

The call died away. Horns sounded and the Wesmen charged

The ground was firm, clear and easy beneath Faleen's feet, allowing her to reach a prodigious speed. The temptation to drop into the shetharyn was great, but they would need that in due course if they were to escape with their lives. Her Tai of Haloor and Jyrrian struggled to keep pace and she looked across to the Tais of Oryaal and Dodann, seeing their strides lengthen as they coursed across the ground.

It was a thrilling run. Ahead she could see the tail of the Wesman force. The supply wagons were drawn up in a line, their backs to her approach. A few guards were scattered about them, but her prize was the Wesman reserve and Ystormun's carriage, which lay beyond them.

Away to the east she saw swift movement over the grass. Merrat and Merke's cells cruised towards the enemy. The picture was complete. All they needed from the village was . . .

A rippling series of detonations eclipsed the war cries of the Wesman attackers. Smoke billowed into the air and flames grasped at the sky. There were screams of pain and roared orders. Bodies were flung high to land broken and burned on the ground. As one, the Wesman reserve force, over a hundred warriors, turned to stare at the carnage meted out to their brethren.

The three cells formed a fighting line on the sprint, racing around the right-hand side of the wagon line. Faleen drew her twin blades and attacked. She chopped a blade into the lower back of a guard, pacing on to smash her other blade into the buttocks of another.

She was past them both before they had a chance to cry out. Haloor spear-kicked another in the back of the neck, landed and swept a blade into the skull of a second, clearing his path to the reserve. Jyrrian hurled a jaqrui at his target, missing him by a breath.

The blade mourned away, thudding into the shoulder of a reserve warrior.

The Wesman yelled his pain and turned just as his comrades awoke to the attack. At a barked command they drew their weapons and faced Faleen's nine. Oryaal took his cell left and Dodann's split right. Faleen crashed into the centre of them, and simultaneously Merrat and Merke hammered into their left flank.

Blades clashed and sparked and the Wesmen yelled for support; the shamen would not be long in coming. Faleen dropped to her haunches and swept the legs from her opponent. He fell heavily, and she stepped on the blade of his axe and thrust a sword into his throat.

She rose to her feet, blocked a sword strike to her midriff and stepped right, catching the flat of an axe on her right-hand blade. She forced the weapon up and thrust her second blade into the warrior's armpit. Haloor's blade deflected a stab at her exposed left flank. He kicked out straight, forcing a small space. Jyrrian came through into it, planting a roundhouse kick into the temple of his target and sending him stumbling back. Faleen followed up, opening his gut and dumping his entrails into the dust. She paced back and moved left with her Tai, leaving the Wesman to scream and fall to his knees, staring at his own innards.

'Shamen incoming!' called Dodann.

'Break and cover,' shouted Faleen. She ducked an axe swing and drove a kick into her attacker's knee, forcing it backwards, breaking bone and ripping tendon and muscle. 'Shetharyn at your discretion.'

Haloor and Jyrrian came to her shoulders. The Wesmen had backed up a pace. Orders sang through their chaotic lines. To her left the fighting remained intense where Merke and Merrat were pressing.

'Don't give them room to get the shamen at us,' said Faleen. 'Oryaal, push on!'

Faleen raced in again, her speed of foot and hand difficult for the Wesmen to counter. Haloor paced up and leaped, his heels connecting with an enemy chest, knocking his target over. He rode the fall, swiping his blades to the left and right, having one blocked and the other cut a Wesman face from cheek to cheek.

Faleen followed him in, Jyrrian at her left. Wesmen began to close about them, seeing in Dodann's withdrawal the chance to bring pressure on the TaiGethen for the first time.

Faleen's right blade struck the sword hand from a warrior aiming a blow at Haloor. Her left fenced away a quick stab to her groin and she swayed left to avoid another, feeling it slice her jacket and nick the flesh over her ribs.

Faleen gasped at the sudden pain. She ducked another swing. The blow was beaten upwards by Jyrrian, who followed it with a killing thrust to the chest. Haloor turned a backward somersault and landed next to her.

'Tai, we need out of this press,' said Faleen. 'Where's Dodann?'

Haloor moved right to force a little room. Jyrrian felled another Wesman, whose overhead strike had left him off balance and exposed. The three of them took a pace back. Oryaal was a few paces to their left. Pannos, of his Tai, was bleeding from a cut to his head, blood running down into his eyes.

Oryaal pushed him from the path of an oncoming warrior pair. He fielded one blow; Jyrrian's jaqrui lodged in the neck of the other. Oryaal nodded and his Tai fell back.

'Dodann's in the clear, running the right flank.'

In front of Faleen the Wesman line had solidified. They were well drilled and courageous. The bodies of their comrades littered the ground and they had barely touched an elf, but there was no fear in their eyes. They held their ground, waiting. Faleen frowned.

She backed up another pace, crouched and drove up, leaping as high as she was able. Over the heads of the reserve she could see why they were so confident. Shamen were moving fast to her right, obscured by the fighters. Others were moving through the lines. Dodann was running into deep trouble.

'Shamen in the lines!' called Faleen as she landed. 'Oryaal, break to Merrat. Tai, with me to Dodann.'

Faleen sprinted right, drawing a response from some Wesmen who broke ranks to chase her despite the orders howled by their commanders.

'Dodann, break off!' shouted Faleen, but he could not hear her. 'Get back into the fight. You've got to get among them. It's the only way to be safe!'

She ran harder, the Wesmen beginning to break in larger numbers, seeking to cut her off.

'If that's the way you want it,' she muttered. 'Tai, break them.'

Faleen planted her right foot and drove back into the Wesmen. She could see Dodann, Valess and Myriin moving steadily on out of blade range. Faleen thrashed both her blades right to left, forcing the

Wesmen to take evasive action. Jyrrian drop-kicked one in the gut and Haloor came up on the right, swaying beneath an axe before rocking back and flattening the nose of his target with a straight kick to his face.

'Push!' shouted Faleen. 'Dodann! Turn!

Wesmen were at their backs as Faleen surged forward. The Wesman line ahead was thin and beyond them, shamen waited for Dodann's cell. Faleen punched the hilt of a blade into the mouth of one warrior, knocking his head back, then she opened his throat with the same blade.

Faleen ran into the gap, shouldering another aside and onto Haloor's swords. A third blocked her path. She took a pace and leaped above him, cycling her blades in her hands and chopping down onto his head and shoulder as she passed. Faleen landed behind Dodann's cell just as he ran into the sight of the Shamen.

Black rods of energy, each thick as a fist, skewered his cell, each one finding the heart. She watched helpless as the TaiGethen were plucked from their feet and hurled back. The shamen held them in the air for a moment before tossing their bodies aside like discarded dolls. This was no broken black fire and its potency was extreme.

Faleen turned, and as she did saw the back cloth of the single carriage twitch.

'Speed!' she howled. 'Tai, with me!'

Faleen called on the shetharyn, and the world slowed around her. The shamen were looking for new targets. The Wesmen were closing around her cell. Jyrrian and Haloor turned to follow her. She saw a Wesman with his back to her sweep out an arm. Jyrrian ran straight into it, his attention on Haloor. He tumbled to the ground, his speed gone.

Faleen began to turn. An axe came down slowly. Jyrrian was rolling aside, trying to get his feet under him. Faleen dived headlong. The axe blade passed in front of her face. She grasped at it but her reach was not enough. Jyrrian raised his hands but the blade took them with it into his chest.

Faleen landed, rolled and stood.

'Shorth will take you all,' she hissed.

She shot off after Haloor, tearing across the front of the Wesman lines. Beams of dark energy shot out, blistering the air. Faleen shivered, dreading the bite of the malevolent magic.

'Oryaal! Break and go.'

On the left Merrat and Merke still fought, but ripples in the Wesman lines told of shamen approaching. Faleen fell back into the battle, her blades sweeping ahead of her. Wesman blood sprayed into the air.

'Merrat! Merke!' Faleen thrashed a blade into the neck of a Wesman, who collapsed forward. Merrat stood there, blood across his face and a cut on his left arm. His blade was cocked to strike. 'Break and go! We can't take these without magic.'

Merrat's Tai fought around him, giving him a moment's pause.

'We're among them,' he said. 'We can win this.'

'No. Dodann's Tai is gone, downed by a new power. Please, we have to get out of here and take the message to Auum.'

Merrat looked at the battle about them and back into Faleen's eyes.

'I trust you,' he said.

'Speed,' whispered Faleen.

Chapter 34

Here's the thing. It isn't just that a TaiGethen in the shetharyn is much faster than a galloping horse, it's the speed of thought that goes with it. That's what makes them really frightening.

Stein, Mage of Julatsa

The wards did terrible damage. While Sentaya's Wesmen sheltered inside the stockade, sending prayers to their spirits and cursing human magic, their enemies had run headlong into the wide arc of wards Stein had placed to encircle the village and had made active when all were either inside or gone south for safety.

Explosions reverberated through the ground and howling flames glared in the sky. Tribesmen were slaughtered in large numbers and Auum saw the sense of injustice burning bright in Sentaya's eyes.

'I should not have allowed you to do this,' the Wesman chief said, his face taut and the muscles of his neck corded and proud under his skin. 'Now human magic stains my hands. These are my brethren, the people I wish to rule, and they will not forget this day.'

Outside the advance had halted, the roaring charge losing all impetus to be replaced by wails of pain, the cries of dying warriors and the crackle of multiple fires.

'Think, my Lord Sentaya,' said Stein. 'They are nine hundred blades, outnumbering you six to one. No one doubts your courage or skill but those odds are not survivable. What your subjects won't forget is how you faced the Wytch Lord, Ystormun, and won, and how some chose black fire to further their own selfish ambition.'

Sentaya knew Stein was right, but Auum could see him wrestling with himself, for a moment unable to provide the leadership his warriors needed. Some were frightened, some angry, and none relished what was being done in their name.

'They're advancing again,' called Thrynn from her perch on a barn overlooking the field. 'The shamen are moving up closer behind their warriors. It's a slow advance to the last line of wards.'

Auum could hear orders carried on the breeze and feel the vibration of marching feet through the ground.

'I need a distance countdown,' said Auum.

They were as ready as they would ever be. A line of warriors, mainly Sentaya's, stood ten paces back from the stockade ready to attack the moment it was breached, to engage and to break off in an attempt to bring the enemy into the village. The rest of the force was scattered in and around the buildings, much to Sentaya's dismay.

'We need chaos, not line on line, or we'll lose,' Auum had said. Sentaya had wanted to lead his warriors in a charge.

Stein's mages were set behind the warrior line, sending shivers down the spines of the Wesmen, who had sworn never to turn their backs on human magic. And the Il-Aryn were in three groups, charged with providing as much defence as they could muster against the black fire as the warriors charged. Beyond that, planning was pointless.

'Seventy-five,' called Thrynn.

'Closing on the obscurement ward grid,' said Stein,

'I wish those had all been fire walls now,' said Ulysan.

'Stamina is a finite thing. This was the best we could do in the time,' said Stein a little testily.

'Just saying,' said Ulysan.

'Isn't it time you went to your place?' said Stein.

'I think you'll find my place is next to Auum. Always has been.'

Auum held up his hands. 'Will you two stop it? What is this?'

'Sixty-five,' called Thrynn. 'Wards in five.'

'It's called bickering,' said Stein. 'It's what brothers do.'

Ulysan enveloped him in a bear hug and gave him a big wet kiss. Stein pushed him away and wiped at his cheek.

'That's disgusting,' he said.

'It's for luck,' said Ulysan.

'Does he do that before every battle?' asked Stein.

Auum shook his head. 'It's a first.'

'I'm . . . honoured.'

'Just get casting,' said Ulysan.

A series of dull thuds was heard. With the triggering of the first ward, the rest followed in sequence. Thick oily dark grey smoke spread in all directions like the deepest of winter fogs, rising thirty feet into the sky.

'Go, go!' called Sentaya.

His forty or so archers ran through gaps opened in the stockade on the three land-facing sides of the village. The Julatsans followed, already preparing spells. In the village the Il-Aryn began their work, ready for the inevitable.

'Speak to me, Thrynn.'

'Nothing to see, Auum. The smoke is too thick. Arrows are flying into it all across the arc. Spells away too . . .'

Auum saw them go as well as the black shafts of arrows, twenty orbs of fire trailing smoke and plunging out of sight just before impact. Auum closed his eyes. Like the wards, the Wesmen would not have seen them coming. More arrows shot across the gap. A handful were returned, but such was the confusion within the smoke that nearly all were poorly directed, falling harmlessly towards the lake or even back down among their own.

Above the smoke huge drops of fire began to fall from the clouded sky. Auum scanned across the arc of the attack front. Like burning leaves falling in a rainforest fire, they tumbled into the fog. And like many of Gyal's tears, the fire rain was torrential but short-lived.

Auum shuddered. How many were perishing blinded by the smoke and with claws of fire digging into their heads and backs? Again orders were ringing out above the sounds of pain. Still they had order and courage, and Auum could only respect them for that.

'I see figures!' called Thrynn. 'Smoke thinning at thirty yards.'

'Back inside!' called Auum.

The call was taken up by elven and Wes throats, bringing archers and mages scurrying through the gaps, which were immediately closed. Well directed arrows started to come over the stockade, sending defenders hurrying for cover. Thrynn lay prone on the barn roof, still calling out the closing distance.

Sentaya roared for his warriors to get back into line. Bows were discarded, swords and axes bristled. Stein's voice in his most melodious elvish reorganised his mages, bringing them back towards the houses before turning to prepare again.

'Twenty.'

Auum looked up. 'Thrynn, don't—'

A bolt of pure black the thickness of an arm crossed the space faster than an arrow and struck Thrynn square in the forehead. Her skull burst, her body twitched and fell from the roof of the barn, leaving blood and brain smearing the thatch. For a heartbeat Auum struggled to understand what he had seen.

'Il-Aryn, barrier, now! Stein, get some spells over that wall. Anyone in the open, get to cover!'

Auum ran across the central oval. A breathless hush fell in the village as Julatsan mages launched orbs over the stockade. A moment later the Il-Aryn barriers shimmered into place, each covering a third of the stockade the enemy threatened. Sentaya's warriors backed up a pace or two but ignored Auum's advice to seek cover.

Auum turned a full circle, checking positions and trying not to think about Thrynn and what her death meant for them all. He trotted back towards Ulysan and Tilman, both peering from the door of Sentaya's house. Tilman was looking nervous, but Ulysan's face was set hard, the loss of Thrynn firing his desire to fight.

Across the arc shaman fire slammed into the barriers, Auum imagining the thick black rods like spears of magic lancing into the magical construct. He heard Rith yelling for the Il-Aryn to hold and could see the adepts, with arms about each other in their horribly vulnerable positions, bowing their heads to focus harder.

Again and again the fire came in and the barriers shimmered, bowed and steadied. Auum prayed that their adaptation of Takaar's original casting had eradicated the weakness which had previously brought them down, and that the Wesman warriors would be forced to attack the stockade. After the fifth attack the bombardment ceased.

'Hold!' called Rith. 'They haven't gone anywhere. Keep the bindings secure.'

The temptation to look above the stockade was almost overwhelming, but Thrynn's demise was raw in their memories and the defenders held their positions. Orders were called beyond the stockade. Arrows flew into the village in disciplined volleys, Auum estimating the archer strength at around seventy – enough to cause problems. Sentaya's warriors raised their shields.

Auum felt the weight of magical energy heavy across his shoulders, pressing down on his head. Beside him Ulysan felt it too, and out in the village the Il-Aryn had hunched closer together.

'That doesn't feel—'

The light dimmed momentarily in front of the northern section of the stockade. Dark energy engulfed the Il-Aryn barrier without warning, scattering it to twinkling shards. The stockade was obliterated along a length of some sixty yards, sending splinters through the village on a cloud of choking dust. Mage, Il-Aryn and Wesman alike threw themselves down while the hideous energy rolled over them only to be snatched back and swallowed by the hands that had cast it. It was gone as quickly as it had come.

Auum sprinted out into the open, racing across the ground to Rith, who was flat on her back. The dust was clearing away and through it he could see enemy warriors making their charge. To the right more shamen moved into position while those who had broken the Il-Aryn retreated to recover. On the shallow rise where the carriage stood a single tall figure gazed across the land. It was thick with the corpses of his fighters, while magical fires picked at bodies, some of which were moving grotesquely, grasping at nothing and hoping for death.

'Yniss preserve us,' breathed Auum.

He stared down at Rith, whose face was smothered with confusion and shock. Other TaiGethen ran to help the Il-Aryn.

'Up,' he said. 'Enemies coming. Come on, Rith, get to your other teams. More incoming power. You have to help them.'

Auum hauled her to her feet and she stared at him while the world swam into focus. She nodded and turned away to see to her Il-Aryn. Auum ran to the shattered stockade.

'Tais, with me!' he called. The Wesmen were only twenty yards away and running in hard. 'Jaqruis!'

Ulysan came to his left shoulder with Tilman the other side of him.

'Face front, trust the TaiGethen,' said Auum, wondering how vulnerable his right flank would be. 'This is your chance to be one of us. Arrows!' Auum grabbed Tilman and dragged him flat. Arrows flew overhead. 'Up, up!' Tilman jumped to his feet, no fear on his face but a wild excitement in his eyes and pride fit to burst from his chest. 'Remember your training.'

Marack, Nokhe and Hohan joined his right. Auum saw Evunn and Duele moving left with more coming, bolstered by Sentaya's Wesmen roaring their fury and holding weapons high. Archers behind them sent arrows into the midst of the attackers, downing one or two. Auum estimated their strength at around six hundred. A third of them were down, but it was nowhere near enough.

Without warning the central section of the stockade exploded inwards, scattering Il-Aryn and Wesman fighters alike. The pressure of the blast blew across Auum and his defenders. Wesmen poured towards the new gap as the last section was blown apart. Sentaya could he heard ordering his warriors back to their feet.

'Ulysan, hold them here,' said Auum. 'We need a diversion.'

He turned and ran back into the village, hearing the first swords clash, the first cry of a dying fighter. He prayed it wasn't Tilman. The Il-Aryn were exposed and vulnerable. Enemies were driving in across the arc, buoyed by the devastating power gifted their shamen by Ystormun. TaiGethen cells were moving to their aid but he needed more than that.

'Stein! Where are you!' he roared.

'Auum.' It was Grafyrre with his cell of Ferinn and Lynees. 'What do you need?'

They were standing in the centre of the oval, their plan in tatters. Their withdrawal should have been much more controlled and gradual.

'I need the Il-Aryn up, defended and under cover. They have to get barriers back up when the shamen are ready to cast again. And I need Stein.'

'Stein is by Sentaya's barn.'

Auum looked to his left. Stein and seven of his mages launched orbs of fire across the defence to slam into the enemy line at the third section.

'Good. Get two cells . . . Truun and Gyliaar's . . . put them in charge of the Il-Aryn. Then get to Stein. You're heading out on his signal to take Ystormun.'

Grafyrre took his cell and sped away. Auum raced over to Stein.

'We can't hold them when the shamen come back,' said Auum. 'But Ystormun is poorly defended.'

Stein looked at him and nodded. 'Now is as good a time as any.'

'It might be our only chance,' said Auum. 'Grafyrre will be with you. We'll try to sweep up any survivors of the strike cells and send them back in.'

'I'll take twenty with me, fly out and hopefully turn a few shamen away from the village.'

'I can't risk you,' said Auum. 'Send your best deputy.'

'I've trained for this all my life,' said Stein.

Auum nodded, still reluctant. 'Just don't die, brother.'

'I have no intention of doing so.'

Auum turned and ran back to Ulysan and Tilman. Despite the shock of the shaman power, Sentaya's warriors were up and fighting, the line thin but just holding with the help of the TaiGethen, who worked the left and right flanks to contain the attack. Auum saw Sentaya front and centre, his axe sweeping through low into the legs of an enemy and reversing to batter its spike into the face of another. For a Wesman beyond his physical peak, he had the energy of someone half his age.

Running in hard, Auum saw Ulysan close to Tilman, tipping away a blow meant for the human and savaging his second blade into the neck of an opponent. Tilman had a short blade held two-handed and displayed good speed, knocking aside an axe aimed at his skull and riposting swiftly, lacing a cut into the Wesman's chest.

Auum called Ulysan's name, leaped and soared over the big TaiGethen's head, his blades in hand. He landed behind Ulysan's next opponent and drove one of his blades backwards through his thigh, ripping it clear through the side of his leg. He turned and spun right, driving his left foot up into the mouth of the attacker facing him and his bloodied blade into the chest of the one moving in beside him.

Auum completed his turn, stabbed his right blade into the kidney of the Wesman closing on Tilman and rejoined the line.

'We missed you,' said Ulysan.

The Wesmen came on again after a moment to compose themselves. Beyond them the shamen were gathering themselves for another assault while overhead Stein flew out and to the right heading for his showdown with Ystormun. Down on the ground Grafyrre and his cell would be under the shetharyn and following him through the enemy.

'This had better work,' muttered Auum. 'Die old, Stein, not today.'

Grafyrre could see fingers pointing up into the sky and Wesmen and shamen turning. Auum was going to get his diversion. He led his cell through the lines and away to the right beyond the reach of shaman fire, where he knew the strike teams were to muster before returning to the village.

Grafyrre called Ferinn and Lynees from the shetharyn, and they dropped to a sprint. Almost immediately Stein swept overhead, indicating ahead and to his right. Grafyrre changed direction, ran over a low rise and into a small stand of trees, where TaiGethen stood over the prone forms of two others.

'Faleen,' he said, sliding to a stop and kicking up dust. 'How many can come with us?'

He looked down and saw Pannos, over whom Oryaal crouched offering words of comfort. Next to him Merrat stroked the hair from Nersini's face. Both injured elves were lying on their sides and had scorches across their bodies where fires had burned through their clothes and into their backs.

'This is what we face,' said Merrat. 'Dodann's cell was gone in a taipan's strike.'

'Jyrrian?' asked Grafyrre.

Faleen shook her head. 'At least it was steel that killed him, not this new evil.'

'We have no time to grieve,' said Grafyrre, feeling heartless. 'Any who can run with me, we're after Ystormun. Stein's mages are in the sky.'

Merrat and Oryaal stood. Faleen and Merke joined them.

'What we have, we'll bring.'

'Then let's run.'

Grafyrre led them out towards Ystormun's carriage, twelve of them in all to take on whatever Ystormun threw at them. The elven mages were ahead and had been seen as they landed. Wesmen and shamen were advancing on them from the carriage guard some two hundred yards away.

Stein spread them wide apart and all walked forward steadily, preparing. Ystormun stood proud in front of his carriage, barely even looking in their direction. Shamen and Wesmen in their dozens were heading back to join him while the remainder battered at the village defenders.

'Break around the mages and target the warriors first,' Grafyrre said. 'Stein will take the shamen.'

Orbs of fire shot from the hands of Stein's mages, arcing over the warriors and falling on the carriage, Ystormun and into the midst of the shamen. The carriage roof blew off and the axles broke as the vehicle collapsed into an inferno. Shamen were blown apart, others had dived and rolled away, some caught by flame, others unscathed. Ystormun did not so much as flinch when the fire was diverted harmlessly across the shield he had created for himself. He continued to stare downslope as if searching for something, or someone.

Grafyrre sped past the mages, who were advancing again after casting their spells. He nodded at Stein, who was staring straight at Ystormun, already working on his next and pivotal construct.

Grafyrre drew a jaqrui and hurled it. His Wesman target ducked and it slashed past him and struck a shaman thirty yards behind him square in the forehead. Grafyrre drew his twin blades and launched into the attack, Ferinn and Lynees on his flanks.

Grafyrre swivelled and launched a side kick up to block an axe blade. He moved forward after the kick, sweeping his left blade into the warrior's midriff. Lynees was airborne, spear-kicking his target, catching him on the jaw. The Wesman's axe jerked up and back and lodged in the skull of the warrior behind him.

Ferinn spun on her heel and unwound a heavy blow to the shoulder of her target with her right heel, sending him sprawling. Grafyrre pounced on him, slicing his throat open. He rolled under a scything axe sweep and chopped both his blades into the groin of the fighter. Grafyrre stood as the Wesman collapsed. Ferinn dodged a cut to the face, failed to stop a sword slicing across her chest and stepped back, blood seeping through her shirt and jacket.

Grafyrre surged right, battering the hilt of one blade into her attacker's temple and jamming the other up under his ribcage. Ferinn nodded she could continue. To Grafyrre's far right, Merke, Siraaj and Dysett were making short work of the flimsy warrior line. Left, Merrat and Faleen were working their depleted cells as a four while Oryaal and Lyrrique swept up the left flank.

Lynees came past Grafyrre at head height, piling into three Wesmen protecting a casting shaman. Grafyrre hurdled the knot of flailing bodies and struck the head from the shaman in a clean blow. He turned. Lynees had killed one and wounded another, and now scrabbled backwards only to have an axe blade bite into his ankle from a downed warrior. Lynees fell forward. Grafyrre slashed a blade into the third man's back, staying his killing strike.

'Get yourself away to the other injured,' said Grafyrre. 'We'll find you.'

Grafyrre turned to find his next target. He saw Merrat kill two with simultaneous strikes to the left and right then duck for Artuune to hurl a jaqrui into the face of a shaman. This fight was done, and with the fall of the last shaman body, Ystormun turned.

Grafyrre felt those ancient eyes cross his body and he shivered.

'Tais, with me!' he called. 'Stein, it has to be now!'

Grafyrre ran hard straight past the Wytch Lord to the slope where

James Barclay

the returning Wesmen and shamen were almost on them. He longed
to strike the bastard but knew he was invulnerable to steel.

'Spread wide,' called Merrat as he strode up to Grafyrre's shoulder. 'If only Katyett was here. She'd have loved this.'

'Old times and all times, we could do with her strength,' said
Grafyrre.

He looked down the slope and breathed hard. He didn't fear the
fifty and more warriors who came at them, it was the shamen moving
in their wake who were worrying. Their fate was in Stein's hands.
The first shaman prepared his black fire.

'Speed!' called Grafyrre.

'Focus on the casting and only on the casting,' said Stein.

His mages were spreading to encircle Ystormun. The Wytch Lord
had finally taken notice of them and would soon be able to feel what
they were bringing to bear on him. Ystormun's filthy gaze swept
across them, within it the contempt of centuries and the memory of
humiliation.

Stein.

Stein jolted and almost lost his construct.

'Push out,' said Stein to his mages. 'He's going to resist. Be ready.'

I can trace your line through the centuries to your first betrayal.

Stein's heart was pounding in his chest. He shook his head to
dislodge the voice. He linked his construct to those of his mages and
could see the spiked net they had created just beyond the bounds of
Ystormun's subconscious. They were ready, but then so would he be.

You cannot hurt me, not here. Let it go. I seek others today.

They are my brothers, said Stein to himself and he felt a chill inside
his skull. *I will not let you harm them.*

*Brothers. Is that what they told you? You have no power here,
Stein.*

Then do your worst and prove it.

'Advance,' ordered Stein. 'Press and then hold. Do not let him in,
do not look at him – he will be seeking your soul.'

The elven mages tightened their arc and sought to encircle Ystormun. Stein could feel his eyes tracking across them, seeking weakness
he could exploit. Stein felt as if he was toying with them and anxiety
flooded him briefly before he quashed it, knowing it was what
Ystormun desired.

'Strike,' said Stein, his word carrying across the construct and into the mind of each mage. 'Strike hard.'

They pushed out and forward. The construct came into contact with Ystormun's aura, sick and malevolent. Stein crushed his eyes closed and heaved with his mind. Spikes pierced the aura and darkness flooded out.

That is far enough.

Stein pushed again. His mages were with him, all of them using every mote of energy they possessed. But they could go no further, as if cement had hardened across the surface of their net, holding it secure and immovable.

Now it is my turn.

Stein's eyes snapped open. Ystormun was staring at him.

'I warned you,' he said. 'No one stands in my way.'

Sickness flooded into the construct and Stein dropped back into the mana spectrum to see the net tangled with a mass of grasping black tendrils. Each found purchase, locked on tight and hardened. The darkest of night pulsed within Ystormun's aura and flashed towards them.

'Out!' screamed Stein.

He dropped the construct, risking dire psychological damage, and turned, barrelling into the mage next to him, clawing at a third and reaching for a fourth. But he only had moments, and as his hand reached out to the serene figure her expression turned to dread. She saw what was coming.

Her body turned to blood and burst asunder.

Chapter 35

It will for ever be a source of sorrow and regret that the Sundering which gave wing to the powers of the four colleges also gave wing to that of the Wytch Lords.

Sipharec, High Mage of Julatsa.

The screams stopped the fighting. Shamen staggered back feeling the force of something ricocheting through their bodies. Wesman warriors stared past the TaiGethen, backing up, fearing something more than the unseen cut of an elven blade.

Grafyrre paused in mid-strike, spinning to look back at Stein and Ystormun. The Wytch Lord was gesturing towards the mages as if shooing children gently from his path. And they were standing there, transfixed and shuddering, unable to move, and their expressions tore at his heart.

Their screams gained in volume, splitting the sky with the purest terror he had ever heard, and one by one their faces reddened, darkened and split open as if smashed from the inside. Grafyrre started to run to their aid but Merrat grabbed his shoulder.

Grafyrre turned, barely taking in the surreal scene of Wesman and TaiGethen standing almost shoulder to shoulder, beguiled by the horror Ystormun had unleashed. Movement among the mages caught his eye, and he saw three get to their feet and flee. But the rest could not break themselves free. Seeing their friends die one by one, they died too, shrieking their terror, consumed by the darkest of magic and taken to a place where even Shorth would fear to tread.

The last of the transfixed mages perished, and a merciful peace replaced the dread cries. Ystormun raised his head, glanced at the three escaping mages, turned and strode towards the village, towards Grafyrre and his TaiGethen. Merrat's hand tightened on Grafyrre's shoulder, who swallowed, a chill coursing through his veins as the Wytch Lord's eyes fell on them.

He had never experienced fear before but he did now. In that moment he understood what it was to be truly helpless in the face of your greatest terror. You could not strike a thing like that. You could not do it harm or defeat it. You could only do one thing.

'Run.'

For the briefest of moments Auum thought Stein would succeed at the first attempt. The shamen moving to strike at them had stopped and turned as if lacking direction, and the press of magic had eased. Seizing the moment, Auum had led a counter-charge which Sentaya had joined.

Stein's remaining mages had dumped fire on the shamen they could reach and blasted ice through the Wesman lines. If the numbers he was facing were anything to go by, they had killed a third of the remaining enemy warriors and reduced the shaman numbers by half. Not enough, given the casualties among Sentaya's people.

Auum sidestepped a downward chop, jabbed his right elbow into the Wesman's temple and carved his left blade across the back of his neck, half-severing his head. He dragged his blade clear and kicked the body aside. Tilman, gaining in confidence and using Auum's knife as a second weapon, jabbed his blade into the mouth of his opponent and drove him back and over with a decent kick to the gut.

Auum was weighing up his next foe when the screams rolled across the battlefield. The tenor of the sound cut across the roar of the melee, and the fighting stopped. Auum stepped back and jumped into the air to see the scene further up the shallow rise. He saw blurred shapes streaming towards them, TaiGethen under the shetharyn; and behind them he saw Ystormun marching towards the battle.

Auum landed, pirouetted and smashed a kick into the face of his enemy. He felt cold. Stein was gone, then, and most of his mages with him. Ystormun had destroyed them in the blink of an eye and was moving to finish the job.

'Hold!' he yelled, hearing Sentaya pick up the call. 'Break on my word.'

The shamen had turned and the Wesmen ahead of them returned to the battle with renewed energy. The defensive line was forced back by weight of numbers.

'What's happened?' shouted Tilman over the din.

Auum angled his right blade and deflected away a strike meant for the human's flank. He thrashed his left blade into the enemy's neck and reversed it immediately back across the face of his next opponent, who jerked back, avoiding the cut by a hair.

'Concentrate!' barked Auum. 'Ulysan!'

Ulysan snapped a side kick high into the face of his enemy, stepped into the space and rammed a blade into his gut.

'With you, skipper.'

'He was waiting for it,' said Auum. 'That bastard was waiting for us to go for him.'

'What now?'

'Go for the skirmish points. Wait for the signal. Make sure the left flank watches the shamen.'

Auum blocked an axe blade left, reached in and nicked his right blade through the leather jerkin of his enemy and slashed it up across his chest. He stepped back and let the axe crash back down. He stepped on the haft and chopped down into the Wesman's shoulder, putting him on the ground.

Tilman took a heavy blow on his blade and staggered back. He was off balance and his knife arm was flailing to recover. The axe man circled his weapon ready for the decapitating blow and Auum moved fast right, leaning over hard and swiping his blade in to out, chopping into the axe man's arm, carving deep. His left flank was exposed. A Wesman stepped in, hacking with his sword. Auum snapped his left leg up and kicked under the warrior's wrist, holding the blade high. Ulysan jammed a blade under his arm. The Wesman fell back, and the axe man dropped his weapon.

'Thank you,' managed Tilman.

'A TaiGethen is never alone,' said Auum. 'Ulysan, shamen approaching. On my go . . .'

Ulysan yelled a command to the TaiGethen holding the left flank. Sentaya understood it and carried the word to his people. In moments it had travelled to the elves on the right flank too. Some of Sentaya's warriors broke away and ran back into the village. The Julatsan elves lined up with them in the oval.

'Il-Aryn, barriers ready!' called Auum.

He couldn't afford the time to look towards the back of the village where Rith and her people were under cover, but the word was carried back. Auum fenced with a powerful swordsman, cutting him across both arms. Tilman was tiring next to him and under pressure again. Ulysan struck an enemy's arm off at the shoulder, spraying blood across all three of them as the shamen gathered, almost ready.

'Go!' called Auum.

Ulysan roared the command to break. Auum turned, grabbed Tilman and, half-carrying the youth, sprinted away to his position behind Sentaya's house. They ran through a line of archers whose bows were tensed and ready and on through mages waiting to cast.

Auum heard Sentaya order the release and arrows shot away. Moments later six orbs of fire flew over the oncoming enemy to scatter the shamen, catching some and destroying their concentration. Hailstorms flew out across the arc of the charge, ripping leather and furs, flaying the skin from faces and slicing the flesh from fingers.

Sentaya's men dropped their bows once more and charged back into the fray, a thin line of courageous warriors knowing their chances of survival were minimal. The mages dropped back to cover among the sixty or so buildings making up the village. The enemy broke around to the left and right of Sentaya's warriors and the TaiGethen streaked back out to get among them.

'Stay here,' Auum ordered Tilman.

Auum and Ulysan scaled Sentaya's stockade and stood to look out beyond the village. The shamen were gathering again, but behind them the TaiGethen from Stein's failed attempt on Ystormun were approaching. Auum smiled, watching them streak in behind a group of shamen close to the village readying to attack the Il-Aryn and Julatsans behind the right flank.

'Count the shamen. We need them down fast.'

Ulysan began counting as the TaiGethen struck the shamen, dropping out of the shetharyn. Wesmen turned to their aid but were far too late. Seven went down at a stroke. Auum watched as Merrat, Graf, Merke and Faleen led the group of eleven TaiGethen at a run back towards the village.

Auum sensed Ystormun switch his attention to them. He saw the Wytch Lord raise a hand and jab the heel of his palm out. Auum tracked across to the right and for a moment nothing happened. Then one of the dead or dying shamen moved, his body jerking and convulsing. Soon the others began to do the same, twitching where they lay. And from their bodies rose a wave of dark energy, broad at its base and with grasping fingers at its leading edge.

Auum didn't even have time to shout the warning they wouldn't have heard. The wave snatched across the gap of some fifty yards to the escaping TaiGethen and broke over them, grasping at them, dragging them down, enveloping them and reducing their bodies to bloody fragments.

Auum almost fell from the stockade. Only Ulysan's strong arm kept him upright as the two of them stared at the scene in horror. Four were still running. One paused to turn, hoping to help his fallen brothers and sisters.

'No,' whispered Auum. 'Keep moving. Who's still standing?'

'Faleen, Siraaj, Grafyrre and Merke,' said Ulysan. 'He took seven for seven.'

'He killed Merrat just like that. How can we beat such power?' asked Auum.

Ulysan's grip tightened on Auum and they jumped down back into cover next to Tilman.

'We take the last eleven shamen, we isolate Ystormun, and the Il-Aryn and Julatsans must hold him until—'

'Until when, Ulysan? No one is coming. Not soon enough.'

'Then we fight to the last man,' said Tilman, his voice tremulous but his grip on his weapon strong. 'And elf of course. And we show him no fear.'

Auum managed a fleeting smile. 'You'll make a fine warrior.'

Tilman blushed. There was a commotion over to their right. Julatsan spells were falling behind the enemy lines and in front of the Wesmen forming up to join the attack on that flank. An Il-Aryn barrier flashed into place and black fire slammed into it, picking at its edges. It held for a moment before shattering.

'Come on,' said Auum.

He led his unique cell across the oval, seeing Sentaya still up and fighting. The Il-Aryn had changed tactics and so far they were working. Small domes shimmered into existence over the two remaining groups of shamen every few paces, forcing them to break the wards before moving on. Auum could see Rith crouched on a rooftop at the back of the village directing their placement. It would only delay the inevitable, but it was smart and bought Sentaya a few precious moments.

Auum ran around the right flank, where Marack was organising the dwindling TaiGethen into five cells.

'What's going on?' asked Auum on the way past.

Marack smashed her blades into a Wesman face and stomach,

turning her head briefly as the blood splattered across her features. Her grin was fierce.

'TaiGethen survivors incoming,' she said then raised her eyebrows. 'And the Senserii.'

Auum's heart leaped. Marack turned back to the fight. Wesmen were running in again, too many to hold off.

'Break with them,' said Auum. 'Get fire on the shamen if you can. Protect the mages.'

'It's done,' said Marack.

Auum sprinted away. He could see a group of elves tearing across the ground, light glinting from the blades tipping their staffs.

'Where's Takaar?' asked Auum when he reached them.

Gilderon pointed past him. 'Already in the village with the Il-Aryn. He had some ideas.'

'I think I've seen one of them already. We have to get him to Ystormun. Can he destroy him?'

'He plans to hold him until the Xeteskians arrive.' Gilderon indicated a smudge of dust away to the east. 'They can cage him.'

'Then let's get him to Ystormun, it's a reunion that's long over-due.'

'Which way?' asked Gilderon.

'There. Ystormun's heading in from the north.'

Auum looked back across the village. Spears of black slapped into Sentaya's line, scattering burning and blistered warriors across the oval. A black sphere the size of a boulder and shot through with pure white crashed into the first buildings, shattering wood and bursting through stone walls, smearing the bodies of the Communion mages inside across the stone.

Ystormun was at the gates.

The enemy warriors surged forward as their remaining shamen sought targets among the survivors. The defensive line, already compromised by Ystormun's intervention, was shattered along two thirds of its length, and with enemies pouring in behind them the rest of the line broke too.

Auum glanced back at the mage and Il-Aryn positions, seeing Grafyrre leading his surviving TaiGethen towards them, cutting off the advance of attacking Wesmen. Auum could see the fury in Grafyrre's face and in every blow he struck. Merrat had been his closest friend for three thousand years, and his death in such a manner would be hard avenged on his enemies.

'Tilman, get to the mages, find Takaar and bring him back to us. We're cutting a path to that bastard.'

'I want to fight with you,' said Tilman, fearing a slight.

'And so you shall, but your task is critical. Takaar must join us or Ystormun will kill us all.'

Tilman nodded and hurried away. Auum winked at Ulysan.

'Gets him out of harm's way,' he said. 'Takaar will see Ystormun long before Tilman finds him.'

Two Senserii had gone with Takaar. Auum led Ulysan and the twelve others back into the fight. The battle line had dissolved into a confusion of skirmishes across the oval and around buildings, paddocks and yards. This reduced the effectiveness of the shamen, forcing them to seek out individual enemies for fear of striking their own. But behind them, directing them, was Ystormun, his eyes everywhere, always seeking his greatest adversaries.

'I'm coming to you, you bastard,' muttered Auum.

The TaiGethen and Senserii flowed across the ground, spreading through the fighting. Auum took the centre with Ulysan and Gilderon. Auum watched the enemy tactics evolve. They outnumbered Sentaya and the elves by three to one at least, allowing them to keep one-on-one fights going while moving the shamen steadily to the right, under the guard of good numbers of fresh warriors.

'They're heading for our casting positions!' called Auum. 'Drive on, but help Sentaya on our way.'

Auum was about fifty yards from the first knot of shamen, which was moving quickly to an open position. He sprinted forward feeling the comforting presence of Ulysan at his left shoulder and the strength of Gilderon to his right. The oval was crowded with fighting and dying. Auum raised his blades above his head and both he and Ulysan stepped up to leap high over the heads of the combatants. Auum brought his legs into a tuck and hacked down with his right blade, feeling it bite into the top of an enemy skull.

He landed, bent his right knee and battered a kick into the chin of a warrior getting the better of one of Sentaya's men. The flash of a blade on his right was Gilderon. His ikari speed was without equal. The petrified wood, strong as steel, levered between three enemies pressing a single warrior.

The flow of Gilderon's arms and the balance of his body were perfect. He struck the leftmost in the face with one blade, stabbed the rightmost in the throat with the other, and his momentum carried him forward to butt the third square on the bridge of the nose.

Auum ran on, dropping and cutting his blade through an enemy's hamstrings, kicking out sideways to crack into knee joint or hip. Ulysan beside him was using his fists and body among the flailing steel, snapping out punches to kidneys, rolling and thudding fists up into groins and shouldering enemies off balance. Everywhere they and the Senserii passed, Sentaya's men could close and counter-attack.

But the body count was high. Defenders, people Auum had seen hugging their children, lay burned or run through, blood pooling before it soaked into the ground. Auum burst through the last of the fighters and into clear space, acutely aware he was momentarily turning his back towards Ystormun.

He took a glance at the Wytch Lord, who was surveying the battlefield. He opened his palm and another black orb seared out to demolish a building on the edge of the village. Wesmen surged into the space, racing towards the defenders' casting positions. Auum had to assume Grafyrre would see them.

Auum charged towards a running group of five shamen encircled by Wesmen. He pulled a jaqrui from its pouch.

'Gilderon, the warriors. Ulysan, with me.'

'As you command,' said Gilderon.

The Senserii lifted his staff and circled it above his head. His brothers moved in on either flank to form a semicircle and drove in as the shamen shouted warnings and ran on. Wesmen stopped to intercept the attack and the Senserii engulfed them. The shamen slowed and turned, already casting.

Gilderon fenced away an overhead blow and jammed a blade tip into his attacker's gut. Auum hurdled the falling body and flung his jaqrui at the shaman in his path. It caught his shoulder, knocking him to the dirt. Ulysan's crescent fared better, lodging in his target's throat. The other three opened their hands.

Auum readied to leap but a shimmering barrier snapped into place in front of him. Thick rods of black fire burst against the barrier, destroying it but getting no further. Auum had time to raise hand in salute towards Rith before stepping in and hammering his left blade into the mouth of one of the shamen. Ulysan decapitated another, swivelled and kicked the third in the side of the head, knocking him into Auum's path. Auum glared down at him.

'How's that for magic?' he said.

His blade pierced the shaman's chest, and the holy man spewed blood from his mouth before his eyes dimmed. Behind them came an inhuman howl, and Auum's blood chilled. He spun around. Gilderon whirled his staff in front of him and lashed one tip across the throat of his enemy. Beyond him Ystormun had stopped and was staring straight at them.

Auum replayed the death of Merrat.

'Ulysan!'

But Ystormun had already turned away and was moving rapidly towards the defenders' casting positions. Auum saw barriers placed in his way at every step, but he simply beat them aside.

'Dammit,' muttered Auum 'He's after Takaar. Marack!'

Marack was deep in action on the right flank with the second knot of shamen heading her way.

'The shamen!' roared Ulysan. 'Get the shamen!'

Auum saw her indicate she'd heard with a flick of her head.

'Gilderon, it's time.'

The TaiGethen and the Senserii ran together for Ystormun.

Chapter 36

If Shorth wills it, Merrat will strike the first blow of Ystormun's eternal torment beyond death.

Grafyrre, TaiGethen

Tilman was scared. Leaving Auum's side was like taking off his armour and lying down before the enemy. He ran as fast as he ever had back to the cluster of six buildings at the southern edge of the village, noting with dismay how small the open space was between the relentless advance of the enemy and the casting positions.

The remaining ten Julatsan elves were gathered in three groups spread across the buildings. He could see from their positions that they were holding shields in place over the Il-Aryn, as they would do little good against Ystormun and the shamen.

The Il-Aryn had survived in good numbers, he thought, and were scattered inside the buildings, hidden behind walls and under window openings. They cast barrier after barrier. All of them looked tired but still they responded to Rith's calls from the roof of the central building, a stone and thatch barn with a hayloft. Takaar was in the loft by the opening, beneath the block and tackle, two of his guard elves with him.

Tilman raced inside and hared up the ladder. He moved through the tight bales of hay and looked through the opening, gasping at what he saw. There was Ystormun, destroying buildings and making space for his warriors to advance from the left. There were Auum and the elves with the masks over their mouths and their bladed staffs moving through the chaos with such speed and precision he was glad Auum had sent him away. And there on the right, where the fighting was the fiercest, stood most of the surviving TaiGethen, preventing the enemy from overwhelming the casting positions but being driven back by weight of numbers. Further away but closing fast was a large number of horsemen under a heavy cloud of dust. No more than a mile distant. Xetesk was almost here.

'My Lord Takaar!' called Tilman, swallowing his nerves and speaking in elvish as best he could. 'Auum has asked that I escort you to him for the attack on Ystormun.'

As soon as he said his words Tilman blushed, realising how preposterous and stupidly formal they must have sounded, given the path to Ystormun they would have to take. Takaar said something in elvish he could not understand and turned to Tilman. His eyes were ablaze with the power he held within himself and yet he smiled in the warmest and most disarming fashion. Tilman felt his nerves dissipate.

'I see he has sent me his best guardian to see the job done,' said Takaar in fluent Balaian, but his tone did not mock. 'But, forgive me, Auum seems to be going the wrong way if he wishes to attack the Wytch Lord.'

And Auum was. He was heading to the right after a group of shamen. Tilman thought quickly.

'Yes. He wants to take the shamen down and isolate Ystormun as the last enemy caster. Otherwise I think the shamen will destroy us here.'

Takaar scanned the battlefield briefly. 'Good. He thinks clearly. But let's wait until he turns back towards our target and then we will move.'

Tilman moved to get a better view of the scene. He was uncomfortable with Takaar's decision. Auum was a long way from them and Ystormun was advancing at the pace of someone who knew he was invulnerable. Tilman watched Auum, Ulysan and the Senserii attack the shamen and saw Takaar follow their assault and move a barrier into place at the critical moment.

'Which is why we must wait,' Takaar said.

Ystormun howled, paused briefly and ran towards them.

Tilman shut out his fear. 'Please, we should go now.'

Takaar stayed where he was. 'He has sensed me. He will come to me.'

Tilman took another look and knew they were about to die. Ystormun stared straight at them. He moved his hands apart and brought the heels of his palms together; Tilman was moving before they struck. He dived at Takaar, catching him around the waist and bearing him down. The two of them rolled once and fell from the hayloft.

Halfway down to the dusty floor and anticipating the pain, Tilman saw the black orb blot out the light of the hayloft opening and destroy the front of the barn in a single blast. Bales of hay were incinerated, the two Senserii, moving right, were caught in the blast and hurled against the wall, dead before they struck it. The thatch burst into flame and the front wall bowed inwards, threatening to collapse.

The impact on the ground never came. Takaar had turned them in the air and he landed on his feet, taking the force of the drop for both of them. He grabbed Tilman's collar and ran them both out of the back of the barn, others of the Il-Aryn with them. Reaching open air, Takaar paused briefly. He shouted commands to the Il-Aryn and held Tilman at arm's length.

'You have the survivor in you,' he said, 'but you can't come with me – he is too powerful. Defend the Il-Aryn, stand with Grafyrre. What's your name?'

'Tilman.'

'You saved me, Tilman, and you might just have saved us all. Garan would have been proud of you.'

Takaar moved away at startling speed, and Tilman wondered momentarily who Garan was before recalling his history, smiling to himself and running off to find Grafyrre.

One moment the barn was there and Rith was calling castings, the next she and the whole frontage of the building were gone, blasted away by Ystormun. Auum shouted at his impotence and ran harder for the tall striding figure in his tattered robes, brimful with hideous magic.

An enemy Wesman stood in his path having downed his opponent. Auum feinted left, ran right and lashed a blade up into his lower jaw, barely breaking stride. Ahead Sentaya still stood, his legs astride a fallen warrior who Auum recognised as one of his sons. The Wesman lord bore the grief on his face and used it to power his axe. He was roaring for his men to stand, and they did wherever they could. Not one had run in the face of his enemy, but they were going to lose this battle because Auum had entirely misunderstood Ystormun's power here in his hinterland. Stein had known; Stein had said, and Auum had ignored him.

'Defend the casters!' called Auum on his way past. 'Ystormun attacks.'

Sentaya nodded to him. Auum indicated his son and put a hand to his heart in sympathy. Sentaya seemed to understand and Auum felt a weight of guilt. He had brought this on Sentaya.

Breaking into open space, the Senserii spread out and moved up to take on Ystormun's warrior guard which was already turning towards them. Ulysan and Auum went directly for the Wytch Lord, neither knowing what he could do beyond buying a moment's delay for Takaar, should he still be alive.

Ystormun poured his hate into another casting and obliterated a barn, the house adjoining it and all the souls within it. It was enough. Auum couldn't help himself.

'Hey!' he shouted. 'Over here, you bastard. Come and get me!'

He and Ulysan dropped into the shetharyn, streaking past the Senserii moving to engage the Wesmen. Auum paced easily around an enemy warrior, who knew he was coming but couldn't follow him, and kept his eyes on Ystormun. The Wytch Lord was turning his head in their direction and bringing up a hand.

Auum changed direction, but the hand and eyes tracked him despite his speed. Ystormun opened his palm then closed his fist. A sheath of black flame encased it for a blink before shooting out at incredible speed, fast even within the shetharyn. Auum couldn't dodge it. He felt an impact about his midriff and flew sideways, Ulysan's arms about him, the big TaiGethen's body pressed against his and sent the pair of them tumbling over and over in the dust and bowling into the legs of warriors.

Auum came to rest on top of his friend and pushed himself to his feet. His swords were gone and he was amid enemies. He lashed a kick into the face of one, drew a jaqrui and slashed it into the body of another. He squared up for another blow and the Senserii flowed past him.

Auum reached down a hand to Ulysan to help him up. The big TaiGethen's chest heaved in breaths fast and let them out in a rush, his body juddering each time. Auum looked down and saw the black wound all along his right flank and the blood pooling beneath him. Auum wanted to roll him on to his side but he was terrified what he would see.

'Ulysan? Please, speak to me.' There was no response and Auum roared, 'Stein! Stein, please be alive, I need you here! *Stein!*'

Ulysan lay there, his eyes closed and his breathing so pained. Auum straightened, his mind submerged by fury. He turned and ran, the shetharyn taking him just as it had when Elyss had fallen. Ystormun was close, distracted for a moment by the Senserii wiping out his guards. He killed one and sent another flying back, screaming and encased in a sheath of black.

Auum ran for him. Belatedly the Wytch Lord turned. Auum leaped and powered in a spear kick which caught the bastard square in the mouth and sent him staggering. Auum landed, dimly aware of the Senserii's ikari weaving their patterns as they kept Ystormun's guards away.

Ystormun snapped his head round, glared at the elf and raised a hand, but Auum was on him again. He lashed a roundhouse kick into his temple, continued the movement and thudded a heel into Ystormun's groin. Auum planted his feet, slapped Ystormun's hand aside and smashed his fists into Ystormun's face again and again, feeling his skin rasp against the inhuman creature's hide.

Ystormun retreated under the onslaught as Auum powered forward, now thumping a kick into his midriff or up into his chin but wanting nothing more than to feel his fists pounding away at that face, his nose, his teeth, his eyes. And with every blow he prayed that Ulysan would live, that the black fire had missed his vital organs, and with every blow he was so scared by the memory of his ragged breathing that he dared not hope.

Auum drew back his fist again as Ystormun reeled back, his face looking bruised through the greyness of his skin but unbroken. Auum punched his jaw. A skeletal hand, skin mottled and stretched tight over the bones, shot out and clamped on Auum's neck, lifting him from the ground. He clawed at the hand, tried to angle his head to bite it and chopped at his wrist with a jaqrui blade he grabbed from his dwindling supply, but he could not cut Ystormun's skin. The Wytch Lord held him at arm's length, his legs flailing uselessly.

'Enough,' rasped Ystormun. 'Seven hundred years and now I have a prize.'

'You will die today, you bastard,' spat Auum.

Ystormun squeezed a little harder and Auum choked.

'You cannot kill me,' he said. 'But I am not impervious to pain.'

'Then all my blows were worth my death,' said Auum.

Ystormun pulled Auum close and the TaiGethen hung limp, his

breath hard to draw and his strength beginning to fail. Still the sounds of battle carried to him and the day was not yet lost.

'It is over, Auum of the TaiGethen; for you, for man and soon enough for all of your kind. What strength remains when I have wiped you out here?'

'Come to Calaius and find out,' said Auum.

'I have every intention of doing just that,' said Ystormun.

The Wytch Lord studied Auum's face while he squeezed. Auum tried not to panic, but every breath sounded like fear and he could no longer force the words out. He stared into Ystormun's eyes, wishing upon him the most enduring agony that Shorth could inflict while commending his own soul to Yniss for the struggles yet to come beyond the halls of the ancients.

'Put him down.'

Auum wasn't sure if he'd imagined the words, so full was his head with the thumping of his heart and the roaring of his blood. His chest heaved but so little came in and he felt his consciousness slipping away.

'Ah, my second prize. Another who thought to hurt me only to find he could not.'

'Wrong.'

Auum felt a sudden rush of energy. Ystormun gave a shriek and Auum was airborne, flying backwards, gulping in air through the raw agony of his throat. The Senserii flowed around him. He felt a brief touch on his shoulder and looked up at Gilderon while the rest of them threw a screen of whirling death around Takaar as he circled Ystormun.

'We will protect him. See to your brother.'

Auum frowned and looked to where Gilderon had indicated before joining his people. The *thwack* of wood on blade and the singing of the ikari were rejoined. Auum heard both Takaar and Ystormun cry out, and a huge pressure of magical energy settled across Auum's shoulders.

Ulysan lay on the ground where Auum had left him. Auum scrabbled over to him and took his hand. He was still breathing but it was in short whistling gasps now. The blood seemed to have stopped, but the wound, dear Yniss, the wound was horrible. Auum could see a great gash that led from beneath Ulysan's ribs all the way down his right leg in which burned flesh and bone were visible.

Auum felt the tears rush and fall down his cheeks. He didn't care that the fight for Balaia, for Calaius, the whole dimension was going on right behind him. This was his fight right here, to save his greatest friend, his conscience, his rock . . . his life beyond the haunting pain of the loss of Elyss.

'Stein!' he roared. 'Where are you?'

Auum heard footsteps run towards him and stop. He looked up, but it was not Stein; it was Marack, Nokhe and Hohan.

'The right is holding,' said Marack. 'I . . . Oh, Auum, no. We'll . . . we'll stand over you. See to him. Tai, with me.'

'I need Stein,' said Auum, weeping and hoarse. 'Please bring me Stein.'

Auum looked down on Ulysan and the pain that crossed his face every time he breathed.

'It's all right, old friend,' he said. 'Help is coming.'

'Liar,' said Ulysan, his eyes flickering open.

Auum gasped. Elyss had said the same thing, and she had died.

'He'll be here,' said Auum. 'Just don't die, Ulysan, please don't die.'

Auum gulped, and the tears fell on Ulysan's face. The big TaiGethen focused on him anew and frowned, clutching his hand tight.

'It was you who saved me, wasn't it? Back in Hausolis? It was you.'

Auum nodded. 'And you've been saving me ever since.'

'Are we even?' asked Ulysan.

'Yes, old friend, we're more than even.'

Ulysan smiled. 'That's good. Can't go dying if I still need to save your sorry hide.'

'You're not dying,' said Auum.

Ulysan's hand slipped from his and his eyes closed. His body, so tortured by pain, relaxed. He was at peace.

Auum bent forward and kissed his eyes, his forehead and his mouth.

'Shorth's embrace will be eternal for you, my brother.'

Here on the battlefield, surrounded by his friends and beset by his enemies, Auum sat down next to Ulysan's mercifully undamaged face and stroked the top of his head while the tears rolled unchecked down his face. There was nothing left. Marack was fighting right in front of him. The Senserii were fighting behind him. The elves he'd brought here were struggling to save the lives of countless thousands, and he had nothing left.

Auum wept.

Chapter 37

You cannot kill a Wytch Lord, only remove him to a place where he no longer has the capacity to do you harm. Thus, you can never be free of the fear of his return and you must remain watchful because he will never cease his search for a way to break free.

Bynaar, Circle Seven Master, Xetesk

Ystormun gave an ululating cry and every head turned towards him. *Bring blades. Bring the fire. Break him.*

Wesman warriors, weak of mind but strong of body, turned and ran from their petty squabbles. But the fire was gone. No shaman touched his mind. Ystormun pushed back against the wall Takaar had erected about him and experienced what he had to assume was fear.

The words of his cadre echoed in his memory. How he longed for their chiding now, their thundering voices in his head, because they would be able to lend him the strength to unpick the casting that threatened to bind him. But inside the spell they were lost to him.

Ystormun opened his eyes. His arms were outstretched and the fire roared from them only to be swallowed by the shimmering sphere that dipped below the earth as if Takaar knew he could attack through the rock itself. But Takaar was not a Wytch Lord and had neither their strength nor their stamina. Again he battered his fire at the construct and Takaar winced, standing holding his palms open and his wrists side by side.

Ystormun looked at the burn on the arm that had held Auum. Another moment and he would have seen the warrior's light go out. The pain had been a shock. It had blistered his skin and he had thought only his brothers could channel such energy. He flared again, and this time Takaar moved back across the ground.

There. A pin hole. A place to work myself free.

'You are weak, Takaar. You cannot destroy me and you cannot hold me. You will fail and then I will tear out your heart with my bare hands.'

Takaar opened his eyes, stared at Ystormun, and Ystormun flinched. There was no sanity within, just a strength born of madness and of a desire he could only guess at. The hatred matched his. Ystormun's heart, for he still thought of it as such, trilled with anxiety.

'I don't have to hold much longer. I know you will kill me, but here I stand. Look and see what is coming for you. Pound with all your might and know it won't be enough. We have you.'

Ystormun looked and this time his shriek was of desperation and panic.

Gilderon whirled his staff in front of his face too fast for any foe to track, too strong a defence for their swords and axes to pierce. He stilled the motion and snapped out left and right, striking his blades into his foes, seeing great cuts open up in their faces, across their chests or across their necks.

Helodian was next to him, Teralion on his other side, and their brothers made a lethal web of wood and steel, protecting their master, whose struggle they could feel inside their minds. The Wesmen were relentless and Gilderon could see many more coming, chased by TaiGethen and the painted warriors who fought with them.

To his left Auum was protected by a cell of TaiGethen hard pressed by a group of a dozen or more enemies, but Gilderon could offer them no help. At a call from the rear of the Wesmen, they surged forward, fifty against ten.

'Brace!' yelled Gilderon.

They attacked, yelling cries of death. Gilderon held his ikari on the diagonal as four came at him. He snapped his staff out straight-armed, catching one in the face and another across the knees. Weapons came through the defence. Gilderon swayed inside a sword thrust that nicked his left arm and ducked his head as an axe flew past, its haft clattering against his ikari.

He pulled back the staff and jabbed out, taking one in the chest, who fell back, clutching the weapon to him. Gilderon went with it, leaping as he fell and kicking high into the nose of one who thought to strike him while he was exposed.

Gilderon came down on the chest of the fallen warrior, pulled his blade clear and swiped down hard to the right, slicing deep into the arm of his target. He jumped back, an axe whispering past his midriff. The Wesmen fell back as one.

'Hold,' said Gilderon.

Behind him Takaar grunted with exertion and said something to Ystormun that made the Wytch Lord squeal. Gilderon glanced left and right. Two Senserii were down, eight were left. He could see the Xeteskian force sweep towards the village, bare moments away from beginning their casting.

TaiGethen were attacking the rear of the Wesman lines, deflecting significant numbers, but at the front the enemy had changed tactics. Through came thirty or more archers while warriors spread wide left and right, waiting to exploit any move to run or to attack the bowmen. They knew nothing of the Senserii.

'Ready defence!' called Gilderon. 'Close the net, defend the master.'

The Senserii closed up, moving forward or back half a pace. The archers stretched their bows.

'Execute!' ordered Gilderon.

Eight ikari whirled, their speed making the air hum around them. The arrows flew. Some missed but most were straight enough. Gilderon felt one slap away from his staff, but near him Cordolan grunted and fell forward with a shaft jutting from his chest.

'Close!' ordered Gilderon.

It was a matter of time and luck now. Gilderon needed both friends and faithless allies to move faster.

Bynaar rode in behind the cavalry, feeling the slap of every hoofbeat through his ageing back. He hardly cared. The gallop had been an extraordinary thrill across ground made for horses. He had fliers high in the sky, who had reported back that Ystormun was destroying the defence but a few moments later that Takaar had trapped him. It seemed that the mad elf had not been lying after all, and now time was short.

They drove into the village across fields littered with bodies to buildings reduced to rubble where a ferocious fight still continued. Ystormun was battering his hideous magic against some construct or other thrown up by Takaar, a handful of whose guard was trying to shield him from a good number of archers, but their whirling staffs were only having limited effect. The rest of the defence was being held at the rear and on the flanks. This was no time for mages.

His cavalry commander knew exactly what was required. On a command taken up by a hundred voices, he wheeled his riders and drove straight through the archers and those clustered around them, scattering them, breaking their bows and their bodies alike. They circled and came back, driving a deeper wedge, then pulled up, ready to move in again. Bynaar halted them.

'This is not our fight,' he said. 'Cage team, dismount and prepare. And every one of you with a blade defend us with your lives.'

'And Takaar?' asked the commander.

'He has friends. Stay out of his and their way.'

Tilman raced across the field in the wake of the cavalry charge and of Grafyrre and Faleen, both of whom sought Auum. His sword was dripping with blood, he was cut on both legs and his chest was ablaze with agony. He thought the axe had nicked his ribs. He was lucky to be alive and wasn't about to waste that luck.

He tried to keep up. The battlefield was a total mess now, and he hardly knew who was an enemy and who an ally. Wesmen still fought among themselves, the painted, Sentaya's people, gaining in strength. Ahead a large group of the enemy was attacking TaiGethen protecting two elves sitting on the ground.

Tilman followed Grafyrre into their rear, splitting the skull of one before they began to turn. Grafyrre's strength seemed inexhaustible and his speed undimmed by his exertions. He jumped and smashed both feet into the back of a Wesman's head, rode the body down, rammed a blade through its back and thrashed the other into the side of the warrior next to him.

Tilman threw himself to the side to dodge a huge axe swing and lost his footing, going sprawling. The Wesman came at him as he scrambled back, trying to make the space to get to his feet. His chest was agony and blood flowed from the cuts on his legs. The Wesman was on him quickly. Tilman held up his blade, which was contemptuously batted away so the warrior could chop down at his chest. The blow was deflected by a blade and thudded into the ground right next to him. The second blade beheaded the enemy.

Grafyrre reached down a hand.

'Ulysan is dead,' he said. 'You must not die too.'

Tilman was hauled to his feet. The fighting still raged across the oval, Wesman on Wesman for the most part. Tilman looked at Auum and his heart was pained. The elf was surrounded by his friends but was so alone, so lost. Ulysan lay next to him, Auum's hand stroking the top of his head. He barely registered what was going on just a few paces away. Four of the Senserii stood guard around Takaar, who was plainly losing the battle with Ystormun, though the Wytch Lord himself appeared significantly weakened.

Takaar was forced back by another of Ystormun's attempts to break him. Black fire flooded the inside of the construct the elf held against the awful might of the ancient creature. But it couldn't go on. Tilman looked further to his right, seeing the Xeteskian mages kneel in a circle and prepare their casting. The moment they did so, Ystormun screamed. It was a sound of bestial fury and ripped at Tilman's soul, threatening to steal his courage.

Auum's TaiGethen looked around and began to fan out. Tilman made his way to Auum, wondering how long Takaar could hold the Wytch Lord. He found two elven blades on the ground and picked them up on the way. He knelt by Auum, who did not seem to notice him. Tilman's heart heaved.

'Auum, you're going to have to fight him,' he said quietly.

Ystormun sent a wave of dark energy smashing against his enemy's construct. Takaar wailed and berated himself as he began to lose it. Tilman could see it shudder violently, and holes appeared through which the black fire roared. Ystormun laughed and prepared to strike again.

'I have had my fill of fighting,' said Auum.

'I brought your blades. You will need them,' said Tilman.

'What for?' asked Auum, looking down at the blades.

'Ystormun will break free. You are the only one he fears.'

'Those are Ulysan's blades,' said Auum.

'The perfect weapons,' said Tilman.

Auum looked up at Tilman, down at Ulysan, and he took the blades.

Perhaps it was because he was dead inside that he could feel everything. Away to his right the Xeteskian mages created their cage, and the pulses of raw energy were like bars drawn across his soul. It was a construct that sought its victim. It was tuned to him but not strong enough to take him. Not yet.

Auum pushed through the line of TaiGethen, his few precious

TaiGethen, and they let him come, no one seeking to stand with him. He watched Ystormun and saw the fatigue in him and the rage keeping him standing. He saw Takaar, and Takaar was spent.

Auum shouted to Takaar, who was talking to his other self, trying to hold his focus while the last of his strength ebbed away, 'For all that you have done, today is your day, and all who survive do so because of you. I misjudged you.'

Takaar turned his head, and Auum saw the exhaustion in his eyes and the sweat on his face.

'No, you didn't,' he said. 'I am all that you accused me of being.'

'I forgive you it all,' said Auum. 'I would be proud to walk by you again.'

Takaar relaxed and his face cleared. A smile crossed it and the pain left his eyes just for a moment. Inside the construct Ystormun heaved his black fire at the walls again. It spewed from his mouth and burst from his fingers. The holes in Takaar's casting widened to yawning rips, and the fire slapped into the elf's chest, picked him up and threw him into the backs of his Senserii.

Ystormun stood hunched but his face shone with his victory. He was breathing as if each was his last, and each exhalation rattled his chest. He was shivering all over, and here and there his skin was broken, thin blood leaking out. He looked at Auum and smiled.

'Your best is not good enough. We will meet again.'

Ystormun began to cast and Auum rushed him, lashing a blade into his arm. Ystormun yelled his pain and looked at the cut. He stumbled back, and Auum followed him.

'That is what elven magic does to evil,' said Auum. 'And this is what real pain feels like.'

'You cannot kill me!' screamed Ystormun.

'I do not need to.'

Auum paced in and laced a cut into Ystormun's cheek.

'That is for Ulysan.' Another into his forehead. 'And that is for Merrat.' A third into his other cheek. 'And that is for Takaar and Thrynn and for every elf whose life you blighted.'

Auum dropped his blades and moved around the creature, who was still trying to gather a casting that would let him escape. Auum roundhoused him in the side of the head and followed up with a snap kick to the chin that sent him sprawling.

Auum put a foot on his throat. Ystormun grabbed his boot and tried to twist it away. The elf could feel the Xeteskian casting seeking him.

'You can feel the magic coming for you too, can't you?' Auum said.

Ystormun's eyes were blank with fear. He shrieked and scrabbled away. Auum let him go. Ystormun stood and began to intone something, his hands moving fast. Auum bounced on one foot, then jumped and drove both feet hard into Ystormun's mouth, smashing teeth and gagging his words. Ystormun's hands flew up, his concentration broken. He tripped and fell. A yawning chasm opened up behind him. The Wytch Lord tried to scramble away, but claws of deep blue shot out and clamped on to his skull and shoulders.

Black fire exploded around Ystormun. More bindings surged from the chasm, wrapping his arms and legs. He screamed and convulsed, his cries resonating through the ground and sending hands to ears. He bellowed and roared his defiance, and his fire lashed at his bindings.

A final claw snaked from the chasm and clamped his mouth shut. He stared one last time at Auum, his hate as abiding as ever. Auum stared back, his heart cold, the ashes of victory in his mouth. And as the bindings retracted, dragging Ystormun to his cage, Auum turned away.

He reached Ulysan and sat by him again as the door slammed shut on the Wytch Lord for good.

Chapter 38

Ulysan's death would bring the ClawBound to a halt to sing a lamentation in his honour, such was his standing. His life was given to save the elven race from its enemies, and in his death he goes to Shorth knowing he has achieved exactly that. His was a great heart, and the halls of the ancients will for ever reverberate to the sound of his name.

Auum, Arch of the TaiGethen.

Takaar lay on his back. The Senserii had made him comfortable, but in truth he could feel very little. He thought his back was broken. Either that or the shock of the impact had entirely numbed his body. He smiled up at the sky, and Auum's words played over in his mind. He heard a chuckle.

You're dying.

'Yes,' said Takaar.

Then I got what I always wanted.

'So did I. And at last we can be one again. Let us walk with gods together.'

'Graf?'

'Yes, Auum.'

'How many are we?'

'You don't want to know.'

'Tell me.'

Grafyrre sighed. 'Marack, Nokhe, Hohan, Merke, Faleen, Evunn, Duele, Siraaj. You and me, of course. And Tilman.'

Auum didn't look up from Ulysan.

'You're in good company, old friend,' he whispered.

The capture of Ystormun had seen the surviving enemy Wesmen break and run, and Sentaya had let them go. Peace had descended on the village only to be broken by angry shouts from the direction of the Xeteskian cavalry and mage force, which was resting far too close to the village oval and its dead. Auum heard swords drawn from scabbards and the sounds of men running and he felt a growing tension.

'But they won't let you rest.'

Auum stood and looked at the scene of the trouble, almost instantly breaking into a dead run. There was a knot of men pushing and shoving: Xeteskians, Wesmen including Sentaya and a man he had thought dead. With his anger burning bright again, Auum, followed by his surviving TaiGethen, turned a high somersault in the air and landed right in the midst of the argument. Battle-weary angry TaiGethen with painted faces made a very efficient barrier. Both sides moved back a few paces.

Auum took in the Xeteskians – the pompous-looking old mage, his powerful cavalry captain and the melee of other soldiers and mages wanting in on the argument – and turned, his grief lifting a degree for a moment. There stood Sentaya, bloodied, bruised and exhausted. He was supporting Stein, who had an arm around the tribal lord's shoulders and Sentaya's about his waist. Stein looked in a bad way. Burned and spent, with what was clearly a broken arm and a foot he could barely place on the ground.

'You're supposed to hate each other,' said Auum.

'We'll do it again tomorrow,' said Stein. 'What do you say?'

Auum dragged himself over and embraced Stein. 'It's good to see you, brother.'

'You too.'

'Whatever's going on here, it can wait.'

Stein's face coloured. 'This sweaty supercilious bastard and his murdering filth have to answer for their crimes.'

'It can wait.'

The pompous mage said something Auum didn't understand, but the tone was contemptuous. Auum's scalp prickled and he spun round, his weary TaiGethen following his lead. The mage shrank back a pace, his gaze flicking to his cavalry captain.

'The dead lie unattended. Those we love are alone under the sky while you posture and strut like ageing stags chasing powers long faded. Brave men, brave elves, have died today. You will show them proper respect.'

Auum didn't take his eyes from the mage, who looked to Stein for the translation he needed. His understanding did nothing to soften his face. He opened his mouth to speak but Stein got there first.

'They *betrayed* us, Auum. Think of how many you lost because they allied with the bastard they have belatedly caught.'

The Xeteskian responded with a furious outburst of his own and had to be pushed back again by Marack and Grafyrre.

Auum rounded on Stein. 'Yes, look how many have died!' He gestured back towards Sentaya's ruined village. Sentaya himself looked bemused, the grief for his loss beginning to shroud his mind. 'Wesmen, elves and Julatsans, and yet here we stand and they are lost without us beside them. We must attend to our dead now, so your reckoning will wait.'

Auum waited until Stein nodded before turning to the Xeteskian once more. Stein translated for him.

'And you will accord us the proper respect. You will allow us the space and the peace to prepare our dead and see them to their eternal rest. And we will accord you and your dead the same respect. And when dawn breaks tomorrow, you and I and Stein will speak.'

The mage wafted a hand. 'Do as you will. Your primitive rituals hold no interest for me.'

It was Stein's hand on Auum's shoulder that stopped the Tai-Gethen killing the mage then and there. He shook the hand off and nodded to Marack and Grafyrre that he intended only to speak.

'The blood of every elf and every one of Sentaya's dead is on your hands. You are guilty in the eyes of Shorth, and if you utter one more ignorant word I will send you to stand before him. Knowledge has been lost today that we could not afford to lose.' Auum's anger left him and he squeezed his eyes shut against the tears that threatened. 'Ulysan is dead.'

'Oh, Auum, I am so sorry,' said Stein. 'I grieve for you.'

'Grieve for them all,' said Auum. 'I can't stand here any longer.'

Auum walked away, his TaiGethen with him. He heard the mage speak and Stein reply.

'Graf, Marack, we have to scour the field from the enemy camp to the borders of the village. We have to bring all our dead together. Some of them we will never find. You know what to do. I'm going to sit with Ulysan.'

Grafyrre and Marack melted away, taking the TaiGethen with them. Auum walked alone.

*

Ulysan was not alone, and Auum felt a rush of relief. But it was not one of the TaiGethen with him, nor was it one of the Il-Aryn, who were utterly spent and sitting in a single group for comfort. It was Tilman who stood as he approached, looking anxious as if caught stealing.

'I thought he . . . needed . . . company. I'm sor—'

Auum embraced him hard while the tears fell down his face and the sobs racked his body. After a nervous pause, Tilman gripped back.

'Thank you,' whispered Auum. 'Thank you.'

He broke the embrace and, holding Tilman's shoulders, looked deep into his eyes.

'There is soul in you,' he said and kissed Tilman's forehead. 'And now . . .'

'I know. You need solitude. I'll make myself useful elsewhere.'

Auum sat by Ulysan.

He watched Tilman walk off, looking for someone to help. 'Humans are fools. With some exceptions. But you already knew that.'

Around him survivors were moving among their fallen comrades, checking for signs of life. Occasionally a shout would go up, but mostly a touch was followed by a shake of the head. He looked at Ulysan's face. It was relaxed and untroubled but pale.

'I would kill every Xeteskian for just one of your jokes.'

A tear dropped onto Ulysan's cheek. Auum made to wipe it away then left it, watching it track down the side of his face, life travelling across death. There was so much he wanted to say, but admissions of guilt were as pointless as they were wrong. Ulysan would have chided him for expressing them.

'Among all the souls that have crossed my path, yours was the warmest, the one possessed of the most joy, passion and care. But it didn't ever stop you taking the right path as a TaiGethen warrior. How did you walk that narrow path so effortlessly? I have so many questions. Stupid, isn't it? I have known and loved you for three thousand years and yet I never found the time to truly mine your wisdom.

'But don't worry; it won't be wasted because I can recall every conversation, every combat and look we shared and every act Yniss bade us perform to protect his blessed rainforest. And your wisdom binds them all, doesn't it? All I have to do is remember and your knowledge will be there.'

Auum smiled and rested a hand over Ulysan's heart, desperate to feel it beating. 'You know there was a time I thought you would challenge me to be the Arch. You were walking with Silent Priests, you were loved by them and by every TaiGethen, every Al-Arynaar. I wondered why you didn't speak up – I even thought to prompt you because I thought you would be the perfect Arch – but it's obvious now. Now it's too late to tell you I understand.

'You already were a leader, weren't you? Spiritually, emotionally and paternally, they all followed you and your purity of mind and action. I cannot thank you enough for knowing your better role. You made my life as the Arch one of brotherhood and not isolation. No elf can put a value on that.'

Auum's hand moved to Ulysan's head and stroked his hair. He strained to hear his voice, his breath, anything to bring him from this awful reality to the one he desired more than anything. Auum was hollow, and every breath he took felt like betrayal.

'You know what I saw that day in the Arish mountains? What has stayed with me every day since? No, of course you don't. I was always too busy to tell you. Probably thought your ego would get too heavy and break your neck or something.' Auum chuckled briefly. 'There you go. I can't escape your jokes even though you can't tell them.

'You were cold, and it was so dark that our sight was challenged. You were exhausted, your eyes were closed and your breathing was so terribly shallow. You must have been so close to the end, but your hand, your freezing hand, was still locked around that root.

'And that's what I saw. The elf with more belief, more strength and more determination than any I have ever met, before or since. And you just a whelp too. I cannot begin to voice the scale of the tragedy that is your passing.

'I just thought you should know,' whispered Auum. 'Now let's sit together and let the world soak into our souls like we have so many times before.'

Evening was coming, and there was a chill on the breeze that grew as the light faded. Auum had barely lifted his head in the last few hours though he had remained dimly aware of the activity going on all around him. He knew he should have played his part but he really did not feel he could be anywhere other than by Ulysan's side. Apparently everyone else had felt so too.

But now Marack, Grafyrre, Stein and Sentaya were heading his way, looking every bit the deputation. Stein, though still limping, was looking considerably better, having clearly benefited from some healing magic, but the other three wore their grief like yokes across their shoulders. Auum felt a sympathetic pain in his heart. He squeezed Ulysan's shoulder and stood up.

'Thank you for—'

Stein had begun to translate Auum's words, but Sentaya held up a hand and talked over him, Stein obliging.

'When a warrior has lost a brother he loved for three thousand years, scant hours are not enough, but they are all we have.'

Auum put a hand to his heart. 'I am humbled,' he said.

Sentaya inclined his head.

'Auum,' said Grafyrre. Auum knew what he was going to say but didn't want anyone to say it. 'You know we can't take them with us.'

Auum couldn't speak for a moment. He looked back at Ulysan, gestured at his body and frowned. This felt like the ultimate betrayal.

'The rainforest is home. We can't lay him for reclamation *here*. None of them.'

'No, we can't,' said Grafyrre. 'But Sentaya has another way and I think you should hear it.'

Auum nodded though he failed to see how there could be such a thing.

'I have spoken with your warriors and I respect your way of honouring your fallen though I don't understand it,' said Sentaya. 'And I don't expect you to understand mine. But the soul travels to its resting place however it is honoured. We build pyres for our dead because the soul escapes the body through fire. The ashes that remain are scattered on land or water to spread the memories of the dead for the benefit of all who travel through them for eternity.

'Our peoples fought and died as brothers. It would be an honour to lay your dead with my son and my fallen warriors, as brothers in the afterlife.'

Auum had expected to be revolted by Sentaya's words or at the very least dismissive of his beliefs, but he wasn't. Indeed, here in this barren ugly land, Sentaya's imagery had a stark beauty and a reverence that was wholly fitting. Ulysan would have agreed, and that was all that really mattered.

Auum stepped up to Sentaya, and the lord allowed himself to be embraced and kissed on the forehead.

'Tell Sentaya that it would be an honour fitting of the TaiGethen dead to move to the afterlife beside his son and his warriors. We will pray together and we will grieve together. Tell him that the thanks of all elves are with him and his people today.'

Three large flat rocks close to the lakeside were traditionally used as bases for pyres, but more than twenty other temporary structures had been built around the water's edge either side of the rocks, where the prevailing breeze would blow the smoke away from the village.

The fallen enemy had been readied for return to their tribes, and the concerns of the surviving elves and Wesmen around the joint ceremony had been eased and agreement reached. In the deepening twilight Sentaya's fallen son was laid in the middle of the central stone atop a pyre of sticks and the ruined timbers of buildings. Ulysan and Takaar flanked him, and with other senior Wesmen dead next to them went Merrat and Rith.

And so it was on every pyre: TaiGethen, Il-Aryn and Wesman lay side by side. Auum had initially wanted the races separated, but Sentaya had spoken of his desire for elven ashes to bless his lands and for Wesman ashes to fall on Calaius. The fierce Wesman lord spoke with such emotion that Auum could do nothing but agree that it was the right way, the only way.

Auum had carried Ulysan himself and laid him on the pyre. The smell of lantern oil was strong, and the liquid shined on the timbers and firewood.

'It is not as you may have dreamed, but your soul will be freed. Yniss will see you safely to Shorth's embrace and the calls of the ancients will bring you home. Goodbye, Ulysan, hero of the Tai-Gethen, hero of the elven race, my oldest and most loved friend. Where you go now, I cannot follow. It is not yet my time.'

Fresh tears fell on Ulysan's face. Auum stroked his cheeks, smoothed his hair one last time and kissed his forehead and eyes. He took Ulysan's cold hand in his, still unable to comprehend why the big TaiGethen had no grip.

'I can't believe I'll never hear your voice again,' he whispered.

He laid Ulysan's hand back down by his side and stepped back to stand shoulder to shoulder with Lord Sentaya and Grafyrre. To his left and right the surviving TaiGethen lined up with Wesmen. Torches flared in the darkening sky.

'Auum,' said Sentaya.

Auum looked. Sentaya was holding two torches, one of which he proffered to the elf. Auum nodded and took it, then surprised himself with the warmth of his smile when Sentaya spoke one word in elvish.

'Together.'

Sentaya and Auum stepped forward, followed by every other torch bearer. Sentaya checked Auum was ready and the two of them laid their flames against the wood of the pyre, moving around it to set an even fire. Sentaya leaned over and dropped the torch onto his son's body and Auum did the same for Ulysan.

Auum had to force himself to watch as the fire intensified quickly, accelerated by the light oil. He saw it touch Ulysan's clothes, his jaqrui pouch still full of his crescents and the swords crossed over his chest. His skin began to blacken and smoulder and Auum had to convince himself afresh that this was the right way. He sent a silent prayer to Yniss for forgiveness and understanding before letting his voice carry for all his people to hear.

'Where you walked, the ground was blessed. Where your voice was heard, the air rejoiced. Your name will ever warm the throats of Tual's denizens and echo in the halls of the ancients.'

The Wesmen were singing. To Auum the words didn't matter, but the emotions of sorrow and hope lifted him as the flames consumed Ulysan, Takaar and so many TaiGethen and Il-Aryn the elves could not afford to have lost. And when they were done, the elves added their song: a dirge for the departed, beautiful and brimming with grief.

Auum lost track of the passage of time. He stared into the mesmerising flames, letting them obscure his eyes from their task. He was aware that the Wesmen were beginning to drift away. Many of them threw mementos into the fires – brooches, knives and buckles – as a final show of respect.

Sentaya placed a powerful hand on his shoulder. Stein was there as ever, waiting to translate.

'It is done, Auum. The fires will fade and die, some ash will blow on the wind across the water, and at dawn we will gather what remains and share it between us. Now it is time for sleep and for the grief to begin to settle.'

Auum nodded. 'May your dreams be full of glad memories, but

for the elves it is not done. Not until the sun crests the horizon tomorrow.'

'What will you do?'

'We will pray.'

Auum watched Sentaya walk away, envelop his wife in his arms,
lift and carry her back to the ruins of his village, his shoulders
shaking, her head tucked into his neck. At an unspoken word the
TaiGethen gathered, and how few they were. The Il-Aryn would not
partake in the warrior tradition.

'You can stay,' Auum said to Stein and Tilman. 'I'm sure Yniss will
forgive me.'

Stein shook his head. 'Not this time, Auum. This time is for you
and your TaiGethen. I'll see you in the morning.'

'You're a good man,' said Auum.

'And you are the finest of souls, Auum. I feel so deeply for your
loss.'

Auum smiled. 'Your loss too. Never going to get an Ulysan kiss
again, are you?'

'I shall never wash this cheek,' said Stein, placing his hand on it.
'Send a prayer for me.'

'I'll do that.'

The TaiGethen sat in a circle and prayed until dawn.

The Xeteskian camp was busy preparing for departure on a cold
cloudy morning. Horses were being walked, fed, watered and saddled.
Tents were coming down, wagons were being loaded and ugly human
voices rang out in shouts, tainting the air.

But there were words to be spoken, and not even the Xeteskian
mage Bynaar thought to ride away with them unsaid. However, his
reluctance was plain as he arrived, along with four guards, to speak
with Auum, Sentaya and Stein. He refused to sit, and so the quartet
stood to talk in the centre of the village. Stein translated for them all.

'I want assurances of safe passage for my people in your lands,'
said Bynaar without preamble.

Sentaya wiped a hand across his mouth and shrugged.

'Is that really your opening gambit?' asked Stein. 'You have committed crimes against man and elf and you think you can simply walk
away?'

'I acknowledge no crimes. We are at war, and yes, I think I can
simply walk away.'

Auum closed his eyes briefly. He was exhausted after a day and a night of prayer and tears following a day of fighting. His patience was gossamer-thin.

'You are a lying treacherous pig and you and your college will face justice,' said Stein, his face red and his eyes wide and wild.

Bynaar started to reply, but Auum rounded on him, staring at him with such undisguised malice that he stopped. Auum turned back to Stein.

'And you need to calm down too. And translate for me. Try not to get upset by what he says.'

'Yes, I'll translate, and no, I won't get any angrier than I already am.'

'Bynaar,' said Auum. He swung back to look at the mage, who was flushed and flustered. 'You dishonour our dead. Wesman, elf and Julatsan have fought here for the lives of everyone, and your posturing sullies the passing of their souls.'

'The dishonour is all his. Consorting with our enemies, standing arm in arm like brothers in battle,' said Bynaar, pointing to Stein, whose translation was spoken very carefully in a monotone.

'And so they were,' snapped Auum, stepping very close. 'Stein risked his life to come here and make our case, and the Lord Sentaya trusted him and us enough to do what had to be done. We drew Ystormun out and we held him so that you could capture him. And now it is done, and we will never forget what your people did to us at Triverne Lake. For that you have my abiding hate.'

'We did what had to be done,' said Bynaar.

Auum grabbed his chin. The Xeteskian guards tried to force him away, but Bynaar waved them back. Auum stared into Bynaar's eyes and studied him while his anger settled.

'You really don't understand, do you? I should hate you. But instead I pity you.'

He let Bynaar go, and the master mage backed off a pace, unable to stop himself rubbing his chin, where Auum's fingermarks were coming up red on his skin.

'I do not care for your pity,' said Bynaar.

He made to turn away, but Auum's next words stopped him even before Stein translated them, their tone cold, quiet and steeped in the authority of great age.

'You will listen to me.' Auum waited for Bynaar's eyes to meet his. 'We have never sought conflict with others, yet it has been visited upon us, first by the Garonin and then, for the last thousand years, by humans. You risk our lives by your carelessness and your ignorance.'

Bynaar's eyes narrowed, and he opened his mouth to speak. Auum shook his head, a minute gesture.

'Your desire for dominance over your enemies has consequences for us all, and you are either oblivious to them or you choose to ignore them. For three thousand years I have walked the rainforest with my people. Three thousand years of love and care and knowledge, and most of it before your college was even dreamed of, before Ystormun and his bastards. Before human magic.

'But your unquenchable desire for power means so many have died. Elves with wisdom none of us could afford to lose. Takaar has died. Ulysan has died.'

Auum's voice threatened to break and he saw Bynaar's eyes twitch.

'You sought a spell you could never find to grant yourselves power you could never own, and now you are left with nothing but hate.'

'Who are you to lecture me?' said Bynaar, his voice teetering on bluster. 'I am of the Circle Seven.'

'That office has not conferred any wisdom on you, has it?' Auum regarded him for a moment. 'I am Auum. I am Arch of the Tai-Gethen. I have seen more sorrow than I should have even in my long life, and these last days have been the worst of all. Dread powers clashing and tossing life aside. So many men leave their families without fathers. So many brothers and sons dead here and across the mountains, testament to a battle that should never have been fought because no one had the wit to wonder whether the victor could enjoy his spoils.

'You assumed your power allowed you to grasp whatever you wanted. You were wrong and those I loved above all are dead as a result.' Auum stared into Bynaar's eyes. 'There is only one reason you are still alive and that is to finish what Takaar started. You have five more Wytch Lords to catch. This land must have peace so my people can have peace too.'

'And supposing we do not do as you demand, Auum of the TaiGethen?'

'I had sworn never to come back here,' said Auum. 'I swore it to Ulysan, but now he is dead and his death will not be in vain. So if I must return to deal with you I will bring power with me such that you will wish you had never crossed paths with me, my TaiGethen or the Il-Aryn.

'My warriors are faster than your eye can track. They can kill you before you know you are attacked, and the Il-Aryn can reduce the walls of your precious college to dust before your eyes and then do the same to your skull.'

Bynaar made a contemptuous noise. 'A ridiculous assertion.'

Auum put an arm around Bynaar's shoulders and held him very tight. Sentaya growled at Bynaar's guards and they fell back.

'Then I will demonstrate.' Auum raised his voice. 'Ephemere! Ephemere!'

Of the elves gathered in front of the last of the village buildings, one stepped forward.

'Yes, Auum.'

'This man doesn't believe you can make dust from that broken barn.'

'Doesn't he? Well I'll see what I can do.'

Ephemere gathered four Il-Aryn to her including her sister. Bynaar cleared his throat noisily, and Auum held him a little tighter, tight enough to make him wince. The five elves stepped towards the barn on which Rith had died and prepared. It was a relatively quick casting in the making. The barn was in ruins, its roof burned away and its timbers so much ash, but its stone walls still stood. Ephemere's team teased out the energies, grabbed them with their minds and pulled. The stone vanished, replaced by a dust cloud that settled slowly, revealing the extent of their skill. Bynaar had tensed in Auum's grip, and when he was released regarded the Arch with a deal more wariness and a modicum of respect.

'Impressive,' he conceded.

Stein was looking as if he had won the war on his own. Auum turned to him.

'None have come out of this with any honour except Lord Sentaya, who risked everything on the say-so of an elf. This is not your victory.' Auum swung back to face the Xeteskian mage. 'You will incarcerate the Wytch Lords?'

Bynaar nodded. 'We have never wanted anything else. It is for that we demand safe passage. Ridding the Wesmen of the Wytch Lords will free them, and only we can do it.'

'For that and that alone I will organise safe passage,' said Sentaya. 'Word of Ystormun's capture will spread like a wildfire through the tribes. The tribal lords will rise and the shamen will be cast down. I,

Sentaya, Lord of the Paleon, promise this. You will ever be my enemy but I will not strike at you while you complete this task.'

Bynaar studied him and inclined his head.

'How quickly can you organise this?'

'A few days,' said Sentaya.

'I must bring reinforcements,' said Bynaar. 'The Wytch Lords remain strong.'

Sentaya hesitated a few moments. 'So be it, but your actions will unite the tribes. We will be watching and our blades will yearn for the taste of Xeteskian blood.'

Bynaar shrugged. 'It is not in our plans to attack your country – nothing else of value lies here – but you should be warned that enough strength remains in the east to destroy any who seek to take advantage of our absence.'

Stein exploded, trying to get past Auum, but was held back by Sentaya.

'What is wrong with you?' hissed Auum.

'He's lying. He means Xetesk to be master of this whole country, the east and the west. You cannot trust him!'

'Of course I don't trust him.' Auum turned back to Bynaar, feeling tired and desperate to breathe rainforest air. 'Stein is a brother of the elves. Julatsa is an ally of the elves. They have our ear and they enjoy our protection. Do not make me come back here because you will be the first I seek out. As Yniss is my witness, this is my pledge.'

'You don't believe I will keep my word?' said Bynaar.

'I believe you will do whatever is in the best interests of Xetesk. Ensure none of my friends is damaged by those interests.' Auum turned to go and then had a last thought. He swung back and tapped a finger on Bynaar's chest. 'You might want to pass that on to your sons, their sons and the sons of the next hundred generations.'

'Why?'

'Because I am immortal, and I have a very, very long memory.'

Bynaar opened his mouth to speak, but a strange look came into his eyes and he seemed to relax, holding up his hands.

'The threat eternal,' he said. 'It is well made. Now, unless there is anything else, I must leave to set about ridding the world of Wytch Lords and saving us all in the process.'

'How dare you cast yourself as the world's saviour,' snapped Stein. 'You are a butcher and your college wallows in deceit. We will never trust you.'

'Then at last perhaps we understand each other, Stein of Julatsa. Give my regards to Kerela.'

Bynaar turned and walked away, his guards with him.

'He will betray us,' said Stein.

'Of course,' said Auum. 'And so you and Lystern and Dordover must be ready, mustn't you?'

'Neat idea getting Ephemere to demonstrate, by the way, though I thought you hated magic and never wanted to see another elf cast a spell,' said Stein.

'Don't you start. I get enough of that from—' Auum gestured over his left shoulder, which was cold because Ulysan was not there. 'Anyway, even I have to admit it has its uses. Come on, let's get back to the others.'

'I can't imagine life without him,' said Auum.

The elves were gathered to eat breakfast. The mood was sombre and quiet.

'The rainforest will certainly be quieter,' said Grafyrre.

Auum chuckled in spite of himself.

'You know he always said that I should let him do the jokes. Who's going to do them now?'

No one had an answer. No elf, anyway.

'I will,' said Tilman.

Auum smiled at him. 'Your place is here with Stein. But you are always welcome in the rainforest. I'll even stop it killing you.'

'Is that a joke?' asked Tilman.

'Not entirely,' said Grafyrre.

Auum sighed. 'I lost my cell here.'

'Anyone would be proud to run with you,' said Faleen.

'I have my eye on one or two,' said Auum, 'but I think I'll walk the path of the Silent until I can face it all without Ulysan.'

Faleen and Grafyrre were staring at him, Merke and Marack too.

'What?' he asked.

'You're seriously not going to tell us who you have your eye on?' said Marack.

'All right then. Duele is good, but he might make a more useful cell leader. Evunn too. Fast, accurate. Ulysan liked them both.'

'Then that's enough, isn't it?' said Grafyrre.

'When the time is right,' said Auum. There were fresh tears

threatening, and Auum shook his head, not wanting to wallow any more. Ulysan would have chided him for it, after all.

Auum heard a brief exchange of words in tribal Wes, and two more figures moved into the circle. Auum stood and Sentaya enveloped him in a huge bear hug. When the Wesman let go there were tears in his eyes and he wiped them away angrily. Though surprised at the embrace from a man normally so in control of himself, Auum's heart beat for the feelings they both shared so keenly.

'Tell Sentaya that to cry is to let the essence of your soul comfort those of the departed. There is no shame in it, only love of the most precious kind. Tell him his son will be the greater for it where he has travelled.'

Stein translated and Sentaya smiled, letting fresh tears drip down his cheeks.

'I have brought you three boxes full of the ashes of the fallen. Part of my son is in there along with your Ulysan.'

Auum nodded, the reason for the sudden tears now plain.

'Is there anything else you want to say to Sentaya?' asked Stein.

'Tell him that, with his blessing, we will rest here today, but as dawn breaks tomorrow we will be leaving him to rebuild his life as we go to rebuild ours.' Auum smiled and felt hope as well as a yearning to feel the canopy above his head. 'Tell him we want to go home.'

Acknowledgements:

To Gillian Redfearn, Robert Kirby, Jon Weir, Charlie Panayiotou, Steve Diamond and Marc Aplin – thank you for all that you do. To Clare, Oscar and Oliver thank you for putting up with my occasional grumpiness and being a wonderful family. And to Sarah Pinborough, if it hadn't been for your friendship and many authorly lunches, I'd probably have gone quietly insane.